VI
BRIDES

Three novels from international
bestselling author

LYNNE GRAHAM

brought to you

With Love

VIRGIN
BRIDES
LYNNE GRAHAM

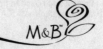

M&B™ and M&B™ with the Rose Device
are trademarks of the publisher.
Harlequin Mills & Boon Limited, Eton House,
18-24 Paradise Road, Richmond, Surrey TW9 1SR

VIRGIN BRIDES © Harlequin Enterprises II B.V./S.à.r.l. 2009

Married by Arrangement, Mistress Bought and Paid For and *The
Cozakis Bride* were first published in Great Britain by Harlequin Mills
& Boon Limited in separate, single volumes.

Married by Arrangement © Lynne Graham 2005
Mistress Bought and Paid For © Lynne Graham 2006
The Cozakis Bride © Lynne Graham 2000

ISBN: 978 0 263 87534 8

010-0909

Harlequin Mills & Boon policy is to use papers that are
natural, renewable and recyclable products and made from
wood grown in sustainable forests. The logging and
manufacturing processes conform to the legal environmental
regulations of the country of origin.

Printed and bound in Spain
by Litografia Rosés S.A., Barcelona

Married by Arrangement

LYNNE GRAHAM

A collection of bestselling novels
from some of our favourite writers,
brought to you

With Love

Lynne Graham was born in Northern Ireland, and has been a keen Mills & Boon® reader since her teens. She is very happily married, with an understanding husband who has learned to cook since she started to write! Her five children keep her on her toes. She has a very large dog, which knocks everything over, a very small terrier, which barks a lot, and two cats. When time allows, Lynne is a keen gardener.

Look for an exciting new book
from Lynne Graham,
Desert Prince, Bride of Innocence,
in October 2009.

CHAPTER ONE

'But why didn't Belinda tell us last year that she had given birth to Pablo's child?' Antonio Rocha, Marqués de Salazar, demanded of his grandmother, lingering astonishment etched in the hard set of his sculpted cheekbones, his lean, darkly handsome face grim.

'We barely got to know Belinda while your brother was alive.' Doña Ernesta's fine-boned features reflected her regret over that state of affairs. 'How could we expect her to turn to us for help after he had abandoned her?'

'I tried several times to set up a meeting with Belinda. She always made excuses,' Antonio reminded the older woman. 'Finally, she insisted that she didn't need our help and she made it clear that she no longer regarded us as being related to her.'

'Her pride may have spoken for her. I imagine Pablo left her with little else. Now that we know that he must have deserted her when she was pregnant, my heart is even heavier,' Doña Ernesta confessed. 'Yet when he married her, I truly believed that he might finally settle down.'

Being an incurable cynic, Antonio had had no such hopes. After all, his younger brother had broken the heart of his own family long before he had graduated to wreaking havoc beyond that select circle. Although born with every advantage into the most élite stratum of Spanish high society, Pablo had started getting in trouble at an early age.

5

His parents had found it impossible to control him. By the time Pablo had reached his early twenties, he had dissipated a substantial inheritance and defrauded several relatives and friends of large amounts of money. Throughout those troubled years, countless people had made repeated efforts to understand, correct and solve Pablo's problems. All such attempts had been unsuccessful, not least, Antonio believed, because his brother had got a huge kick out of breaking the law and swindling the foolish.

It was three years since Pablo had come home to mend fences and announce his intention of marrying his beautiful English girlfriend. Overjoyed by his return, Doña Ernesta had insisted on throwing the wedding for the happy couple while at the same time making them a very generous gift of money. The marriage, however, had failed and Pablo had returned to Spain twelve months ago. Soon afterwards, the younger man had lost his life in a drunken car crash.

'It astonishes me that Pablo could have kept such a secret from us,' Doña Ernesta lamented. 'It is even more sad that Belinda could not trust us enough to share her child with us.'

'I've made arrangements to fly over to London tomorrow morning,' Antonio told her, frowning when the elderly woman seated by the elegant marble fireplace continued to look deeply troubled. 'Try not to dwell on your sorrow. As a family, we did all that we could and we will now do our very best for Pablo's daughter.'

It was only that afternoon that Antonio had received an urgent call from the family lawyer, who had in turn been contacted by Belinda's solicitor in England. Antonio had been sincerely shaken by the news that his brother's widow had not only given birth to a child six

months earlier, but had died from pneumonia just a fortnight ago. He had been relieved that, independent
though Belinda had evidently intended to be, she had
still had the foresight and sense to nominate him in her
will as the guardian of her daughter, Lydia. At the family lawyer's instigation, however, Antonio had also
agreed that, even though he had no reason to doubt that
the little girl was his brother's child, DNA testing, dis-
tasteful though it was, would be a sensible precaution.

The lawyer had then informed him that Belinda's sister, Sophie, was currently looking after the child.
Dismayed by that information, Antonio had appreciated
that his own intervention was immediately required.
Sophie was far too young for such a responsibility and
he thought it unlikely that her lifestyle would be con-
ducive to the care of a baby.

Antonio had met Sophie when she had acted as a
bridesmaid at her sister's wedding. The pronounced differences between the two sisters had disconcerted his
conservative family. While Belinda had had the confident gloss and clear diction of the British middle class,
Sophie had appeared to hail from a rather less privileged
background. Indeed Antonio's English had been much
more grammatically correct than hers had been. As he
recalled those unexplained discrepancies his incisive
gaze veiled. An involuntary memory of Sophie with her
tumbling fall of blonde curls and glinting green eyes
assailed Antonio. Not a beauty in the classic elegant
style of her sister, certainly. Even so, Antonio had found
his attention continually returning to the youngest,
smallest bridesmaid that day and he had been equally
quick to notice that there wasn't a man in the room
impervious to her appeal.

But her apparent appeal had been very short-lived,

Antonio reminded himself grimly, his expressive mouth curling with disdain. Sophie had been sparkling, sexy and intensely feminine. But as he had discovered she had also been a slut. Watching her trail back into her hotel at dawn with her youthful lover and with her clothing dishevelled from a night of passion on the beach had been a salutary lesson. Clearly, she had been no more particular in her habits than the many tourists who came to Spain to indulge in rampant casual sex and an excess of alcohol.

'A little girl. My first great-grandchild,' Doña Ernesta remarked with a tentative smile softening her rather severe features, her well-modulated speaking voice breaking into what was a rare moment of abstraction for her grandson. 'Lydia. It is a pretty name. A baby will transform the *castillo*.'

Antonio resisted a dismayingly strong urge to wince while inwardly acknowledging that he had been in no great hurry to embrace fatherhood. He was barely thirty years old. He had yet to experience the faintest glimmer of a desire to produce the next generation and had never had the slightest interest in babies. In fact he generally gave the rug rats a fairly wide berth at family events. Doubtless the perceived charm of a howling baby lay in the fond eye of its parent and magically enabled the parent to overlook the fact that babies were horrifically noisy and messy.

'I imagine so,' Antonio murmured wryly, resolving to have the nursery suite in the little-used east wing renovated at speed. He would also ensure that a full complement of staff was hired to service the child's every need.

He was not ashamed to admit that he liked his life just as it was. He had had to work incredibly hard for a very long time to repair the damage done to the Rocha family fortunes by Pablo's ceaseless depredations. While his brother had been running wild and free on his ill-gotten gains, Antonio had been working eighteen-hour days. Self-indulgence, personal interests and relaxation had all been luxuries out of Antonio's reach. Having since amassed sufficient wealth to be judged a billionaire, Antonio now relished his own highly sophisticated existence, his fantastic social life and his freedom to do exactly as he liked.

But he was equally well aware that change was in the air: Pablo's daughter was now his personal responsibility. It was his duty to take charge of the orphaned infant and bring her back to Spain. It was right and fitting that this should be the case, Antonio conceded. The baby was of his blood and part of his family and he would raise her as though she were his own daughter.

'You'll have to get married, of course,' his grandmother murmured in a voice as soft and light as thistledown.

Startled by that disconcerting assurance, Antonio swung back to survey the old lady, who was carefully addressing her attention to her needlework. Grudging amusement glinted in his clear dark golden eyes, for he was well aware that his grandmother was eager for him to take a wife. 'With all due respect, *Abuela*…I don't think that a sacrifice of that magnitude will be necessary.'

'A baby needs a mother. I'm too old to take on the role and the staff cannot be expected to fill the gap. You travel a great deal,' Doña Ernesta reminded him. 'Only a wife could ensure the continuing level of care and affection which a young child will require.'

As Antonio listened the amusement slowly evaporated from his gaze. 'I don't need a wife.'

Glancing up without apparent concern, Doña Ernesta treated her grandson to an understanding smile. 'Then, I can only offer you my admiration. Obviously you've already thought this matter over—'

'I have and in depth,' Antonio slotted in rather drily, for he was unimpressed by his wily grandmother's pretence of innocence.

'And you're prepared to sacrifice all your free time for your niece's benefit. After all, with only you to depend on, she will need so much more of your attention.'

That angle had not occurred to Antonio. His brilliant eyes grew bleak. He was most reluctant to contemplate that level of commitment. He could not imagine assuming the role of a hands-on parent in constant demand. The very idea of such a thing was ridiculous. He was the Marqués de Salazar, head of an ancient and noble family line, as well as being a powerful and influential businessman on whom many thousands of employees depended. His time was too valuable. His importance to the success of his business projects was limitless. What did he know about children? Babies?

At the same time the very idea of embracing the imprisonment of marriage banged the equivalent of a sepulchral cell door shut in Antonio's imagination and made him pale.

In the act of changing Lydia's T-shirt, Sophie succumbed to temptation and blew a raspberry on her niece's tummy. Convulsing with chuckles, Lydia held up her arms to be lifted, her little face below her soft brown curls lit by a sunny smile.

'I don't know which one of you is the bigger kid!'

Norah Moore quipped while her stocky, well-built son, Matt, set the old highchair out beside the pine kitchen table.

Tiny in stature and slender as a ribbon, Sophie thrust her own curls back off her brow in a rueful gesture and resisted the urge to admit that grief, stress and a heavy workload were combining to make her feel more like a hundred years old. Staying financially afloat was a constant struggle and since Lydia's birth had required her to do two jobs. Her main income came from working as a cleaner for the Moores. Mother and son owned the trailer park where she had lived for almost four years. At present she cleaned the caravans that were rented out as holiday lets. But quite a few were lived in all the year round by people like herself who could not afford more expensive accommodation. She made extra cash from embroidering clothes for an exclusive mail order firm. Her earnings might be poor in comparison to the hours she put in but she was grateful for any work that she could combine with caring for Lydia.

'But I know which one of you is the prettiest,' Matt declared with a meaningful look in Sophie's direction.

As Sophie strapped Lydia into the high chair she contrived to evade his admiring gaze and wondered why Mother Nature was always encouraging the wrong men to chase her. She liked Matt. She had tried, she really had tried to find him attractive because he was hardworking, honest and decent. He was everything her irresponsible father had not been and a solid gold choice for a sensible woman. As always she wished that she were less fanciful and more prudent.

'Right now, I should think Sophie's more concerned about what this solicitor might have to say to her,' Norah, a thin woman with short grey hair, told her son

brusquely. 'I can't understand why Belinda even bothered to make a will when she had nothing to leave.'

'She had Lydia,' Sophie pointed out to the older
woman. 'Belinda had the will drawn up after Pablo
died. I think it must've been her way of making a new
start and showing her independence.'

'Yes, your sister was very keen on her independence,'
Norah Moore said with a sniff. 'And not so fond of
being tied down to a kiddie once Lydia was born.'

'It was hard for her.' Sophie lifted a slight shoulder
in a noncommittal shrug because it hurt that she could
not actively defend Belinda's rash behaviour during the
last months of her life. At least, not to a woman who
had repeatedly helped her out with the task of caring
for Belinda's daughter. But then that was what she most
liked about the Moores, she reminded herself. They
spoke as they found and there was nothing false about
them.

'It was even harder for you,' Norah told her squarely.
'I felt very sorry for Belinda when she first came here.
She'd had a tough time. But when she took up with that
new boyfriend of hers and landed you with Lydia, I lost
patience with her silliness.'

'I loved being landed with Lydia,' Sophie declared
staunchly.

'Sometimes what you love may not be what's good
for you,' the older woman retorted crisply.

But at a time when Sophie's heart still ached from
the cruelly sudden death of her sister, her baby niece
was her only real comfort. Although Sophie and Belinda
had had different fathers and had not met until Belinda
had sought Sophie out. Sophie had grown very fond of
her older sister. Belinda had, after all, shown Sophie the

first family affection that the younger woman had ever known.

Yet the stark difference between their respective backgrounds might more easily have ensured that the two sisters remained lifelong strangers. While Belinda had grown up in a lovely country house with her own pony and every childhood extra her parents could afford, Sophie had been born illegitimate and raised in a council flat by a father who was always broke. Sophie was the result of their mother, Isabel's extramarital affair. After her infatuation had subsided, Isabel had won her estranged husband back by leaving Sophie behind with her lover. Sophie's feckless father had brought her up with the help of a succession of girlfriends. She had learned when she was very young that her wants and wishes were rarely of interest to the self-seeking adults who surrounded her.

At first meeting, Sophie had been in awe of her beautiful, sophisticated sister. Five years older, Belinda had been educated at a fancy boarding-school and she had talked with a cut glass accent that put Sophie in mind of the royal family. Her warm and affectionate nature had however soon won Sophie's trust and love. Perhaps more slowly and rather more painfully, Sophie had come to appreciate that Belinda was not very clever and was extremely vulnerable to falling for handsome men who talked big and impressed her. But wild horses would have not have dredged that unhappy truth from Sophie, who was loyal to a fault.

Leaving her niece in Norah Moore's capable care, Sophie climbed into Matt's pick-up. He gave her a lift into Sheerness and, stopping right outside the solicitor's office, he offered to wait for her.

As always in a hurry to escape Matt's hopeful air of

expectation, Sophie had already jumped out onto the pavement. 'There's no need,' she said breezily. 'I'll catch the bus.'

Matt behaved as if she hadn't spoken and told her where he would be parked.

A young car driver waiting at the lights buzzed down his window to call, 'Hiya, sexy!'

Sophie flung him a pained glance from eyes as deep and rich and green as old-fashioned bottle glass. 'Shouldn't you be in school?'

He looked startled by the comeback. Sophie pondered the decided embarrassment of still looking like a sixteen-year-old when she was almost twenty-three years old. She blamed her youthful appearance on her lack of height and skinny build. She kept her hair long because, although she would not have admitted it to a living soul, she was always terrified that her slender curves might lead to her being mistaken for a boy.

As she entered the legal firm's smart office she tugged uneasily at the hem of her denim skirt, which rejoiced in floral cotton frills. The skirt was well out of fashion and she had worn it only because she thought it looked more formal than the jeans that filled her limited wardrobe. All her clothes came from charity shops and none were of the designer cast-off variety. Without complaint, she hovered while the receptionist chatted to a colleague and answered a call before finally deigning to take note of her arrival.

In the waiting room, Sophie took up a restive position by the window. She watched a limousine force its passage along the street outside and cause traffic chaos. The long silver vehicle came to a halt and a uniformed chauffeur emerged. Impervious to the car horns that protested the obstruction that the limo was creating, he opened a rear door for his passenger to alight.

As the passenger sprang out and straightened to an imposing height the breath caught in Sophie's throat. Her green eyes widened with disbelief. It couldn't be, it simply couldn't be Pablo's autocratic big brother, Antonio Rocha! She shrank back to the side of the window but continued to stare. It was Antonio all right. He had the impact of a tidal wave on her self-command.

There he was: the male who had made mincemeat of her every prejudice, overpowered her defences and reduced her to a level of eyelash-fluttering, giggly compliance. She suppressed a quiver of shame at that recollection. For nearly three years since that awful day, Sophie had told herself that Antonio could not possibly have been half as devastatingly attractive as she had believed him to be. And now here he was in the flesh to destroy even that comforting lie with his smooth aristocratic façade that set her teeth on edge and his altogether more disturbing quality of raw sexuality.

His gleaming black hair was cut fashionably short. His lean, classic features were stamped with a bold masculinity that attracted female admiration wherever he went. He was a work of art, Sophie acknowledged grudgingly. Not only did he look like some mythical Greek god, he was also built like one with broad shoulders, a narrow waist and long, powerful legs. Dressed in a trendy dark designer suit, he looked achingly handsome. Only when he strode into the same legal practice did she break free of her paralysis and sincerely doubt the evidence of her own eyes.

Why would Antonio Rocha be over in England? What was he doing on the Isle of Sheppey where the titled rich were scarcer than hens' teeth? Surely he could only be in Sheerness on this particular day to keep the same appointment that she had been asked to attend? No other reason could rationally explain such a coincidence.

Sophie hurried over to the door that led back into the reception area where an alarming amount of activity had broken out. The once laconic receptionist was standing to attention with a megawatt smile of appreciation and a well-dressed older man was greeting Antonio with a horrendous amount of bowing and scraping. 'Your Excellency,' he murmured obsequiously.

As though some sixth sense warned him of her presence, Antonio turned his proud dark head. Eyes as rich as gold ingots in sunlight encountered hers. Her tummy flipped and her mouth ran dry and her heartbeat escalated as though she were trying to run up a hill. It was like being hit by a truck at breakneck speed and she reacted with panic.

'Just what the heck are *you* doing here?' Sophie asked belligerently.

Taken aback though Antonio was by her unexpected appearance, he betrayed no visible sign of the fact. In the space of a moment, he had absorbed every facet of the slender woman poised by the door. She had the fine bones and grace of a dancer and the transient air of a butterfly ready to take wing at the first sign of trouble. Her toffee-blonde hair fell in a riotous mass of curls round her delicately pointed face, framing wide green eyes bright and sharp as lancets, a freckled nose turned up at the tip and a full sweet cupid's bow mouth. His keen gaze semi-cloaked by the lush density of his lashes, he tore his attention from the provocative appeal of that very feminine mouth and struggled to suppress a primitive and infuriatingly inappropriate flare of pure lust.

Sophie folded her arms to hide the fact that her hands were shaking. 'I asked you a question, Antonio—who asked you to come here?' she demanded.

'His Excellency is attending this meeting at my request, Miss Cunningham,' the solicitor interposed in a shocked tone of reproof.

Antonio moved a step closer and extended both his lean brown hands. His stunning dark deep-set eyes met hers in a head-on collision. Before she even knew what she was doing she was uncrossing her defensive arms and freeing her fingers to make contact with him, for a yearning she could not deny had leapt up inside her.

'I know how close you were to your sister. Allow me to offer you my deepest condolences on her death,' Antonio breathed with quiet gravity.

Hot colour rose like a flood tide to wash Sophie's pale complexion. Her small hands trembled in the warm hold of his. Ferocious emotions gripped her and threatened to tear her apart. She could not doubt his sincerity and his compassion pushed her to the brink of tears. With his immaculate sense of occasion, social sophistication and superb manners, he had put her in the wrong by answering her less-than-polite greeting with courtesy. For that alone, Sophie could have screamed at him and wept in rage. She refused to be impressed. She also refused to think about how much he had hurt her almost three years earlier. Instead she concentrated on a more relevant line of attack. Where had Antonio Rocha and his rich, snobby family been when Belinda had been desperate for help and support?

She jerked her hands free in stark rejection. 'I don't want your precious condolences!' she told him baldly.

'Nonetheless they are yours,' Antonio purred smoothly, marvelling at the level of her aggression and the novelty value of her rebuff. Women were never aggressive towards Antonio or ungrateful for his consideration. Sophie was the single exception to that rule.

'You still haven't told me what you're doing here,' Sophie said stubbornly.

'I was invited,' Antonio reminded her gently.

'Your Excellency…please come this way,' the solicitor urged him in a pained tone of apology.

Although Sophie had grown increasingly pale with discomfiture and nerves, her chin came up. 'I'm not going anywhere until someone tells me what's going on! What gives you the right to hear what my sister said in her will?'

'Let's discuss that and other issues in a more private setting,' Antonio suggested quietly.

Once again Sophie's face flamed pink with chagrin. Squirming embarrassment afflicted her when she unwillingly recalled the consequences of her visit to Spain nearly three years earlier. His rejection had hurt like hell and devastated her pride. She had been too pathetically naïve to recognise that the blue-blooded Marqués de Salazar was simply amusing himself with a bit of a flirtation. It was an effort for her to repress that wounding memory and concentrate on the present.

Her slender spine stiff, she sank down in a seat in the spacious office. Determined to emulate Antonio's cool, she resolved to resist the temptation to give way to any further outbursts and she compressed her lips. At the same time she was frantically striving to work out why Antonio Rocha should have been asked to come all the way from Spain. After all, Pablo's haughty brother had not bothered to get in touch before, nor had he shown the smallest interest in the existence of his infant niece. An enervating frisson of anxiety travelled through Sophie.

The solicitor began to read the will with the slight haste of someone eager to get an unpleasant task out of the way. The document was short and simple and all too soon Sophie understood why Antonio's presence had been deemed necessary. However, she could not accept what she had heard and questioned it. 'My sister nominated Antonio as a guardian as well?'

'Yes,' the solicitor confirmed.

'But I'm more than capable of taking care of Lydia,' Sophie proclaimed brightly. 'So there's no need for anyone else to get involved!'

'It's not quite that simple,' Antonio Rocha slotted in smooth as a rapier blade, but a faint frown line now divided his ebony brows. He was surprised that the will had made no mention of the disposition of Belinda's property and was about to query that omission.

Sophie spared the tall Spaniard her first fleeting glance since entering the room. Her troubled green eyes telegraphed a storm warning. 'It can be as simple as you're willing to make it. I don't know what came over Belinda when she chose to include you—'

'Common sense?' Antonio batted back drily.

'I suppose Belinda must've been scared that both her and me might be involved in an accident,' Sophie opined heatedly, fingers of pink highlighting her tautening facial bones as she fought to maintain her composure. 'We're talking worst-case scenario here, but luckily things aren't as bad as that. I'm young and fit and well able to take care of Lydia all on my own.'

'I would take issue with that statement,' Antonio murmured.

Her teeth gritted. 'You can take issue with whatever you like but it's not going to change anything!' she shot back at him.

'Your sister nominated you and the marqués as joint guardians of her daughter,' the solicitor expanded. 'That means that you have equal rights over the child—'

'Equal rights?' Sophie gasped in rampant disbelief.

'Equal rights,' Antonio repeated with a silken emphasis he could not resist.

'No other arrangement is possible without application to the courts,' the solicitor decreed.

'But that's utterly outrageous!' Sophie launched at Antonio.

'With all due respect, I would suggest that my family is entitled to assist in the task of raising my brother's child to adulthood.'

'Why?' Sophie slung back wrathfully as she leapt to her feet. 'So that your precious family can make as big a mess of bringing up Lydia as they did with her father?'

Angry disconcertion had tensed Antonio's lean, darkly handsome features. 'Both our siblings are now dead. Let us respect that reality.'

'Don't you dare ask me to respect Pablo's memory!' Sophie flared back at him in disgust. 'Your brother wrecked my sister's life!'

'May I speak to Miss Cunningham alone for a few minutes?' Antonio enquired of the solicitor.

The older man, whose discomfiture during that increasingly heated exchange of views had been extreme, got up with relief at the request and left the room.

'Sit down,' Antonio instructed coolly, determined not to rise to the bait of her provocative accusations. 'Appreciate that I will not argue with you. Recriminations are pointless and wrong in this situation. The child's interests must come first—'

Sophie was so furious that only a scream could have expressed her feelings. Denied that outlet, she coiled her hands into tight little fists of restraint by her side. 'Don't you dare tell me what's right and what's wrong. Let me tell you—'

Antonio rose upright with unhurried grace. 'You will tell me nothing that I do not ask for, as I will not listen. You will lower your voice and moderate your language.'

'Where do you get off talking to me like that? Like I'm some stupid kid?' Sophie launched at him. 'You walk in here, you start laying down the law and acting like you know best—'

'I most probably do know best,' Antonio incised and not in a tone of apology. 'I recognise that you have suffered a recent bereavement and that grief may well have challenged your temper—'

'That's not why I hate your guts and that is not why I am shouting at you!' Sophie informed him fiercely, green eyes bright with fury. 'Your rotten brother robbed my sister of everything she possessed and left her penniless and in debt. He was a hateful liar and a cheat. He took her money and threw it away at the gambling tables and at the racetrack. When there was nothing left he told her he'd never loved her anyway and he walked!'

Antonio was perturbed but not that surprised by those revelations. He felt it would be tactless to point out that, even before Belinda had wed his brother, he had made an unsuccessful attempt to warn Sophie's sibling of her future husband's essential unreliability when it came to money. 'If that is the truth I am sorry for it. Had I been made aware of those facts, I would have granted Belinda all the help that it was within my power to give.'

Sophie snatched in a jagged breath. 'Is that all you have got to say?'

Antonio had a low tolerance threshold for such personal attacks. In his blood ran the hot pure-bred pride of the Spanish nobility and a long line of ancestors to whom honour had been a chivalrous, engrained concept of prime importance. He had lived his own life within those tenets and his principles were of the highest. He had a profound dislike of being upbraided for his brother's sins, for which he had too often paid a high personal price. His strong jaw line squared. He had no intention of getting dragged into an exchange that was only likely to exacerbate hostilities.

'It is an unhappy fact that I cannot change the past,' Antonio pointed out flatly. 'The only subject I'm willing to discuss at this moment is your niece's well-being.'

Eyes glinting a ferocious green, Sophie surveyed him in raging frustration. Nothing fazed him. Nothing knocked even a chip off that cold, smooth, marble façade of his. He was neither shamed nor affronted by his younger brother's appalling mistreatment of her poor sister. Indeed there he stood, all six feet three inches of him, wonderfully insulated by his great wealth and aristocratic detachment from the harder realities of those less fortunate in life. He lived in a castle with servants. He had a private jet and a fleet of limos. His fancy suit had probably cost as much as she earned in a year. He would never know what it was to struggle just to pay the rent at the end of the month. He had even less compassion to spare for Belinda's sufferings.

'I'm not going to discuss Lydia with you!' Sophie

LYNNE GRAHAM 23

snapped in the feverish heat of her resentment. 'You're as much of a bastard as your sneaky brother was!'

Dark colour accentuated the superb slant of Antonio's fabulous cheekbones. His brilliant eyes suddenly flared gold as the heart of a fire. 'On what do you base your abuse? Ignorant prejudice?'

'I've got personal experience of what kind of a guy you are!' Sophie declared in a tempestuous surge of hurt and anger. 'Not my type anyway!'

'Sorry, I'm just not into tattoos,' Antonio murmured in a sibilant tone designed to wound.

'Tattoos?' Sophie parroted in response to that particular taunt, feeling the image of the butterfly she had acquired at eighteen burn through the flesh of her shoulder like a brand. A fresh spurt of angry mortification took hold of her. 'You total snob and snake! How dare you sneer at me like that? You act like you're so superior and so polite, but you strung me a line and let me down and misjudged me that night!'

Antonio's intent dark golden gaze was welded to her flushed heart-shaped face and bright green eyes. Her passion fascinated him. Temper was running through her like an electric current and she could not control it. He was grimly amused and unexpectedly pleased to discover that his justifiable put-down that night still rankled with her nearly three years after the event.

'I don't think so. I think you resent the fact that I saw you for what you were—'

Sophie was trembling with the force of her feelings. 'And how did you see me?' she challenged.

'You don't want to know,' Antonio asserted lazily, dangling that carrot with every hope of provoking her further. She was already so mad she was practically jumping up and down on the spot and he could not resist the temptation to see just how much further he could push her before she lost it altogether.

Sophie took a hasty step closer and stared up at him with outrage stamped in her delicate features, her hands on her hips like a miniature fishwife. 'Tell me…go on, just tell me!'

Antonio lifted and dropped his wide shoulders in an infinitesimal shrug of dismissal, deliberately prolonging the moment to the punchline. 'In common with most men, I confess that I can really enjoy a wanton woman, but I'm afraid that promiscuity is a real turn-off. You missed your chance with me.'

Sophie hit him. She tried to slap him, but she was not tall enough. His reactions were also faster than her own and he sidestepped her so that her palm merely glanced off his shoulder, leaving him infuriatingly un-harmed. 'You pig!' she seethed up at him. 'You think I care about missing out with you?'

'Attempted assault on that score nearly three years later rather speaks for you, *querida*,' Antonio shared in his dark-timbred drawl, only dimly wondering why he was enjoying himself so much.

White with shock and chagrin at her own behaviour and the biting effect of his derision, Sophie headed to the door. 'I refuse to have anything more to do with you.'

'Perhaps just once you could exercise some discipline over your temper and think of the child whose future is at stake here.'

Sophie froze as if his words had plunged a dagger into her narrow back. Guilt and shame engulfed her. Stiffly she turned and tracked back to her seat without once looking in the direction of her tormentor.

'Thank you,' Antonio Rocha murmured smoothly.

Her fingers carved purple crescents of restraint into her palms. Never in her life had she hated anyone as she hated him at that moment. Never in her life had anyone made her feel so stupid and selfish. He invited the solicitor back in. Initially she was silent for fear of letting herself down by saying the wrong thing, but she had been planning to ask questions. However, there was no need for her to do so. Antonio requested the clarification that she might have asked for her own benefit and the answers told a chastened Sophie what she least wished to hear.

All arrangements for Lydia would have to be reached by mutual agreement between her and Antonio. Either of them could refuse the responsibility or relinquish rights to the other. But, as executor, the solicitor was empowered, if he thought it necessary, to invite social services to decide how Lydia's needs would best be fulfilled. Adequate security and funding to support a child would naturally have to be taken into consideration.

'So as I'm poor and Antonio's rich, I can't possibly have equal rights with him over my niece, can I?' Sophie prompted tightly.

'That is not how I would view the situation, Miss Cunningham.' Dismayed by such blunt speech, the solicitor glanced at Antonio for support.

Antonio Rocha, Marqués de Salazar, rose unhurriedly upright a split second after Sophie scrambled to her feet, eager to be gone. 'I see no reason why Miss Cunningham and I should not reach an amicable agreement,' he drawled with all the controlled calm and cool of a male who knew he had beaten an opponent hollow. 'I'd like to see Lydia this evening. Shall we say at seven? I'll call at your home.'

'I'm sure you're not giving me a choice,' Sophie framed bitterly.

Having taken complete charge, Antonio accompanied her out to the narrow corridor. 'It doesn't have to be this way between us,' he murmured huskily.

'How else could it be?' she heard herself prompt.

He was so close that she could have reached out and touched him. The very sound of his rich, deep-pitched drawl was incredibly sensual. She let herself look up and it was a mistake. He took her breath away and rocked her world on its axis. In the blink of an eyelid it was as though time had slipped and catapulted her back almost three years. Meeting the slumberous darkness of his spectacular eyes, she trembled. Treacherous excitement seized her and made a prisoner of her. For a wild, endless moment, she was so fiercely aware of him that it was agony not to make actual physical contact with his lean, powerful frame. She heard the roughened catch of his breathing and imagined the burn of his beautiful mouth on hers. Only the humiliating memory of his comments earlier forced her back to solid earth again and left her bitterly ashamed of her own weakness.

'Do you honestly think I'm stupid enough to fall for the same fake charm routine you used on me the last time?' Sophie asked with stinging scorn, sliding sinuously past him with the quicksilver speed that characterised all her movements. She had vanished round the corner at the foot of the corridor before he was even properly aware that she had gone.

Antonio swore long and low and silently and with a ferocity that would have astounded those who knew him.

CHAPTER TWO

ON THE drive back home, Sophie gave Matt a brief update on events and then fell silent. She was too upset to make conversation.

Shattered by the contents of Belinda's will, Sophie was simply terrified that she was in serious danger of losing Lydia and shell-shocked by meeting up with Antonio Rocha again. How could her sister have chosen Antonio to be her child's guardian? After all, Belinda had had virtually no contact with her Spanish in-laws after her wedding. She had once admitted to Sophie that Pablo had never got on with his relatives and that that was why he preferred to live in London. When Antonio had contacted Belinda after Pablo's death, Belinda had been almost hysterical in her determination to have nothing further to do with her late husband's family. Even when Belinda had mentioned the will she had made, she had not admitted to Antonio's place in it. Sophie had been totally unprepared for her sibling's evident change of heart.

Nevertheless, Sophie could also understand exactly why Antonio had been selected: Belinda had always had enormous respect for money and status. It was rather ironic that her sister had actually been rather intimidated by the sheer grandeur of her husband's family, who lived on a palatial scale. She thought that Belinda had most probably been hedging her bets when she had named Antonio in the will. Knowing that Sophie was poor as a church mouse, she could only have hoped that including the mega-rich Antonio might result in his offering to contribute towards his niece's support. Sophie clutched at that concept and prayed that Pablo's brother would have no desire to become any more closely involved in Lydia's life.

Sophie had come to love Lydia as much as if her niece had been born to her. The bond between Sophie and her infant niece would always have been strong because, having suffered leukaemia as a child, Sophie was painfully aware that the treatment that had saved her life might also have left her infertile. Her attachment to her sister's baby had been intensified, however, by the simple fact that from birth Lydia had been almost solely in Sophie's care.

Initially Belinda had not been well and she had needed Sophie to look after her daughter until she was stronger. Within a few weeks, though, Belinda had met the man with whom she had been living at the time of her death. A successful salesman with a party-going lifestyle, Doug had shown no interest whatsoever in his girlfriend's baby. Having fallen for him, Belinda had been quick to pass all responsibility for Lydia onto Sophie's shoulders.

On many occasions, Sophie had attempted to reason with her sister and persuade her to spend more time with her baby daughter.

'I wish I'd never had her!' Belinda finally sobbed shamefacedly. 'If I have to start playing Mummy and staying in more, Doug will just find someone else. I know I'm not being fair to you but I love him so much and I don't want to lose him. Just give me some more time with him. I know he'll come round about Lydia.'

But Doug did not come round. Indeed he told Belinda that there was no room for a child in his life.

'That's why I've reached a decision,' Belinda told Sophie tearfully two weeks before she died. 'You probably can't have a baby of your own and I know how much you love Lydia. You've been a terrific mother to her, much better than I could ever be. If you want Lydia, you can keep her for ever and that way I can at least see her occasionally.'

That day Sophie deemed it wisest to say nothing, for she was convinced that Belinda's affair with Doug was already fading and that her sister would soon bitterly regret her willingness to sacrifice even her child on his behalf. Sophie had grown up in a household where her father's lady friends had almost always had children of their own. She knew that there were plenty of men who refused to take responsibility for anyone other than their own sweet selves. Her father had been one of that ilk, a work-shy charmer of colossal selfishness, but he had never been without a woman in his life. All too often those same women had put his needs ahead of their child's in a pointless effort to hold on to him.

'My goodness…fancy Belinda not even telling you!' Norah Moore exclaimed in astonishment when she heard about Antonio Rocha's appearance at the solicitor's office. 'That sister of yours was a dark horse, all right.'

Engaged in cuddling Lydia close and rejoicing in the sweet, soft warmth of her niece's weight in her arms, Sophie sighed, 'Belinda probably put Antonio's name down and never thought about it again. She didn't keep secrets from me.'

'Didn't she?' the older woman snorted, unimpressed. 'I reckon Belinda only ever told you what she thought you wanted to hear!'

Sophie stiffened. 'What's that supposed to mean? Are you teasing me?'

Reddening, Norah looked discomfited. 'Of course I am,' she said awkwardly.

It was not the first time that the older woman had hinted that Sophie might not have known her sibling as well as she thought she did. Sophie was irritated but placed no credence in that suggestion. She was well aware that Norah and Belinda had merely tolerated each other. Norah had been too rough and ready for Belinda's refined standards and had been hurt and offended by the younger woman's coolness.

With Lydia in her pram, Sophie left the Moores' neat little bungalow and walked back to the static caravan where she lived. Belinda had totally loathed living there and had been delighted to move into her boyfriend's smart apartment in town. But Sophie looked on the caravan as her home and loved the fact that the big front window looked out on a field where sheep sometimes grazed. Indeed, high on her agenda was the dream that some day she might be in a position to stop renting and buy a more up-to-date model.

Changing back into her jeans and gathering up her cleaning materials, Sophie was in a hurry to make up the time she had lost from her day's work. Try as she might, she found it impossible to lock her memories of Belinda's wedding and her first meeting with Antonio out of her thoughts...

Sophie had been thrilled when she was asked to be a bridesmaid. Some of her enthusiasm had waned, however, once she'd realised that Belinda wanted her to conceal her humble beginnings and avoid any close contact with Pablo's blue-blooded family. Only her sister's frantic pleas for her to share that special day with

her had persuaded Sophie to overlook those embarrassing strictures.

Belinda had paid all her expenses and it had been
cheapest for Sophie to travel to Spain on a five-day
package holiday at a nearby resort. Sophie's father, his
then girlfriend and her son had decided to take advantage of the low prices and share the same apartment.
The day of their arrival, and the night before the wedding, Sophie had accompanied Belinda to a social evening at the imposingly large home of one of Pablo's
relatives.

Sophie had felt like a prune in the fancy pink suit
that Belinda had insisted on buying for her. Worried
that she might mortify her sister by saying or doing the
wrong thing in such exalted company, Sophie had taken
refuge in the billiards room. It was there that she had
met Antonio for the first time. Glancing up from the
solo game she had been engaged in, she had seen him
watching her from the doorway. Drop-dead gorgeous in
an open-necked black shirt and chinos, he had simply
taken her breath away.

'How long have you been standing there?' she asked.

Antonio laughed huskily. 'Long enough to appreciate
your skill,' he replied in perfect, accented English. 'But
you're not playing billiards, you're playing snooker.
Who taught you?'

'My dad.'

'Either you're a born player or you must have practised a great deal.'

Sophie resisted the urge to admit that when she was
a kid her father had often kept her out of school so that
he could take her into bars at lunchtime and place bets
on her ability to beat all comers at snooker. Her father
had only stopped that lucrative pastime when the au-

thorities had given him a stern warning about her poor school-attendance record.

'I guess…' she muttered, biting her lower lip while all the while studying him from below her lashes and feeling horribly shy. She had an innate distrust of handsome men and he was dazzling. She was also noticing the subtle signs of expensive designer elegance in his apparel and going into automatic retreat. 'I shouldn't be in here.'

'Why not? Are you not a friend of the bride's?'

Remembering Belinda's warning, she nodded grudging agreement.

'And your name?' Antonio prompted, strolling silently closer.

'Sophie…'

He extended a lean brown hand. 'I am Antonio.'

Awkwardly she brushed his fingertips and backed towards the door. 'I'd better get back to the other room before I'm missed. I don't want to insult them—'

'Them…?' He quirked an amused dark brow. 'All those terrifying Spanish people next door?'

'It might seem funny to you, but I don't speak the lingo and the ones that speak English can't seem to understand *my* English and keep on asking me to repeat things… It's a nightmare!' she heard herself confiding, desperately grateful just to find someone who could follow what she was saying.

'I shall go and tell them off immediately. How dare they frighten you into hiding in the billiard room?' Antonio teased.

Sophie lifted her chin. 'I don't hide from people.'

'Let's play…' He presented her with the cue she had abandoned. 'I'll teach you the game.'

'I'll beat you hollow,' she warned him.

His stunning dark eyes gleamed with pleasure at that unashamed challenge to his masculinity. 'I don't think so.'

In fact she played the worst she had ever played. She was so intensely aware of him that she was quite unable to resist the need to keep on looking across at him. She was terrified of the strength of his attraction for her. Young though she was, she was painfully aware of the havoc that tended to result from such wayward physical enthusiasms. It was almost a relief when Belinda interrupted them, aghast to find her little sister in Antonio's company. Making an excuse, Belinda was quick to separate them.

'Didn't you realise who he is?' she scolded Sophie. 'You shouldn't even be talking to him. That's Pablo's big brother...the one with the title and the castle... the Marqués of Salazar.'

For a real live Spanish marquis, Antonio had, on first brief acquaintance at least, seemed refreshingly hip and normal. Sophie was savagely disappointed to discover how far he was out of her reach and annoyed that Antonio had not spelled out exactly who he was. Impervious to Belinda's clumsy attempts to keep them apart, Antonio intervened to sweep Sophie off to meet some of the younger people present. When the evening came to a close, it was Antonio who had to drive Sophie back to the holiday resort: in all the excitement of being the centre of attention as the bride, Belinda had forgotten about her sister's transport needs.

'I can't understand why you are not staying with your sister at my grandmother's home,' Antonio admitted, assisting her into a long, low-slung fire-engine-red sports car that would have looked at home in a Bond movie.

'I didn't want to intrude—'

'I'm not happy that you should be staying in an apartment alone. I do not wish to imply criticism of your sister, but you should be relaxing and enjoying my family's hospitality. I'll wait while you pack,' Antonio imparted with the quiet but absolute authority of a male accustomed to instant obedience to his every expressed wish.

'But I'm not alone…er, I'm with friends,' Sophie protested awkwardly, recognising the impossibility of naming her father when Belinda had begged her not to tell a living soul that they were actually only half-sisters because their late mother had had an extramarital affair. Her sibling had been ashamed of that history, had already refused to share it with Pablo and had been determined that his aristocratic relatives should not find out about it either.

'Friends?' Antonio queried, his bewilderment visibly growing.

'Yes, I decided to make a holiday out of my trip over here…nothing wrong with that, is there?'

'No, there is not,' Antonio drawled in a measured tone. 'But you only arrived in Spain this morning and are perhaps not the best judge of good accommodation. My cousin owns a local business and he tells me that the tourist complex where you are staying has a bad name. The police are often called there to deal with fights and drunks.'

She resisted a flippant urge to tell him that her father would be very much at home there. 'I'm not a delicate flower…I'll manage.'

'But you should not have to manage,' Antonio murmured gently.

The idea that she might look to a man to protect her

from the evils of the world was a really novel concept to Sophie. She lay awake that night on her uncomfortable sofa bed in the apartment's tiny reception area. While she strove to block out the noise of the argument between her father and his girlfriend in the room next door she discovered that she could not stop thinking about Antonio.

At every point where she had consciously expected Antonio to reveal his male feet of clay, she had been confounded. He had listened to every little thing she'd said as if he was interested. He had not once shouted at her or sworn at her or eyed up other girls. He did not drink and drive. Nor had he at any stage attempted to ply her with alcohol or make a pass at her. Indeed Antonio Rocha had in some mysterious and romantic way contrived to make Sophie feel special and cosseted and worthy of attention and care for the first time ever.

At twenty years old, Sophie had never had a serious boyfriend. She was a virgin because she was totally terrified of sliding down the same slippery slope that had wrecked the lives of most of her father's girlfriends. Unlike them, she hadn't had to worry about becoming a mother at too young an age. But she had observed that placing faith and energy in countless casual relationships could result in low self-esteem, even a disrupted education and poor employment prospects, thus trapping one in poverty. She had told herself that she was too clever to succumb to the dangerous allure of casual sex, but the real truth was that she had never been remotely tempted to succumb to the coarse advances she had met with.

Never before had she lain awake until dawn counting the hours until she would see a guy again. Never before had she agonised over whether or not a man liked her or whether in fact he was simply being polite. Never before had she fantasised like mad over what it would be like if that same man were to kiss her. In fact her imagination was so extravagantly exercised by Antonio that when she saw him face to face again embarrassment afflicted her with blushes, stammers and painful shyness for the first time in her life. She had floated through Belinda's wedding festivities on a cloud of such intense happiness that the wake-up call of cruel reality had been all the harder to bear twenty-four hours later...

Antonio stayed behind at the solicitor's to clarify certain matters for his own benefit. Even the vague facts that he was able to establish stamped the kind of reflective frown to his lean, dark features that put his employees on their mettle.

Evidently, Belinda had been penniless at the time of her death and working as a barmaid. Yet when she had married Pablo, the beautiful blonde had been a receptionist in a London modelling agency, her comfort and security ensured by the healthy amount of cash and property she had inherited from her parents. Antonio had little need to wonder who or what had been responsible for bringing about Belinda's reduced circumstances and angry regret gripped him. That his late sister-in-law had been living with another man did go some way to satisfying his need to know why Belinda had apparently been determined not to ask her late husband's family for help.

It took a lot to shock Antonio but he was stunned when, having asked for Sophie's address, he learned where exactly she was living. He could not initially credit that she resided in a trailer park. Was his criminally dishonest brother responsible for her impoverishment as well? The limousine paused outside the entrance while his chauffeur double-checked his destination with his employer. Alighting outside the run-down office, Antonio decided that Sophie was a problem best cured by the liberal application of money.

Sophie was cleaning the floor in one of the smarter mobile homes on the site when a brisk knock sounded on the door. Scrambling up, she pushed it open and froze when she clashed with dark-as-midnight eyes set below level black brows. She knew she should not but she stared, drinking in the dark, sexy symmetry of his bold, masculine features. Her heart started to beat very, very fast. 'You said seven o'clock,' she reminded him. 'What are you doing here this early?'

'Is this not a good time for you?' Antonio enquired, his keen gaze raking from the torrent of her curls gilded to gold by the sunlight to the vivid intensity of her animated face and then back to centre on the soft, ripe curve of her mouth. Taken individually her features were ordinary and flawed, he reflected grimly. But that did not explain why she continually gave him the impression of being ravishingly pretty.

'No, it's not... I mean, I'm working and Lydia's asleep and it's just not convenient,' Sophie broke into an enervated surge of protest.

'I appreciate that but I have nothing else to do in this locality while I wait. I'm also understandably eager to meet my niece,' Antonio responded without apology. There was a brooding coolness in his decisive scrutiny as he suppressed the absurd spark of desire she always generated. He could only think she had the deceptive allure of the unfamiliar for him. 'May I come in?'

Feeling ridiculously flustered, Sophie edged back into the trailer's small lounge area and surreptitiously moist-

ened her dry mouth. He strolled up the steps and took
up what felt like every square inch of space.

'You'll have to wait until Lydia wakes up from her
nap.'

Impatience tautened Antonio's striking bone structure. 'Meeting her uncle should be rather more fun than
sleeping. I haven't got much time to spend in the UK.
I'd be grateful if you tried not to make matters more
complicated than they need be.'

By the end of that little speech Sophie was breathing
a little heavily. She had put Lydia down for a nap so that
the baby would be less tired when Antonio made his
visit. His early arrival had thrown that schedule into
chaos. Her small, slight body stiff with annoyance and
concern, she bent her curly head and pinned her lips tight
on the tart comments eager to flow from her ready
tongue. Antonio Rocha, Marqués of Salazar, was loaded.
The solicitor had treated him like royalty and had treated
her like trash to be tolerated. The warning was clear: she
could not afford to make Antonio a bitter enemy. If push
came to shove, he would always win the upper hand by
virtue of his wealth and status. Therefore, even if it
choked her, she had to be polite for Lydia's sake and
swallow Antonio's every demand with as much grace as
she could manage.

'Lydia will be a little cranky if we waken her before
she's ready,' Sophie said hesitantly.

'I want to see my niece now,' Antonio decreed, having decided that Sophie responded best to firm authority.

After a pause for consideration, Sophie nodded, for
she wanted to be fair. There had been a lot of little boys
and girls at Belinda's wedding and her sister had once
told her that the Spanish were particularly fond of chil-

dren. Antonio was obviously accustomed to babies and confident of being able to handle his niece. She pushed open the door of the narrow bunkroom where she had stowed Lydia to sleep undisturbed in her little travel cot.

Antonio gazed down at the small hump under the blanket, which was topped by a fluff of light brown curls. His niece looked worryingly tiny. Both Pablo and Belinda had been tall. On the other hand Sophie barely reached the top of Antonio's chest, so it was perfectly possible that the baby was naturally undersized and still quite fit. He reminded himself that when he took Lydia back to Spain she would be checked over. The family doctor, who was an old friend, had suggested that giving the baby a full medical examination would be a wise precaution: one or two babies in the most recent generation had been born with heart murmurs.

Mastering his own reluctance, Antonio decided to show an appropriate level of interest in the child by lifting her out of the cot for a closer inspection. He brushed back the blanket and scooped the baby up.

Almost instantly, the baby went as stiff as a tiny steel girder and looked up at him with enormous stricken brown eyes. Her mouth opened wide enough to treat him to an unwelcome view of her miniature tonsils and a yell that would have roused a graveyard exploded from her. Her face turning scarlet, the baby shrieked blue murder as if she were being attacked. Antonio stared down at his niece in paralysed horror.

'What's wrong with her?' he demanded.

'Have you ever been snatched out of bed by a stranger and dangled in mid-air like a toy?' Sophie asked fiercely, resisting the urge to haul Lydia from his inept and unfeeling hands.

Hearing Sophie's voice, Lydia twisted her little head round. The baby squirmed like mad and stretched out her hands towards her aunt in a movement that was as frantic as it was revealing.

'Perhaps you should have made the effort to introduce us first,' Antonio censured, and without further ado he deposited the screaming bundle into Sophie's waiting arms.

His sculpted mouth curling, his ears still ringing from that appalling bout of shrieking, he watched his tiny niece clamp onto Sophie's shoulder like a limpet restored to its favourite rock. An immediate and very welcome silence fell. While the baby clung with what he considered to be quite unnecessary drama, Sophie rewarded that show of extreme favouritism with an enormous amount of petting and kissing and soothing whispers.

'I had no idea that the child would be quite so attached to you,' Antonio admitted flatly.

'I've been looking after Lydia since she was born.' Restless with tension, Sophie moved out of the bunkroom and back into the lounge. 'Belinda was ill at first...and then later, well, there were reasons why she wasn't able to spend as much time as she would have liked with her daughter.'

'What reasons?' Antonio prompted.

'Belinda started seeing a bloke who wasn't fussed about kids and when she moved in with him, Lydia stayed on with me,' Sophie explained grudgingly.

'Here...in this place?'

'We should be so lucky.' Sophie loosed an uneasy laugh. 'This is a luxury holiday home. The one I live in is at least twenty years older and without frills.'

Antonio spread his attention round the confines of a

room that he found claustrophobically small. Frills? What frills? The décor was abysmal and so jazzy and cheap it offended his eyes. *This* was what she called luxury? He bit back an incredulous comment.

'If you don't live in *this*, why are you here?'

'I'm cleaning it for the holiday-makers coming to stay tomorrow.'

Appalled by that admission, Antonio stared at her with concealed disbelief. 'You are employed on the park as a cleaner?'

Sophie curved Lydia even closer to her taut length. 'Have you got a problem with that?'

His strong jaw line squared, for he had hoped she had been joking. 'Of course not. You said that my brother robbed your sister. Did you lose money too?'

'I've never had money to lose,' Sophie answered in surprise, and then, realising that he did not understand why that should be the case, she sighed and surrendered to the inevitable. 'There's a skeleton in my family cupboard and Belinda didn't like me to talk about it. Belinda and I may have had the same mother but we had different fathers. I didn't meet my sister until I was seventeen.'

'All families have their secrets,' Antonio murmured, relieved to finally have some explanation on that score. 'Let us be candid with each other.'

Sophie tensed again. 'I wasn't going to tell you any lies.'

Picking up on her anxiety, Lydia lifted her head and loosed an uneasy little cry.

Antonio spread expressive lean brown hands. 'I do not want to argue with you.'

'Good…but between you and me and the wall there, you and I would always argue.'

'I don't accept that.' Antonio angled a smile at her, dark golden eyes cool and confident. 'A child's future is at stake here and after what you've undergone in recent months, it is natural that you should be under stress.'

'I haven't undergone anything,' Sophie asserted tightly. 'I love Lydia and I enjoy looking after her. Worrying about what's going to happen now that you're in the picture is all that's stressing me out.'

Two pairs of eyes, one green, one brown, were anxiously pinned to him, both fearful. For the first time in his thirty years of existence, Antonio felt like the wolf in the fairy tale, guilty of terrorising the innocent and the vulnerable. At the same time being treated like the bad guy infuriated him and stung his strong pride. He decided that it was time to drop the diplomatic approach. If he made his intentions and his expectations clear there would be no room for misunderstandings.

'Why should you worry about what's going to happen now that I'm here to help? I must assume that you intend to insult me—'

'No, I didn't intend that!' Sophie interrupted in dismay at that interpretation of her words.

Lean, strong face hard, Antonio dealt her a stony appraisal. 'My intervention can only be of advantage to my niece when she is currently living in appalling poverty. You have done your best in most trying circumstances and I honour you for your efforts on the child's behalf and thank you for your concern,' he drawled smooth as glass. 'But Lydia's best interests will be met only when I take her back to Spain and ensure that she receives the care and privileges which are hers by right of birth.'

As he spoke every atom of colour slowly drained

from Sophie's shattered face. 'We don't live in appalling poverty—'

'On my terms, I'm afraid that you do. I do not wish to offend you but I must speak the truth.'

'You can't take her away from me…and back to Spain,' Sophie breathed shakily, feeling so sick at that threat she could hardly squeeze out sound. The very idea of losing Lydia hit her as hard as a punch in the stomach, winding her, driving her mind blank with gut-wrenching fear.

'Why not?' Antonio quirked an ebony brow. She was white as snow and clutching the baby to her like a second skin. A mixture of frustration and anger gripped him, for he knew that his intentions were pure and his solution the only sensible one. 'I can see no alternative to that plan. If you love the child, you won't stand in her way. I will give her a much better life.'

Sophie took a step back as if she could no longer bear to be that close to him. 'I honestly think I will die if you take her away from me,' she framed unsteadily. 'I love her so much and she loves me. You can't just throw me out of her life as though I'm nothing just because I'm poor.'

Antonio stilled. Faint dark colour illuminated the spectacular slant of his carved cheekbones. He was severely disconcerted by the tears swimming in her eyes and her raw emotion. She had abandoned all pride, dropped her tough front. She looked like a tiny teenager striving to stand up to a bully. The baby, evidently picking up on her aunt's distress, was sobbing into Sophie's slight shoulder.

'It is not a matter of throwing you out of her life… This is the language of emotion, not of intellect,' Antonio censured in exasperation.

Sophie dragged in a deep, tremulous breath and treated him to a look of fierce condemnation. 'I'm not ashamed of that...as far as I'm concerned love would win over money every time—'

'According to what I understand, you've never had any money, so are scarcely qualified to make such a sweeping statement—'

'I love her...you don't!' Sophie launched at him.

'If you love her why don't you restrain your temper and stop scaring her?' Antonio asked with lethal effect.

Sophie gave him an anguished look and turned away, soothing the anxious child in her arms.

Antonio decided that it had been a definite mistake to try to cut to the baseline as if he were dealing with a business issue. There was nothing businesslike about Sophie. Nothing practical, nothing sensible, nothing controlled. In fact he had never seen a woman betray that amount of emotion and the freedom with which she showed it held an almost indecent fascination for him. She was a powder keg of passionate feeling. Sexual curiosity threatened to seize him and he fought it off, angry with her, angry with himself. But even anger could not make him unaware of a very powerful urge to just grab her up and flatten her to the nearest bed. Scarcely an appropriate response to her distress, he acknowledged. He despised the primitive reactions she had always stirred in him.

'I want you to think over what I've said,' Antonio continued, deciding that attempting further discussion in the current atmosphere would be unprofitable. 'I'll come back tomorrow morning at eleven. If you need to talk to me before then, you can reach me at this hotel.' He passed her a card. 'Tell me where you live.'

'In the blue van at the far end…the one parked right by the field,' Sophie told him chokily.

'I have no desire to sound like an actor in a bad movie but I can improve your life as well as Lydia's. You don't need to live at this level.'

'Oddly enough, I've never met any baby thieves living like this, only decent people who don't think money and social status is the be-all and end-all of life!' Sophie tossed back accusingly.

Antonio decided to prove his maturity by not responding to that taunt. 'I think it would be less upsetting for the baby if she was…resting when I call tomorrow.'

'Perhaps you'd like to think about how much Lydia will be upset if I suddenly vanish out of her life,' Sophie retorted thickly.

Antonio was sufficiently impressed by that warning to glance at the baby. He could not evade the suspicion that his brother's child had inherited Sophie's overly emotional temperament and was more sensitive than most. He had only lifted the child and it had gone off like a burglar alarm on hyper alert. For a split second he imagined carrying the baby away with both Sophie and the baby screaming and sobbing at high volume and he barely managed to repress a very masculine shudder.

Discovering a depth of imagination that he had not known he possessed, he even considered the risk of tabloid headlines and interference. *Baby thief.* No, he would be careful to do nothing likely to rouse such hysterical publicity. He was, he reminded himself, a highly intelligent and shrewd businessman. He was renowned for his logic and subtlety and his willingness to consider fresh and innovative approaches to find workable solutions. He was confident that he would find a way to persuade Sophie to accept the inevitable with good grace.

'You don't care about how I feel or how she feels, do you?' Sophie accused as she thrust wide the front door, descended the steps and proceeded to buckle Sophie into her buggy.

'I care enough to want to ensure that my niece does not grow up with your disadvantages.'

Shooting him a shocked glance from pain-filled green eyes, Sophie lifted her head high. 'Isn't it strange that even with all your advantages—your money and title and education and success—you are a ruthless bastard with no consideration for anyone's feelings but your own?'

Hot temper unleashing, Antonio surveyed her with thickly lashed eyes that shimmered a biting gold. 'But then I'm not a hypocrite. I know that you're not the fragile little flower that you look, *querida*. You're the same sleazy little liar who told me she was ill and then went out to get drunk and shag some loser on the beach,' he reminded her with icy derision. 'What you could never grasp about a guy like me is my good manners.'

'Excuse me? *You?* Good manners?' Sophie slung back at him in a hissing undertone selected to bypass Lydia's hearing.

'You said you were unwell. Naturally I went to see you to offer you my assistance.'

'Nah...that wasn't good manners, Antonio. You didn't trust me, so you called round to check up on me and you couldn't wait to jump to the wrong conclusions about me!' Sophie hurled with the bitterness she had never managed to shake off. 'Well, for your information, I told a polite lie to avoid embarrassing you with the truth of why I couldn't see you that night. And by the way, that loser you refer to was Terry, the son of my father's girlfriend, and he might have been very tall for his age but he was only fourteen years old! Not my lover, not my anything, just a scared kid worried sick about his mum!'

Having delivered that final rebuttal with spirit, Sophie stalked down the path with the buggy. To Antonio's eyes, she seemed to dance as she moved. Her golden corkscrew curls bounced and tumbled round her shoulders and down her narrow back. The worn fabric of her jeans accentuated the suggestion of a pert swing to her small, heart-shaped derrière. She did not have much of any particular attribute, but what she did have had an explosive effect on his libido. He was not proud of his base instincts. Willing his inappropriate arousal to hell and back, Antonio breathed in very slow and deep.

But he still wanted to haul her back and voice his scorn for that foolish story that only an intellectually challenged male would swallow. He wanted to ask her where she got off speaking to him in that impertinent tone. He wanted her to listen to his every word when he spoke to her. He wanted to teach her respect. He wanted to drag her into his arms and demonstrate sexual skills that he had never practised on a beach…at least, not a public one. Being who he was, however, and proud of his tough self-discipline, he chose instead to watch her walk away. He could no longer ignore the obvious: shameful though it was, it could only be her sluttish qualities that attracted him.

CHAPTER THREE

ANTONIO was planning to take Lydia from her and bring her up in Spain, Sophie reflected in agonised panic. How dared he start telling her how the baby that she loved should be brought up?

Frantically determined to keep herself busy so that she did not have time to fret, Sophie fed Lydia and put her to bed. She tidied up the static caravan that had been her home for over three years. She would make an early start tomorrow to finish that mobile home. She opened the box of cardigans the mail order firm had sent her to be embroidered and sat down to begin work on the intricate flowers.

How was she supposed to fight Antonio? A real live aristocrat? Was her lifestyle really one of appalling poverty? They had a secure roof over their heads and enough to eat. Admittedly the mobile home could be rather cold in winter and their clothes were rarely new, but Lydia was a happy, thriving child. How was she supposed to demand equal rights over her niece when Antonio could offer so much more in every material way?

Norah Moore called in at nine that evening. As soon as the older woman realised that Antonio was returning the next day, she offered to take care of Lydia while he was there. 'That way you'll be able to talk in peace. Where did you say this Antonio was staying?'

'I didn't say...the card's on the table,' Sophie mum-

bled, dimly wondering why the older woman wanted
to know.

'Quite a way away...the hotel looks very fancy,'
Norah remarked. 'You should take yourself off for a
walk along the beach. That always calms you down. I'll
mind Lydia.'

'How can I calm down? Antonio is going to take
Lydia off me,' Sophie breathed in a tormented whisper.
'He's already made up his mind.'

'You can't be sure of that. Wait and see what happens. You might be surprised,' Norah remarked cryp-
tically.

'I don't think so. Antonio was pretty blunt.'

The older woman gave Sophie's arm a comforting
squeeze and departed without further comment.

Sophie trudged down to the beach and let the breeze
toss her hair into a wild mass. Antonio had not changed
one atom, she thought feverishly. He had not had a clue
how to handle Lydia, but had been far too arrogant to
admit it. In fact he appeared to know precious little
about young children, a reality he had been happy to
ignore while picking on her shortcomings. And, worse
still, Antonio was still as prejudiced against her as he
had been at their last meeting in Spain almost three
years earlier...

Her memories of that period in her life were still
surprisingly fresh and raw and her thoughts swept her
back in time. Her sister's wedding had turned into a
dream event for Sophie as well as the bride. Throughout
that day, Antonio had smoothed Sophie's passage in a
whole host of ways. He had complimented her on her
appearance in the fussy purple dress that she had secretly absolutely detested. He had chatted to her while
the photographs were being taken, arranged to have her

sit near him at the reception and acted as interpreter and translator so that she could mix with the other guests. He had introduced her to lots of people, danced with her and acted as if her pleasure was his primary objective.

All that attention had been a very heady experience for Sophie, who would have felt vastly out of her depth in such smart company without Antonio's support. Her feet had barely touched the ground.

Belinda had been concerned enough to take Sophie aside to warn her off. 'Antonio's being very kind to you, but I don't want you to get the wrong idea about him—'

'I'm not getting *any* ideas about him,' Sophie protested in severe embarrassment, wondering if she had been making a fool of herself. After all, she had been doing all those despicable girlie things like batting her eyelashes at him and going for the giggle rather than the belly laugh.

'There's no way that Antonio would be attracted to you. Pablo says his brother's standards are so high that a saint couldn't make the grade with him,' her sister pointed out apologetically. 'But Antonio does have fantastic manners. Obviously he felt sorry for you when he found you on your own last night. I'm sure that's why he's making so much effort to ensure that you have a good time today.'

'Push off,' Sophie told Antonio when he next asked her to dance. 'When I need the sympathy vote, I'll let you know.'

'What are you talking about?' Antonio demanded with incredulity.

'I hear you're being kind to me because you took pity on me last night—'

'No, I'm really not that nice and unselfish.' His shimmering dark golden eyes connected with hers and held her entrapped. For the space of thirty seconds she was as out of touch with planet earth as a rocket powering into space. 'Was it your sister who told you that? I did notice her anxious looks. It's natural for her to want to protect you.'

Having driven her back to the apartment complex that night, he insisted on escorting her right into the shabby reception area. Once there, he quite casually suggested taking her out to eat the following evening and giving her a tour of a less busy part of the coast. Striving hard to match his cool, she accepted with a shrug and went into the lift with a light wave. Hopefully he hadn't noticed that she was so dizzy with excitement that she bumped her nose on the back wall of the lift.

Like Cinderella without the fairy godmother to help, Sophie toiled from dawn to dusk the next day striving to beautify herself for Antonio's benefit. Early that evening, however, her father and his girlfriend, Miriam split up. Miriam found Sophie's father with another woman and a huge argument took place. After listening wretchedly from the balcony to the fight that concluded in their separate departures, Sophie crept back indoors.

Ten minutes later Miriam's teenaged son, Terry, appeared. The boy was desperate to find his mother and prevent her from drowning her sorrows in drink. Only then did Sophie learn that Miriam was a recovering alcoholic. She was bitterly ashamed of her father's behaviour towards the poor woman. She also knew that she would not be able to live with her conscience if she did not help Terry look for his distraught parent.

Telling Antonio the full sordid truth of the goings-on at the apartment that day was not an option as far as

Sophie was concerned. It broke her heart to phone him and cancel their night out with the polite fiction that she had taken ill. He made no mention of an alternative arrangement and time was running out fast, for her flight home was only twenty-four hours away.

That search for Miriam through all the many bars in the resort was long and unsuccessful. Footsore, exhausted and too broke to afford a taxi, Sophie and Terry walked home by the beach in the early hours of the morning. Her heart leapt with joy when Antonio stepped out of a car parked across the street from the entrance. She told Terry to go on up to bed.

'I was so scared that I wasn't going to see you again,' she confided, too delighted by his appearance even to remember that she had pleaded sickness as an excuse for not seeing him earlier.

'You won't see me again.' Lean bronzed face hard, Antonio raked contemptuous dark-as-jet eyes over her.

Bewildered, she stared up at him, suddenly horribly conscious that she was looking even less glam than usual. 'But...but you're here now—why not?'

'How many reasons do you need? That you pretend to be ill when there's nothing wrong with you?'

'There was a reason for that—'

'*Sí.* I saw you with your arm round the young man in the Union Jack shirt. You've been on the beach with him,' Antonio murmured with mesmerising sibilance, letting a brown forefinger casually flick a stain on her vest top. 'And rolling in sand. I don't have to be a detective to know that you've been screwing outdoors.'

An argumentative drunk on the beach had kicked wet sand at her and soiled her white top and shorts. 'No, you've got it wrong—'

'*De veras?* I'm not into liars or tattoos.' Antonio angled a brief look of derision at the tiny colourful butterfly etched into the skin of her bare shoulder before concluding with succinct bite, 'Or for that matter, sluts.'

Sophie did not like to recall that she had been so keen on him that even after that rejection she had tried to contact him by phone to plead her innocence. Her initial calls had been unsuccessful and then he had phoned her to dismiss the whole situation with galling casualness.

'Stop worrying about this,' Antonio advised with nonchalant cool. 'There is no need for you to make any explanations to me. I had no right to criticise your behaviour. You went out on a date and told me a little white lie. It was nothing and now that we are related by marriage, even less than nothing.'

She discovered that his good manners could be the unyielding equivalent of an immoveable stone wall. He was equally firm about wishing her a good trip home and ending that brief conversation. It was a very long time before Sophie recovered from that disappointment. Foolish though it was, she had fallen madly in love within the space of forty-eight hours. So many times after that she wished that she had never laid eyes on Antonio Rocha. What she had never known she could not have missed. Nor would she have found herself pointlessly comparing the rough-and-ready males she met with a high-born Spanish noble.

Drifting back to the present, Sophie rediscovered her sense of purpose and hope. She was being too pessimistic. She had not really tried to reason with Antonio. Why should he want to take on the burden of a baby? He was a single guy, for goodness' sake! When Lydia had begun crying, Antonio had been totally unnerved. All she had to do was convince Antonio that she was capable of giving Lydia a loving and secure home. Maybe she would have to find fancier accommodation to please him, but if he was willing to contribute even a small amount towards Lydia's upkeep that would be possible. Surely then a compromise could be reached?

Antonio had decided to breakfast in the public restaurant rather than in the isolation of his suite. He had just finished eating when the head waiter approached his secluded table to inform him that he had a visitor waiting to see him in the lounge.

A gaunt older woman with grey hair scrambled up to introduce herself as Norah Moore. 'You don't know me, but I've known Sophie for years,' she proclaimed nervously. 'I know it's early but I wanted the chance to have a private word with you before you saw Sophie again.'

Antonio extended his hand. 'Antonio Rocha. Please sit down. Would you like something to drink? Perhaps tea?'

'Sophie said you had lovely manners...she was right. I don't need tea...thanks,' Norah told him anxiously. 'I'm here because I'm worried about Sophie.'

'How may I help you?' Antonio enquired.

'Sophie's wonderful with Lydia and terribly fond of the kiddie. You mustn't try to part them.'

'I only want what is best for my niece,' Antonio fielded gently.

'Sophie and your niece are as close as any mother and child. There's also the fact that Lydia's own mother wanted her sister to keep her child for good. I was a witness to that being said by Belinda,' the older woman continued squarely. 'Were you aware of that?'

'No, I was not,' Antonio conceded.

'There's something else too,' Norah continued heavily. 'Something I don't want to tell you but I feel I should tell you for Sophie's sake.'

'I can be discreet.'

'Well, Sophie can't have children of her own. She had leukaemia when she was a kid and the treatment messed her up. Did you know about that?'

'No, I was not aware of it,' Antonio said flatly, his strong bone structure tightening, the pallor of shock spreading below his bronzed skin.

Indeed he felt almost sick at that revelation. He was appalled to think of how she must have suffered as a child. He also knew how much Sophie would have loathed his knowledge of such a very personal matter. He did not question how he knew that. He was both angry and relieved that the older woman had decided to betray Sophie's confidence. His ignorance of just how vulnerable Sophie was had made him behave like a cruel bastard.

'So obviously that baby is very precious to Sophie. She's had a rotten life, you know,' Norah Moore continued accusingly. 'She works her fingers to the bone seven days a week trying to give that baby something better than she had herself. It may not look like much on your terms, but don't underestimate the sacrifices she's made. She looked after that daft sister of hers as well—'

'You have made your point, Mrs Moore.'

Having escorted the older woman out to her car, Antonio strode back into the hotel. What had Sophie said? *I honestly think I will die if you take her away from me.* He had preferred to be cynical about the depth of her affection for the child. Now, and thanks only to a stranger's intervention, he was being forced to face the probability that Sophie was very deeply attached to the child and with good reason if she could not have a baby of her own. He was dealing with a much more complex situation than he had appreciated. If he was to deprive Sophie of Lydia, might grief drive her into doing something foolish? He breathed in slow and deep and then out again in a measured hiss of acceptance. That was not a risk he felt it would be reasonable for him to take. For the first time he acknowledged that Lydia was as much Sophie's niece as his.

CHAPTER FOUR

LATER that morning, Sophie saw the limousine first. Antonio swung out and unfolded to his full intimidating height and she had eyes only for him. Immaculate in appearance and stunningly handsome, he was wearing a formal charcoal-grey suit teamed with a white shirt and a blue silk tie. Dragging her enthralled attention from him, she smoothed damp palms down over her most presentable T-shirt.

She was so nervous she started talking before she even had the door properly open. 'A friend is looking after Lydia for me...I thought we could talk on the beach... It's a lovely day.'

Lovely? Antonio thought the sky was cloudy, the wind rather strong and the temperature distinctly on the cool side. But then even at its best the British climate could not compete with the sun-drenched heat of his own country, he conceded ruefully.

'We would have more privacy indoors,' he suggested.

Sophie tensed. 'I don't want you to see where I live,' she admitted.

Antonio raised a bemused brow. '*Por qué*...why?'

Sophie began walking along the path that led down to the strand. 'After that crack you made about poverty, I just wouldn't feel comfortable entertaining you in my home. It may not be much but I like it. Why should I have to put up with you acting like I'm living in a hovel?'

'I hope I would not be so rude,' Antonio drawled flatly.

'Well, you were yesterday,' Sophie could not resist telling him. 'On the beach, we'll be equal.'

Antonio was not dressed for the beach. He wondered if that was supposed to be part of the great levelling exercise or if she was secretly hoping that he would freak out when he got sand on his shoes. He watched her race to the edge of the water like an eager child, her every movement fired with mercurial energy. Beautiful to look at, but almost impossible to handle. She was unpredictable, hot-tempered, impulsive, wildly emotional: she was driving him mad. The proposition he was about to outline, however, would restore the status quo. She would become much more amenable to his guidance when she was living in Spain...

'I've worked out a compromise since we talked last night,' Antonio imparted in his smooth honeyed drawl.

'Oh...?' Her spirits lifted by the bright reflection of the sun on the sea, Sophie pinned hopeful eyes to his bold bronzed profile.

'You can move to Spain.'

'No way!' Sophie gasped in disconcertion.

'Try not to interrupt me.' Dark golden eyes levelled on her mutinous face. 'Lydia will have to live at the *castillo* with me, but I own many properties nearby. Finding you accommodation would not be a problem and it would be free. You could see the child whenever you liked and she would find it easier to adapt to her new home if you were there to provide support.'

Sophie folded her arms with a jerk. She could not believe his nerve. 'So I give up my life here, move abroad and live in limbo on your property like some charity case. Thanks, but no, thanks! I'm not unreasonable. I'm happy to share Lydia with you but I refuse to hand her over to you lock, stock, and barrel. I mean, what are you planning to do with her?'

'Engage childcare professionals to take care of her every need.'

Her green eyes flamed. 'That really says it all, doesn't it? Why can't you just be honest? You haven't the slightest personal interest in your brother's child. You think it's your duty to give her a home, but you resent it—'

'That is not true.' But there was enough of a grain of truth in that accusation to flick Antonio on the raw.

'You'll never love Lydia the way I do because you're always going to see her as a burden!'

'You're wrong,' Antonio incised almost fiercely.

'Of course you will. She's not your baby and you didn't ask for her and you're not that fussed about kids anyway…and if you get married Lydia's likely to be as popular as rat poison with your wife!'

'I have no intention of getting married—'

Adrenalin pounding through her veins, Sophie stalked over to him to look up at him, her eyes bright with conviction. 'But she needs a mother, Antonio. Not people you pay to wash and feed her.'

'I'm not ready for marriage.'

'Then let Lydia and I alone and send us the occasional postcard!' Sophie advised thinly, her temper rising at her inability to gain an emotional reaction from him. 'You're too selfish to take charge of a baby. You'll neglect her. You'll be too busy wheeling and dealing at the office and socialising with your harem of women to make time for her!'

Brilliant eyes shimmering into a hot golden blaze, Antonio closed long fingers round Sophie's wrist to urge her closer. 'Harem?' he prompted with subdued mockery.

Angry, mortified colour burnished Sophie's cheeks. 'Pablo used to tell Belinda all about your exploits with your string of women.'

'Pablo would have known nothing. We were not close. I did not confide in him. But while I may not talk of my conquests I'm not ashamed of my sex life. Did you think I would be?' Arrogant dark head high, Antonio gazed down at her, lush black lashes semi-screening his disturbingly intent gaze.

'I don't give two hoots about your flippin' sex life!' Sophie flung in affronted denial, her cheeks burning.

'I think you do…' Antonio breathed soft and low, the dark timbre of his deep, rich drawl feathering down her slender spine like a hurricane warning. 'I think that nearly three years ago I was too much of a gentleman for your tastes—'

'Gentleman is not a word I would label you with,' Sophie cut in unevenly, a hunger she could not suppress licking up in her pelvis and freezing her where she stood bare inches from him. Every inch of her was taut and screaming with so powerful an awareness of her own body that she felt light-headed. All she needed from him was one kiss, she was telling herself. One kiss just to see what all the fuss was about and she was convinced that he would be as much of a disappointment as every other guy she had kissed. But in Antonio's case, it would be a glorious, wonderful disappointment that would for ever banish her unease around him.

'But, whatever the label, you're still hot for me, *mi cielo*,' Antonio murmured huskily.

Sophie trembled. 'Curious...' she admitted in a breath of sound, her throat dry and tight.

Antonio never kissed women in public. He gazed down at her, his attention welded to the darkened emerald of her expectant eyes and the ruby allure of her luscious, parted lips. He lifted a hand to close his fingers into her curls, learning that her hair felt soft as silk and picturing the rebellious golden-toffee waves spread across his pillows. Thought had nothing to do with what happened next.

His mouth touched hers; she stopped breathing. He brushed her lips light as a butterfly and then slowly deepened the pressure. She was torn by delight and impatience and a mortifying desire to grab him with both hands. Tantalised beyond bearing, she leant towards him, wildly conscious of the aching heaviness of her breasts below her T-shirt, the swelling sensitivity of the rosy crowns abraded by the rough cotton. She knew she wanted his mouth there too and the very thought shocked her rigid, but she could no more pull back from him and temptation than she could have stemmed the tide.

'Antonio...' she whispered.

'I don't want this...' Antonio growled, but he went back for more of it all the same.

Passion banished restraint as he used his tongue to delve deep into the moist interior of her mouth. That invasive tactic had the most extraordinary effect on Sophie. The taste and feel of him drove her wild. An excitement close to the edge of pain shot like flame through her slender length. She shivered violently and locked her arms round his neck, kissing him back with unconditional fervour. The heat and strength of his lean, powerful body hard against her softer curves left her breathless and gasping.

In an abrupt movement, Antonio wrenched himself back from her. Stunning eyes a scorching gold, he was breathing heavily. For a split second, Sophie was lost in a time slip, still craving that intoxicating tide of sensation. Then self-preservation kicked in and she spun away, digging shaking hands into the pockets of her jeans and dragging in oxygen in a greedy gulp. He was dynamite. She hadn't wanted to find that out. But equally quickly it dawned on her that the attraction was not one-sided, as she had once naïvely believed.

Her body felt electrified and deprived, but her mind was racing. A wicked sense of triumph put her embarrassment to flight. Antonio Rocha, Marqués de Salazar might think that he was vastly superior to her in every way, but he still fancied her. Whoopee! Yay! She was tempted to dance round the beach and sing. In one fell swoop, in the space of one revealing kiss, almost three years of believing that she had made an outsize fool of herself in Spain had been wiped out. Antonio was more into tattoos than he was ever likely to admit.

The silence stretched like an endless cavern where light never shone.

Feeling indecently smug and ashamed of herself, Sophie veiled her sparkling eyes and reflected dizzily that she had never imagined a kiss could be that volatile.

'We were talking about you taking up residence in Spain,' Antonio reminded her drily.

He sounded so cool and calm that her buoyant mood deflated as if he had stuck a pin in her. All right, maybe he was only a teensy weensy bit attracted to her. It took enormous effort for her to recapture her ability to concentrate. 'Spain…that idea's not on,' she countered in a flat undertone. 'We'd be in your country and Lydia would be in your home and I wouldn't have any rights. You would be making all the decisions about her. You could easily change your mind about allowing me to see her—'

'You would have to trust me.'

'I don't,' Sophie confided without hesitation. 'I'd have too much to lose. And I just know you'll get married and that would change everything—'

'I am not about to get married. What is this obsession?'

Sophie was unimpressed. She shot him a sidelong glance. Her heartbeat speeded up. He really was breathtakingly handsome. 'Now or five years from now, what difference would it make to me? I'd still be powerless and no wife of yours is likely to allow me to stick my oar in where Lydia's concerned. Your wife would have far more say in her upbringing than I would ever have—'

'*Por favor Dios*... I enjoy my freedom. I won't take a wife for at least ten years!'

'I just want to be with Lydia. That's *all* that I want,' Sophie stressed with pained dignity. 'I love her...you don't. I mean...maybe you're always going to look at her and remember your brother. Don't tell me that he was your favourite person!'

His strong jaw line squared at that inflammatory statement. But he was no hypocrite. As she spun away to hide the tears burning her eyes he tugged her back round to face him, his every move redolent of the confidence that powered him. 'Come back to my hotel with me for lunch...'

Suddenly shy of him again, terrifyingly sensitive to

the intimate tone of his accented voice, Sophie coloured. 'You're not thinking of food.'

Antonio gave her a hard, devastating smile that was quite unrepentant. 'You're so direct—'

His lack of self-consciousness infuriated her and her whole face stiffened. 'I imagine I'd disappoint you.'

'I don't think so.' His stunning dark, deep-set eyes flared reflective gold.

'Purely as a point of speculation, how much would you give up to be with Lydia all the time?'

Her smooth brow pleated. 'I'd do anything for that.'

The silence eddied around her like a dangerous current.

Antonio surveyed her without expression. 'If you had constant access to Lydia and security, would you be prepared to do everything I asked in return for that privilege?'

'Short of crime, yes,' she agreed urgently, but her bewilderment was growing. 'Why are you asking me that?'

'If Lydia needs a mother twenty-four seven, then I should marry. But I like my life as it is. That's the problem,' Antonio admitted with a candour he had never employed with a woman before.

'That you don't want a wife?'

'If I opted for a marriage of convenience instead the problem would vanish. That kind of marriage might last between five and ten years max before ending in an amicable divorce.'

Sophie was hanging on his every word but she was totally confused. 'Why are you telling me this?'

'I think there's a possibility that we could reach a mutually beneficial agreement,' Antonio murmured thoughtfully. 'The wife I choose would have to know the score. I would expect to retain my freedom to come and go as and when I liked and with whom I pleased.'

'You're talking about a fake marriage?' Sophie pressed uncertainly. 'Are you suggesting that you and me—?'

'You would gain Lydia and financial security and my life would continue as normal. That would be the deal.'

Green eyes huge, she stared up at him, transfixed by the concept of marrying him. 'The deal? *But—*'

'You'd be insane to turn me down,' Antonio asserted, examining the arrangement from every angle and more and more impressed by his own creative ingenuity.

He believed that it was as close to perfect as a solution could be. Even so it would only be a temporary solution and he would have to have a watertight prenuptial contract drawn up. Sophie, however, would have no illusions as to the nature of their agreement. She would make her home on his country estate and take full charge of their niece and his conscience could be easy. As soon as he had learned that Sophie was infertile, he had known that it would be indescribably cruel to deprive her of Lydia. But only by marrying Sophie would he be able to watch over the child's interests without being unduly troubled by further responsibility.

His grandmother, however, might well be aghast when Sophie, with her poor background and education, became his bride, but Doña Ernesta was a strong woman and she would get over her disappointment. The rest of the family and his friends would be shocked as well. Always an individual, he decided he could live with that. In any case he was finally willing to recall just how many people had been charmed by Sophie's vivacity when they had met her in Spain. Doña Ernesta would very probably take charge of her and teach her anything she needed to know. His grandparent would also benefit from having full access to Pablo's daughter without the burden of having to worry about the quality of the child's care.

Sophie stared up at Antonio in unconcealed wonderment. He was asking her to marry him so that he could offer her a home with Lydia in Spain. It certainly would be a marriage of convenience, she thought breathlessly, for she could not imagine two people with less in common. Yet it was also a very practical answer to the problem of Lydia's future welfare. Even so, she was still amazed that he should be willing to marry her for Lydia's sake and that he should have come up with that idea quite so quickly.

'*Dios mio!* Say yes and let's get off the beach,' Antonio urged with masculine impatience.

Sophie blinked. 'You can't just throw something like that at me and expect—?'

Antonio dealt her a bold look of challenge. 'Why shouldn't I expect an immediate positive response? You're cleaning floors to put food on the table. You live in a home with wheels under it and it's so shabby you won't let me see it. I have offered you a ticket out of hell.'

Sophie reddened and shifted worriedly off one foot onto the other. 'It's not that simple...this isn't hell—'

In the cool breeze, Antonio suppressed a shiver: he was freezing. He looked out at the grey sea under the grey sky and then down at the even duller shingle below his feet. 'It *is* by my standards.'

'But you're rich and spoilt—'

'Wouldn't you like to be rich and spoilt too?' Antonio murmured smooth as silk, planting a lean brown hand to her narrow back to gently press her back towards the path.

'I can't imagine being rich…but I think I'd like being spoilt,' Sophie confided tightly. 'Is this a joke? Or are you serious?'

'If you can accept a marriage that has a finish date in sight and a husband who is a free agent, I'm serious.'

A husband who was a free agent was a contradiction in terms, Sophie reflected abstractedly. Her head was buzzing with too many thoughts at once. She was astonished, fearful, excited, distrustful and confused all at one and the same time. But she had not been exaggerating when she had said that there was nothing she would not do to be with Lydia.

Marry Antonio? Learn how to be a demure wife? Overlook his infidelity? Her gut reactions warned her that that was wrong and absolutely against her own principles. But then she reminded herself that Antonio was not suggesting a normal marriage. She could scarcely apply the usual moral standards to an arrangement that he had referred to as a 'deal.' A wholly self-centred deal calculated to cause the least possible interference with his enjoyment of his life, she conceded ruefully. But how could she blame him for that? His lack of interest in being a proper parent to Lydia was the only reason he was willing to make it possible for Sophie to continue filling that role for their niece's benefit.

'You have until tonight to decide your answer. I'll send the limo to pick you up and bring you back to my hotel for dinner.' Having reached the top of the path, Antonio was already signalling his chauffeur to indicate his readiness to depart.

Sophie could not help recalling the heady few minutes on the beach when Antonio had awarded her his full attention. That kiss had rocked her world. Now his spectacular dark golden eyes were cool and distant again. His indifference was a slap in the face, a rejection as much as an acknowledgement that their kiss had not been equally special on his terms. In comparison, Sophie was all too well aware that for her the kiss had been seriously addictive stuff. Just thinking about that wicked blaze of excitement made her feel incredibly hot and quivery and very unwilling to look at him.

'What time?' she asked, striving to match his cool with her own.

'Eight.'

'I don't have anything fancy to wear,' she warned him.

'It's not a problem. We'll dine in my suite.'

Sophie got the message. Unless she could present what he deemed to be an acceptable image, she would not be seen in public. Or was she being over-sensitive? Even a little unfair? After all, she would have Lydia with her, and if the baby became sleepy Antonio's suite would be quieter than a public restaurant. She watched him smile, spring into his opulent limousine and depart. It was the sort of throwaway smile he might have given anybody. She was conscious of a deep-seated need to see him smile and know it was just for her.

That evening, and only half an hour late—which was really good going for Sophie in terms of promptness— she travelled up in the lift to Antonio's suite. She had Lydia cradled by one arm on her hip. 'Now remember…lots of smiles. You've got to make the running with Antonio and sell yourself,' she instructed the baby gazing up at her with trusting brown eyes. 'He's sensitive to screams, so you have to take the fear out of fathering for him. If you cry again, he's going to avoid you like the plague...okay?'

A middle-aged guy dressed like a waiter ushered her into the suite.

'Is Antonio in?' Sophie asked nervously and the man responded in what might have been Spanish with an apologetic shake of his head.

She hovered in the centre of the fabulous reception room, shook her head when a sofa was indicated and did so again when the drinks cabinet was spread invitingly wide. A communicating door opened and Antonio appeared. Relief and tension struggled inside her. 'I thought maybe you were out.'

In one skimming glance Antonio took in the unexpected presence of the baby and settled his attention on Sophie. In a shabby cord jacket with a fur-trimmed hood and black trousers ornamented with an embarrassment of zips, she looked painfully young. Her sudden vivacious smile lit up her heart-shaped face and for a split second he forgot what he was about to say and simply stared.

'I'm sorry I wasn't available when you arrived,' Antonio responded, his recovery almost immediate while on another level he sought to solve the riddle of her appeal. 'I was taking a call. Did Maureo offer you a drink?'

'Is that his name? I didn't want anything. It's nice of you not to say anything about me being late.'

'I have a great respect for punctuality,' Antonio sliced back softly.

'We're going to have a problem,' Sophie forecast with unblemished good humour. 'I try really hard to be on time, but things tend to hold me up. Everywhere I go I'm always running against the clock—'

'Better organisation will improve that.'

Sophie wondered if he had any idea how hard it was to organise a baby.

'Maureo would like to take your coat,' Antonio explained as the older man hovered nearby.

'Would you like to hold Lydia?' Sophie asked brightly, ignoring the tautening of his spectacular bone structure and moving closer to helpfully tug up his arm and pass her niece deftly into his grasp. 'Smile and talk to her…she loves people.'

Antonio marvelled at how little Lydia seemed to weigh. He could not recall ever taking a close look at a baby before. With her soft fluff of curls, creamy skin and big brown eyes, she was really quite pretty, he decided in surprise. He could see no resemblance to Pablo. His mobile phone rang. The baby jerked, her face screwing up as she loosed a plaintive howl of fright. Antonio stuffed Lydia back into Sophie's arms with unconcealed haste.

'Perdón…' He took his call.

Sophie soothed Lydia and interpreted Maureo's gestures to take a seat at the table by the window. Antonio was talking in a foreign language, moving his hands to accentuate certain points with a confidence that she found irresistibly attractive. His lean, darkly handsome features were intent with concentration. Some day, Sophie thought fiercely, I want him to ook at me like that. Like I'm important and interesting. n shock at that lowering aspiration that had come out of nowhere at her, she froze. Shame-faced, she cleared her mind and refused to think about it again. She would marry Antonio because that was the price of keeping Lydia. That, she assured herself firmly, was the only reason she had for marrying him. Only a real idiot would get romantic ideas about a guy who said he wanted to be a free agent.

Maureo reappeared toting a highchair for Lydia. Thanking him warmly, she strapped her niece in and put some toys on the tray to keep her occupied.

'You're a very busy guy,' Sophie remarked brittlely when Antonio sat down opposite and the first course had arrived.

'Invariably.'

'Well, like you forecast, I'm about to say yes to the deal. But I have a couple of conditions to make,' Sophie told him while she opened the small container she had brought with her, put some finger foods on her side plate and set them down in front of Lydia.

'Conditions?'

'I want to have a proper wedding,' Sophie advanced uncomfortably. 'Nothing fancy, just us and the witnesses with a few frills…a dress and some photos to make us look like a *real* couple. I don't want Lydia to know this is a deal and not an ordinary marriage.'

'She's six months old,' Antonio murmured drily.

'But she won't always be. I don't ever want her to know that I had to marry you to keep her because that would make her feel bad—'

'Why should it?'

'I remember how I felt knowing I was just a burden to the grown-ups who looked after me.' Sophie set a feeding cup down on the tray of the highchair, her delicate profile taut. 'So, what do you think?'

Antonio recognised that he had not thought through every angle. He had no plans to go public with an announcement that he was making a marriage of convenience. Consequently, he would have no choice but to act out a charade of normality. Appearances mattered little to him, but to the majority of his family appearances were everything. 'The frills aren't a problem but I would like the wedding to be quiet and discreet. What other conditions?'

Sophie worried at her full lower lip with her teeth before speaking. 'Just one… I want you to promise me that you'll try to be a father to Lydia.'

Antonio flung back his arrogant dark head and dealt her a searing look of indignation. 'Who are you to address me on such a subject?'

Sophie was very pale but she persisted. 'This is just a deal for you. You've made that clear. But you're still likely to be the only father Lydia ever has.'

'The deal is between you and I only. My niece's position in my life is unassailable,' Antonio spelt out with cold clarity. 'I will naturally make every effort to fulfil a paternal role.'

The main course arrived in the tense silence that followed.

'I will not apologise. You were offensive,' Antonio drawled when Maureo had departed again.

Watching Antonio look challenged as Lydia grizzled because she was over tired, Sophie tried not to wonder when his parenting efforts would begin.

'I have certain conditions too,' Antonio affirmed. 'Before the wedding can take place you will have to sign a pre-nuptial agreement.'

Unexpectedly Sophie grinned. 'Like a Hollywood star?' she prompted in visible excitement. 'Are you really that rich? Crazy!'

'The agreement will specify financial arrangements and—'

'Yeah, yeah, yeah… Do we have to talk about that now?' Lifting Lydia down onto her lap to soothe her fractious whimpers, Sophie ate her meal with a fork in one hand, quite unconscious of Antonio's amazement at her dexterity. He watched his niece's eyes drift shut in contentment and marvelled at Sophie's remarkable control over a baby whom he considered to be as volatile as dynamite. He congratulated himself on having made a very wise decision: Sophie was worth five nannies.

'We can leave any discussion of the terms of the prenup to our lawyers.'

'I don't have any—'

'You must engage one for independent advice.'

Sophie wasn't listening. She gazed across the table at Antonio, dazzled by the stunning symmetry of his lean bronzed face, and her eyes took on a dreamy cast. 'What do you want me to wear for the wedding?' she asked softly.

'I have no wish to be rude,' Antonio confided silkily, 'but why should I have an opinion on what you might wear?'

The mental soap bubble in which Sophie was floating her make-believe world burst with a bang that hurt and humiliated. Her face went pink and hot.

'You blush like a schoolgirl,' Antonio mocked.

'Fancy that!' she tossed back and pushed away her plate, all appetite ebbing.

Sophie was really annoyed with herself for that brief flight of foolishness. If Antonio had decided he needed to deliver a reality check, she could hardly blame him. After all, why *would* he be interested in how she dressed for their fake wedding? Why had she even asked that stupid, stupid question?

'So, apart from what's already been agreed, what are the rules of this deal?' Sophie enquired briskly.

'Mutual respect and cooperation, *querida*.' Antonio signalled Maureo and the wineglasses were topped up for a toast.

Sophie interpreted his objective without difficulty. She might fancy Antonio Rocha rotten, but at his most basic she understood his expectations as clearly as if he had voiced them: she was to respect him and strive unceasingly to fit in with all his wishes, reasonable and otherwise. He was noble, he was rich and he was successful and she was poor and illegitimate and lived in a home with wheels under it. Equality could not exist in such diversity. Antonio exuded the proud benevolence of a male convinced he was making a hugely generous sacrifice for which she ought to be undyingly grateful.

Soft, full mouth set mutinously taut, Sophie dropped a kiss down onto Lydia's little drooping head and rejoiced in the baby's soft, trusting weight against her. Her pride might be stinging, but she had to be more sensible and less sensitive, she scolded herself. If Antonio ensured that she and Lydia had a comfortable home and a secure future, he *did* deserve her gratitude.

CHAPTER FIVE

'VERY colourful...very unusual,' Norah finally selected with obvious difficulty.

It was Sophie's wedding day and, as she fully expected that it would be the only wedding day she ever had, she was keen to make the most of the occasion. Refusing to be deflated by the older woman's lack of enthusiasm, Sophie twirled yet again just for the fun of seeing her dress flounce round slim legs enhanced by perilously high pink diamanté-trimmed shoes. She was overwhelmed by the pleasure of wearing the latest fashion for the first time in her life. Although she adored clothes she had never had the money to follow design trends. Determined not to pose as a conventional bride and run the risk of awakening Antonio's derision, Sophie had decided to be more audacious in her choice of outfit. She was even more proud of having used only a tiny bit of the money in the bank account that he had insisted on opening on her behalf.

It was three weeks since she had dined at Antonio's hotel and three weeks since she had seen him. Norah Moore had made no secret of her concern over Sophie's decision to marry Lydia's uncle and even though the ceremony was due to take place in less than an hour she still could not hide her disquiet.

'Please cheer up and be happy for Lydia and me,' Sophie begged.

'But you shouldn't be marrying Antonio for Lydia's

benefit,' Norah muttered uncomfortably. 'I'm afraid I never imagined *this* happening.'

'Who did?' Sophie asked breezily. 'But if I have to share Lydia with Antonio, this is the best way to go about it. He wouldn't let me bring her up here on my own. And how could I have moved to Spain and coped with just being a visitor in her life?'

'But perhaps leaving your options open that way would have been more sensible at first. From what you've said about Antonio...well,' Norah continued awkwardly, her worn face rather stiff, 'he sounds like a trustworthy man—'

'Don't put those two words together. I wouldn't trust Antonio out of my sight.'

'You can't judge all men by your father's example.'

Sophie shrugged. 'Antonio doesn't owe me any favours, so I had to be suspicious of his motives. I also have to look out for Lydia—'

'It's still not too late to call this wedding off. I don't feel that it's right for you to marry Antonio Rocha.'

Amazed by the older woman's persistence on that score, Sophie frowned in bewilderment. 'Why not? Antonio knows exactly what he's doing. I bet he divorces me even faster than he said he would and shunts Lydia and I off to live somewhere well out of his way. He doesn't care about Lydia the way I do—'

'He hasn't had the chance or the time. A lot of men feel uncomfortable around babies—'

'Why are you so against me marrying him?'

Norah flushed and turned away, her discomfiture unconcealed. Sophie reckoned she knew why, but she was too fond of the other woman to hurt her feelings by being too blunt. Understandably, Norah did not want her to move to Spain. Sophie also suspected that Norah had secretly hoped that Sophie might eventually have a change of heart and start dating her son, Matt. Even though she had never given Matt the slightest encouragement, Sophie had always felt rather guilty about him. His stoic air of misery as the wedding day drew closer had made her feel worse.

'I just thought there might be some other way of bringing up Lydia other than marrying the marqués,' Norah muttered evasively.

'This way Lydia will find out about the Spanish side of her family and learn how to be really exclusive and up-market like…well, like some rich kid,' Sophie pointed out. 'She's going to pick up all sorts of stuff I could never teach her. It's what Belinda would have wanted for her—'

'Yes, it probably is.' Norah nodded thoughtfully. 'Your sister did set great store by that sort of thing. I shouldn't have kept on nagging at you. I can see that belonging to a rich family like Antonio's will give Lydia a terrific start in life and opportunities that she would never get here.'

'She deserves the best.' Sophie was grateful that the older woman was finally thinking along the same lines and accepting her reasons for marrying Antonio. 'That's the only reason I'm doing this…for *her*.'

Forty minutes later, Sophie studied the crowd of people waiting outside the church with some surprise. Had a previous wedding started late and overrun its time? Oh, dear, she thought, Antonio would not like that. Well, they would just have to wait their turn. She checked her reflection to see that the tiny concoction of pink chiffon and feathers perched on top of her curls was still at the right angle. She smoothed nervous hands down over the fitted skirt of her dress, which was made of an exuberant fabric covered with big splashy roses. The limo driver pulled in right at the church steps and jumped out to open the door.

With Lydia in a carrier seat, Sophie climbed out. Noisy people shouting piercing questions and waving cameras surrounded her.

'What's your name?' someone asked.

'Friend of the bride's?' someone else shouted from the back.

'She's not a guest, she *is* the bride!' Norah proclaimed sternly. 'Now move and let us inside the church...we've got a baby here!'

'Are you Sophie Cunningham?' a voice demanded in astonishment.

Momentarily transfixed as she was by the sound of her name on a stranger's lips, a nervous giggle escaped Sophie. Taking advantage of the gap that had appeared in the crush as Lydia's presence was acknowledged, she hurried on up the steps and into the porch. The elderly priest greeted her warmly.

Norah took charge of Lydia. Sophie's heart started beating very fast. She sucked in a steadying breath and took a peek down the aisle. Sunlight was pouring through the stained-glass windows and bathing the interior in beautiful jewelled streamers of rich colour. Antonio was at the altar, another smaller, slighter man standing to one side of him, probably the lawyer he had mentioned. She was more interested in staring at Antonio. Even in profile, he looked incredibly handsome. His formal dark suit and white shirt were exquisitely tailored to his tall, powerful frame. As usual he exuded the quiet, distinguished elegance that seemed so much a part of him.

When she drew level with him, she wanted so badly

for him to acknowledge her arrival with a look, a smile, the merest touch, but nothing happened. He had phoned her several times over the past three weeks but the calls had been brief and businesslike. As the nuptial mass began she listened carefully to every word. Each of them made their responses, her voice uneven with a sense of the gravity of the occasion, his cool and firm. He slid a gold ring on her finger without betraying a hint of proper masculine hesitance.

Only with the greatest difficulty was Antonio restraining his ire. The paparazzi were encamped outside. The discreet event he had had organised had been blown wide open. His family avoided publicity like the plague. Who had talked? One of his own staff? A hotel employee? Someone attached to the church? Or his bride? He had expected Sophie to show up in a very frilly over-the-top long white dress complete with veil. In a funny sort of way that he was reluctant to analyse, he had been rather looking forward to seeing her in a wedding gown. Instead she was sporting the most extraordinarily inappropriate apparel. Her outrageously floral dress was flashy enough to stop rush-hour traffic. He studied her ridiculously tiny perky hat. He knew he was being punished for not giving her the advice she had asked for: it was his own fault.

'Stop right there…' Norah instructed, holding up her camera as the bride and groom turned away from the altar.

Antonio looked down into Sophie's misty green eyes fringed by curling dark lashes. Her soft pink mouth was the same shade as the hat and it was amazing how well that particular colour became her, Antonio reflected grudgingly.

'Sorry about this…but there's times when you have

to bite the bullet and just do what you have to do,'
Sophie whispered apologetically, gripping hold of his
arms to stretch herself up to him. 'Act like you're going
to kiss me…this one's for the album I'm going to make
for Lydia.'

Antonio closed long, lean fingers into the toffee-
coloured curls tumbling down her spine, tugged her
head back and brought his hungry mouth down hard on
hers. In shock, she jerked against him and gasped as if
she were being ravished. Even as pure lust leapt through
him he wanted to laugh. It was time she accepted that
he was a Rocha and like every Rocha right back to the
sixteenth century: he didn't take orders; he handed them
out.

His tongue delved deep in a bold invasion. A piercing, unbearable sweetness shot through Sophie followed
by a fierce wave of heat. Dizzy, she locked her arms
round his neck to stay upright, and as he released her
tingling lips she struggled to catch her breath against
his shoulder. He set her back from him in the thrumming silence. Norah was staring wide-eyed. Crimson
with embarrassment, Sophie stared into space, her mind
blanked out by shock at her own wanton behaviour.

Impervious to that kind of discomfiture, Antonio introduced her very briefly to the lawyer, who, having
acted as their second witness, was already making his
departure. The official photographer, whose services
had been arranged, awaited them in the church porch.
At Antonio's request he produced his driving licence as
proof of his identity.

'I'm sorry but the presence of the journalists outside
means that a photographic session will not be possible,'
Antonio imparted gravely. 'That will not, of course,
make any difference to your remuneration.'

Emerging from her fog of self-loathing over that kiss, Sophie exclaimed, 'But you can't cancel the photographs!'

'I can do whatever I like, *mi rica*.' His quiet tone audible only to her ears, Antonio gazed down at her with grim dark eyes. 'If you're responsible for that rabble of reporters out there, you're likely to be very disappointed by the coverage they gain of our wedding. We're leaving now by the rear exit.'

'Those people are newspaper reporters?' Sophie was bewildered by his speech. 'Why are you suggesting that I might have something to do with them being here?'

'We'll discuss that later,' Antonio informed her at a pitch that would have frozen volcanic lava in its tracks.

Sophie thought that perhaps she had misunderstood what he had said and returned to her main source of concern. 'You *can't* just cancel the photos!'

'Might I suggest,' the photographer dared in a deferential murmur, 'That a change of location would suffice?'

Considerably more interested in heading direct to the airport and his flight home to Spain and normality, Antonio set his even white teeth together at that unwelcome suggestion.

'Look,' Sophie said urgently, 'Let me go out and tell those reporters to get lost!'

Seriously taken aback by that suggestion, Antonio studied his bride. She might be five feet nothing in height, but there was a definite suggestion of belligerence in her irate stance. She was confrontational and naïve. He had a disturbing image of the headlines that would erupt if his wife waded in to exchange insults with a posse of paparazzi. It began to dawn on him for the first time that being married to Sophie might not be the equivalent of a walk in the park. It was a sobering reflection for a male who had intended to safeguard his freedom by taking a wife.

'You can't let them ruin the day,' Sophie protested at his elbow. 'That would be like giving way to blackmail.'

Antonio stifled a derisive desire to admit that all of a sudden he knew exactly how that felt. 'We'll use the grounds of the hotel.'

His reward for that peace-keeping concession was immediate and startling. Sophie flung both arms round him and gave him an enthusiastic hug. 'Thanks. *Thanks!* You won't regret it.'

Before the bridal couple left the building, however, Norah Moore also insisted on taking her leave of them. 'No, I'm not coming one step further to play gooseberry,' she responded wryly when Sophie took her off to one side in an effort to persuade her to accompany them to the hotel. 'You should just have said that you and Antonio...well, that kiss said it all for you, didn't it? I didn't know where to look!'

Reminded of what an exhibition she had made of herself, Sophie squirmed in shame and chagrin. 'It wasn't like you think.'

'It was just as it should be. Your getting married will be good for my Matt too,' the older woman informed her bluntly. 'He's been trailing after you like a lovelorn puppy, but now he'll have to get over you.'

In the limo on the way to the hotel, Sophie turned to Antonio and said, 'Why did you suggest that I might be responsible for all those journalists turning up at the church?'

Stunning dark eyes unflinching, he looked levelly back at her. 'Someone tipped them off.'

'Not me…for goodness' sake, I didn't even know the newspapers would be interested in what you get up to!'

Antonio said nothing.

Her temper roused, Sophie watched him from below her lashes. 'Aren't you going to apologise?'

'If I misjudged you, I'm sorry—'

'*If?*' Sophie was outraged by the wording he had chosen to use.

'I don't yet know who's responsible for alerting the paparazzi,' Antonio countered silkily, as immoveable as solid rock in his resolve not to yield the point.

'Well, it wasn't me and we're not going to have a very friendly relationship if you keep on accusing me of things I didn't do!' Sophie warned him in high dudgeon.

'Who said we have to be friendly?' Antonio drawled with deliberate provocation, lounging fluidly back in his corner of the limousine to enjoy the entertainment. He liked watching her vibrate with emotion, for that intense capacity for feeling was as rare in his experience as a genuine Stradivarius violin.

'But you just married me!' Sophie condemned furiously.

'Since when did matrimony and friendship go hand in hand?' Having made that statement to keep her simmering, Antonio surveyed her from below lush black lashes. Once again his analytical mind was engaged in attempting to dissect the mystery of her pulling power. It wasn't just her passion. Inexplicably that tiny hat anchored to her mane of curls now struck him as the very essence of femininity. His wide, sensual mouth compressed. In fact she looked amazingly sexy.

'That's a horrible thing to say!' Sophie condemned.

'I have a whole host of lifelong married ancestors who cohabited with hatred.'

'That doesn't surprise me one little bit!' Sophie slung back.

Antonio was now endeavouring to work out why she looked so sexy. He still thought the dress was a mistake, but it did somehow contrive to accentuate her delicate grace to perfection. The neckline revealed only a modest hint of shadowy cleavage. She had surprisingly full breasts for her slender build. Even overblown roses could not conceal that ripe, rounded swell from his attention. At that point and very much to his annoyance, his libido kicked in with almost painful enthusiasm. She shifted position, her hemline riding up to expose a slim length of thigh. A wolf to the slaughter, his gaze lingered to trace the limb's progression into a shapely knee and slender calf that concluded in amazingly narrow ankles and very small feet. Suddenly he wanted her under him with a ferocity that astonished him.

'Pablo was cruel to Belinda,' Sophie breathed abruptly. 'I just want you to know I won't put up with that kind of treatment!'

All desire stifled by that disquieting revelation, Antonio settled brilliant dark golden eyes on her. 'What did he do?'

'What didn't he do?' Sophie traded heavily with a slight shiver, her anger with Antonio ebbing while she remembered what her sister had told her. 'He killed her confidence. He was always criticising her and telling her how stupid she was and cutting her off in front of other people.'

'I am not my brother,' Antonio spelt out with measured clarity.

'Oh, I know that. Pablo wouldn't have cared what

happened to his niece. He would only have got involved if there was money in the offing,' Sophie ceded grudgingly.

She was not in the mood to say anything that Antonio might construe as a compliment. But there it was, whether she liked it or not—Antonio was a positive prince among men when set next to his late brother.

'I dislike being compared to Pablo,' Antonio informed her with cold emphasis.

Feeling snubbed for having been generous enough to point out that he was much more responsible and caring, Sophie flushed with annoyance and pointedly devoted her attention to Lydia. Soon after that they arrived at the hotel.

The photographer had a tough time with the bridal couple. Although the hotel gardens were superb and the sun was shining, his clients refused to act like blissful newly marrieds. Sophie only came alive when the baby was in the picture and became as flexible as a stick of rock when Antonio had finally been induced to curve an arm round her. The photographer was not quite quick enough to hide his surprise at the complete absence of a bridal bouquet. Sophie said nothing, but the speaking glance that she cast in the groom's direction would have withered a less powerful personality.

Unaccustomed to such a ferocious lack of appreciation, Antonio looked so scornful when asked to smile tenderly down at Sophie that Sophie gritted her teeth and hissed like a spitting cat, 'Don't bother yourself!'

Silence simmered all the way to the airport. Sophie was more out of sorts than she could remember being in years, but not at all sure why she felt quite so angry and humiliated and wretched. Antonio received a melodramatic call from his current mistress. She asked him to deny the ridiculous rumour flying round that he, a Spanish noble of ancient lineage, had just got married to the British equivalent of trailer trash. What his mistress said in response to his icy rebuke in defence of his bride's honour led to her being unceremoniously dumped. At that point, Antonio truly felt himself to be a saint among men beset on all sides by unreasonable women.

At the airport, Sophie parted from Antonio to take care of Lydia's needs. She was engaged in changing Lydia into a fresh outfit when the public address system announced her name and asked her to go to a certain desk. Instant panic assailed Sophie. As she frantically finished dressing her niece she was convinced that something utterly ghastly had happened to Antonio. He had fallen down dead in the concourse and she had never got to say goodbye. Businessmen died of heart attacks all the time, didn't they? Antonio seemed to have so much money that he was a sure fire candidate for overwork and stress. On the other hand, perhaps she had been called to the desk to receive a message from Antonio. Could he have abandoned them at the airport because he just could not face taking the two of them back to Spain with him?

A helpless prey to her own fear, Sophie raced up with the buggy and identified herself with breathless urgency. But even as she did so she was frowning in surprise at the stockily built young man standing several feet away.

'Matt…?' she exclaimed. 'What are you doing here?'

Matt Moore went very red in the face. Inarticulate at the best of times, he pulled out the flowers he had been hiding behind his back and held the small bunch of candy-pink marguerites out to her like an offering.

'Oh, Matt…' Sophie said chokily, astonished that he had asked for her name to be announced.

'You come back and visit now,' Matt told her doggedly as she accepted the bouquet.

'Did you come all the way here just to tell me that?' Sophie gasped, tears burning her eyes and overflowing, for she was touched to the heart that he should have made so much effort when there was no prospect of reward. She reached for his hand and squeezed it tight, a sob catching in her throat.

'Look after yourself and Lydia,' Matt urged and then, without giving any hint of his intention, he gathered her into a clumsy bear-hug and kissed her.

It was as thrilling for Sophie as a wash with a wet flannel. But she felt very sorry for him and very guilty that in spite of all his nice qualities she had never fancied him. So she stood still and tolerated that one brief close-mouthed kiss because she could not bear to reject him yet again and it felt just then like the only consolation she could offer him.

Twenty feet away, Antonio was paralysed to the spot. He had headed to the relevant desk to investigate the instant he had heard Sophie's name being called. He had however believed that that message might have been intended for another Sophie with the same name. Now seeing her share a passionate embrace with Norah Moore's son, he felt betrayed beyond belief. She was his bride, his wife, the Marquesa de Salazar, and she was kissing another man and sobbing over him in a public place. His lean brown hands were clenched into furious fists of restraint. The dark, dangerous tide of rage consuming Antonio almost splintered through his hard self-control and provoked him into a violent intervention.

'Thanks for the flowers…see you some time.' Sophie pulled back from Matt and stoically resisted the temptation to wipe her mouth.

Barely a minute later, Antonio strode up while she was struggling to tighten Lydia's safety harness. She felt hot and bothered and messy and had been planning to steal five minutes to freshen up before rejoining him.

'Where did you come from?' Sophie enquired, pausing in her endeavours to throw a dirty look at the gorgeous blonde eyeing him up from across the concourse. It was far from being the first such appraisal Antonio had attracted. He turned heads, female heads in particular and far too many of them, Sophie acknowledged miserably. His spectacular dark good looks seemed to entitle him to the same attention a movie star might have expected. In her vulnerability, she was not alone. She wanted to lock him up in a cupboard or, at the very least, put a paper bag over his head.

'I heard your name over the public address system,' Antonio imparted, his attention welded to the lush fullness of her lower lip. He was very much taken aback by the fierce sting of desire that assailed him in spite of what he had witnessed.

'Oh…er, it was a friend just wanting to say goodbye,' Sophie mumbled, wrenching at the harness in frustration. 'I think this wretched thing is broken—'

'Allow me…' Antonio murmured flatly.

'It's very fiddly,' she warned him.

Antonio sorted it using only one hand. Somehow the sight of his easy success infuriated Sophie even more. In the VIP lounge, she sat feeding Lydia out of the jar of prepared food she had brought with her for emergency use.

'Couldn't that wait until we've boarded the jet?'

Antonio asked as though it were the height of bad taste to be seen feeding a baby.

Sophie shook her head and buttoned her soft pink mouth. She had to. If she hadn't she would have thrown a screaming fit. She had started the day with a crazy sense of adventure and happiness and her mood had gone steadily downhill ever since. Just then she was hitting rock-bottom. Antonio was gorgeous but she hated him. She hated fancying him like mad and she hated being married to him. At that moment she was convinced that a divorce from Antonio could not come quickly enough to satisfy her. She could have signed on the dotted line right there and then without a shred of regret.

He hadn't even bothered to offer her lunch at the hotel and her stomach was meeting her backbone. He had treated her like wallpaper most of the day. And when he wasn't treating her like wallpaper and ignoring her, he was either accusing her of doing something dreadful or criticising her. Sophie breathed in very deep, pent-up tears of self-pity clogging her throat. Here she was travelling off into the unknown to live in a different country, which was a quite terrifying prospect, and the only guy she had to depend on was behaving like an arrogant, insensitive bastard!

They boarded the private jet. Sophie cast a jaundiced eye over the luxury appointments and wondered what Antonio would do if she fainted from hunger. How bad would it make him feel? She reckoned she would have to die to get a real reaction from him. The jet took off. Her heart-shaped face adorned by two high spots of colour, Sophie was shown by the flight attendant into a sleeping compartment where a cot had already been se-cured in readiness for Lydia's occupation. She tucked her niece in for a nap and surveyed the opulent bed for the grown-ups. How many women had Antonio had in there? She bit her lip painfully and screwed her eyes up tight in a desperate attempt to hold back the tears ready to flood out. The level of her own distress shocked her.

Although it was rare for Antonio to touch alcohol before evening, he was contemplating the non-existent joys of matrimony over a brandy. Getting married had proved to be the hell he had always dimly suspected it would be. Sophie had allowed him to put a wedding ring on her finger and had then allowed another man to put his hands on her. That betrayal struck at the very roots of his masculinity and plunged Antonio right back into the same elemental rage that challenged his rapier-sharp thinking processes. His rational mind endeavoured to point out that it had been a kiss exchanged in public, but the conviction that passion had overpowered common sense and decency was not a consolation.

He pictured her tear-stained face afresh, her green eyes like wet jewels as she clutched that pathetic bunch of flowers. A heartbeat later she had had her arms wrapped round the vertically challenged gorilla from the run-down shop on the caravan site. As he recalled from his first visit when he had been looking for Sophie, the guy tended to grunt rather than speak, Antonio reflected with raging incredulity. He tipped his brandy back in one fiery gulp. Why had she not told him that she had a boyfriend? Did she think she loved the gorilla? Were grunts really that appealing? Why had she kept quiet about the relationship? Was she in fact expecting to continue the affair in secret? He set the glass down with a hard snap that sent a crack travelling up the crystal stem.

To his knowledge no Rocha wife had ever been un-

faithful, although there had been a few rather unexpected deaths over the centuries. Death before dishonour. For the very first time Antonio found himself in
sympathy with distant ancestors who had ridden off to
war for months on end leaving young and beautiful
wives behind at home. How was he supposed to go
away for weeks on business? In the space of a moment,
a new horrific dimension had been added to Antonio's
outlook on matrimony. He tried to regard the potential
problem of his bride's future behaviour as a basic security issue. Careful supervision and geographical location would reduce the chances of any similar offence
occurring.

When Sophie returned to the main cabin, Antonio slid
upright with the grace of a panther ready to spring at
an unwary prey. Having looked her fill at his bold
bronzed profile before he registered her reappearance,
Sophie ostentatiously ignored him, screened a fake
yawn and picked up a magazine for good measure.

'I saw you with Norah Moore's son at the airport,'
Antonio murmured with icy cool.

'Did you?' Sophie was surprised but not concerned.
'Matt can be so kind and thoughtful. Maybe you assumed that I bought those flowers for myself. I *didn't*,'
she declared with emphasis. 'Matt gave them to me.'

Antonio listened to that irrelevant and aggravating
response with an amount of disbelief that did nothing
to cool his ire. 'Do you seriously think that I am interested in where the flowers came from?' he enquired
grittily.

'Oh, no, I'm sure you wouldn't be interested,' Sophie
countered with a hint of acidity, still without having
deigned to glance in his direction.

'Put the magazine down and look at me when you speak to me,' Antonio instructed grimly.

Sophie kept her attention on the magazine and turned a page very slowly and carefully. Antonio brought out a defiant streak in Sophie that had remained dormant and unknown even to her until she had met him. She wondered why it was that he had only to address her in a certain tone or raise an aristocratic eyebrow to excite her even temper to screaming pitch.

Provoked beyond bearing, Antonio swept up the magazine and slung it aside.

'So now you're going to add bullying to all your other sins,' Sophie commented in a tone of immense martyrdom. 'I can't say I'm surprised—'

'What other sins?' Antonio raked at her incredulously.

'Oh, let's not get into that right now,' Sophie advised, rising to her full, unimposing height and pausing to hurriedly cram her feet back into the high heels she had removed. 'Unless you've got all day to listen. And, of course, even if you did magically have the time or the good manners to listen, I might drop dead from hunger first.'

'Hunger?' Antonio growled, black brows pleating.

'Obviously I shall have to get used to my comfort being ignored in favour of yours. I haven't eaten since eight this morning and I am starving,' Sophie tossed back at him accusingly. 'And you couldn't care less, could you? Because you've made it very clear that if you're not hungry, I'm not supposed to be hungry either!'

'The detour back to the hotel for the photographic session meant that there wasn't time for lunch,' Antonio informed her drily, striving not to notice how the vivid colour of anger enhanced the brightness of her eyes.

Sophie folded her arms and sent a flashing look of scorn at him. 'So, in other words, starving me was deliberate—'

'How the hell do you make that out?' Antonio launched back at her wrathfully.

'I argued about the photographs being cancelled and that annoyed you and so lunch went off the menu—'

'How could you think that I am capable of being that petty?' Antonio's disgust at the allegation was convincing. 'I did not wish to reschedule our flight. For that reason I arranged for a meal to be served to us now.'

Chagrin rather than relief at that news gripped Sophie. 'Couldn't you have explained that to me back at the hotel?'

'You were sulking—'

'I don't sulk!' Sophie hurled.

'—and if you want to sulk like a little girl you will be treated like one,' Antonio completed without hesitation, while wondering how she would react if he just lifted her off her absurdly high-heeled shoes and kissed her into merciful silence.

'Try that on me again and you'll see what happens!' Sophie threw feverishly.

Infuriated by the weird thoughts and ideas interfering with his concentration, Antonio resisted the temptation to rise to her bait. Stunning dark eyes cool as a winter lake, he surveyed her with intimidating self-command. 'I believe you think that you can distract me from your own inexcusable behaviour at the airport. You haven't a prayer on that score. I saw you kissing Norah Moore's son.'

Sophie went pink and jerked a thin shoulder and studied the floor for about twenty seconds. That sufficed for the amount of discomfiture she experienced at that assurance. Indeed after the heartbreakingly hurtful day she had endured she was actually quite pleased that he had been forced to register that one man at least had thought her worthy of his attention. She glanced up again, green eyes rebellious. 'So?' she queried.

Antonio was incredulous at that unapologetic reaction. 'Do not dare to treat it as nothing,' he warned her, his accent thick with anger. 'Sharing a very public embrace with your lover on the day you became my wife is not acceptable behaviour by any standards.'

Her defiance ebbed a little and she squirmed, no longer able to meet his proud dark golden eyes. 'For goodness' sake, Matt's not my lover or *my* anything—'

'I know what I saw,' Antonio incised icily.

'Matt's fancied me for ages but I only ever thought of him as a friend,' Sophie admitted reluctantly, angry at being forced to make an explanation. 'He was upset about me marrying you and he came to the airport to say goodbye. I couldn't face rejecting him again. I like him and I felt sorry for him, so I put up with him kissing me!'

'I might have found that a convincing story if you hadn't been weeping all over him when I saw you,' Antonio derided with a curled lip.

In that instant, temper and hurt reached flashpoint inside Sophie. 'I was crying because you had made me so miserable!'

'I had made you miserable?' Antonio repeated in thunderous disbelief. 'What had I done?'

'Matt being upset about me leaving and giving me those flowers was the first nice thing that happened to me today. Think about that, Antonio...this was supposed to be my wedding day. And it's been totally horrible!' Sophie condemned tearfully, all the wounded feelings she had suppressed throughout the day suddenly coalescing and finally making sense to her.

'How has it been horrible?' Antonio demanded fiercely.

'I'll probably never have another wedding day,' Sophie proclaimed grittily, pride helping her to swallow back the tears that had been threatening. 'I know it couldn't have been romantic in the circumstances, but you could at least have made it pleasant and friendly. I spent two whole days trailing round London finding this outfit and you couldn't even tell me that I looked OK—'

Dark blood had risen to emphasise the sculpted line of his hard cheekbones. 'I—'

'It's OK...don't worry about it. Do you think I haven't worked out for myself that I couldn't ever reach your standards? But I made the effort; I *tried*. You didn't even try to be nice. You accused me of tipping off the reporters at the church. You didn't give me flowers or anything and the entire time you acted like being with me and Lydia was just one big, awful bore. Matt was so sweet and the comparison between you and him was too much—'

'The comparison between me and that gorilla?' Antonio grated between clenched teeth, seizing on that line because her previous comments had hit too many raw nerves in succession to even be considered in the midst of an argument.

'You're a hateful snob,' Sophie told him fiercely. 'You treat me like dirt...but he treats me like I'm something special!'

A brisk knock sounded on the door and broke the silence that fell in the wake of that last bitter rebuke. A flight attendant entered with a trolley of food. Sophie dropped her head, heavy curls tumbling across her delicate profile to conceal her tear-wet eyes from notice. Trembling with emotion, she sank back down into her seat and cringed over the last revealing words she had flung at him. *You treat me like dirt...he treats me like I'm something special!*

Why don't you be honest with yourself? a snide little voice was mocking inside her head. The truth, which she only recognised in retrospect, cut her pride to ribbons. Her wedding day had been a disaster because she had forgotten it was a 'deal' rather than a joyous occasion to be celebrated. She had got carried away with bridal fervour. She had absolutely craved personal attention and notice from Antonio. She would have crawled over broken glass for a single compliment. Her distress had stemmed from her pain and disappointment when he had neglected to meet her unrealistic hopes and treated her like wallpaper instead.

Did she have the right to complain about the way he had treated her? Or was she being unfair to him? After all, it hadn't been a real wedding for two people who cared about each other. Antonio didn't care two straws about her and she had to learn to live with that, didn't she? Someone like him was never, ever going to think of someone like her as special, she thought wretchedly. Having to put up with her all day had probably been a taxing enough challenge for him. Her aching throat convulsed. She stared down at the inviting meal that had been laid before her and discovered that she was no longer hungry. A tear rolled down her cheek and splashed onto the plate.

'Sophie…' Antonio breathed tautly.

'Leave me alone!' she gasped strickenly and, scrambling up, she fled down the aisle and vanished into the sleeping compartment.

CHAPTER SIX

BY THE time that Antonio entered the compartment Sophie was fast asleep. Curled up in a ball, tawny-blonde curls tumbling over a delicate cheekbone, she looked very young, incredibly pretty and alarmingly vulnerable.

She was also his wife. *His wife.* It was a disturbing moment of truth for Antonio. She was now Sophie Cunningham de Rocha, the Marquesa de Salazar. She had had grounds for complaint, he acknowledged, his handsome mouth hardening on that admission of self-blame. He was not accustomed to finding himself in the wrong. But he had censured her behaviour as his wife without once accepting her right to be treated as though she was his wife.

A slight movement in the cot attracted his attention. He glanced down and met Lydia's big hopeful brown eyes. The baby flashed him a huge gummy smile of welcome and wriggled with excess energy. Without words, Lydia was letting him know that she wanted out of the cot and that she was expecting him to supply the means of her escape from captivity. He was amused until the baby let out a little bleating cry of disappointment when he turned back to the door.

'If I took you out of there, I wouldn't know what to do with you,' Antonio pointed out in his own defence.

The melting brown eyes stayed pinned to him.

'Yes, of course I can learn, but in easy stages,' Antonio murmured in what he was hoped was a soothing tone that might send her back to sleep. He took another step away from the cot.

The brown eyes glistened and the rosebud mouth trembled piteously.

At the threat of tears, Antonio tensed. He glanced back at Sophie, who was clearly enjoying the very sound sleep of exhaustion. Breathing in deep and mustering his legendary ability to deal with the unexpected, he reached down to lift Lydia out of the cot. She wriggled with pleasure and smiled like mad at him in return.

'You know how to get your own way,' Antonio informed the baby wryly. 'But success is not always followed by the reward you expect. We're going to watch the business news together.'

Sophie wakened only when her shoulder was gently shaken. Feathery lashes lifting, she focused slowly on Antonio's darkly handsome face and her mouth ran dry. Try as she might, she could not suppress her response to his mesmeric attraction.

'You may want to get up,' he murmured softly. 'We'll be landing in fifteen minutes. Did you sleep well?'

'I don't remember even putting my head down,' she confided, glancing down at her watch. 'I'm amazed Lydia let me sleep this long!'

'I've been entertaining her.'

Before she could comment on that surprising information, he had gone. Ten minutes later she joined him in the main cabin. Lydia was enjoying a peaceful nap in her baby harness, a sure-fire sign of contentment.

'How did you manage with her?' Sophie asked uncomfortably.

'Consuela, one of the crew, is a parent. She lent me some assistance when Lydia needed a drink,' Antonio admitted modestly. 'But Lydia was very good and easily amused.'

'Thanks for letting me sleep.' Sophie studied her linked hands and cleared her throat. 'I owe you an apology for the way I lost my temper earlier.'

'No, you don't owe me anything,' Antonio contradicted with quiet assurance. 'You were right to complain and I am sorry that I made the day a difficult one. I must confess that I was nourishing a certain resentment of the situation which I needed to deal with.'

It came entirely naturally to Sophie to reach across the aisle to touch his lean brown hand with her own in an instinctive gesture of sympathetic understanding. 'Of course you felt bitter, but you don't have to apologise for being human. It must've been so hard for someone like you to put up with a brother like Pablo. Then to be landed with responsibility for Lydia into the bargain, well, obviously you felt fed up.'

That sudden gush of generosity from her corner was too much for Antonio's innate reserve about his own feelings. His expression of regret, honest admission of fault and the explanation he had believed she was due had cost him dearly. Her unexpected compassion stung his strong pride like acid.

'You mistook my meaning,' Antonio replied icily. 'Never at any time since I learned of my niece's existence have I wished that her care fell to someone else. There is no more proper person than I to undertake that task and I would never attempt to avoid the responsibility. I don't expect you to understand it, but loyalty to my family is as integral a part of me as my honour.'

Sophie coloured hot pink and then white, mortification at that unabashed snub biting at her frail self-esteem. No matter how hard she tried she always seemed to say or do the wrong thing with Antonio, she reflected wretchedly. He appeared to believe that she was too vulgar and common to comprehend the more refined sensibilities of a Spanish aristocrat.

'That's a hateful thing to say,' she whispered with scorching fervour, for once again he had hurt her. 'I was every bit as loyal to Belinda as you are to your precious family!'

An hour later, she was seated in a long, opulent limousine being driven through the Andalusian countryside. Up until that point she had rigorously ignored or crushed Antonio's conversational attempts to redeem himself.

When he tried to tell her a little about the history of Spain, Sophie said tartly, 'Save yourself the trouble. Buy me the book!'

When the country road wended through silvery olive groves, Antonio informed her that they were now on the family estate. After what felt like a very long time to Sophie, the olive trees gave way to orange orchards and a picturesque whitewashed village straggling over the lower slopes of forested hills. Locals peered out of the houses and stopped in the narrow, winding street to stare at the limousine and wave acknowledgement.

'Are we still on your family estate?' Rampant curiosity finally forced Sophie to abandon her stony silence and ask that question as the limo traversed a shaded road surrounded on all sides by dense evergreen woods.

'*Sí*. My great-great-grandfather planted those oak trees,' Antonio told her with unhidden pride.

'It's like the fairy tale of Puss-in-Boots,' Sophie muttered helplessly and, when Antonio angled a look of incomprehension at her, added, 'Puss-in-Boots wanted to impress the king with the idea that his master was hugely important and rich. So, he pretended all the land they passed belonged to this character he made up called the Marquis of Carabas.'

'The Marquis of Carabas,' Antonio repeated with only the slightest tremor of amusement disturbing his dark deep drawl.

'Of course that marquis belongs in the fairy story and he was only for pretend and you're real,' Sophie conceded absently. 'But all this feels very unreal to me...'

There was a reason for the way she suddenly fell silent. The limousine had turned a corner and through the trees she caught a glimpse of an ancient stone building. Adorned with as many towers and turrets as any palace in a fairy tale, it sat in an oasis of lush green vegetation. It was indescribably beautiful and she was enchanted from that first moment.

'What do you think?'

Sophie veiled her stunned eyes and shrugged with studied casualness, too self-conscious to display her true reactions. 'It's very big...I'm not going to be tripping over you every five minutes, am I?'

'It's unlikely. Perhaps I should have mentioned before now that a nanny has been engaged to help you care for Lydia,' Antonio advanced with caution.

'As long as I like the nanny, that's fine with me.' Sophie was grateful that an extra pair of hands would be available. All too often she had been forced to rely on Norah Moore's good nature. A nanny to help out with Lydia would be a real luxury.

The limo came to a halt in a timeless courtyard ornamented with palm trees in vast pots. The soft sunlight of evening illuminated the stone arches and columns that made an arcade on three sides. Water droplets sparkled and fell from the fountain that played near the massive wooden doors that stood ajar on a floor that, even at a distance of several feet, was clearly polished to a mirror finish.

Lydia supported on one slight hip, Sophie crossed the threshold and froze at the sight of the throng of people filling the giant entrance hall.

With wonderful assurance, Antonio cupped a light hand below her elbow and drew her on to greet an elegant little old lady who might have been chipped out of frozen granite.

'My grandmother, Doña Ernesta...Sophie.'

Doña Ernesta gave a regal nod and said that it was a great joy to welcome her grandson, his bride and her great-granddaughter home. Sophie was not deceived. She knew that she was about as welcome in her role as Antonio's bride as the bad fairy. Attention was quickly focused on Lydia, who was greeted with a sincere warmth that quite transformed her great-grandmother's frozen granite exterior. A young smiling nanny was brought forward, introduced, and Lydia was handed over to an enthusiastic reception.

'Come and meet the rest of the staff,' Antonio urged Sophie then, ignoring her dismay as she registered just how many people appeared to fall within that category.

Everyone who worked inside the *castillo* was waiting to pay their respects. Antonio carried her through the introductions with the sure confidence that seemed to accompany everything he did and she really appreciated his support.

Afterwards he closed his hand over hers and walked her up the carved stone staircase. 'You must be incredibly hungry,' he murmured.

'Yes...I should've eaten when I got the chance.' Sophie sighed, her attention locking to the ancient stone walls and gothic arches surrounding them. It was a real castle, a one hundred per cent genuine medieval castle, and she was fascinated by it.

His handsome mouth quirked at her fatalistic outlook. 'I upset you. In the hope that you'll forgive that I've arranged for a meal to be served in your suite. I want you to be happy here at the *castillo*.'

'Your grandmother wouldn't agree with you.'

'It's a shame that she didn't have the opportunity to get to know you at your sister's wedding, *querida*. She would never be unkind and will soon become accustomed to our marriage.'

Sophie was less confident.

'By the way, I should warn you that I have told no one of our marital agreement. Secrets shared soon lead to a wider circle becoming acquainted with what was once private—'

'You mean Doña Ernesta thinks we're like…*really* married?' Sophie interrupted in dismay. 'You should tell her the truth!'

'It would only complicate matters. Allow me to know my own family best. To all intents and purposes it is wisest if at this point at least our marriage appears to be normal,' Antonio decreed.

Sophie disagreed but took the hint. It was obvious to her that Doña Ernesta was hopping with rage and disappointment over the fact that her grandson appeared to have thrown his title, his wealth and his giant castle away on a penniless nobody from England. Sophie did not blame his grandmother one little bit for her annoyance. Antonio was just about the equivalent of a prince and a prince deserved a princess.

Upstairs, Antonio showed her into a beautifully furnished and enormous sitting room, which led into a huge bedroom that in turn had a fabulous bathroom and dressing room attached.

'All this is just for me?' she gasped.

'Dinner will be served here in forty minutes,' he imparted.

'Here…? ' Her relief was palpable. She had been afraid that she might have to dress up to eat in some fancy dining room and she had nothing suitable to change into.

'*Sí.* I've organised an informal meal of your favourite foods—'

'But you don't know what I like…'

'I phoned Mrs Moore to find out, *querida.*' Antonio gazed down at her, stunning dark golden eyes very serious. 'You have eaten hardly anything today. That's my fault. I want you to relax and feel comfortable at the *castillo.*'

Sophie vented an awkward laugh. 'I'm never going to relax in a place like this!'

'Of course you will,' Antonio declared, long brown fingers tilting up her chin to persuade her to look up again. 'You're my wife and this is your home and you must treat it as such. Your comfort is of prime importance to me and to our staff.'

For a long, timeless moment, she was conscious only of the spectacular power of his gaze. His concern for her sent a sudden dangerous flare of happiness winging through her slight frame. The faint citrusy aroma of the shaving lotion he used flared her nostrils. She wanted to drink the scent in like a drug, for it was already wonderfully familiar to her. Something tightened low in her pelvis and an awareness so acute it hurt seemed to make every inch of her feel unbearably sensitive. She wanted to lean closer to him, retain that fleeting physical contact of his fingers against her throat. But she rebelled against her weakness and literally forced herself back for him with a brittle smile fixed to her flushed face. 'Right, so if I'm to make myself at home, I'll have a bath before the food arrives,' she framed not quite steadily. 'So first you'd better tell me where Lydia is, because I want to check she's OK without me.'

For a split second, Antonio was very taut as he mastered the raw hunger that had leapt as high as a burning brand in him. All it had taken was her proximity and that reference to a bath and his imagination had gone crazy. His gleaming gaze veiled while he fought an outrageous desire to simply grab her like a Neanderthal cave dweller. Lust had never controlled him to such an extent that he almost forgot who he was. Exhilarated by the very power of that sensation, he suspended all rational thought on the issue.

It was sex, just sex, nothing to get worked up about. She was amazingly sexy and the very fact that she didn't even seem to appreciate the strength of her own attraction only added to her appeal. He could not recall when he had last been with a woman capable of walking past a mirror without looking in it. Not to mention one so devoted to a baby's interests that her own needs took second billing.

Sophie peeped in on Lydia, who was blissfully asleep in a large cot. Her niece was being watched over by what appeared to be a good half of the female staff. A little while later, her concern laid to rest, Sophie sank into the warm, scented water of the sunken bath that had so captured her interest. She rested her head back against the built-in pillow and surveyed the other luxurious fittings with impressed-to-death eyes. She could see that the misery of being married to Antonio was going to be alleviated by certain small consolations. So, she couldn't have him and other women were going to have him...*but*, she rushed to remind herself, she had Lydia, a bath to die for and at least the promise of food. On the downside this was her wedding night and she was alone? So what was new about being alone, she asked herself, struggling not to give way to self-pity. Unhappily she was all too well aware that Antonio would never have left a princess alone...

Thoroughly refreshed, Sophie emerged from the bathroom with a white towel knotted round her and a riot of tousled curls falling round her shoulders. Her nose twitched at the faint enticing aroma in the air and she followed it.

Antonio was standing by the balcony doors in the sitting room.

'Oh!' Sophie jerked to a disconcerted halt a few feet from the table that was now set with sparkling glasses and cutlery and the catering trolley standing by. 'Did *you* bring the food?'

Antonio was immediately aware that he was staring. With her blonde hair in damp disarray, her fair skin pink and only a towel screening her slim curves between breast and knee, she looked incredibly appealing. 'No...I'm here to dine with you.'

Sophie stared back at him in surprise.

'If we're hoping to pretend that this is a normal relationship, we can't spend our wedding night in different rooms,' Antonio pointed out.

'Oh, right...yeah,' Sophie mumbled, appreciating that he was only joining her because he had no choice in the matter. That meant that his presence was nothing to get thrilled about. 'I'd better get dressed, then.'

Antonio resisted a schoolboyish urge to tell her that

he thought she looked great just as she was and countered with studied casualness, 'A robe will do.'

'I don't have one and it's too warm for my jeans. I
don't have much else yet—'

'Just stay as you are,' Antonio suggested huskily.

The simmering tension in the air danced along her
nerve endings. He had changed as well, into black chinos, which accentuated his long, powerful legs, and a
casual but very elegant blue open-necked shirt. He managed to look impossibly sophisticated and gorgeous.

'You don't look as stuffy as you usually do!' Sophie
exclaimed before she could think better of such frank-
ness.

Faint colour demarcated the spectacular cheekbones
that gave his lean bronzed face such intense power and
beauty of line. Stuffy? His keen intellect threw up every
possible meaning and none was complimentary. It was
a word he associated with some of his more stodgy
relatives, the ones boringly trapped in convention and
habit. Was that how he seemed to her? *Stuffy?* She was
seven years younger than he was. Was it such a gap?

'We should eat,' Antonio murmured flatly, determined not to react to what he knew had been a thoughtless remark.

Sophie knew she had offended. 'It's just the way you
talk and the suits… I'm not used to businessmen and I
guess all of them wear suits—'

'What way do I talk?' Antonio discovered that he
could not silence that question as he spun out a chair
for her to sit down.

'I really didn't mean to suggest anything critical,'
Sophie muttered anxiously, sitting down on the very
edge of the upholstered antique dining chair. 'You've

got fantastic manners and of course you can't help being formal… I mean you're a marquis—'

'And stuffy,' Antonio breathed and shrugged, the ultimate gesture of Mediterranean cool, but that word she had used had been etched like acid into his soul. 'Let's eat.'

Sophie leapt up to examine the contents of the trolley and exclaimed in delight at the sight of the barbecued ribs, pizza and French fries. A multitude of other options was also available. 'You have an in-house take-away?'

'I wanted you to have food you felt comfortable with.'

'I eat loads of more healthy things too, but Norah wouldn't have had a clue about that. To be honest, Norah and Matt eat stuff like this most of the time. I only like it occasionally.' As she spoke Sophie was scooping up cushions and throws and piling them on the carpet in an untidy heap. Then she flung open the balcony doors on the cooling night air.

In a trice the superbly elegant room became disorganised and yet more full of life. It dawned on Antonio that sitting at a table when the hard wooden floor was available might be deemed stuffy. While Sophie emptied the trolley and knelt down among the cushions to arrange containers and plates in the style of an impromptu indoor picnic, he uncorked the champagne and filled the flutes. She ate without cutlery, licking her fingertips clean like a delicate cat. She tore a strip off the pizza, tipped her head back and bit off tiny pieces. Never until that moment had it occurred to him that watching a woman eat could be a sensual experience. He was absolutely fascinated.

'What would you like to talk about?' she asked cheer-

fully, flopping back against the piled-up pillows to finish her champagne.

'My stuffy good manners prevented me from asking
how you and your sister came to have different fathers,'
Antonio admitted.

Sophie tensed, but tried to laugh off her discomfiture.
'Oh, that's no big deal. Belinda's father was married to
our mother, Isabel. He was an oil executive and he
wasn't home much. Isabel met my father when he was
painting their house—'

'He was an artist?'

'He painted walls, not pictures,' Sophie told him
thinly. 'Well, he got her pregnant with me and she left
her husband for him...'

'And?' Antonio prompted as the silence dragged.

'My father was no great catch and Isabel soon realised her mistake. When I was a month old, she went
back to her husband and left me behind with Dad.'

'That must have been hard for your father—'

'Dad would do just about anything for money and
Isabel sent him money every month until I was sixteen.
She never visited me. Apart from the handouts, she just
blanked out the whole affair like it and I never happened.' Sophie tipped up her chin, a defiant glint in her
expressive green eyes.

'She was probably ashamed of what she had done,'
Antonio murmured gently, seeing the pain that she was
struggling to hide. Reaching over, he linked his fingers
with hers in a comforting gesture that was as instinctive
as it was unusual for him. 'You did very well without
her, *querida*.'

'You really think so?' Antonio was so close that
Sophie could hardly catch her breath.

'You bend but you don't break,' Antonio breathed a

little thickly, leaning over her to let a soothing fingertip score the soft pink fullness of her lower lip in a touch as light as silk.

The faintest suspicion of a breeze was ruffling the curls against her shoulder. She was very still, heart pumping like crazy below the towel. Her breasts felt tight and confined and a restive energy was filtering through her. Her whole focus was on him. If he didn't kiss her she thought she might die from the cruel disappointment of it.

A masculine thumb brushed against a springy blonde loop of hair in a movement so subtle she wasn't quite sure it had happened. His scorching golden eyes collided with hers and the knot of tension deep down inside her tightened. 'I love your hair…it has a life of its own.'

'Antonio…' she whispered, stretching back against the pillows, letting her head fall back, bright corkscrew curls spilling out and catching the light of the sinking sun. She felt shameless but she was being driven by a craving much stronger than she was.

His breath fanned her cheek. He took his time and let his mouth toy with hers. Longing snaked through her in a fierce, almost frightening surge. Without even knowing what she was about to do she pulled him down to her. He resisted and laughed huskily, gazed down at her with shimmering dark golden eyes full of satisfaction.

'I don't respond well to the whip and chair approach,' he mocked.

She felt foolish and exposed and temper leapt into the chasm. In a split second she had rolled away and sat up. 'I'm not a joke!'

Stunned by the immediacy of her rejection, Antonio sprang up in concert. '*Por dios*, I was teasing—'

'No, you weren't…you were crowing!' Sophie accused tempestuously. 'Well, before you get carried away with the idea that I'm too enthusiastic—'

Antonio reached out and tugged her straight back into his arms. 'You firebrand…you could never be *too* enthusiastic for me. You turn me on so hard and so fast that I can't think this close to you,' he admitted in a roughened undertone.

On the brink of fighting loose again, Sophie paused and fixed huge anxious green eyes on his lean, strong face. 'Truthfully?'

He spread long brown fingers to frame her cheekbones and his hands were not quite steady. 'I'm burning for you, *querida.*'

She felt the truth of it in his raw urgency and she trembled. 'Then stop playing games—'

'I'm not playing.' Antonio claimed a long, hard, potent kiss that made her grip his arms for support and left her head swimming. 'Believe me, I didn't bargain on this—'

'You can't plan everything—'

'But I *do*,' he growled in frustration, coming back for another fierce and hungry taste of her. 'This shouldn't be happening—'

Her small fingers delved into his luxuriant black hair to pull his head back. 'Then…stop!'

His smouldering golden gaze struck sparks from hers. 'I can't…I wanted you the first time I saw you nearly three years ago. Now I want you even more.'

At that admission, her troubled eyes shone like stars and she screened them. But she still wanted to shout her joy from the rooftops. What he felt wasn't love, but then she had never hoped for love from Antonio. His desire was enough to satisfy her deep, desperate need for some kind of response from him. It wouldn't last, naturally it wouldn't, she thought feverishly. But a desire to match her own was there for the taking now and she was not too proud to seize the moment.

He crushed her lush lips beneath his again. The sweet, stabbing invasion of his tongue in the tender reaches of her mouth made her gasp out loud. He lifted her effortlessly up in his arms and carried her into the bedroom. His strength left her breathless. Resting her down on the bed, he undid the towel. Unprepared for that instant unveiling, she crossed her arms over her nakedness in an instinctive movement.

Antonio surveyed her startled eyes and hot cheeks in surprise. 'You can't be shy with me...'

'I'm not shy,' Sophie denied to the best of her ability, taking advantage of his momentary stasis to shimmy away. Pulling back the bedding, she slid speedily under it with more than a suggestion of a crab scuttling below a rock for cover. 'Not the slightest bit shy,' she added with determined emphasis, and she sat up to embark on the buttons on his shirt in an effort to distract him.

'Let me look at you, then.' Antonio closed long fingers into the sheet she had wrapped below her arms and tugged it down before she could even guess his intent. The tantalising jut of her pert breasts provoked a ragged groan of appreciation from him. He caught her to him with one powerful arm, bent her back against him and explored the firm creamy swells with unashamed expertise. His slightest touch set her tender flesh on fire. Her teeth clenched, her hips shifting on the sheet beneath her. When he toyed with the rosy crests that were swollen and sensitised by his attention, she was unable to suppress the moan rising in her throat.

'You're even more beautiful than I thought you

would be, *querida*,' Antonio breathed thickly, hungry dark golden eyes welded with all-male admiration to the ripe, rounded curves he had revealed. 'And a hundred times more responsive.'

Straightening up to his full height, he finished unbuttoning his shirt and peeled it off. As he shifted position sleek, strong muscles flexed in his strong brown torso and accentuated the powerful breadth of his chest and the rock-hard flatness of his abdomen. Ebony curls liberally shaded his pectorals. She pulled in a sudden gulp of air to her starved lungs. Her heartbeat had quickened to a pulsing thump behind her breastbone: he was spectacularly male. She couldn't drag her mesmerised attention from him until he unzipped his trousers and embarrassment claimed her, forcing her to drop her gaze.

'Come here,' Antonio urged softly.

She scrambled up on her knees, glancing up at him from below her curling lashes, her face burning from the awareness of her nudity. With a husky groan, he just reached for her as though she were a doll. With his hands spread across the feminine swell of her hips, he raised her higher and clamped her hard up against his lean muscular frame. Warm and silky smooth and interestingly rough, his body was an electrifying mix of different textures against her softer skin. She was insanely aware of the hot, hard thrust of his erection and of her own feverish yearning for his touch. She felt programmed, enslaved by the wanton promise of the pleasure he had already given her.

'Touch me,' she mumbled shakily.

'Until you beg me to stop.' He tumbled her back across the bed and came down to her, strong and bronzed and pagan in his sexual intensity. He lowered his proud dark head to the prominent pink buds of her breasts and let his tongue lash the straining tips. She arched her spine and cried out when he intensified that sensation with the graze of his teeth and his knowing mouth. Heat burned low in her pelvis.

'Don't stop,' she whispered urgently, shifting her hips in a restive movement against the sheet, wildly, wickedly conscious of the growing ache at the very heart of her.

Golden eyes molten with desire, Antonio parted her thighs. With sure skill he parted the cluster of curls crowning her womanhood and touched her where she had never been touched before. That intimacy smashed her tenuous control to pieces. He found the most sensitive spot in her entire body and a burning, drowning sweetness of sensation took hold of her and blanked out all other awareness. As the twisting spiral of pleasure tightened to the edge of near pain inside her, she writhed.

'Antonio…' His name was like a prayer on her lips. She could no longer contain the wildness sweeping over her in potent waves. Her hips squirmed up in a sinuous rhythm as old as time, tiny whimpers breaking low in her throat.

'*Enamorada*…you intoxicate me,' he confessed fiercely as he came over her. 'I intend to give you more pleasure than anyone has ever given you.'

When he drove into the slick, wet depths of her, excitement roared through her every skin cell with the ferocity of a forest fire. The sudden sharp pain induced by that bold invasion took her entirely by surprise. Her eyes widened in shock and she muffled her involuntary cry against his shoulder.

Antonio stilled and looked down at her. 'Did I hurt you?'

'No…'

He stared down at the luminous clarity of her beautiful eyes. 'I know I hurt you,' he breathed huskily. 'Was I too rough?'

Hot pink washed her hairline, for she was mortified but far too proud and cautious to admit that he was her first lover. 'Of course not—'

'You excite me beyond all control,' Antonio confessed thickly, sinking by slow, skilled degrees into her now more receptive body. 'I forgot how small you are, how fragile.'

His every subtle movement engulfed her in hot, sweet pleasure. The tempo stepped up. Passion gripped her in a flashing surge of high-voltage sensation. He sank his hands below her hips and tipped her up to him, plunging back into her with raw, demanding urgency. Her heart hammered and she fought to breathe in short little spurts. Need and excitement had combined and the ache for fulfilment was a torment. Her hunger peaked in a shattering release. Losing herself in the voluptuous shock waves of convulsive pleasure, she cried out in joy and amazement.

In the aftermath, Antonio curved her round him, kissed the top of her head and studied the ornate ceiling with brilliant golden eyes. He had both arms wrapped round her in a possessive hold. He had never had such fantastic sex. And she was his, signed, sealed, delivered, even ringed. He wanted to punch the air and shout. Indeed he felt hugely satisfied with life in general. He had ditched a mistress who had been downright boring and, if truth be told, a whiner, only to discover that his bride had a magnificent gift for passion. And unless he was very much mistaken his bride had brought him a very special gift that he had never dreamt he might receive on his wedding night: she had been a virgin. He thought that was absolutely amazing. He thought it was fate that she had miraculously conserved her perfect body for him. He did indeed owe her a humble apology for assuming the worst that night he had seen her coming off the beach. At about that point he remembered their agreement and he was stunned that he could have forgotten it...

Sophie was happy. In fact she could never recall feeling quite so happy except of course in those dreams she sometimes recalled when she first wakened. Wonderful dreams in which she wandered hand in hand through sunlit places with Antonio. Antonio had had a starring role in her best dreams for so long that he was almost a fixture there. And now she had learned that he lived up to every secret fantasy she had ever had about what he might be like in bed. His future in her dreams was now assured for a lifetime, she conceded buoyantly and snuggled closer.

For the first time in almost three years she was letting herself recall the fact that she loved Antonio. Although he was destined never to know it, he had stolen her heart at their first meeting. She had yet to decide what she found most attractive about him. His cleverness, his looks, his wonderful manners, his fabulous smile? Whatever, even though she had known even then that loving him was stupid, no rival had managed to supplant him. That was why she was so oversensitive and prone to losing her temper around Antonio, she acknowledged ruefully. He could hurt her so easily and when it came to him she lost all common sense. Did that explain why she had just given her virginity to a

male who had announced up front that he wanted to be
a womaniser at the same time as he pretended to be a
husband? So what was he pretending to be now? Her
happy feelings dive-bombed faster than the speed of the
light.

Antonio decided that he was doing far too much
thinking. Why complicate things? Why look for trouble
that wasn't there? He rolled Sophie off his chest, confined her beneath one powerful arm and kissed her
breathless. 'You should have warned me that you were
a virgin, *querida*,' he told her softly. 'I could have made
it less painful.'

Emerging from a kiss that made her head swim and
her toes curl, Sophie was aghast at that comment, for it
meant that he had noticed what she had assumed he
would not. 'What gives you the idea that I was a virgin?' She forced a laugh, for she was convinced that
there was no way he could know for sure. 'I mean, how
likely is that at my age?'

'Very unlikely,' Antonio agreed silkily, pinning her
against the pillows and rearranging her into a rather
more intimate position. 'But please don't get the idea
that I'm complaining about your lack of form in the
bedroom—'

'No?' Sophie's interruption was a little jerky because
her teeth were gritted. That reference to 'form' which
was normally applied to a horse and its racing perfor-
mance, struck her as the ultimate in humiliation. Any
minute now he'd be slapping her on the rump and offering her extra oats.

In fact Antonio seemed delighted that she had proved
to be a complete novice in the sex stakes. But Sophie
was unnerved and mortified by the speed with which he
had deduced that reality. If she didn't watch out he

would soon be questioning the significance of why she had yielded her precious virginity to him. He would guess that she was a lot keener on him than appearances might suggest. And if that happened, she knew she would die a thousand deaths from shame and never look him in the face again.

'Not at all, *enamorada*,' Antonio confirmed with lazy cool, running a confident and appreciative hand along the quivering line of one slender thigh. 'I suspect we're going to have a huge amount of fun filling in the blanks in your education.'

Employing all the self-control she could muster, Sophie pulled back from him. 'You've got me *so* wrong. I may have acted the innocent to amuse myself, but there is just no way I was a virgin and I can't believe you should think that I was.'

'Why are you trying to deny the obvious? Why should you be embarrassed about the fact that you didn't sleep around? Why would you want to persuade me otherwise?' Brilliant golden eyes full of incomprehension rested on her. 'I think that you being a virgin on our wedding night is an amazing achievement. You should be proud.'

Her small hands coiled into fierce fists. He knew what he knew and her secret was a secret no more. Her clumsy attempt to blow dust over her tracks had failed. His awareness that he had been her first lover made her feel horribly exposed and vulnerable. Gripped by the growing suspicion that she had behaved very stupidly with him, she scrambled out of the bed.

Snatching up the towel on the floor, she dragged it round herself again as though it were her only cover in a life-threatening storm. 'Look, stop going on about it!'

'Come back to bed,' Antonio murmured as gently as if he were dealing with a wild creature.

'No, been there, done that,' Sophie slung with jewel bright green eyes full of angry defiance, dull coins of pink burning over her cheekbones. 'You were great and you did me a favour, but let's leave it at that!'

'A favour?' At that contemptuous dismissal, Antonio went rigid and any desire to humour and soothe left him.

CHAPTER SEVEN

'You said I did you a favour. Explain what you mean by that,' Antonio instructed with lethal cool.

Playing for time, Sophie dragged in a ragged breath. 'Can't you guess?'

Hard dark golden eyes rested on her with uncompromising force. 'Answer my question, *por favor.*'

'OK.' Sophie lifted and dropped her slim shoulders, attempting to strike a casual note while she frantically plumbed her imagination for a suitable explanation. She was totally terrified that Antonio would guess why he had found it so easy to get her into bed. 'I set you up,' she claimed daringly.

Unimpressed, Antonio elevated an aristocratic black brow. '*No me diga...*you don't say!'

His apparent calm only made her more desperate than ever to save face. 'I'm nearly twenty-three years old and I thought it was way past time I stopped being a virgin,' she spelt out, 'so I picked you to do the deed.'

That brazen claim hit home and outrage powered through Antonio. 'You did...*what*?' he raked at her in raw disbelief.

The atmosphere could have been cut with a knife and Sophie was so nervous she was trembling. Forced to defend her story, she paled. 'You've been around,' she muttered in haste. 'So I reckoned you'd make the experience reasonably pleasant...and you *did*. Can we drop the subject now?'

Antonio might have dismissed that fantastic claim

had he not remembered her walking in to join him clad only in a towel and then virtually luring him down into the cushions. Scorching golden eyes lit on her like lightning bolts. 'You selected me like some kind of stud to have sex with you?'

'Look, least said, soonest mended,' Sophie mumbled, hot-cheeked, while wishing that she had come up with a less inflammatory story.

In a towering rage, Antonio sprang out of bed and began to get dressed at speed.

The intense claustrophobic silence intimidated and frightened Sophie.

'Antonio—?'

'*Silencio!*' His tone of derisive distaste sliced back at her, his lean, darkly handsome face grim. 'I had begun to think of you as my wife. *Qué risa*...what a laugh! I won't make that mistake again. I may have misjudged you the night after your sister's wedding, but you think like a slut and behave like one. It will be a cold day in hell before I share a bed with you again!'

All the colour bled from Sophie's heart-shaped face. 'Don't be like that. Stop being so angry with me—'

'What else did you expect? Approval?' Antonio dealt her a chilling appraisal. 'Your standards are not mine. From now on, we stick to the deal we agreed.'

Her hands were shaking. She had really offended him. She spun away so that he could no longer see her shaken face. Her eyes were hot and scratchy with tears and she was stiff with shock. It was better this way, she told herself wretchedly. They should not have gone to bed together. She should have had more self-control. Almost three years back she had listened to Pablo talking enviously at his own wedding about his older brother's phenomenal success with women. Naturally

the act of sex would be a minor event to a guy like
Antonio. Women were too easily available to him and
who valued what was not in short supply? But what she
could not bear was that Antonio should be so angry with
her that he thought badly of her and condemned her for
thinking like a slut.

She locked herself in the bathroom and studied herself with tear-filled eyes of pain and regret. If only the
dream could have lasted a little longer, if only she had
not settled on that stupid, shameless story of having
slept with him purely to get rid of her virginity. Why
had he believed that? Didn't he know how irresistible
she found him? But when and how had she forgotten
that he had only married her in the first place so that
she could take care of Lydia? She had promised to leave
him free to live exactly as he pleased. That recollection
suddenly became the source of deep distress.

After a very poor night's sleep, Sophie got up soon
after seven the next morning: Lydia would be awake
and looking for her. She was really disconcerted to find
Antonio in the nursery. He had Lydia in his arms and
he was talking to her in soft Spanish.

Sophie hovered, determined to take the opportunity
to clear the air between them. 'I wasn't expecting to
find you in here.'

His keen dark-as-midnight eyes were level, his lean
bronzed features unreadable. 'I thought I ought to say
goodbye to Lydia—'

'Goodbye...you're going somewhere?' Sophie interrupted in dismay. 'Thanks for not waking me!'

The instant she made that crack she regretted it, for
even to her own ears it sounded juvenile.

'I saw no reason to disturb you this early. I intended
to phone later,' Antonio imparted with unassailable as-

surance. 'I have business to take care of. I had hoped to take a couple of days off and remain here, but it is not to be.'

Sophie had become very pale and tense. 'When will you be back?'

'I'm not quite sure,' he admitted calmly. 'I'm flying to Japan and then on to New York. After that, I must attend to matters in Madrid.'

'Antonio…' Hurt and disappointment and frustration were roaring through Sophie's slight frame. 'Don't you think we should talk?'

'I think that all that needed to be said was said last night,' Antonio countered with chillingly courteous finality.

Pride and intense insecurity silenced the apologetic tale of woe and explanation on Sophie's lips. She had met with rejection and disillusionment too often in life to deliberately court them. Why had she assumed that he would even be interested in what she had to say? After all, she was not an important element in Antonio's exclusive world. Why risk exposing herself to more of his contempt? If he was still angry with her, she reasoned unhappily, maybe it was better to let the dust settle for a couple of weeks before tackling him again.

'*Buenos días*, Sophie.' Doña Ernesta walked out onto the shaded upstairs loggia where Sophie was sewing while Lydia played on a rug at her feet. 'You must be the most industrious bride ever to enter this family. You are always at work.'

'But this isn't work…it's enjoyment.' As she placed a stitch in the fabric stretched over her embroidery frame Sophie glanced up. 'I'm not used to being lazy.'

'May I see your embroidery?'

Sophie obliged.

The old lady sighed in admiration over the intricate stitches and the fluid pattern of leaves and birds. 'You must know that this is work of an exceptional standard. You are extremely talented. Who taught you? Was it your mother?'

'I never knew my mother. It was a neighbour I used to visit as a child.' Sophie's eyes clouded with sadness as she remembered the elderly woman who had given her a much needed creative outlet. The chance to escape the noisy chaos of her father's home and visit, however briefly, a peaceful, organised household had been equally welcome. 'She taught me to sew when I was four years old and I was still learning from her ten years later when she died.'

'You must have been a rewarding pupil. Perhaps some day you will consider taking a textile conservation course.' Doña Ernesta lifted Lydia up onto her lap, smiling down at her great granddaughter with unconcealed pleasure. 'There are many very old pieces of needlework here which would benefit from your attention.'

'Even if I did a course, I don't think Antonio would want me touching family heirlooms,' Sophie muttered awkwardly.

Her companion regarded her in surprise. 'But you are a part of this family now.'

A maid arrived with a tray. 'I asked for English tea,' Doña Ernesta confided. 'And scones.'

At the old lady's request, Sophie poured the tea into fine china cups. Over the past week an increasing number of Antonio's relations and neighbours had made formal visits to meet Sophie and Doña Ernesta had been very supportive. Indeed the older woman was clearly intent on getting to know her grandson's wife. Sophie felt guilty that her own unhappiness was making it hard for her to respond with greater cheer to Doña Ernesta's more forthcoming manner.

'Have you heard from Antonio?' Doña Ernesta enquired gently.

Feeling very vulnerable, Sophie reddened. 'No…not for a couple of days.'

'He must be exceptionally busy,' Doña Ernesta immediately assured her in a soothing manner.

But with whom was Antonio busy? Sophie wondered wretchedly before she could suppress that unproductive thought. What was the point of tormenting herself? She had no control over what Antonio did. The sick sense of misery that she had been struggling to suppress threatened to rise up and overpower her. It was no comfort to know that her own hasty words had destroyed the fragile new relationship developing between her and Antonio. It was eight days since he had left the *castillo*. Although he had phoned several times the conversations had been brief and any attempt to stray into more intimate areas had been mercilessly snubbed.

'Sophie…may I speak freely to you?' Doña Ernesta asked then.

Sophie tensed. 'Of course…'

'You seem unhappy. I have no wish to pry,' the old lady assured her anxiously, 'but is there anything wrong?'

Sophie made a harried attempt to mount the cover-up that she knew Antonio would expect from her. 'Of course, there's nothing wrong.'

'It is natural that you should miss Antonio and very sad that you should be parted so soon after your wedding.'

Tears stung the back of Sophie's eyes in a dismaying

surge. It had not occurred to her that she would miss
Antonio quite so dreadfully. But admitting even to herself that she had fallen very deeply in love with Antonio
almost three years earlier and that indeed she had never
got over him had destroyed all her natural defences.

'It is too dull here for you when he is away,' Doña
Ernesta opined. 'Why don't you stay at our house in
Madrid for a few days? You could shop and mix with
the other young people in the family there. I believe
you met some of them at your sister's wedding.'

Sophie was disconcerted by that suggestion but immediately aware of its appeal. Sitting around doing
nothing was draining her confidence and depressing her.
But if she went to Madrid without Antonio having first
invited her there, it might look as if she were chasing
after him. He might also be annoyed. The terms of their
marriage deal did not allow her much room for independent manoeuvre, she reminded herself unhappily.

Whether she liked it or not, she had agreed that
Antonio could do as he liked. All she had asked for in
return was the right to care for Lydia and she had received that. In fact in material terms she really was doing very nicely indeed out of their marital agreement.
She had Lydia and she was living in luxury. To top it
all, in spite of her worst fears, even Antonio's grandmother was being really kind to her. So, really, she castigated herself, from where did she get the nerve to
imagine that she had grounds for complaint?

On the other hand, hadn't the wedding night she had
shared with Antonio blown that original agreement of
theirs right out of the water? Everything felt so incredibly personal now. By making love to her, Antonio had
turned their platonic relationship inside out. Everything
had changed and that was his fault as much as hers.

Obviously she felt differently about him now and the chasm that had opened up between them truly frightened her. Overnight Antonio had become chillingly polite and unapproachable. The misunderstanding between them had to be sorted out, she reflected worriedly.

She decided that it would be best if she arrived in Madrid while Antonio was still abroad on business. That way her presence might look coincidental and he would not even need to know that he was being chased. If he were to ask her what she was doing there she would be able to say quite truthfully that neither she nor Lydia had anything to wear. Before the wedding, she had been too scared to spend his money on anything other than absolute necessities. Now, however, she was aware that Antonio was accustomed to perfectly groomed women. So, she too would get groomed to within an inch of her life. The hair, the nails, the cosmetics, the waxing, the whatever—she would go for the entire package. There was, Sophie acknowledged shamefacedly, very little she wouldn't do to get close to Antonio again. And if she failed, well, it wouldn't be for want of trying. After all, what did she have to lose?

Striding through Barajas airport, Antonio checked his watch with rare impatience. He would be at his Madrid home within the hour. It was almost three weeks since he had left the *castillo* and he was eager to see Sophie.

Not only to *see* her, his more honest self acknowledged, and a slightly rueful smile curved his handsome mouth. He could not understand how he had managed to make such a mess of things with her. Everything he had done had been out of character. But then he could never remember getting quite so angry with a woman before. The brooding bitterness of spirit that had followed had been equally new to his experience and profoundly disturbing for a male who prided himself on his self-discipline. He was neither moody, nor bad-tempered, and he was not one to hold a grudge. In short, his was not a volatile temperament and yet how else could he explain the explosive nature of his own behaviour on their wedding day?

With his customary cool logic restored he knew that Sophie's declaration that she had chosen him to be her stud was ridiculous. In a normal frame of mind he would have laughed that insult off. That had been Sophie putting him in his place. What had happened to his sense of humour that night and over the subsequent days when he had still seethed to such an extent that even speaking to her on the phone had been a challenge for him? Where had his even temper and his shrewd ability to read a situation gone? *Dios mio*, how could he have believed that nonsensical claim for longer than thirty seconds?

The knowledge that Sophie was in Madrid had increased his keenness to get home. It had been six days since he had even contrived to speak to her. He had been working very long hours and the time difference had forced him to phone at awkward times. Then, when he had called, Sophie had always been out. He assumed his grandmother was trotting Sophie and Lydia out to meet every friend and distant relative they possessed.

His chauffeur was so intent on the colourful celebrity magazine he was reading that he did not notice his employer's approach until the last possible moment, Antonio noted in some exasperation. Muttering embarrassed apologies, the older man rushed to open the passenger door and dropped the magazine. On the front cover it carried a picture of Sophie in the floral dress she had worn for their wedding. Antonio snatched it up in disbelief.

An article several pages long liberally spattered with photos of his wife greeted Antonio's incredulous gaze. The dress he had hated was rated as the cutting edge of true bridal style. There was Sophie looking improbably demure and dignified seated in the salon of his house in Madrid. She had let cameras into one of his homes! He breathed in very deep. There was Sophie prancing along a catwalk arm in arm with his cousin, Reina, at some charity fashion show…Sophie arriving at the opening night of a musical wearing a glittering red evening dress that fitted like a mermaid skin…Sophie showing the most shocking length of leg in a striped pink miniskirt as she climbed out of a Ferrari. *Whose* Ferrari? *Whose bloody Ferrari?*

He phoned his city home and learned that Sophie was out. He asked where she was and a hip nightclub was entioned as a possibility. He directed his chauffeur there instead and called his grandmother to ask her why he hadn't been informed that his wife was in town alone.

'Does Sophie need permission?' Doña Ernesta enquired.

'No. However, I understood that you were here with her.'

'Only for the first two days. Madrid exhausts me and Sophie makes friends so easily. She's an original and she has a great sense of style.'

Antonio replaced the phone with a strong sense of dissatisfaction. He began to read the gushing text in the article in the hope of finding out whom the Ferrari belonged to as well as an explanation for his wife's presence in it.

'Your Excellency...when you are finished, could I have the magazine back?' his chauffeur asked apologetically. 'My wife is keeping a scrapbook on the marquesa. You must be so proud of her. So much beauty and life!'

Sophie smiled when Reina's friend, Josias, urged her back onto the floor to dance and resisted the temptation to check her watch.

Whatever time it was scarcely mattered. By now, Antonio had to be back from the airport. She was proud that she had respected the rules that he had laid down at the outset of their marriage. She had done nothing to embarrass herself. Although she was absolutely desperate to see Antonio again, she had been strong. She had neither surrendered to her overpowering desire to rush to the airport to welcome him home, nor stayed in eagerly awaiting her lord and master's return.

From his stance at the top of the steps that led down onto the dance floor, Antonio scanned the crowds for Sophie. When he saw her, his intent gaze narrowed. Her dress bared her slender back and arms and slim, shapely legs. The fine fabric that clung to her delicate curves was the colour of polished pewter and it glistened below the lights as she spun, her mane of hair rippling round her. She was laughing as she danced and the young dark male smiling down at her was...Josias Marcaida, son of one of Antonio's biggest business rivals. A shark circling Sophie could not have filled Antonio with greater disquiet. He took the steps two at a time and forged a direct path across the floor to intercept the couple.

Sophie was enjoying the music and then she saw Antonio and froze. His commanding height and superb carriage brought him maximum attention. As she focused on his dark, lethally handsome features her awareness of everything else external fell away. She met scorching dark golden eyes and her tummy flipped as though she were being spun on a giant wheel. Suddenly she could hardly catch her breath and her pulses were racing. Anticipation held her so taut that she tingled and a little twist of heat flared in her pelvis.

Antonio closed one lean brown hand over hers. 'Tell Josias goodbye, *querida*,' he told her huskily as the thunder of the music quietened down for the DJ to talk.

Every nerve in her body was leaping and jumping like a soldier on parade. He had come to find her. Had he climbed Everest for her, she could not have been more thrilled.

'I have to go...' she framed dizzily in the general direction of her dance partner.

CHAPTER EIGHT

ANTONIO curved a powerful arm to Sophie's spine to urge her in the direction of the exit. She was almost there before it occurred to her that she could hardly leave without telling his cousin, Reina. Although the two women had not known each other long, they got on so well that Sophie already thought of Reina as a close friend.

'I have to tell Reina that I'm going—'

'You can phone my cousin from the limo—she'll understand.'

'No, that wouldn't be right. Just give me two minutes,' Sophie pleaded, pulling free to hurry back to the table where Reina was seated.

'Sorry, but I have to leave—'

'I saw Antonio arriving,' the elegant brunette acknowledged wryly.

Sophie gave her a relieved smile, for she had few secrets from Antonio's cousin. It was largely thanks to Reina, an up-and-coming fashion designer, that Sophie had managed to get to know so many people and step straight into a busy social life. She sped back to Antonio's side, but the wry quality of her friend's farewell had dented her buoyant mood. Although she was still intoxicated to be with Antonio again, Reina's non-committal reaction had left her wondering if she should have responded with greater cool to Antonio's arrival.

Inside the limousine, Antonio reached for her with both hands. She had no thought of resisting him. Indeed a delicious little shiver of expectancy ran through her and her breath caught in her throat.

'Kiss me…' she whispered shakily.

Antonio did not get up close and personal in limos. He gazed down at her rapt face. Her amazingly green eyes clung to his. The ripe pout of her peach-tinted lips was pure, tantalising invitation.

'Antonio…' Sophie linked her arms round his neck.

Without any warning at all, Antonio found himself mentally picturing her spread half naked across the leather seat. His arousal was immediate and almost insufferably strong and all restraint vanished. Framing her cheekbones with spread fingers, he captured her mouth with hard, hungry intensity and his tongue delved deep.

He might as well have pressed a button and set Sophie on fire. Her entire body burned and she responded to that sensual assault with helpless enthusiasm.

Breathing raggedly, Antonio exerted every atom of control he could muster and dragged himself back from the brink of trying to live the fantasy pictures playing out inside his head. 'Let's chill until we get home…'

Belatedly conscious that the chauffeur could see them, Sophie reddened with embarrassment. She had grabbed Antonio. Why had she done that? She wanted to cringe and die there and then. Did she never learn? Why was she continually tempted to make a fool of herself around him?

Antonio dragged in a steadying breath and decided that if he talked, he would manage to keep his hands off her long enough to get home. 'You look amazing in that dress.'

Any desire to play it cool left Sophie at spectacular

speed and her soft mouth stretched into a huge smile. 'Thank you...'

'But...' Antonio intertwined his fingers with hers again and paused for a second, lean dark features reflective '...I have to admit that I also think the dress is too revealing for my wife to wear.'

'Oh...' Sophie framed in dismay and surprise at that unexpected criticism. 'But it's not that short and it's not see-through or anything like that.'

'It attracts too much attention, *mi rica*,' Antonio informed her gravely. 'A lot of men were staring at you.'

Sophie blinked and hurriedly dropped her lashes before he could read her expression. But she almost burst out laughing. He was so deadly serious. Men had been looking at her and therefore her clothing had to be at fault. 'Maybe they just thought I was pretty,' she dared to suggest.

'Whatever...I don't like it when other men watch you in that way,' Antonio affirmed without hesitation.

It was like the sun was rising inside Sophie and she was trying to contain the wonderful golden heat of its rays, for, unless she was very much mistaken, Antonio was jealous of other guys so much as looking at her!

'In point of fact,' Antonio continued, retaining a hold on her hand, 'it's not a good idea for you to be at a nightclub with a crowd of singles.'

Her fine brows drew together, for she was mystified by that statement. 'Why not?'

'Josias Marcaida is a womaniser—'

'Oh, I know that,' Sophie broke in. 'Reina warned me, but she also said that Josias wasn't a patch on you!'

Antonio stiffened at that unwelcome response. 'I do not think you should be discussing me with other family members.'

Her expressive mouth tightening, Sophie tugged her hand free of his. 'Right...so you don't like the dress, don't like me talking to your relations, don't like me going out to a club—'

'I think what I'm trying to say,' Antonio delivered smooth as silk and in no way apologetically, 'could be summed up in one sentence.'

'So say the magic sentence and save time,' Sophie advised curtly, temper licking up inside her in little orange flames hungry for sustenance. As she turned her head sharply away she realised the limo was already coming to a halt outside the hugely imposing dwelling that was the Rocha family home in Madrid.

'You're no longer single...you're my wife.'

Sophie breathed in so deep she honestly thought her lungs might burst. But the deep breathing helped her to emerge from the car, climb the steps with a fixed smile on her lips for the benefit of the hovering housekeeper and head straight for the stairs.

'Sophie...?' Antonio questioned with calm authority.

Sophie spun on the stairs, treated Antonio to a look that should have sent him up in flames and murmured tight and low, 'One more word and I'll be up for murder...'

'I've said nothing to which you should take exception,' Antonio countered, beautiful dark golden eyes daring her to argue.

'You...total hypocrite,' Sophie whispered, green eyes wild with raging reproach.

'Spain is civilising you, *querida*,' Antonio responded in retaliation, for he felt that he had been extremely tolerant and understanding. After all, he had found his provocatively dressed wife dancing the night away in a nightclub with a notorious playboy. 'A month ago you would have shouted that at the top of your voice and you wouldn't have cared who heard you.'

It was an unfortunate remark. Her jewel-bright eyes raked over him in a tempestuous surge.

'You may not be very tall…but in your own special way, you're quite magnificent,' Antonio remarked, his brilliant gaze welded to her with raw appreciation. He mounted the stairs with the subtle predatory grace of a big game hunter closing in on a target. 'I missed you.'

'I don't care!' Sophie launched back down at him even though she knew she did care very much and her angry voice echoed round the landing like a crash of feminine thunder. 'It's at times like this that I hate you!'

Having flung that declaration, Sophie headed with fast and furious steps for the sanctuary of her bedroom. She wanted to punch something. She really wanted to punch him, but he was off limits because she would not have liked it had he punched her. How dared he remind her that she was his wife in that superior tone of censure? How dared he even refer to her with that label?

Antonio strode into her room only a split second in her wake. 'You don't hate me,' he told her with infuriating confidence.

'We had an agreement and you made that agreement. You told me that you wanted to hang onto your freedom!'

Antonio lifted and dropped a broad shoulder in fatalistic style. 'I'm not denying it.'

'And then out of the blue you show up and you start telling me that I have to behave like a *real* wife!'

'But you *are* a real wife,' Antonio asserted.

'Maybe technically speaking…but that angle doesn't matter,' Sophie told him heatedly. 'We need to talk about you practising what you preach.'

Antonio was fascinated by the way she was laying down the law. She employed neither flattery nor feminine guile to state her case. She was not afraid to say exactly what she thought. But no woman had ever utilised such a direct approach on Antonio and he was impressed. 'Is that a fact?'

'Yes, it is,' Sophie confirmed with vehemence, her heart-shaped face flushed with anger. 'You said you wanted your freedom but that means…that *has* to mean that you're not entitled to interfere with mine…right?'

'Wrong. *En realidad*…you are very wrong on that score,' Antonio declared, lean, powerful face taut. 'Tonight I could not even stand by and watch you dance with another man without feeling that something was wrong.'

Sophie's eyes opened to their fullest extent. 'I can't believe I'm hearing this.'

'You're my wife. You wear my ring on your finger. You live in my home. You cannot be my wife and independent of me—'

Her hands knotted into fists, Sophie argued, 'Oh, yes, I can be!'

'It is a contradiction in terms—'

'Like husband and free agent?' Sophie fenced back with saccharine sweetness.

'A good comparison. But every time you shout at me, I feel married, *querida*,' Antonio confided with a glint of raw mockery in his golden gaze.

Incensed by his levity, Sophie treated him to an unamused appraisal. He need not think that she was about to be swayed by the simple fact that he was an outrageously good-looking guy with a killer smile. 'Obviously a lot of women have let you away with this sort of nonsense, but I won't let you away with anything,' Sophie warned him. 'There is no way I will ever accept this one-rule-for-you-and-another-rule-for-me attitude—'

'But that is not what I advocate.'

'But that's exactly what you're advocating...' She stumbled over that unfamiliar word and in the interim he pronounced it correctly for her. A sense of humiliation stormed through her anger and brought hot tears to her eyes. 'That's what I mean about you...you're impossible. You are Spanish and you're correcting my English!'

'That was thoughtless,' Antonio acknowledged.

'No, it wasn't. You think about everything, you always know exactly what you're doing—'

'I *didn't* know exactly what I was doing when I married you. I didn't look for the bigger picture. I must have been insane; I was certainly guilty of poor judgement,' Antonio countered grimly. 'I did not even foresee the complications that would arise from the consummation of our marriage. But from that night, my desire for freedom was inequitable and unrealistic.'

A pounding silence had fallen. Sophie was listening to his every word and she was trembling. 'As far as I'm concerned you can forget about what happened on our wedding night. You wanted to keep your freedom and you can still do that!' she told him boldly. 'You don't owe me anything and, if you stay away from me from now on, we can go right back to that agreement we made. All we need to do is be sensible from now on and we'll soon forget that we ever strayed from the deal.'

His dark golden eyes flared bright as sunlight at that frank proposition. He held her strained gaze levelly.

'That's a very generous offer in the circumstances. But there's a problem—'

'Nothing's perfect, Antonio!' Sophie riposted fiercely, because her heart felt as if it were breaking inside her. It had cost her a lot to make that generous offer. In truth she could have happily chained him to her bed.

'I know, but I can't forget our wedding night and I can't stay away from you either. I suspect that being "sensible" might well be beyond my power at present.'

Utterly unprepared for that statement and thrown into a loop by it, Sophie stared at him in confusion. 'Sorry?'

'You're incredibly tempting. I'm very attracted to you. I fought it every minute of the day the whole time I was away from you, *querida*,' Antonio heard himself admit harshly, for the knowledge that he had lost that battle still rankled like salt in a wound. 'That attraction is not sensible and it's not the deal we agreed either. But, right now, I don't want to be with any other woman; I want to be with you.'

'But...but that's not how it's supposed to be,' Sophie mumbled in shock.

'That is how it *has* to be,' Antonio affirmed, his strong jaw line squaring. 'We should forget how it was supposed to be. I can't stand back and watch you enjoy the same freedom that I once intended to take for myself. For now, let's enjoy being married.'

Sophie was no fool. There was a big smile trying to break out across her lips, for he was offering her a lifeline but she had picked up on his every qualification as well. *Right now...I want to be with you.* He was already accepting that there would be a time when he no longer wanted her. *For now, let's enjoy being married.* Again, a suggestion rooted very much in the present without any reference to the future. He was not suggesting that their marriage become a proper marriage, not really he wasn't, she reasoned painfully. What Antonio was really proposing was that they treat their marriage as if it were an affair. Basically, if she stripped everything he had said bare and got down to the basics, all he was offering her was fidelity in the short term and sex.

'Tonight, I would have liked you to meet me at the airport,' Antonio admitted so that she would know the next time. 'When you weren't there, I was determined not to come back here without you. Perhaps only then was I allowing myself to admit how much I had been looking forward to seeing you.'

As though drawn by an invisible magnet, Sophie was moving closer to him with slow, tentative steps. To the conditions of fidelity and sex, she was adding in airport meetings and thinking that that latter request was rather sweet and unexpected. 'I've hardly even spoken to you since you went away—'

'You avoided my calls—'

She coloured because it was true. 'Yeah…but you were very cold on the phone—'

'I was at war with myself, *querida*. I'm not now and I will never be again,' Antonio promised huskily.

Sophie felt light-headed with relief. She reckoned that she could probably drown and die happy in his gorgeous eyes. Nothing lasted for ever, she reminded herself dizzily. Life offered no certainties. But she loved Antonio and she was ready to take what she could have rather than hang out for what she could not. He was never going to ask her to stay married to him for good. He wasn't in love with her. He was in lust with her.

But then they could never have had a future together anyway, she reflected with a stab of pained regret. He didn't know it and she saw no reason why she should ever tell him, but she was all too wretchedly aware that she was unlikely to ever be able to have a baby. And there he was with his title, his ancestral castle and centuries of family history. He might not be that keen to tie himself down for ever yet, but some day Antonio would be very keen to hand on that title and that rich and ancient heritage to a child of his own. Understandably he would want a wife who could give him children in his future. A future in which she could not and would not feature.

Far from impervious to the distanced look that had darkened her gaze, Antonio eased her up against his lean, powerful frame with the sure hands of a male to whom sensuality was an art. 'You look unhappy,' he murmured.

'I'm not...I'm not,' Sophie insisted, stretching up to tug loose his tie and unbutton his collar.

Refusing to be distracted, he caught her active fingers up in his, turned up her palm and pressed his mouth there for a moment. He glanced back up at her heart-shaped face to see if her eyes still held that same poignant look of sorrow. 'Why are you sad?'

'It's a secret...nothing you'd be interested in—'

'Try me,' Antonio urged, for the instant she mentioned that fatal word, the instant she admitted that she was holding back something from him, he was on fire with the need to know what the secret encompassed.

'No, some things are private,' she whispered ruefully, letting a questing fingertip rub along the hard, masculine angularity of his jaw line. A faint dark bluish shadow of stubble roughened his bronzed skin and somehow made his beautiful, sensual mouth seem even more appealing, she reflected dizzily.

Antonio lowered his arrogant dark head and let the tip of his tongue flick the swollen pinkness of her lower lip. She gasped at his touch and her legs wobbled. 'If the secret relates to a problem there is a very good chance that I could sort it out for you,' he intoned gravely.

Sophie squeezed her eyes tight shut to rein back the stinging surge of tears his offer had unleashed. She loved his pride and his confidence and his immediate conviction that he could come up with a cure for everything short of death. Not to mention his very traditional assumption that it was somehow his duty and responsibility to deal with anything that worried her. 'Not this particular one,' she told him gruffly.

'Trust me...' But even as he said it he was wondering if her secret related to her inability to have children. He did not want to think about that. Never before had he experienced that reluctance to consider an issue. But he discovered that he did not even want to think about *why* that particular issue was such a hotbed of sensitivity even for him.

'No...' Her voice was muffled because she was pushing her tear-wet face into his shirtfront and fighting to get a grip on her strong emotions.

There was no need for him to know that she was barren, no need at all. Who could tell how he would react? She could not bear the idea of him pitying her. Even worse, he might begin viewing her as flawed, less of a woman and not quite so attractive. She had learned that, without really thinking about it, people tended to associate fertility with all sorts of other feminine attributes.

'Some day you *will* trust me, *gatita*,' Antonio swore with fervour and, closing his arms round her, he lifted her right off her feet. He crushed her to his hard, muscular chest and sealed his mouth to hers in a passionate, drugging kiss. Her ribs complained and oxygen was in short supply, but she loved that enthusiastic demonstration of all-male strength and protectiveness.

With immense care he laid her down on the bed and then cast off his jacket and tie where he stood.

'There really hasn't been anyone since…?' Sophie prompted shyly.

He ripped off the shirt without ceremony and smiled down at her. 'For the first time in my adult life, I've lived like a celibate.'

Sophie kicked off her shoes and lay back against the pillows like an old-style temptress, back arched, bosom prominent, knees slightly raised to display her legs to their best advantage.

'You've been practising the seduction pose,' Antonio breathed with amusement.

Sophie shifted a narrow shoulder in a languid movement to let the strap of her dress slide down, allowing just the hint of a pouting breast to be seen.

'And the effort has paid off,' Antonio conceded in another tone entirely, much impressed until he was assailed by an uneasy suspicion. 'You haven't been doing this for any other guy…have you?'

Sophie shot him a shocked look. 'Of course not…I've been behaving myself too!'

Antonio breathed again. 'I should have flown back and sorted this out more than a week ago.'

'Maybe you weren't ready.'

Antonio was still not sure that he was ready for the enormous complexity that had disrupted his once smooth and calm existence. He had not chosen the situation, but now at least he felt in control of it again.

He surveyed Sophie with unashamed masculine posses-
siveness. He could not comprehend how he had ever
dismissed her as only very pretty. Her slanting cheekbones were distinctive and her clear bright eyes were
beautiful and her skin had the creamy bloom of perfection.

'Why are you staring at me?' Sophie whispered anxiously.

'I like looking at you, *querida*,' Antonio murmured
thickly, sinking down on the edge of the bed and lifting
her on to his powerful thighs.

A tiny shiver ran through her as he undid the tiny
hooks holding up the delicate bodice of her dress. He
brushed the fragile fabric out of his path and discovered
that she was not wearing a bra. Her face flamed and she
stopped breathing altogether, madly conscious of the
jutting swell of her bare breasts and the straining prominence of her rosy nipples.

'You are perfect,' Antonio groaned, bending her back
over a strong arm and letting his hungry mouth roam
over her tender flesh with a skill that wrenched shaken
little cries of helpless response from her. 'The entire
time I've been away I've been thinking about making
love to you...I've hardly slept for wanting you.'

'I dream about you,' she muttered feverishly.

Antonio stood her up between his spread thighs and
sent the dress skimming down to her feet. He hooked a
finger into her pale pink panties and sent them travelling
in the same direction. Wide-eyed, she stared at him, her
face hot. Scorching golden eyes melded to hers, he
nudged her thighs apart and explored the warm, damp
entrance below the caramel curls crowning her feminine
mound. A fiery, raging ache stirred low in her belly.

Excitement clenched every muscle in her body and her legs shook.

'You're ready for me, *enamorada*,' Antonio husked with raw, masculine satisfaction.

He swept her up and tumbled her down again on the foot of the bed. Her heart was pumping fast; she was quivering, unable to stay still. Her body was super sensitive and burning up with painful longing. He was magnificently aroused and he plunged his hot, hard heat into the tight, tender core between her legs. She lifted up to him in a torment of wild pleasure. Then nothing existed for her but his passionate dominance and the frenzied climb to the peak of ecstasy. He drove her out of control and inhibition into a world of voluptuous abandonment. She clung to him as the sweet convulsions of heart-stopping excitement claimed her and released her from her own body in an intoxicating explosion of sensation.

'Don't even think of going to sleep, *querida*,' Antonio warned her, pinning her flat under him to capture her reddened lips in a sensually savage kiss.

Sophie gave him a dazed smile. Her body was still humming and purring with wicked little after-quakes of pure pleasure. It was amazing how the mechanics of actual sex had once struck her as being the most ridiculous arrangement ever. Yet when Antonio got passionate, she felt as if intimacy was the most wondrous joy ever and a positive passport to paradise. She linked her arms round him, breathed in the thrilling scent of his damp bronzed skin and marvelled at the feeling that he had been invented and indeed created solely for her benefit.

'You're fantastic,' he drawled, holding her close. 'And the best thing of all is that you're mine.'

'For a while,' she qualified without even thinking, needing simply to remind herself of that reality.

His lithe, strong body tensed from head to toe. 'It could be for a very long while.'

Sadly, Sophie did not think it would be. She did not feel that she would hold his attention that long. Eventually his craving for freedom would surface again. Then he would be grateful that he wasn't in a normal marriage and tied down to a wife and children... Her thoughts switched course at that point. Her smooth brow indented as she realised that on neither occasion on which they had shared a bed had Antonio made use of any protection. She was astonished that he had been so careless. My goodness, had he assumed that she was on the contraceptive pill?

She lifted her head, but not high enough to meet his eyes. 'You haven't taken any precautions...er, you know, in case of pregnancy,' she muttered awkwardly.

Suddenly Antonio was very still and calling himself a fool, for that oversight might well have betrayed his knowledge of her condition. He did not want to distress her by admitting the truth. 'My mistake...I thought perhaps you might have taken care of that.'

'No.' Relaxing again, she nestled her head back in below his shoulder.

'I promise that I'll be more careful from now on,' Antonio swore and his arms tightened round her. He smoothed a soothing hand down over her tumbled curls until the tension had left her small, slight frame and pressed his mouth to the tiny vivid butterfly tattooed on her shoulder.

But Sophie could not get over how careless he had been. Then she thought of all the babies born to men who seemed to want nothing to do with them and decided that such recklessness was possibly a common male trait. Was there even the slightest possibility that she might conceive? For the first time in her life she allowed herself the indulgence of toying with that unlikely prospect. When she was twelve years old, her father had told her that the doctor had thought it was doubtful that she would ever have kids of her own.

'Isn't there even a chance?' she had asked then.

'Yeah, he said there's always a chance, but not much of one. Why are you worrying about it? Kids spoil your life. You'll be better off without them.'

So maybe there was a one-in-ten-million chance that a miracle might occur and she would conceive. Why was she even thinking such nonsense? Antonio, she thought painfully, would be absolutely appalled if she were to fall pregnant. He would already have an image of the kind of woman he would choose to become the mother of his child. She was willing to bet that the likely lady would be blue-blooded, beautiful and fancy just as he was. But that woman would still be only his *second* wife. Well, at least she'd have been the first wife and nobody could take that away from her, Sophie reminded herself dully. Although she had to remember that she was only a wife because of Lydia and only in bed with Antonio because he had an overactive libido. Wasn't that the most likely explanation of all?

'I've arranged to take a couple of weeks off,' Antonio confessed, striving for a casual note. 'I need to spend more time with you and Lydia.'

Sophie splayed small fingers across the hair-roughened expanse of his virile chest and released a contented sigh. 'You definitely do.'

He rolled over, swinging her under him to gaze down at her with smouldering dark golden eyes. 'Do you think you could keep me entertained for that length of time?'

'I'm not sure.' Sophie surveyed his lean bronzed face from beneath her curling lashes, a newly playful light in her sparkling gaze. 'After all, the boot will be on the other foot.'

'Meaning?'

'Josias might be a tough act for you to follow.'

Reluctant appreciation of that sally lit Antonio's appraisal even as his big, powerful body tensed at the impudence of that challenge and suggested comparison. 'Anything he can do...' Antonio shrugged with magnificent assurance. 'Can you doubt it, *gatita*?'

Her heart swelled with love, for his supreme confidence made her feel safe. 'I have no doubts about you at all—'

'That sounds ominous.' Antonio finally slotted in a question he had been holding back for quite a few minutes in search of the right light moment. 'I saw that interview you did with the magazine—'

'Wasn't it amazing? Didn't the cameraman make me look really special?' Sophie exclaimed with pleasure. 'I did it for a charity...you'd be amazed at the size of the donation the magazine made to their funds. The interviewer said really nice things about me too—'

'Journalists generally do in publications of that nature. If they were unpleasant, people would not give them access to their lives and their homes,' Antonio said drily.

'I never thought of that. But I was hoping you would see the interview and be proud of me. What did you think?' she prompted eagerly.

That, aside of the business news, a Rocha should only receive a mention in print on the occasions of birth, marriage and death. That was Antonio's attitude to all such publicity.

Antonio sidestepped the question. 'I wondered who the Ferrari in the photos belonged to—'

'Josias…'

Antonio was learning that the mere mention of a name could set his teeth on edge.

'He gave me a lift from Reina's apartment to a restaurant. Of course, if you take me out to eat at least once a week, promise to teach me how to drive and constantly tell me that I'm fantastically beautiful and fantastic fun, I could probably get by without Josias,' Sophie told him deadpan, dancing green eyes pinned to his frowning incredulity.

'Yes to the eating out. No to the driving— I'd be a hellish teacher. As for Josias's seduction routine, I don't copy,' Antonio informed her huskily, rearranging her under him to his own very precise requirements and with a sexual intimacy and finesse that made her shiver in wanton anticipation of the pleasure to come. 'I have my own methods, *mi rica.*'

But it was the smile that transfixed Sophie. That dazzling, charismatic smile that was purely for her and the conviction he gave that nothing was more important than her at that moment. It was her dream, and shutting out her misgivings and her fears, she surrendered to living her dream.

CHAPTER NINE

Six weeks later, Sophie sat in the bright and colourful nursery watching Antonio demonstrate in all seriousness to Lydia how to crawl. Amusement was threatening to crack her up, but she managed to keep a straight face. All his life Antonio had been a high achiever and, having read a book on child development, he had learned all the important milestones and was keen to see Lydia sprint ahead of her peers.

'You're wasting your time,' Sophie warned him gently. 'Some babies may crawl at this age, but I don't think Lydia is likely to be one of them. She's too laidback and contented to rush into making that much effort.'

'Perhaps all she needs is encouragement,' Antonio informed her stubbornly while his niece chuckled at the sight of him on hands and knees and held up her arms to be lifted.

'No, Lydia's not the physically active type. You can tell by the way she behaves. Belinda was like that. She loved to be lazy. I could hardly get her out of bed in the morning.'

'But her daughter just might take after my side of the family—'

'I think we'd know by now if that was on the cards,' Sophie interposed. 'We'd have found her barking out orders to the staff through the bars of her cot, setting her own developmental targets and threatening to leave home unless we let her sit up to watch the stock market close.'

A slow grin curved Antonio's handsome mouth. 'I don't bark out orders...'

'Well, you do it very politely, but you are an incredibly bossy person,' Sophie told him, watching him surrender to Lydia's pantomime of pathetic pleading and hoist his delighted niece in the air. 'Just promise me one thing...that you're not going to be disappointed with Lydia if she fails to set the world on fire.'

Antonio shot her a look of reproach. 'Of course not. As her parents we can hope and pray that she enjoys good health and happiness as she grows up. But beyond that her life will be what she chooses it to be.'

His common-sense outlook impressed Sophie and she scolded herself for worrying that he might have too high expectations of Lydia. After all, in recent weeks she had come to appreciate that Antonio was demonstrating all the signs of becoming a fantastic father. For a start, Lydia just adored him. Her little face shone with trust and love and pleasure the instant Antonio appeared. Antonio might have started out spending time with Lydia because he knew that that was what he ought to do. But his niece's enthusiastic response to his attention had swiftly won her his interest and affection for her own sake.

As for Sophie, she was simply basking in the kind of happiness she had never dared to hope might be hers. Six weeks ago, Antonio had swept her and Lydia off to a Caribbean villa for the best part of a month. They had had a wonderful time. He had taught her how to sail and swim and snorkel, and she had taught him how to make the sort of basic sandcastle that Lydia could then be allowed to destroy. Even with a baby in tow the number of staff looking after their needs had ensured that the holiday was a honeymoon in every sense of the word.

There had been long, endless days when they had barely stirred further than the sunlit privacy of the terrace beyond their bedroom. Days they had barely got out of bed and surrendered body and soul to the overwhelming magnetic attraction that kept on welding them back together again when satiation ought to have long since set in. She studied him with a secret smile. He was an incredible lover and in that department they appeared to be a perfect match. He might not be able to keep his hands off her, but she was equally useless at keeping her hands off him, she conceded with hot cheeks. Every time she saw him she wanted to connect with him in some way just to convince herself that he was still hers.

Since returning from the Caribbean they had spent most of their time at the *castillo*. There the more leisurely pace of life and the vast swathe of countryside encompassed by the Salazar estate allowed them a peaceful seclusion that they could have found in no other place. Sophie had got to know the staff, had managed to handle a couple of semi-formal dinner parties and was gradually becoming acquainted with the tenants as well. She now had quite a vocabulary of Spanish words and expressions and had agreed to teach new stitches to the needlework group that met in the village. Her skill with a needle had crossed the barriers of language and nationality and had done more than anything else to help her to win acceptance as Antonio's wife.

Antonio closed his arms round her as she straightened from settling Lydia into her cot. 'Lunch…' he growled soft and low.

The feel and the familiar scent of him hit Sophie like an instant aphrodisiac and she wriggled back shamelessly into the hard, muscular shelter of his lithe, powerful body.

'Keep on doing that and you're likely to go hungry until we dine this evening,' Antonio promised in a husky purr.

Her knees went weak at that sensual threat. She leant back into his impressively male frame, wickedly conscious of the helpless awakening of her own body. He used a certain tone of voice and looked at her with those spectacular golden eyes in a certain way and she just melted into a pitiful puddle of eager longing.

'I would rather have you than lunch…' she admitted, her cheeks warm with embarrassment over her own boldness.

With a throaty laugh of masculine appreciation at that frank confession, Antonio spun her round to face him. 'You must have been made specially for me, *enamorada*.'

'Or you must've been made for me,' Sophie traded.

In the corridor outside the nursery he dragged her into his arms and captured her mouth with a devastating urgency that left her dizzy. 'You've turned my life upside down,' he breathed raggedly. 'But I like it this way.'

His mobile phone started ringing before they even reached the bedroom. They exchanged mutually irritated glances and with a sigh he answered it. She knew by the shadowing of his lean dark features that something important had come up and that he would have to leave.

An estate tenant, an old man who had known Antonio from childhood, had been ill for a long time and was asking for him to visit.

'I must go and see him,' Antonio said gravely.

'I know.' Sophie masked her disappointment and smiled to show that she understood, for she had learned to appreciate his serious side and the strong sense of responsibility that drove him.

She opened the bedroom door and stared wide-eyed at the superb arrangements of white flowers that flourished in several corners. The air was heavy with the scent of blossom. 'My goodness...'

'It was supposed to be a surprise. I should have kept you out of this room until I got back,' Antonio groaned.

'My birthday's still a week away—'

'I know...' Antonio watched her remove the envelope from the biggest floral display. 'But we have now been together for two months and we're celebrating, *querida.*'

Her throat thickened and her eyes misted over with tears as she scrutinised the gift card. It was such a romantic gesture and she was really touched. What had happened to their marriage of convenience? He had said to forget how their marriage was supposed to be and she had needed no encouragement to forget that original businesslike agreement, for she was madly, hopelessly in love with him. He had suggested that they enjoy being married and since then every day, every night had been a joy for her. Nobody had ever made so much effort to bring her happiness. Was it any wonder that she simply adored him? With an unsteady hand she skated a fingertip over a delicate white blossom.

'You don't like them?'

Fiercely blinking back the moisture in her aching eyes, she flung her arms round him, hugged him tight and whispered gruffly, 'I love them, I really, really love them and appreciate the thought.'

Antonio drove out to the isolated farm to visit the old man, who had once been the estate farrier. He was taking his leave of the sick man's family early that evening when his phone rang again. It was his friend, Navarro Teruel, the family doctor.

'Could you come and see me at the surgery?' Navarro sounded unusually stilted. 'I know I usually come up to the castle, but on this occasion you might find my office more suitable.'

Climbing into the dusty four-wheel drive he used on the estate, Antonio frowned. 'I could come right now. Is there something wrong?'

'I'd prefer not to discuss this on the phone,' Navarro told him awkwardly.

Antonio dug his phone back in his pocket. He felt slightly nauseous. Was it his grandmother? Doña Ernesta had been pronounced fighting fit at a recent examination. But a couple of weeks earlier Antonio had allowed Navarro to run a full battery of tests, including DNA, on Lydia. *Dios mio!* Had that medical turned up a disease? But why had it taken so long for Navarro to approach him with the adverse result?

Sophie didn't even know about half those tests. Having arranged to take Lydia to Navarro for a vaccination that had been overdue, Sophie had come down with a twenty-four-hour virus that had confined her to bed and it had been Antonio who had taken the baby instead. Navarro had been very thorough. He had sympathised with Antonio's concern about the risk of a heart murmur and his friend's desire not to worry his wife unnecessarily. But in most cases heart murmurs could be dealt with, Antonio reminded himself. Why had Navarro sounded so bleak and constrained?

Antonio drove to the surgery with the immense care

of someone worried sick. What if there was something seriously wrong with Lydia? Leukaemia, he thought strickenly. Could it run in families? He pictured Lydia, who was the most cheerful baby imaginable, suffering and fighting for her life. His hands gripped the steering wheel with the fierce power of his disturbed emotions. He imagined what that terrible battle would do to Sophie…and to him. He knew that he would have to be strong for all of them. He knew that just at the moment he did not feel strong. He wanted to rage against fate with every atom of his being.

Navarro, a tall, thin, bespectacled man opened the door of the surgery. It was after opening hours and the reception area was empty and silent. 'Come in, Antonio.'

Lean, powerful face pale and grim, Antonio refused the offer of a seat. 'Just give me the bad news.'

'The DNA results on your late sister-in-law's child arrived this afternoon.'

'You invited me here to discuss that DNA stuff?' Antonio interrupted in surprise.

'You asked me to take care of the testing when you brought Lydia to see me,' Navarro reminded him. 'As you know I did the saliva tests on you and her and sent them off. I imagine that, like me, you thought no more of the matter.'

'I didn't…' Antonio agreed, endeavouring to rise above his concern for Lydia to absorb this new and unexpected information. 'I assumed that you had asked me here to tell me that there's something wrong with Lydia.'

'Lydia is a perfectly healthy child.' But Navarro was still frowning when he extended a folded sheet of paper to his former school friend. 'But you had better look at this. I dealt with the DNA testing personally, so none of my staff have had access to this information.'

Antonio flipped open the document and read the typed lines several times over with fierce concentration. 'This can't be true...there must be some mistake!' he contended in flat rebuttal.

'I'm sorry, but the tests prove beyond doubt that Lydia is not your brother's child,' Navarro pronounced with a regretful sigh. 'The child is not related to your family. She carries none of your genes.'

Antonio was so shocked he dropped heavily down onto the chair opposite the other man. He began to speak and then thought better of it. An intensely private man at the best of times, he immediately battened down the hatches of his reserve on his personal reactions. Navarro might be his oldest friend from childhood, but this was a family matter that touched his honour.

'I'm sure that this news will be equally distressing for your wife to hear, which is why I preferred not to come up to the castle. Try not to judge Lydia's mother too harshly, my friend...'

Antonio was no longer listening. Incredulous dark anger was rising in a flood tide inside him, washing away the trusting foundations of the newer ties that had formed in more recent times. The child he regarded as his niece, the baby he had learned to regard as his own daughter, was an impostor, a fake. She had not a drop of the blood of the Rocha family in her veins. Who had put forward Lydia's claim? Belinda—and through Belinda, Sophie. The sisters must both have known the truth. He refused to believe otherwise.

Antonio sprang upright. 'I must go home.'

Navarro looked concerned. 'Take some time to come

to terms with this, Antonio. People do make mistakes and often the innocent foot the price.'

But Antonio was too outraged to embrace such a philosophical view and too close to the sharp end to feel generous. He had allowed himself to become the victim of a scam! What else could it be? He had married a virtual stranger on the strength of his conviction that that little girl was his brother's child. But he should have insisted that DNA tests to prove the child's identity were done first. In retrospect he could not credit that he had been so gullible. He had actually ignored the legal advice he had received at the time. His own lawyer had advised caution and tests, but Antonio had been impatient to get the marriage over and done with and the situation resolved. He had also been ashamed of the part his dishonest brother had played in his late wife's impoverishment. Questioning the paternity of Belinda's child against such a background would have been adding insult to injury.

But wasn't it strange that just at the point when he had decided simply to remove Lydia from Sophie's care something had happened to change his mind? How much had he been influenced by Mrs Moore's well-timed sob story about Sophie's inability to have a baby of her own? Had Sophie even had leukaemia when she was a child? How did he know that she was infertile? That story had not come from Sophie personally and tact had prevented him from approaching her for verification. If Mrs Moore had lied to further Sophie's hope of enriching herself through Lydia, Sophie would be able to disclaim any responsibility for the fact.

Back at the *castillo*, Antonio strode into the vast and imposing salon and poured himself a brandy. As he replaced the stopper on the crystal decanter he noticed that his hand was unsteady. He drained the goblet and strode upstairs to the nursery. He did not know why his steps had automatically taken him up there. The room was dimly lit and the nanny, who was tidying away clothes, slipped away to leave him in peace with her charge.

Lydia was fast asleep, her little face serene below the mop of her curls. She looked very much like Sophie, he acknowledged. Lydia had the same delicate build, facial shape and creamy skin, but her hair was darker than her aunt's and her eyes a different colour. Antonio surveyed the child whom he now knew had nothing to do with him at all. Fierce bitterness laced his mood. He had never had much interest in children but he had still learned to love Lydia. Yet she was a stranger's child even if she did not feel like a stranger and was Sophie not a stranger too? After all, the woman he had believed her to be would never have deceived him in such a manner.

Sophie studied herself critically in the dressing room mirror and decided that she looked downright indecent. If the fire alarm went off and she was forced to jump from a window, she would have to pretend that the reason she was in her underclothes was that she was fresh out of her bath. She was wearing a lace-trimmed blue silk lingerie set adorned with tiny roses and seed pearls. On her terms the flimsy camisole and panties were the last word in erotic presentation and daring. Did she look daft? Women photographed in similar get-ups for magazines always had legs that went on for ever and beautiful faces stamped with superior expressions of extreme boredom. She practised looking bored while struggling to suppress her worst fear: suppose Antonio laughed?

The food she had ordered arrived on a trolley along with an ice bucket and champagne. Casting off her wrap again, she took the trolley into the bedroom and began lighting scented candles. He gave her flowers and a romantic card and she gave him…a rerun of their wedding night with supper on the floor and sex. She winced, green eyes reflecting her mortification over that analogy. Well, she couldn't tell him she loved him, could she? He certainly wouldn't thank her for any soppy confessions of that nature. *Let's enjoy being married,* he had said. There was nothing deep or emotional about that suggestion.

Nervously she fingered the glittering diamond pendant in the shape of a flower at her throat. He had given it to her while they were abroad. He had also bought her an exquisite watch and diamond-studded ear hoops and she had no doubt that she would receive something even more expensive and precious to mark her birthday. He had bought her and Lydia a host of other little gifts as well. He was very generous. Ought she just to have bought him something? No, she decided, when a guy could buy himself anything, a woman had to go that extra mile to make an impression. But did she look cheap…sluttish?

When the door opened, she called out, 'Antonio? Close your eyes before you come in!'

He didn't close his eyes: he looked and he burned with hot anger and even hotter desire. There she was spread across the bed for his benefit, sin in miniature and only minimally clad in silk. And she looked shameless, sexy and stunning. It was a combination that did something quite disgraceful to his healthy libido.

Encountering the chillingly cool light in Antonio's stunning eyes, Sophie flushed to the roots of her hair and sat up with a jerk to hug her knees. She felt like an absolute idiot and almost cringed, for his disinterest was palpable. 'I was getting dressed…and I just decided to lie down for a nap,' she lied in a stricken surge, sliding off the bed in such clumsy haste that she almost fell.

'Did you know that Lydia wasn't my brother's child?' Antonio murmured smooth as silk, his tone conversational.

At that entirely unexpected question, Sophie froze like a fawn in flight and her green eyes opened very wide in response. 'Say that again…'

'If you are trying to convince me that you had no suspicion, you're wasting your time,' Antonio retorted with scornful bite. 'I can't believe you didn't know. How *could* you not have known? Your sister lived with you while she was pregnant and you were best friends—'

'Let me get this straight…out of the blue you are attempting to suggest that Lydia might *not* have been Pablo's kid?' Sophie recounted in strained interruption. 'What is this? Some sort of horrible bad joke?'

'If only,' Antonio riposted, lean, darkly handsome features hard as steel. 'I feel that you should be aware that you'll have to do more than prance round the bedroom in sexy knickers to dig yourself out of this particular tight corner!'

'How am I in a tight corner?' Sophie demanded, striving not to show any response to that mortifying reference to both her appearance and her behaviour. 'Just you explain why you're suddenly throwing all this rubbish at me. Have you any idea how insulting you're being?'

'Is there a polite way to put this? Belinda slept with

someone other than my brother and that man was Lydia's father.'

'Don't you dare try to smear my poor sister's reputation with disgusting lies!' Sophie shouted at him, her temper flaring as she stared at him in bewildered disbelief.

'It may be disgusting but it's not a lie. DNA tests have been carried out on me and on Lydia and I have the paperwork that assures me that there is no question of there being a blood relationship between us—'

'How could you have had DNA tests carried out?' Sophie gasped. 'That's not possible!'

'The tests were done a couple of weeks ago when I took Lydia to see Navarro Teruel—'

'You went behind my back and—'

'It wasn't like that—'

'It was exactly like that!' she flung fierily.

'I knew DNA testing would be necessary even before I came to England to see you. My lawyer warned me that the very fact that Lydia was born after Pablo and Belinda broke up and after his death might awaken doubts about the child's paternity. *Qué demonios!* It is most ironic that I had no doubts but those tests had to be done to protect the child in the future—'

Her head was reeling with the twists and turns of his explanation. 'I can't accept what you're saying. Why would people think such nasty things about an innocent child?'

'When there's money involved even my relatives are not above malicious conjecture.'

Sophie was more confused than ever. 'Money? What money?'

'My grandmother is a wealthy woman. The minute she learned of Lydia's existence she decided to alter her will and leave a substantial legacy to her great-granddaughter,' Antonio clarified coolly. 'For that reason even I saw the good sense of proving now by whatever means possible that Lydia was my brother's legitimate heir.'

'I had no idea about the legacy or your grandmother's plans,' Sophie admitted unevenly. 'But that doesn't excuse you taking advantage of me being ill to have tests done on Lydia that I didn't know about!'

'At the time my main goal was that she should have a full medical examination. I didn't want to worry you with my concern but she seemed very small and frail to me—'

'Thought I'd been neglecting her, did you?' Sophie stabbed jaggedly.

'No, my concern related to the fact that a couple of babies in this family were born with heart murmurs.'

'Right, OK,' Sophie groaned. 'But what is this gobbledegook about Lydia not being Pablo's child?'

'She *isn't* his child,' Antonio asserted grimly. 'DNA tests have proved that.'

'I still don't believe you…either you've picked this up wrong or you're lying for some weird reason of your own!' Sophie condemned wildly in her desperation. 'Belinda was married to Pablo and there was nobody else in her life until after Lydia was born. Somebody has made a dreadful mistake.'

Antonio dealt her a derisive look of distaste. 'You're wasting my time with these empty protests. It is my belief that you and Mrs Moore were well aware that Lydia was not related to me. I also think that you hoped to make money out of the deception—'

'What deception?' Sophie exclaimed so sharply that

her voice broke, for she was feeling increasingly out of her depth.

'I believe you expected me to pay you handsomely to look after the child in England. I'm a rich man. It was well worth your while to try and pass off Lydia as my brother's child—'

'That's the most revolting suggestion I've ever heard and you seem to be forgetting that my sister named you as one of her child's guardians in her will. Was she also in on this deception? Are you saying that my sister knew she was going to die?' Sophie asked him in disgust. 'And what on earth has Norah Moore got to do with all this?'

Antonio vented an embittered laugh. 'She was the ace up your sleeve. Things weren't looking too good for you that day that we talked on the beach, were they? I had every intention of taking Lydia back to Spain and you weren't going to make much profit out of that. So what did you do?'

Sophie jerked a thin shoulder. 'I don't know…you have this amazing imagination,' she breathed curtly, fighting her pain with all her might because it hurt so much that their relationship could disintegrate so fast into a welter of crazy accusations and suspicions. 'You tell me what I supposedly did next.'

'You sent Mrs Moore to see me at my hotel the next morning—'

Sophie fixed startled eyes on him. 'What the heck are you talking about?'

'And the woman made an excellent job of engaging my sympathies.'

'If Norah did come to see you, I knew nothing about it—'

'It was too neat the way it happened,' Antonio countered, unimpressed by her plea of innocence. 'Of course you knew about it. Your good friend, Norah, told me that I couldn't possibly separate you from Lydia because, having suffered childhood leukaemia, you were infertile. I swallowed the sad story and in common with most men I was reluctant to question you about that particular personal tragedy.'

Listening to him, Sophie felt as though she had been kicked in the teeth and betrayed. When he referred to her fertility problems, she turned as pale as milk. The terrible heavy silence lay while she fought to recover from that wounding blow and still hold her head high. 'I had no idea that Norah had sneaked off to see you to plead my case for me. She had no right to tell you my personal business,' she whispered sickly. 'And I'm sorry you were embarrassed like that, but I'd have drunk poison sooner than ask for your sympathy!'

Antonio could not drag his penetrating dark eyes from her heart-shaped face. She looked traumatised. He knew instantly that Norah Moore's visit to his hotel had not been a part of any scam and that what the older woman had told him in confidence about Sophie was true. Appalled at the manner in which he had confronted her on that sensitive issue, he was filled with immediate regret. His superb bone structure taut below his bronzed skin, he made an instinctive move towards her. 'Sophie…if that's true, I'll—'

'You'll what? Yes, it's true about the leukaemia and the infertility, but none of that has anything to do with this conspiracy theory you've dreamt up about Lydia,' Sophie spelt out, stepping back out of his reach and snatching up a wrap to dig her arms into the sleeves and cover her trembling body from view. 'I don't believe what you're saying, but I don't really care either.

Lydia is still Lydia and still my niece and she doesn't need a snobby uncle or a great grandmother's money... She never did need any of you when she already had me. And whatever happens she's *still* got me!'

Having completed that stricken assurance of intent and independence, Sophie vanished into the bathroom and slammed shut and locked the door. He knocked and she ignored it. He tried to reason with her through the door and she told him to shut up and leave her alone. He threatened to get the master key and use it unless she came out of her own volition and she told him she'd scream the place down and make such a fuss the staff would still be talking about it in a hundred years' time.

CHAPTER TEN

SOPHIE sat on the cold mosaic tiled floor and hugged her knees and stared into space.

It was all over. Her crazy romantic hopes, her living for today and not worrying about tomorrow, their marriage. All over. Suddenly Antonio was willing to believe that she was a lying cheat, a greedy, money-grabbing fraudster. She had had no idea just how fragile their understanding was. But now their relationship already seemed as imaginary and insubstantial as a child's soap bubble and she felt terrifyingly as if she were waking up in a living nightmare. In the space of minutes Antonio had taken her love and her pride and even her faith in him and destroyed the whole lot. As if it meant nothing, and obviously what they had shared *did* mean nothing to Antonio.

Sophie suppressed the sob clogging up her aching throat. How could she be so selfish that she was only thinking of her own predicament? What about Lydia? If Lydia was not a Rocha, she stood to lose so much: her new family, her home and her promising future. Nor could Antonio be expected to continue acting as a father-figure. About the only thing that Sophie knew about DNA tests was that they were reputed to be foolproof. Yet she still found it almost impossible to credit that the sister she had believed she knew so well could have been unfaithful to Pablo while they were still living together as a couple.

At the same time Sophie was reluctantly recalling

Norah Moore's crack about Belinda being a dark horse.
The older woman had also suggested that Belinda had
only ever told her kid sister what she reckoned she
would want to hear. Sophie's heart sank as she ran those
revealing comments back and forth inside her head.
Obviously, Norah knew more than she had been prepared to admit about Belinda and Sophie would have
to approach the older woman to see if she could cast
some light on the situation.

But right now Antonio's anger was a painfully convincing body of proof and if he was right, Lydia was
some other man's child. Antonio would not throw
around such damaging allegations without strong evidence. He had been upset too, she acknowledged, her
throat convulsing. He had become fond of Lydia. But
it had been a mistake to forget that Antonio had only
married her to give his supposed niece a mother and a
stable home.

Sophie hugged her knees to her breasts. Norah had
spilled her deepest secret to Antonio. Norah had told
him she couldn't have a baby. She wanted to chase after
him and tell him that her condition wasn't that cut and
dried and final and that she just might have a tiny
chance of conceiving. But what would be the point? Her
face crumpled and she sucked in a quivering breath,
fighting to keep control of her wildly see-sawing emotions.

She even understood why Norah had intervened and
told Antonio. The older woman had been trying to help
Sophie keep the baby she loved. Norah had quite deliberately treated Antonio to a sob story in a desperate
attempt to shame and embarrass him into going away
and leaving Sophie and Lydia alone. Of course, it had
not occurred to Norah that Antonio's response to that

sob story would be a marriage proposal. No wonder the older woman had been so dismayed at the prospect of Antonio marrying Sophie for Lydia's sake. For Norah had known that Antonio's most driving motivation could only have been pity.

The tears overflowed from Sophie's eyes in a hot, stinging flood, but not a sound escaped her, for she was determined not to let Antonio hear her cry. But what she had just been forced to accept was the most painful truth she had ever had to swallow. There it was, whether she liked it or not: Norah had pulled the right strings with Antonio. Antonio did loads for charity. Antonio was stuffed full of decent principles and conscience. And Antonio would have felt desperately sorry for Sophie when he realised that Lydia was likely to be the closest she ever got to a baby of her own. So, he had decided that he could not deprive her of Lydia and that was the only reason he had offered her marriage…the pity vote. She felt hollow with hurt and humiliation and the sheer agony of his rejection and the tears kept on falling for a long time.

Two hours later, Sophie emerged from the bathroom. She was very surprised to find Antonio still waiting. 'What do you want?' she asked, blanking him for it hurt far too much to let herself look directly at his darkly handsome features.

'When I got the news about Lydia, I lost my head…I'm sorry, *querida*,' Antonio breathed tautly. 'It was the shock but that is no excuse for the way I took my anger out on you.'

'Yeah, well, you won't be doing that again,' Sophie responded stonily from the dressing room where she was stuffing a change of underwear into a carrier bag.

'I won't be,' Antonio conceded. 'We will deal with this challenge together—'

Sophie rolled her eyes at her carrier bag. 'No, thanks. This isn't a challenge…trust you to call it something like that. This is the end of something that never should have begun.'

Antonio appeared in the doorway. 'What are you doing?'

'Packing a few things.'

His big, powerful body went rigid. 'Packing…to go where?'

'Back home.'

'This is your home.'

'No, this is *your* home. I want to speak to Norah and find out if she does know more about Belinda than I did. I assume the DNA tests you mentioned are correct and if it's at all possible I would like to know who Lydia's father is.'

'I'll come with you.'

Sophie compressed her soft pink mouth into a line tighter than a jar with a child-proof lid. 'No, this isn't your business any more.'

Antonio released his breath in a hiss. 'Please let me express my—'

'I'm really not interested in hearing you express anything. You married me 'cos you thought Lydia was your brother's kid. She's not his kid, so we can call it a day now—'

'There is much more between us than that,' Antonio argued. 'You're furious with me and you have every right to be—'

'OK, so push off and give me peace to pack—'

'It would be foolish to embark on a journey at this

time of night. We'll rise early and fly over to London tomorrow—'

'I'm not flying any place with you. I already told you…Lydia and I aren't your business any more—'

'You're my wife and I will not let our marriage break down over this,' Antonio asserted fiercely.

Sophie vented a thin little laugh. 'Marriage? What marriage? We never had a marriage! We've had a good laugh and lots of sex, but that's it!'

Antonio reached for her. She twisted away with sufficient violence to persuade him of the need to back off. Green eyes feverishly bright, she shot him a warning glance. 'Stay away from me!'

'If I could take back what I said, I would,' Antonio intoned in a roughened undertone. 'But the very fact that you never told me that you were infertile made me suspect that Norah Moore had told me lies!'

Sophie lost colour, for she had not thought of matters from that angle. Although she was reluctant to admit it, she could see how her silence on that thorny topic would have roused his suspicion that Norah had been shooting him a line. 'I didn't tell you because we didn't have a proper marriage,' she said in an effort to defend herself.

'What do you call a proper marriage?'

'One where the guy doesn't says things like, ''For now, let's enjoy being married,'' like it's a casual affair!'

Dark colour demarcated the slashing line of Antonio's high cheekbones. 'You have a point. But I would still argue that our marriage was as real as any other. All the elements that needed to be there were there—'

'Yeah, *were*…past tense. We had a good time, but

let's quit while we're still speaking!' Sophie retorted with a brittle smile.

Antonio breathed in deep. 'I'm flying to England with you.'

'I don't care what you do as long as you leave Lydia and me alone,' she muttered tightly.

'Lydia won't be accompanying us.'

'Excuse me?' Sophie tossed him a disbelieving look.

'Lydia is staying here at the *castillo* until we return.'

'But I wasn't planning on returning!' Sophie exclaimed. 'I want to take her with me—'

'No. Lydia goes nowhere without my agreement and I will not give it,' Antonio delivered without hesitation. 'You're not in the right frame of mind to make an important decision about her future.'

Her hands clenched into hurting fists. 'What do you care? Lydia's nothing to you now—'

Dark golden eyes sought and held her accusing gaze. 'That's not true. I'm angry that I didn't know the truth. But I care as much about Lydia at this moment as I did when I woke up this morning.'

'Well, whoopee for you…you can visit us every six months.'

'Lydia is not travelling to England with us tomorrow,' Antonio spelt out grimly, brilliant eyes welded to the tight set of her delicate profile. 'Perhaps by then you might be ready to let me talk and say what I really want to say.'

Her soft mouth quivered and she turned her back on him. 'You've said enough for one day.'

'Sophie…' He touched her shoulder.

She shrugged him off. The silence pounded and thudded. Then the door closed on his departure and she wanted to scream and scream to exorcise the agony inside her. She hadn't wanted him to stay. But she could not bear him to leave her. But what was she supposed to say to a guy who had made a huge sacrifice for nothing? He hadn't wanted to give up his freedom and marry. But he had truly believed that he had a duty of care towards Lydia. Yielding to temptation on their wedding night had led to a relationship he would never have sought on his own behalf. So he had made the best of things in the short term.

That was the sort of guy Antonio was...always set on doing the right thing no matter how painful it might be. She loved him a lot, but she didn't want his pity. She felt so ashamed of her sister's behaviour as well. Belinda's will had got them into a disastrous marriage and unfortunately Lydia would suffer the most from the fallout. Sophie could not accept that Antonio could still genuinely care about Lydia now that he knew she wasn't his niece.

The following afternoon, the jet landed in London. After a night spent tossing and turning in misery, Sophie had slept for most of the flight. Antonio watched her the entire time she slept. He covered her up with a rug. He pushed a pillow under her flushed cheek. Without even speaking to him she was putting up signs as big as placards to keep him in touch with her mood. She had left off her wedding ring and even the watch he had given her. She was wearing a T-shirt and shabby jeans that he recalled from his first visit to the caravan site. It bothered him that she should have held onto those garments in spite of her wardrobe of new clothes and the wealth that surrounded her. He could see that he was being not so much airbrushed out of her scheme of things as annihilated as though he had never existed.

'You can stay in the car,' Sophie told him uncomfortably outside Norah Moore's little bungalow. 'If there's anything to find out, I promise that I'll share it with you.'

She had phoned Norah to tell her that she was visiting and she had also told the other woman about the results of the DNA test.

'Did you know Lydia wasn't Pablo's?' Sophie asked baldly as the older woman put on the kettle.

Norah gave her a reluctant nod of assent.

'Why didn't you tell me?' Sophie groaned.

'Belinda begged me not to and after she had passed away I saw no reason to upset you—'

'I can't believe that my sister talked to you and not to me!'

The older woman grimaced. 'She was your big sister and she wanted you to look up to her. She didn't exactly plan to tell me either.'

'It's OK…I'm grateful that she did talk to you because at least now I can find out the truth.'

'Well, I called in one evening and found Belinda drinking. I gave her a right telling-off about drinking with a baby on the way and she just laughed. You know how silly she could be. She asked me if I'd be shocked if she told me that the baby wasn't her husband's kid. She was gasping to spill the beans to somebody.'

'What did she tell you about Lydia's father?'

'That she'd been with a bunch of different men she picked up in bars and didn't have a blind clue which one was responsible.' As Sophie studied her in consternation Norah folded her lips. 'She went off the rails for a while. It happens. Her marriage was breaking up. Pablo was out all the time and having other women on the side and she decided to have some fun of her own.'

Sophie wrinkled her nose. 'What a mess…what an

awful mess. But if she knew right from the start that Lydia wasn't Pablo's why did she name Antonio as a guardian in her will?'

'I bet she only had that will done after Pablo had been killed. I think she was ashamed and wanted to forget what she'd done. She wanted to pretend the baby *was* her husband's. She certainly regretted telling me the truth and took against me because of it,' the older woman reminded Sophie wryly.

'I also know that you went to see Antonio at his hotel,' Sophie admitted. 'He told me about it.'

Norah pulled a face. 'That backfired on me,' she confided ruefully. 'I expected Antonio to let you keep Lydia here and maybe help you out with a bit of money. Instead he went and asked you to marry him.'

'Now I understand why you were so against our marriage.'

'But I didn't want to interfere. How was I to know what was for the best? Antonio meant well by Lydia and I didn't want to be the one who spoilt that for the kiddie.' Norah studied Sophie and raised a brow. 'I was about to ask how marriage is treating you, but I can see Antonio's right and tight with his cash. You're still wearing the same jeans you had before you left. Well, at least he'll not be getting into debt like that brother of his!'

Sophie went very red in the face and hastened to dissuade Norah from the conviction that Antonio was seriously mean with money. Norah informed her with some satisfaction that her son had started dating a neighbour's daughter and that the relationship was looking serious. Sophie walked slowly back out to the limousine.

'You don't have to tell me anything if you don't want

to,' Antonio drawled in a trying-to-be-ultra-sensitive tone.

'Belinda went with a load of different blokes and so we're never going to be able to find out who Lydia's father is,' Sophie responded, determined not to reveal just how affronted she was by her late sister's behaviour.

'I'm her father now,' Antonio murmured very quietly.

'Believe me, if Lydia was grown up enough to know that you're prone to taking pity on little children and cleaners, she'd pretty soon tell you not to bother yourself!'

'What if I was to tell you that I didn't take pity on the cleaner...that I actually wanted the cleaner for myself,' Antonio murmured softly.

Sophie blinked, reran that statement in her mind, examined it from all angles and shot him a furious glance of condemnation. 'I'd know you were just feeling guilty about what you said yesterday and I wouldn't believe you.'

The flight back to Spain seemed endless to her. An evening meal was served on board, but she had little appetite for it. When the limousine was ferrying them through the wooded countryside, she finally succumbed to the lure of watching Antonio. After all, there would be few if any such opportunities in her future, she reminded herself. Their marriage was finished. What reason did they have to be married now? She would pack and return to England with a cheery wave. The cheery wave, the show of happy indifference, was an essential. At least if she walked out with her head high, she would leave with her pride intact. Antonio, on the other hand, was looking very bleak. But then he had amazing tact and a real sense of occasion, she reflected. It would hardly be polite or considerate of him to sit there wreathed in smiles at the prospect of divorcing her and regaining his freedom.

She wondered how long it would take her to get over him. Just then she felt as if the entire world were covered by a big dark storm cloud that shut out all the light. Her past track record on getting over Antonio was not inspiring. Her attention lingered on his bold masculine profile, the springy blue-black darkness of his hair, his classic nose, the ebony sweep of his lashes and the wide, sensual curve of his mouth. Heat prickled low in her pelvis and she found herself wondering if she could tempt him into bed just one more time, and she was so mortified by that thought that she punished herself by looking out the window instead.

By the time the battlemented towers of the *castillo* appeared on the horizon, Sophie was strung up as high as a kite with nervous tension. Set against the backdrop of hills clad with dense green forest, Antonio's ancestral home looked glorious. Grand though the ancient fortress was, it had, without her even realising it, become home to her.

She worried at her full lower lip, keeping her eyes very wide to hold back the tears that were threatening her. She was remembering breakfasts on the ironwork balcony when Antonio had cut up fresh fruit for her and made her feel like a princess. She was remembering how he had driven her crazy when he was trying to teach her to drive. She was remembering how nervous she had been before that first dinner party and how he had teased her out of her worries and boosted her confidence by convincing her that she was much cleverer than she had ever thought she was.

In a silence that echoed and without even needing to discuss a preference, they both opted to go straight up to the nursery. Lydia was fast asleep in her cot, gloriously unaware of the revelations that had rocked the world of the adults selected to care for her.

'Will you visit her?' Sophie heard herself ask Antonio tightly as she walked back out of the room again. It was painful to bear the strained silence where once they would have been cheerfully engaged in talking about Lydia.

'Lydia's not going anywhere,' Antonio retorted, slowing his long stride to match her slower pace.

'You don't have the right to tell me that—'

'This is not about rights. Regardless of what happens between us, I intend to continue playing an active role in Lydia's life.'

'I wonder if you will.' Unhidden cynicism edged Sophie's curt response to that declaration.

'You will find that I keep my promises, *mi amada*. What I say I will do, I will do—'

'Oh, stop being so stuffy and superior!' Sophie lashed out at him, her desperate unhappiness finding a vent in temper.

Antonio swore under his breath, smouldering golden eyes clashing with her defiant scrutiny. 'Don't speak to me in that tone.'

'Why? What are you going to do about it?' Sophie snapped like a cat ready to scratch.

Antonio tugged her to him with one powerful hand and trapped her between the wall and his lithe, powerful body. 'What you like best?'

Her heart started pounding like a road drill, her breath parting her lips in short little spurts. Her pupils dilated, she stared up at him, every sensitive skin cell on fire for him, every nerve ending singing with sexual awareness. She wanted him instantly and desperately.

'No...' Antonio told her with seething derision. 'No talk...no sex!'

Her soft lips fell open. Hot pink flooded her creamy complexion. Shaken eyes veiling, she twisted under his arm and stalked away. 'I didn't want—'

'Don't you dare lie to me!' Antonio launched at her wrathfully.

Sophie was shattered that Antonio had raised his voice. She paled, mortification eating her alive. Just by looking at her he had realised she wanted him. How much else did he know? That she loved him?

'Antonio...'

'But even if you won't talk, you can at least listen,' Antonio delivered, lean, strong face grim and, with that assurance, he bent down and scooped her up into his arms.

'When you're in the middle of having an argument with someone, you don't just lift the person up in the middle of it and carry them away!' Sophie hissed enraged.

Antonio settled enquiring eyes on her furiously flushed face. 'Why not?'

'Because it's disrespectful...that's why!' Sophie declared.

Antonio shouldered open the bedroom door and, pausing only to kick it resoundingly shut behind him, he strode over to the bed and settled her firmly down on the edge of it.

'You want to talk? OK...I'll say it all for you,' Sophie told him jerkily.

'Why didn't I think of that? I really should take you into the office with me—'

'Look, I can't joke about this!' All of a sudden Sophie was finding it impossible to maintain her act of insouciance. 'But you know we only got married because you believed Lydia was your niece.'

'No, I don't know that,' Antonio responded infuriatingly.

Sophie fixed strained eyes on him, her heart-shaped face tight with tension and very pale. 'This is not the time to be smart. You thought you had to be a father to Lydia and you felt sorry for me because Norah had mentioned that I couldn't h-have k-kids...'

Antonio unfroze from his intimidating stance over her and hunkered down at the side of the bed so that their eyes were on a level. 'That's not important, *mi amada*.'

'Of course it's important...how can you say it's not?' Sophie gasped, the tears clogging her vocal cords making every word a challenge, her restive hands twisting together.

'It's sad,' Antonio murmured gruffly, and he unlinked her tense fingers with gentle pressure and held them in his. 'But you survived leukaemia and there was a price to pay. I am very grateful that you are alive and healthy today.'

'Why?' Sophie whispered shakily, in the dark as to where the dialogue was travelling.

Shimmering dark golden eyes captured her bemused gaze. 'I can do without having children but I don't think I could live without you.'

For a heartbeat Sophie was as still as a statue, for she could not accept that he could feel that way. She dragged in a shivering breath. 'You can't mean that...you can't. You're just feeling sorry for me—'

'I don't feel sorry for you. I was sad that you were infertile, but it's not that uncommon these days and there are various remedies like adoption. It's not the end of the world. I can see that it is still a great source of regret to you, but I have come to terms with it,' Antonio imparted intently.

'But how can you?' Sophie mumbled, scarcely knowing what he was telling her.

'People have adapted to far worse news. If our positions were reversed, if I was infertile, would you turn away from me?'

'No!' Sophie exclaimed instantly and then, colouring, added hastily, 'But that's different.'

'How is it different?'

'I don't have a title to pass on.'

'Titles such as mine are not of much use in today's world,' Antonio informed her levelly.

Sophie swallowed convulsively. 'There is a small chance that I might be able to conceive. The doctors don't really know how much damage was caused by the treatment I had when I was ill…but I wouldn't want you to get your hopes up.'

'I wouldn't. In fact I would suggest we don't even think of that slight possibility. Each of us has only one life and should make the most of it. I have found a happiness with you greater than anything I have ever known and I refuse to give that up,' Antonio swore, his keen gaze alight with fierce sincerity.

The silence lasted a long time while she tried to find fault with that far-reaching statement, for she was almost afraid to credit that he might mean it and afraid to believe that happiness might be within her reach after all.

'You refuse…you mean…are you saying you want to stay married to me even though I can't have kids?' Sophie almost whispered.

'*Sí, enamorada,*' Antonio confirmed.

Her green eyes were huge. 'I really make you that happy?'

'You do…'

'So you don't think a divorce would be a good idea?' she pressed unevenly.

'Not a question of it,' Antonio told her boldly and, springing fluidly upright, he drew her up with him. 'I couldn't let you go…ever. It's amazing. I never knew I could feel like this. I am head over heels in love with you.'

Her eyes shone and her whole face lit up. 'Seriously?'

Antonio tugged her to him with possessive hands. 'Very seriously. Lydia gave me the excuse to be with you and I grabbed it. My ability to make rational decisions went haywire the minute I saw you again. I even enjoyed fighting with you. Isn't that crazy? Nothing went according to plan—'

'Our wedding day was awful—'

'I wanted you to wear a long white dress,' Antonio confessed with an apologetic grimace. 'When you wore that flowery outfit, I thought you were making a joke of the occasion.'

'Oh, no, I wish I'd known that. I thought you'd be furious if I went for the full bridal show!' Sophie lamented.

'It's not your fault. I didn't know what I wanted until it was too late.' The regret in Antonio's steady dark golden eyes touched her heart. 'I didn't do any of the stuff I should've done to make the day special for you.'

'But you're brilliant at wedding nights,' Sophie hastened to tell him. 'That was special.'

'I didn't even realise how I felt about you. When you made that crack about picking me as a stud, I was…I couldn't see the joke. I was angry, offended...hurt,' he finally admitted grittily.

Sophie wrapped her arms tightly round him in apology. 'I was too busy worrying about how I could save face to see how you were feeling. When I don't feel sure of myself, I tend to go on the offensive.'

'I stayed away from you and I was incredibly miserable. I didn't recognise what was wrong with me until I came back and saw you again,' Antonio admitted, his fingers tilting up her chin so that he could scan her upturned face with appreciative eyes. 'I realised that I had a lot of work to do to try to turn our relationship round and make you happy.'

'You really succeeded at that...' Her throat tightened on the words for powerful emotions were coursing through her. 'You know, I have feelings for you too but I've been doing everything I could to hide the fact.'

'Like threatening to take Lydia and leave me?' Antonio gritted, but he was stroking gentle fingers across her cheekbone in a caress. 'Don't ever do that again. I messed up when it came to dealing with the DNA tests, but over the last twenty-four hours you almost ripped my heart out. I was so scared I was going to lose you and all over something that doesn't matter a damn.'

'You were shocked when you found out that Lydia wasn't your niece— I'm not blaming you for thinking the worst of me as well. You didn't think that way for long,' she pointed out forgivingly. 'But how can you say that Lydia's parentage doesn't matter?'

'Being Pablo's daughter would always have been something of a poisoned chalice for her. People have long memories and my brother had a bad name,'

Antonio remarked ruefully. 'At least Lydia won't suffer that stigma.'

Sophie was grateful that he was all for an open and honest approach to Lydia's background. 'You'll have to tell Doña Ernesta. Will she be very upset?'

'My grandmother will be disappointed, but she'll cope. I think we should adopt Lydia.'

'Oh, could we? I'd love to do that.'

'I don't think Belinda planned to lie about Lydia,' Antonio said then. 'After my brother's death, I tried several times to persuade her to let me visit and she always put me off. She must've been pregnant then and at that point she evidently wasn't thinking of passing off her baby as Pablo's.'

'That must've come later, probably because she wanted to forget that she'd gone a little wild.'

'Lydia's beautiful. Let's be glad she's ours,' Antonio suggested.

Her smile was as bright as the sun. 'That's how I always feel about her.'

'Would you now like to tell me about those feelings that you said you were determined to hide from me?' Antonio prompted tautly.

Sophie went pink when she realised that she still hadn't told him she loved him. 'I love you…lots and lots and lots.'

Golden eyes ablaze with satisfaction, Antonio snatched her off her feet and kissed her with all the fire of his passionate temperament. One kiss led to another and matters became pretty heated very quickly. A long time afterwards, while they lay secure in each other's arms, Antonio tried to get her to promise that she would rerun the 'fancy lingerie and supper on the floor' seduction routine for his benefit again. She said she'd have to think about that very carefully, while secretly planning to indulge him on his birthday.

Just over a year later, when Lydia's adoption was finalised, Sophie and Antonio threw a massive party at the *castillo* to celebrate the occasion.

Sophie felt a little out of sorts that evening and over the next month she suffered several other minor but irritating symptoms. When she consulted Dr Teruel, she discovered that she was three months pregnant. Her joy and Antonio's knew no bounds. They shared every tiny milestone of the pregnancy with intense interest and gratitude.

Their daughter, Carisa, was born without complications. Lydia was so excited about having a little sister that she brought all her toys to Carisa and was disappointed to learn that it would be some time before the baby could play with her. Doña Ernesta comforted Lydia with the suggestion that she would be able to teach Carisa all her favourite games and tell her stories.

Sophie's grasp of Spanish was by then fluent and she began attending a part-time course on textile conservation. Lydia was almost five years old when Sophie conceived for a second time. Sophie gave birth a month early to two little boys, who quickly gained weight and made up for their premature arrival in the world. They called the twins Francisco and Jacobo. Their christening was celebrated at the Rocha home in Madrid. A very flattering set of photos and a brief interview would later appear in an up-market magazine in return for a sizeable charitable donation. Antonio had come to accept that his wife was something of a celebrity and her public liked to see her in print.

'I have a surprise, *enamorada*,' Antonio confided the

night of the christening when all the children were finally tucked up and asleep and even the most long-staying guest had gone home. He made her close her eyes as he slid a ring on her finger, but it stuck on her knuckle and she had to push a little and peep.

'Oh, my goodness!' she gasped then, impressed to death by the starry sparkle of the huge diamond. 'What's this for?'

'It's your engagement ring...just a few years late,' Antonio teased tenderly. 'Would you still say yes if I asked you to marry me?'

Sophie gave him a huge smile, happiness bubbling through her. 'Yes, I'm still crazy about you.'

Antonio closed her into his arms and met her warm green eyes. 'I will never stop loving you,' he promised her and she believed him, all her former insecurity long since cured by his love and care.

Mistress Bought and Paid For

LYNNE GRAHAM

CHAPTER ONE

CRISTIANO ANDREOTTI, the software billionaire, stood on the topmost deck of the megayacht *Lestara*. Built to his exacting specifications, and already regarded as the most beautiful craft ever built, *Lestara* was a floating palace, complete with twin helipads, a cinema, a freshwater swimming pool and a sleek landing craft tucked in her stern. Yet Cristiano was infuriatingly conscious of the faintest tinge of disappointment with his latest acquisition.

His guests, however, were talking about the yacht in hushed tones of reverence.

'Unbelievable…'

'The most staggering level of luxury I've ever seen…'

'You have a private hospital and you're *never* ill…*wow*, is all I can say…'

'The gym and the basketball court are to die for…'

'The glass viewing area in the hull blew me away…'

'Sixty crew members to sail her and wait on you…you must feel like a king…'

His lean, darkly handsome profile detached, his brilliant dark eyes bleak, Cristiano continued to look out to sea. A king? Not so as he had noticed. He wondered if he had brought company on board to say for him what he no longer said or felt himself. Increasingly, only aggressive takeovers or extreme sports gave Cristiano a genuine buzz. Born into fabulous wealth, he had discovered that few experiences, or indeed possessions, lived up to their initial promise.

'Have you heard the gossip?' the socialite Jodie Morgan was asking in her piercing English upper-class voice when he emerged from his reverie. 'About Lia Powell?' she continued.

As Cristiano tensed at the unexpected sound of that name, female giggles broke out.

'There are rumours all around London. How do you think she'll take to life in prison?'

'Who are you talking about?' his friend, Philip Hazlett, enquired.

'The Powell girl…that model who took off with Mort Stevens. Her career dive-bombed when he was done for drugs and she disappeared off the map,' Jodie reminded her fiancé cheerfully. 'A couple of months ago she tried to make a comeback by doing good works—'

'Yes. I believe she organised a fashion show for some children's charity called Happy Holidays and made a mess of it,' Philip interposed in a suggestive tone of finality.

Impervious to the hint that the subject matter might not be welcome, Jodie continued to tell the story. 'Lia persuaded her fellow models to donate their services free to the show, and the goss is she robbed the poor little kiddies blind by pocketing the proceeds!'

A spark of raw splintering gold flared in Cristiano's brooding, dark gaze. He was grimly amused by Philip's attempt to silence Jodie. Evidently the socialite was not aware that Lia Powell and Cristiano had briefly been an item. For a nanosecond time leapt back eighteen months, to Cristiano's first glimpse of Lia Powell during a Paris show. Slender and sinuous as a willow wand, she had stalked down the catwalk like a warrior princess, her pale blonde hair rippling back from her hauntingly lovely face like silvery streamers of moonlight. Huge eyes the mesmeric blue of lapis lazuli had blanked him when he was introduced. Her smile had been a masterpiece of indifference. Accustomed to instant awe and fawning attention, Cristiano had been intrigued, his lust heightened by that rare sense of being challenged. He had been eager to see just how well she played a game he had assumed was naïvely aimed at increasing his interest.

But, unusually, Cristiano had underestimated the brazen avarice and ambition of his scheming target. Although he had been unaware of it, he had not been the only wealthy male in Lia's sights, and she had been chasing a better offer than a casual affair. After a handful of dates he had invited her to his country house for the weekend. There Lia had come over all virginal and refused to share his suite. At dawn the following day, however, she had eloped with one of his guests: a dissolute rock star more than twice her age, famous for his very expensive habit of marrying his youthful arm-candy. As he chirpily introduced Lia to the press as his new fiancée, Mort Stevens must have seemed the more rewarding prospect in financial terms. Unhappily for Lia, though, cruel fate had intervened to ensure that all her plotting and planning had come to nothing in the end.

With an almost imperceptible signal, Cristiano inclined his imperious dark head and his watchful PA hurried over to receive his instructions. While his guests were served with lunch on the entertainment deck Cristiano was in his office, being briefed with the facts he needed. A discreet phone call to a national newspaper editor revealed, in the time-honoured phrase beloved of the tabloids, that Lia was 'helping the police with their enquiries'. But soon everyone would know the *real* story. Who could have sympathy for a woman accused of defrauding underprivileged children?

A slow, hard-edged smile of satisfaction slashed Cristiano's bold, masculine mouth. He was conscious of an energy surge of pure badness. All boredom had fled. It was said that revenge was a dish best eaten cold, but Cristiano was more into hot and spicy flavours. While she'd played for time eighteen months ago, Lia Powell had faked prudish innocence to stay out of his bed. She had then, with breathtaking impudence, cheated on him beneath his own roof. She was the only woman who had *ever* said no to Cristiano and walked out on him. He knew that the secret of her lingering attraction in his mind could only be that basic.

When it came to sex, Cristiano knew himself inside out. He was much more clued up than his late father, whose life had been destroyed by his hopeless addiction to a woman with as much heart as a carcass on a butcher's block. He had even fewer illusions about Lia Powell. She was a worthless little scrubber with no morals. But she was still a bloody gorgeous one, he mused with ruthless cool, and for the price of her freedom she could be his. He had no doubt of that fact. Any charity would prefer recompense and a handsome donation over an indiscreet and costly court case. He could buy Lia Powell's pardon. He could buy *her*. He had never paid for sex before. Did he want her on such tacky terms? He discovered that the very thought of having leggy Lia tangled within his sheets and eager to please excited him more than anything had in a very long time. She would be on call whenever he so desired, to provide easy and uncomplicated sexual release.

He was willing to acknowledge that where women were concerned he had a low boredom threshold. In fact he was notorious for the brevity of his relationships. But this would be something different—something new and fresh. A contractual agreement would be the best blueprint for such an arrangement. His lawyers would relish that novel challenge almost as much as he would revel in having Lia act out his every tacky fantasy...

The young bespectacled solicitor gave Lydia a troubled look. 'I can't help you if you won't help yourself.'

Lydia dropped her head, weariness engulfing her. 'I know...'

'You must protect yourself,' he warned her equally wearily.

'Not if that means my mother taking the blame,' Lydia countered in a tight, driven voice. 'This is nothing to do with her and I won't have her involved.'

'But as co-signatory on the cheques she *is* involved,' the solicitor pointed out flatly. 'Naturally the police want to speak to her as well.'

Lydia said nothing. During the preceding long and nerve-racking interview with two officers she had been asked repeatedly where her mother, Virginia Carlton, was. Nobody had believed her when she'd said she didn't know, and she had tried not to care. After all, even if she had known she would have protected the older woman by keeping her whereabouts a secret. She was determined not to let her mother pay the price for her daughter's mistakes.

Now, one of the fraud officers reappeared. He told her that, although she was to be released on bail while more enquiries were made, she would have to return to the station in four days' time for further questioning. Even as

her heart sank at that assurance, Lydia was informed that
she would have to leave the interview room and wait in a
cell for the necessary paperwork to be prepared. Her
tummy flipped in dismay. Her solicitor protested, but to no
avail.

The cell door was mercifully closed on her before a
violent fit of shaking overtook her tall, slender frame.
Sinking down on the hard sleeping platform, Lydia
wrapped trembling arms round herself in an effort to get a
grip. There was no point in giving way to the fear and the
panic pulling at her. Matters were only going to get worse,
she reminded herself heavily. The wheels of justice were
grinding into motion to prosecute and punish her, and if she
was found guilty she would serve a prison sentence. Eventually the sight of a cell would be very familiar to her. The
money from the Happy Holidays account was gone, and she
could neither repay it nor borrow it. The conviction that she
could only blame herself for that state of affairs hit her
hard.

Her thin shoulders slumped, guilt racking her. It was a
familiar feeling. Things always went horribly wrong, and
it seemed that it was her fault…

When Lydia had been ten years old she had survived a
boating accident in which her father and her kid brother
had drowned. Her mother, Virginia, had been distraught.
'This is your fault!' she had screamed furiously at her
daughter. 'Who was it who begged and begged to go on
that stupid boat trip? You killed them. You killed the two
of them!'

And, even though other people had hushed the hysterical older woman, Lydia had known that her grieving
parent was only speaking the unpalatable truth. Then,
when her father's business had gone bankrupt, and their

comfortable standard of living had vanished overnight, Lydia had known that she was to blame for that as well. It had been a huge relief when she'd discovered just a few years later that she had the earning power to give that luxury lifestyle back to her mother. Between the ages of fourteen and twenty-one Lydia had made a small fortune as a model.

But then, Lydia acknowledged wretchedly, she had become selfish—stupidly, wickedly selfish. And short-sighted. She'd hated modelling, and a bad experience and a broken heart had persuaded her to leave the fashion world behind and train as a garden designer. Everything that since had gone wrong could be traced back to that single foolish and fanciful decision...

Still in fear of the press cameras that had greeted her arrival at the police station, Lydia walked stiffly out to the reception area. Thankfully the only person to show the slightest interest in her appearance was the small curva-ceous brunette seated there. Her cousin Gwenna stood up, frowning when she saw the exhaustion etched on Lydia's face. Yet the younger woman still looked so incredibly beautiful that even Gwenna found it hard not to stare. The pure lines of Lydia's delicate bone structure, allied to her dazzling blue eyes and the mane of naturally pale blonde hair, took most people's breath away.

'Gwenna?' Lydia was dismayed that the other woman had subjected herself to the embarrassment of coming to the police station on her behalf. 'You shouldn't have come—'

'Don't be silly,' Gwenna scolded her in Welsh as she marched her much taller cousin out into the night and on to the car park, with her head held high and her chin at a determined angle, defying the camera flashes. 'You're family—and where else should I be? I'm here to take you home—'

Lydia was too touched by Gwenna's appearance to be able to find the right words in Welsh, a language that she had only recently rediscovered. She swallowed hard on the thickness in her throat and climbed into Gwenna's ancient hatchback. As a young child she had often stayed in Gwenna's Welsh-speaking home while her own parents were abroad. Eighteen months back, when Lydia's life had been in awful turmoil, Gwenna had phoned to invite her to use the family farm as a bolthole. The generous warmth of that offer had meant a great deal to Lydia at a time when her friends had abandoned her.

'I really appreciate you doing this, but I think you should forget that you know me for a while—'

'I'll just pretend I didn't hear that,' Gwenna interposed, in probably much the same no-nonsense tone that she employed with the teenagers she taught. In her early thirties, she had short dark hair that shone as though it had been polished.

When Lydia unlocked the door of the tiny terraced house where she now lived, Gwenna headed straight for the kitchen. 'I'll make a cup of tea while you nip upstairs and pack a bag.'

Lydia stiffened. 'No, I'm not coming home with you. This is a small community and you have to live and work here. You mustn't get caught up in my problems.'

Gwenna turned. 'Lydia—'

'No…' Fierce conviction made Lydia's soft voice unusually firm. 'I mean it. Think of your father. He's barely over the loss of your mother. Let's not upset him with this as well.'

The brunette's look of disconcertion told Lydia that she had stumbled on the one argument that would work— for Gwenna was protective of her elderly parent.

'But thanks for caring,' Lydia tacked on gently.

Sudden anger brightened Gwenna's troubled gaze. 'But it's not a matter of caring. You didn't take that money and we all know who did!'

Her colour fluctuating at that assertion, Lydia breathed, 'Maybe you *think* you know—'

'Come off it! You're so straight you can't tell a lie without crossing your fingers!' her cousin told her impatiently. 'Do you expect me to keep quiet while you take the rap for a woman who couldn't care less about you?'

Losing colour at that blunt statement, Lydia switched on the kettle. Gwenna had never been able to understand the nature of Lydia's relationship with her mother. The brunette's family had been blessed with a quiet and secure lifestyle, while Virginia had survived tragedy and a succession of thoroughly unreliable men that would have broken a lesser woman. 'My mother has had a very tough life—'

'Look, she was telling you that when you were five years old, making you fetch and carry like a little slave while she moaned about the horrors of motherhood. And let's not overlook the fact that between them your mother and your stepfather have managed to spend every penny you ever earned!'

There was reproach in Lydia's troubled gaze. 'You can't blame them because the nightclub failed and I lost everything last year. I was naïve about the amount of money I'd made as a model. I thought it would last a lifetime—'

'It would have done if you had only been keeping yourself, and not Virginia and Dennis with their huge house and flash cars. I can't believe that you had the slightest personal interest in opening a nightclub either.' Her companion sighed.

Lydia said nothing. When she had stopped modelling she had effectively dispossessed her stepfather of his job managing her career and her money. Agreeing to provide the capital for a nightclub had seemed the least she could do. Sadly, the enterprise had crashed. But Lydia had come to terms with the loss of her financial security. Although she was only twenty-two years old, she was well used to picking herself up after a disappointment.

Busily engaged in making tea, Gwenna was wishing that she could get her hands on Lydia's greedy mother and thieving stepfather. Given the chance she would soon tell them what she thought of them! The couple had turned Lydia into the family cash cow, and had enjoyed the high life on the lucrative proceeds of her modelling career. Although Virginia had never worked herself, she had always been able to spend like there was no tomorrow.

'You have to deal with this,' Gwenna told her cousin impatiently. 'Virginia stole the money you raised from the fashion show and spent it—'

Lydia shook her head in tired disagreement. 'Dennis had left her with a pile of debts. She knew I couldn't help and she panicked.'

'Stop making excuses for her. She forged your signature on the cheques that emptied the Happy Holidays account. She did everything she could to make you look like the guilty party, and now she's done a runner! Don't let her do this to you,' Gwenna pleaded in frustration. 'A criminal conviction will wreck your life. How many people will employ an ex-con?'

When Gwenna had gone home, Lydia retrieved the letter that she'd seen lying on her doormat and read it with a growing hollow feeling inside. It was a brief note from a couple who had accepted her quote to design their garden. They would have been her first proper clients since she had completed her college course. But they had dropped this letter through her letterbox earlier today to say that they had changed their minds. She suspected that what had changed their minds had been news of her visit to the local police station. No doubt her face would be all over the tabloids tomorrow morning.

Later, in bed, she tossed and turned. The evening before she'd had to go out to buy food. An odd little pool of silence had seemed to enclose her as she'd packed her groceries at the supermarket. When she'd looked up, a couple of women had been treating her to a contemptuous appraisal. Evidently rumours of the stolen money had already spread to the highly efficient local grapevine. It had been a disturbing experience.

On the edge of an uneasy doze, Lydia was yanked rudely back to full wakefulness by the sound of a crash and glass breaking. Switching on the bedside light, she got out of bed. Had someone smashed a bottle outside on the street? She went downstairs and found the window in her small cosy sitting room broken. She hovered in the doorway, wondering how such a thing could have happened, and then she saw something lying on the floor in the middle of the shattered glass. It was a stone with a piece of paper wrapped round it. Frowning she spread it out to read.

YOU THIEVING BITCH GO BACK TO WHERE
YOU BELONG!

The brutal capitals were written in red felt-tip. Her heart started to hammer like crazy and she felt physically sick. She made herself fetch a brush and dustpan to clean up the glass. She propped an old cupboard door from the coal shed over the gaping hole and slowly climbed back up the stairs. But if sleep had been elusive before, it was now impossible, and she lay still and quiet and barely breathing, flinching at every sound she heard.

Having finally fallen asleep around seven the next morning, she was still in bed when the doorbell went at ten. She assumed that it was the postman and, knowing that he would not wait long, rose in haste, pulling on her cotton wrap and racing downstairs to answer the door.

As her stunned gaze took in the very tall black-haired male outside on the street, she was gripped by total disbelief and pinned to the spot in complete stillness. Cristiano Andreotti. Even though she thought he could only be a figment of her imagination, the compelling effect of his exotic dark charisma and hard-edged masculinity still knocked her for six. Her heart started pounding and her soft pink mouth opened on a soundless *ooh*.

His magnificent bone structure was accentuated by the smooth olive planes of his high cheekbones. Although he shaved twice daily, faint blue-black shading still emphasised his strong jaw and beautifully modelled mouth. But her mind refused to move on from recognition to acceptance. Because Cristiano Andreotti did not belong on the doorstep of a terraced house in the back street of a nondescript Welsh market town. His natural milieu was much more exclusive, and always redolent of the privilege of the very rich.

Cristiano studied her with unflinching intensity. He had never seen her without make-up before. He saw the changes in her, picked up on every flaw with the eagerness of a man who had dimly expected and possibly even hoped to be disappointed in her. She had lost weight. She was pale, and her tiredness was patent. Her mane of fair hair fell in a tangle round her slight shoulders, no longer glossy and styled into smooth layers of silk by a professional hand. In the midst of cataloguing those differences with the precision of a male to whom no detail was too small, he met eyes as blue as sapphires. Just as suddenly he realised that she was, if anything, more breathtakingly beautiful than ever. Only this time around she was as nature had made her, with glorious eyes, skin like clotted cream and full, pouting mouth. Desire ripped through his big powerful frame with the dangerous force of a storm tide.

'May I come in?' he enquired lazily, his rich, resonant drawl wrapping round her rigid spinal cord like a silk caress. The habit of command and high expectation was so engrained in every syllable that it did not even occur to her to deny him.

CHAPTER TWO

ONLY when Cristiano broke the pounding silence could Lydia credit the reality of his appearance. Snatching in a startled breath, she blinked, her long brown lashes fluttering as she struggled to get a hold on the bone-deep shock gripping her. Even in that very first moment she knew that the flame of her hatred for him burned as bright as ever. Perspiration beaded her short upper lip and her legs felt wobbly. She stared fixedly at him, controlled by a heady mixture of fear and fascination, curiosity and loathing.

Predictably, Cristiano took advantage of her astonishment to move forward, and she automatically retreated. Although she was five foot eleven in her bare feet, he still towered over her by a comfortable six inches. A snaking little frisson of awareness curled somewhere low in her belly, and she went rigid at the novelty of that almost forgotten sensation. All senses on hyper-alert, she could feel the tender tips of her breasts tingle and pinch.

Hot colour flared through her pallor as shame and confusion filled her, and suddenly she found her voice. 'What do you want?'

Cristiano closed the front door with a casual, lean

brown hand. He was feeling his power and enjoying it. 'Don't you know?'

Painfully embarrassed by the way her treacherous body had reacted to him, Lydia tilted her chin in a defiant manner that would have surprised any one of her relatives. She felt trapped and angry and raw. Deep down inside her lurked the wounding recollection of just how much she had once cared for Cristiano Andreotti and how savagely he had hurt her. It didn't show on the surface, but he had changed her—and not for the better. 'How could I know why you're here?'

'I thought some sixth sense survival instinct might kick in…' Cristiano surveyed her with liquid dark eyes full of mockery. 'Might spell out a simple message.'

'Obviously not.' She folded her arms in a defensive gesture and tried to still the trembling aftershock that was threatening to take her over.

'I'm here because I want to see you…*obviously*,' Cristiano traded, his sexy accent wrapping round the syllables in the most extraordinarily melodic way.

Without having realised what she was doing, Lydia found she was staring up at him, at those brilliant, beautiful dark eyes that had haunted her dreams. Eyes that betrayed only the most superficial emotion and her own reflection. He gave nothing away. He was famous for a detachment that veered on indifference, even icy coldness. She had felt ten feet tall when she'd made him laugh or smile.

Fighting that tide of memory, she shook her head as though to clear it. She strove feverishly to blank him out, remembering fearfully how it had been for her for a crazy couple of months when he had been all she could think about, when his mere presence had been enough to ensure that she was blind to everybody and everything but him.

'I don't want you here…' Even as she spoke, she knew that the remedy of asking him to leave was in her hands, but that for reasons she was afraid to examine she could not yet bring herself to actually tell him to go.

Cristiano angled his sleek dark head to one side and studied her with maddening cool. 'Don't you?'

Her tummy seemed to somersault, as if he had punched a panic button. For a crazy moment she worried that he knew her better than she knew herself, and she rushed to fill the silence. 'How did you find me?'

'I obtained some privileged information…'

She turned pale as milk. So he knew about the missing money. *Of course he knew*, an inner voice censured. She wanted to cringe, and a pronounced reluctance to look him in the face afflicted her.

Cristiano Andreotti took advantage of that moment of weakness and stepped past her. He knew her fortunes had been in a steady decline since their last meeting, but it was only now when he saw the shabby, sparsely furnished sitting room, that he appreciated how steep that descent had been. Nothing could more adequately illustrate the vast gulf between their lives, and the reality that she had only ever been a visitor in his world.

'What happened to the window?'

'It got broken,' she mumbled.

'Have you called a glazier?'

'Not yet. It only happened late last night.'

His incisive gaze alighted on the crudely lettered and crumpled note on the mantelpiece and he reached for it. The stone was sitting on the hearth, and he guessed what had happened. A frown drew his sleek dark brows together for a split second. 'You've been threatened? Have you reported this?'

In an abrupt movement she snatched the abusive note from his shapely brown fingers. 'Why don't you mind your own business?' she gasped, more mortified than ever.

'The police should be told. The brute mentality behind that sort of intimidation is liable to get more physical. You cannot stay here alone—'

'And where do you suggest I move to?' she broke in tautly, deeper anxiety assailing her—for if anything the incident last night had made her even more reluctant to take advantage of her cousin's offer of shelter. Gwenna, and her father and brother, lived in an isolated farmhouse, and she would not risk bringing trouble to their door.

'I may be able to provide a solution,' Cristiano murmured without the slightest change in his level of intonation.

Lydia realised that she was trembling. Looking away from him, she struggled for mastery over conflicting promptings of fear, bewilderment and discomfiture. In doing so, she registered for the first time since his arrival that she was standing in front of him wearing an old dressing gown and with messy hair. She almost died of chagrin.

'Look, I need to get dressed…I'm not going to hang around arguing with you.' *What solution?* she wanted to ask, but she wouldn't let herself. She hadn't even told him to get out. Didn't she have any pride? How much lower could she sink?

Watching her climb the stairs, Cristiano caught a flash of a pale, slender silk-smooth thigh, and an instant shaft of heat travelled to his groin. He ground his even white teeth together. The sexual buzz in the atmosphere was sending his male hormones on a primal rampage. That ferocious attraction had been there from the first time he saw

her. But he was convinced that once he slept with her, he
would no longer want her. She was scared. If he offered
her the money without further ado she would probably let
him have her here and now. So what if it was sleazy? So
what if he had never paid for the privilege of bedding a
woman before? *Dio mio,* she wanted him too. Her eyes and
her edginess around him were unmistakably revealing to
a male of his experience. Yet she still seemed to be in
denial of that truth—always backing off, primly avoiding
visual contact. A guy with some class would wait and
prolong the finale, he told himself grimly.

A gardening book lay open on the small dining table
and he studied it with a questioning frown. Restive as a
hungry panther on the prowl, he paced. It was a challenge,
for the room was tiny, the hall non-existent and the kitchen
not much larger. There, however, he came to a sudden
halt, a black brow rising in astonishment. In defiance of
the grim urban outlook, the small back yard had been
transformed into a glorious green patio jungle of contain-
erised flowers and foliage.

Employing his mobile phone, he told one of his staff to
organise a glazier to replace the broken window. He said
the job had to be done immediately.

Upstairs, Lydia darted into the bathroom and ran a
brush violently through her tousled hair, while at the same
time trying to clumsily clean her teeth. She was all fingers
and thumbs as she shed her nightwear and yanked a pair
of jeans and a vest top from a drawer. How could she be
calm and controlled? Downstairs was the guy who had
won her trust and made her love him. Downstairs was the
smooth, slick operator who knew how to fake romance and
act as if he was serious. But it had all been a con. She had
been the victim of his cruel, demeaning charade! A dupe,

a joke for macho males who got in touch with their crude masculine selves by comparing the number of notches on their bedposts. She zipped up her jeans with a trembling hand. Unfortunately, she had been so hurt and angered by that betrayal she had made herself a victim all over again. She had fallen for the stupid suggestion that she might take revenge and at least emerge with her pride intact. The consequences of that final foolish impulse had pretty much destroyed her modelling career.

So what was Cristiano Andreotti doing in Wales? Why had he come to see her? A solution? She couldn't see why he would wish to help her in any way. When she'd left his Georgian mansion with Mort she had struck a blow at Cristiano's ego. There had been nothing else to take aim at, she acknowledged painfully. Cristiano Andreotti did not have a heart or a conscience. Had he come to gloat over more of her unending misfortunes?

Slowly, Lydia descended the stairs. 'What do you want with me?' she asked defensively.

'What do most guys want?' Cristiano traded, smooth as glass, while he scanned the silvery pale waves tumbling round her oval face, her luminous blue eyes and her sultry lips, which were slightly parted to show the moist inner pink. He wasn't really listening; he was rejoicing in her visual allure.

Hot colour flooded her cheeks. The direction of his gaze was not lost on her, and she shot him a look of loathing. 'At least you're not pretending to be a nice guy any more!'

Dark eyes flaring to gold, Cristiano inclined his arrogant dark head in acknowledgement. 'You'd take advantage of a nice guy. I'm much more your style.'

'In your dreams!' Lydia slung back at him.

'How often does Mort Stevens figure in yours now?' Cristiano riposted without skipping a beat.

That merciless retort made her blench, and she semi-turned away, presenting him with a view of her delicate profile. 'You still haven't told me what you're doing here.'

Sideways on, her slender build made her look disturbingly fragile. Without hesitation he reached out and closed his hands over hers.

In surprise, she gasped, 'What the heck—?'

'Just checking...' Having scanned her arms for any suspicious marks that might have indicated drug abuse, and satisfied himself that that was not her problem, Cristiano released her again.

'I do *not* do drugs...I never have and I never will!' she protested furiously.

'Glad to hear it.' But she needed to eat more, Cristiano reflected as his attention skimmed from her narrow white shoulders to the pert outline of her small breasts. She wasn't wearing a bra. He tensed, infuriated by his own thoughts and behaviour. What was he? A schoolboy again? Since when had the female form entertained the slightest mystery for him?

'Did you only come here to insult me?'

'No, there is always purpose in what I do. You're facing a prison sentence.'

Taken aback by that unequivocal assurance, Lydia snatched in a sharp breath. 'You don't know that...how could you? You know nothing about it—'

'Crimes that entail cash and deception and female offenders always attract a more severe punishment,' Cristiano murmured silkily. 'Defrauding a charity was not a good idea—particularly one engaged in raising funds for disadvantaged children.'

Her skin felt cold and clammy. 'I don't want to talk about it.'

'Were you in debt? Were you being pursued for payment? You stole a very large amount of money, but I don't see much evidence of ill-gotten gains.'

That Cristiano had no doubt of her culpability cut across Lydia's tender skin like a whiplash. A painful tide of colour lit her face. On the strength of rumour, he had decided that she was guilty as charged.

'Why should you care either way?' she queried, throwing back her pale head, her chin at a truculent angle.

Cristiano surveyed her with eyes as cool and hard as tempered steel. 'I don't. But I *can* keep you out of prison…'

She stiffened, eyes widening, while a crazy little leap of hope surfaced somewhere inside her. 'And how could you possibly do that?'

'By repaying the money you took with the addition of a handsome donation to oil the wheels of charitable forgiveness,' Cristiano explained softly.

'It wouldn't be that simple—'

'Don't be foolish. I never talk about what I can't do.' His wide, sensual mouth curled. 'A discreet approach has already been made to the director of the Happy Holidays fund, and the response to that particular suggestion has been a very positive one.'

Her restive fingers clenched in on themselves with fierce tension. 'But why would you offer to replace the missing cash?'

'Obviously because I want something in return,' Cristiano delivered, soft and low, his dark drawl as erotic as velvet trailing over silk.

Her heart jumped behind her breastbone. She met bold, dark golden eyes shaded by luxuriant black lashes. Breathing normally became a distinct challenge. His lean dark features were wholly intent on her. Something that felt like a tiny hot wire was pulling taut in her pelvis. It was a sensation that fell somewhere between pleasure and pain, and the surge of heat that followed made her tremble.

His sizzling, sexy smile slashed his beautiful mouth. 'And I do believe you will enjoy giving it to me, *cara mia*.'

Lydia was finding it impossible to concentrate. 'I'm afraid I don't understand—'

'Don't you? I'm offering a pretty basic deal. I want you in my bed—'

Shock roared through her, leaving her light-headed. 'I don't believe you—'

'Of course you would have to throw yourself heart and soul into the role of being my mistress—'

'This doesn't make sense—'

His brilliant eyes were ice-cold. 'It makes perfect sense. Watching you endeavour to meet my every wish and need will provide me with considerable entertainment. I'm not an easy guy to please.'

Lydia had turned bone-white. 'You can't despise me and want me like that at the same time.'

'Why not?'

'Because it's immoral!' she gasped.

'When did I say I was moral?'

'I can't believe your nerve. I can't believe you can approach me with such a proposition!' Lydia lanced back at him, burning with furious mortification. 'Maybe you don't have any standards, but I do—'

'I don't steal,' Cristiano proclaimed, in a super-soft undertone.

'Maybe I don't either. But you're only interested in

trying to take advantage of the fact that I'm in trouble, and I think that is disgusting!'

'I've made a fortune from opportunism, *cara mia*.'

'Well, you lucked out when you met me—because I'd sooner go to prison than sink to the level of being your mistress!'

Shimmering dark golden eyes connected with hers. 'I don't think so.'

The force field of energy he projected was all around her, like an invisible web of silent intimidation. Unable to break the hold of his compelling scrutiny, she felt his anger, and it somehow soothed the ache deep down inside her.

'I *know* so.'

As she stepped past him, he curved a light hand to her spine and stilled her. He bent his handsome dark head and the cool, irresistible power of his sensual mouth claimed hers. It was everything she had secretly feared, everything she had ever craved. With the utmost gentleness he let his tongue steal between her parted lips and explore the moist interior. He delved deeper. She moaned low in her throat, heard her own plaintive cry of surrender and acceptance, and wanted to die of shame. But still she couldn't break free of the fierce physical excitement that controlled her. That inner conflict made her quiver, as though she was in the eye of a storm.

Cristiano stepped back. He had not held her. He had not given her that much excuse to succumb. 'Answer the phone…'

Only when she was separated from him did the world crowd back in on her again, and she heard the phone's insistent shrill. She surged in a feverish rush to answer it. Fighting to rescue her smashed composure, but nowhere near strong enough to meet Cristiano's appraisal, Lydia snapped a damp palm round the receiver. It was her solicitor. She stiffened in dismay when she learned that the police had requested a meeting today, rather than in four days' time, as had been previously arranged.

'It's your choice. You don't *have* to go to the station. But evidently they have some new information, and I feel it would be in your best interests to agree to make yourself available today,' her legal adviser informed her.

Lydia breathed in deep. 'Right…yes, I'll go.'

Her lips were tingling and her knees were weak. Perhaps an extra trip to the police station was her punishment for making such a fool of herself with Cristiano Andreotti, she thought crazily. How could he still live and breathe when she hated him with such venom? Or did she hate herself even more? How could she have sacrificed her pride for one kiss? Had stress deranged her wits? What vindictive fate had brought Cristiano back to her door when she was at her weakest?

In one harried step she reached the front door and yanked it wide. 'I have a pressing invitation to have another chat with the police, so you'll have to leave.'

'I've arranged for a glazier to replace the window,' Cristiano informed her.

Her teeth gritted. 'And why the heck would you have done that?'

'Isn't it fortunate that I did, when you nave to go out again?' In a fluid gesture, Cristiano cast a business card down on the shelf to one side of her. 'My number…for when you come to your senses and accept the inevitable.'

'You are not an inevitable event in my life.'

Cristiano looked down at her from the vantage point of his superior height, his slumberous golden eyes glittering down towards hers in a collision course as keen as an arrow thudding into a target. 'Conversation is a much overrated pursuit between men and women. The kiss told me all I needed to know.'

Inwardly she shrank from that humiliating reminder. Her body had responded to him in blatant disregard of her entrenched dislike and defiance. But then how much would Cristiano Andreotti care about that? As he had just admitted, without an ounce of shame, he was more into the physical than the cerebral where women were concerned. She could not help but remember how she'd used to chatter on the phone to him. Had he been bored witless by the way she had rattled on?

While she wondered, Cristiano inclined his handsome dark head, strolled out, and swung into the limousine waiting for him. The long, opulent vehicle purred away from the kerb and disappeared from her view as if it and its owner had never been there.

Five minutes later a glazier arrived to replace the broken windowpane. All smiles, he told her that for what he was being paid he had been more than happy to give her job priority.

As she made her way to the police station that afternoon, Lydia was consumed by a helpless need to rerun Cristiano's visit in her mind over and over again. In a nutshell, he had offered to recompense the Happy Holidays charity in return for her sexual favours. Had he been acquainted with her abysmal lack of experience in that department, however, he might have been rather less keen, she thought ruefully. Yet she could not forget that eighteen months ago she had been so besotted with Cristiano that she had been on the very brink of being whatever he wanted her to be...

She was not proud of that weakness. But then she blamed her susceptibility on the fact that she had first seen Cristiano Andreotti in a glossy magazine spread when she was only fourteen years old. He had been twenty-two. Convinced that he was the most breathtakingly gorgeous guy she had ever seen, she had torn out his picture and kept it. She had not just stuck him in a drawer—no, she had ironed his paper image and put him in a photo frame, and spent seemingly infinite, essentially adolescent moments devouring his picture with wistful contentment. She had much preferred those dreams to the often crude reality of the young men she'd encountered.

In fact more than six years were to pass before she actually met Cristiano—years during which her popularity as a model had gradually brought her to the point where she had an occasional entry ticket into his rarefied world of wealth and privilege. Once she'd had the thrill of seeing him across a nightclub, lounging back like royalty and looking bored, while a bevy of women fought for his attention. He hadn't seen her or noticed her.

A frightening experience when she was only thirteen had made Lydia wary of men. After that she'd found it hard to flirt, and was careful not to bare too much flesh in mixed company. That she was still a virgin was a secret she'd kept very much to herself, for she had moved in circles where casual sex was considered the norm. She had also been endlessly hunted by rapacious men eager to bed her just so that they could add her to a macho tally of conquests. When she'd finally realised that she was being labelled frigid by the men she refused, she had been deeply hurt and embarrassed. It had seemed easier not to date at all. It had not occurred to her that her very unavailability might make her an even more tempting target for a predatory male.

The day she'd peered through the curtains at a Paris fashion show and seen Cristiano Andreotti seated in the very front row, she had been overwhelmed. The teenager who had once cherished his photo as a pin-up had surfaced inside her again. Edgy as a beginner on the runway, she had been afraid even to glance in his direction. In fact when he'd asked to be introduced to her, she'd been so sick with nerves that she hadn't dared to look directly at him. He had asked her for her phone number and she had told him that her mobile had been stolen. A moment later she had had to race off to do a private showing for a VIP. Later Cristiano had had a new phone delivered to her hotel, and his had been the first call, his rich dark drawl coiling round her like melting honey.

He had wanted to see her that night, but she'd had a booking back in London early the following day.

'I'll be in Sydney next week. Phone and say you're ill so that you can stay on in Paris,' he'd urged.

'I can't do that.'

'You can if you want to see me.'

'And if you want to see me you can wait,' she'd heard herself reply.

'Are you always this difficult?'

That had been her first—and not her last—taste of dealing with a very rich and powerful guy, accustomed to the instant gratification of his every expressed wish. Anything less than immediate acceptance or agreement was perceived as a negative response.

Even so, Cristiano had still flown her back to Paris the following evening to dine with him, and they had got on so well that they had still been talking in the early hours. Perfect white roses had awaited her when she returned to London, and he had called her every day for a week afterwards. She had felt cherished and appreciated. Every step of their relationship had struck her as being the very essence of romance. Plenty of people had warned her that Cristiano had a reputation for being notoriously cold-blooded when it came to her sex, but she'd paid no heed. She had ridden the crest of the wave of phone calls and all-too-brief meetings while secretly dreaming, as women had from time immemorial, of love and happily-ever-after. At no stage had it crossed her mind that she might simply be an object to be used and abused in a game being played by a super-rich, egotistical man.

Now, the pain of that final recollection did nothing to ease Lydia's tension as she found herself back in a police interview room.

The inspector gave her a surprisingly genial smile. 'Tell me about your mother's house in France,' he invited.

'France?' Lydia's astonishment was unhidden. 'But my mother doesn't have a house in France.'

'We believe that she does, and according to our source it's quite a luxurious second home. Five bedrooms and a pool, no less. At least, that is what she told a friend last year. That kind of set-up doesn't come cheap in the south of France.'

Lydia shook her head in urgent disagreement. 'The supposed friend is talking nonsense.'

'I don't think so…'

'Of course it's nonsense. If my mother owned another house, I'd have known about it. There's been a misunder-standing.' Of that fact Lydia had no doubt. After all, *had* there been a second property it would have been sold to ease her parent's cash-flow problems, and Virginia would never have made the appalling mistake of spending money that did not belong to her.

'We may not have established the location of that house yet, but we are well on our way to doing so. I think we'll have more answers when your mother is in a position to assist us with our enquiries.'

Lydia had lost colour. She was dismayed by the fact that the investigation now seemed to be changing course to place new emphasis on her mother's role. 'But I've told you before that she has nothing to do with this.'

'I believe that your mother has *everything* to do with this. You were unable to tell me what you had spent the missing money on.' The inspector settled a clutch of plastic evidence bags on the table between them. 'I have a series of cheques that were drawn on the charity account and signed by both you and your mother. One is made out for almost fifty thousand pounds and was used to purchase a four-wheel-drive vehicle. The salesman remembers the buyer well. Where is that vehicle now, Miss Powell?'

Lydia was aghast at the question. Virginia had changed her car before she disappeared? And for a larger, more expensive model? She was disconcerted by the information, but steady in her determination to protect the older woman from the consequences of her crime. 'I don't know…'

'All of the cheques we have retrieved so far relate solely to purchases made by Virginia Carlton, or payments made by her to settle personal debts. When did you sign those cheques?' the inspector queried, but did not wait for her to respond. 'It must've been difficult for you to deal with the day-to-day expenses of the charity fashion show when you and your mother lived so far apart. I gather the financial arrangements were left in her hands as she was on the spot. Did you pre-sign cheques for her convenience?'

'No—*she* did that for *me*,' Lydia insisted, a tad desperately.

The older man sighed. 'If you persist with this stance you will in all likelihood be charged with aiding and abetting your mother to defraud the Happy Holidays charity. All the current evidence, up to and including her careful disappearance, suggests that *she* was the prime instigator of the theft.'

'No—no, she wasn't!' Lydia exclaimed, her hands twisting together on her lap.

'And telling silly tales is unlikely to convince me, or any judge, to the contrary,' he spelt out impatiently. 'Stop wasting our time, Miss Powell. In due course your mother will be found and prosecuted. There is nothing you can do to alter that. I suggest that you go home now and think over your position very carefully.'

Lydia was on the brink of tears of frustration and fear when she left the police station. How could she have made such a mess of things? She had failed to convince the police that *she* was the culprit, and her mother was about to be hunted down to her hideaway—wherever that was— and dragged off to court regardless. Of only one thing was Lydia certain, and that was that her frightened parent could not *possibly* be hiding out in some palace with a pool on the French Riviera!

Although Lydia had been shattered when she'd realised what her mother had done, she had understood how desperate Virgina must have been. In the spring, Lydia had reluctantly agreed to lend her name to the charity fashion show that Virginia had set her heart on staging, and had contacted several other models. It had been around that time too that Dennis had cornered Lydia to ask her for money.

Lydia had been astonished, because her stepfather was well aware that the failure of the nightclub had left her penniless.

'But you know I don't have anything left.'

'Oh, come on. I wasn't born yesterday.' His heavy face had been taut with fake joviality. 'You must have at least one secret account—a cash reserve you keep quiet. Tell me about it—I won't let on to the tax man!'

Lydia raised a brow at such wishful thinking. 'If only…'

'I don't believe you…you've got to be holding out on me. I've been offered a terrific opportunity but I'm short of capital.'

'I'm sorry, I can't help.'

Angry resentment flashed in his pale blue eyes. 'Not even for your mother's sake?'

Lydia winced. 'I can't give you what I don't have.'

'Then isn't it about time you stopped playing at being a garden labourer and got back to the catwalk, where you belong?' Dennis demanded accusingly. 'You could cover the losses we made on the club in a couple of months!'

It had worried her that her stepfather should still be expecting her to provide him with cash when he should have been capable of earning his own healthy crust. It had not occurred to her, though, that anything could be seriously amiss. But, amidst conflicting stories from the Happy Holidays charity director about payments that hadn't arrived and a cheque that had bounced, and her mother's differing explanations for those same issues, Lydia had finally travelled to Cheltenham to visit. There she had been amazed to discover that Virginia had already sold the home that her daughter had purchased for her and moved into a hotel.

'What on earth's going on?' Lydia had asked, when her pretty blonde mother had opened the door of her hotel room. 'Why have you sold the house?'

The older woman treated her to an embittered appraisal.

'I can't believe you have the nerve to ask. After all, *you're* the one responsible for wrecking my marriage!'

Lydia gasped. 'How? What have I done?'

'You put my husband out of work. Now, not surprisingly—because we've had dreadful financial worries and I had to sell the house—Dennis has left me for another woman! Do you have any idea how I feel?'

Lydia experienced such a fierce jolt of sympathy for her deserted mother that she attempted to hug her.

'For goodness' sake, Lydia… Oh, all right.' Stiffly, Virginia submitted to being comforted.

'I'm so very sorry,' Lydia whispered with pained sincerity.

'Well, it's too late for sorry now, isn't it? If you'd gone back to modelling when we asked you, I'd still have a husband and a house I could afford to live in!'

Lydia felt horribly guilty—because she *had* put herself first when she'd refused to abandon her garden design course. Her heart ached for her mother, who adored her second husband. Having accepted Virginia's love and trust, Dennis had hurt and humiliated her. Lydia understood exactly how that felt, because it was barely eighteen months since she'd suffered the agony of a similar rejection at the hands of Cristiano. Fortunately for her, passionate love had turned to energising hate while she tormented herself for her own gullibility.

'What am I going to do?' Virginia suddenly sobbed. 'I'm so scared!'

For an instant Lydia was taken aback by the unfamiliar sight of her mother crying, but she was quick to offer reassurance. 'It's going to be all right. Whatever happens, I'm here, and together we can get through this.'

'But I'm in so much trouble,' the older woman had

confided tremulously, glancing up with a sidewise flicker of her eyes at her daughter. 'You have no idea how much…'

Her anxious thoughts sinking back to the present, Lydia walked home from the police station through the park. The steady rain would serve to conceal the tears on her cheeks, she thought wretchedly. She felt such a failure. She could not help Virginia if the police refused to believe her story. Why was it that she always ended up letting her mother down? And how many times had she already cost Virginia the man she loved? Had there been some curse put on her at birth?

First there had been Lydia's father, who would never have gone sailing in that wretched little boat had it not been for the pleas of his more adventurous daughter. It was true that it had been a terrible accident which nobody could have foreseen, but that did not alter the appalling consequences.

Then there had been Rick, Virginia's boyfriend when Lydia was a teenager. Lydia shuddered when she recalled the ugly ending of that relationship, and the bitter recriminations that had come her way. Whether she liked it or not, she had been the cause of that break-up too, and once again her mother had ended up heartbroken and alone.

With such a history behind them, Lydia had been delighted when Virginia had met Dennis Carlton and found happiness again. Although Lydia had disliked her stepfather, she had been content to pretend otherwise for her mother's sake. If only her mother had foreseen that in her desperation to keep her husband, and lessen the strain on their marriage, she would feel that her only option was to steal to pay the bills.

When Virginia had tearfully confessed the whole sorry tale, Lydia had immediately promised to protect her.

Virginia had been terrified, and so grateful. Recalling the
rare warmth that her mother had shown her that day, Lydia
felt her eyes overflow afresh. Virginia would never be able
to cope with the shame of a legal trial or the rigours of
prison life.

Overnight, however, it seemed that the balance of
power had changed. Lydia's readiness to take the blame
for the stolen cash was no longer enough to save her
mother's skin. The police were intent on finding Virginia,
and there was now only one way that Lydia could keep her
pledge to get the older woman off the hook.

Soaked to the skin and numb with cold, Lydia leant
back against the worn front door of her home and closed
it behind her. She lifted Cristiano's business card. If he
repaid the missing money, the charges would be dropped
and her mother would be able to come home again.
Virginia would be safe—and wasn't that all that truly
mattered?

She chose to text rather than phone Cristiano, because
she could not bear to make a surrender speech.

You've got me if you want me.

CHAPTER THREE

WITHIN minutes, Lydia's phone rang.

'Lia…' Cristiano murmured softly, sounding out and savouring every syllable.

'It's Lydia. Lia was the name the modelling agency insisted I use, and I never liked it,' she told him flatly, while her heart beat very fast somewhere in the region of her throat. 'I need you to pay back the money quickly, so that the charity will withdraw their charges. Can you do that?'

'It's not a problem. Are the police behind your sudden change of heart?'

'Does it matter?'

'No. Winning is all,' Cristiano conceded without hesitation. 'But we can't reach agreement before we've ironed out the finer details.'

Blinking back the hot tears of humiliation washing her eyes, Lydia clutched the phone as though she was hanging off the edge of a cliff. 'That's not what you said earlier today!'

'You should have been more receptive. The necessary formalities can be dealt with tomorrow. You'll have to come to London.'

'What formalities? Now you're making all sorts of conditions!' she condemned, threading shaking fingers through the hair tumbling over her damp brow. What on earth did he mean by *formalities*?

'Yes.'

'But it's not necessary. You can trust me,' she framed between clenched teeth, frightened that if he did not speedily repay the stolen money her mother would be tracked down and arrested.

At the other end of the phone, a sardonic smile of disbelief slowly curved Cristiano's mouth. She was priceless! This was the woman who, while staying below his roof as his latest squeeze, had eloped with another man. This was also the woman who stood accused of defrauding a charity of almost a quarter of a million pounds. Furthermore, loath as he was to recall the fact—for he was famous for his astute intelligence—when he had first known her he had actually been very impressed by that sweet-little-country-girl act of hers. She had been a natural at pretending to be what she was not. If he'd been a tree-hugging, weepy type of guy he would have got all choked up when she walked barefoot through the grass in his roof garden and confided that every day she was in the city she pined for the countryside. She was a real box of tricks, Cristiano reflected grimly.

'I'll arrange for you to be picked up and flown to London early tomorrow. Pack light. I'll be buying you new clothes. And lock up well and say your goodbyes locally,' Cristiano advised in the same even tone. 'If we achieve agreement, you won't be returning for some time.'

Bright blue eyes wide, Lydia shook her head. 'Whatever happens, I *have* to come back here. I rent this place. I'll need to sort that out, organise storage—'

'My staff will take care of the boring stuff for you.'

'But I have relatives here…and if I'm going away, I want to see them before I leave.'

'I'll give you one week after tomorrow, and that's it.'

Lydia sucked in a sustaining breath. The entire dialogue felt unreal to her. If she told him how much she hated him he would naturally want to know why. After all, on the face of it, she had walked out on him for another man. As far as Cristiano was concerned she had no particular reason to dislike him. He, on the other hand, would feel he had ample justification for despising her.

'I can't believe that this is what you want...you have to hate me,' Lydia reasoned tautly.

'How I feel is my business.'

His cool intonation made Lydia feel as cold as though a chip of ice had lodged in her tummy. She shivered in her damp clothes. He wanted revenge. What else could he want? When she had walked out of his superb country house with Mort Stevens, she had quite deliberately set out to make a fool of him. Now it seemed payback time had arrived.

At seven the next morning she was collected and driven to a private airfield several miles outside town. There she boarded a helicopter ornamented with the blue and gold logo of the Andreotti empire. A couple of hours later, she was being escorted from the helipad located on the roof of a contemporary glass and steel office block in London and ushered straight into a large empty office on its top floor. She smoothed down a ruck in the sleeve of the fitted black jacket she had teamed with a white T-shirt and a braided skirt.

'Mr Andreotti is in a meeting,' she was informed by a clean-cut young man in a business suit.

When his PA slipped back in with a shaken nod of confirmation, and rather pink about the ears, Cristiano knew Lydia had arrived and was exercising her usual stunning effect on the male sex. He was very busy. She would have to wait. Of course, she was only on time because he had had charge of her travelling arrangements, he mused, recalling how her unpunctuality had once infuriated him. He did not like to be kept waiting. Even on their first dinner date she had made a late showing. On arrival, however, she had electrified the restaurant with her beauty, approaching him with a wide, engaging smile of apology in a manner that had magically dispelled his exasperation.

In the act of listening to his whiz-kid executives trade facts and figures with a speed and precision which had never before failed to hold the attention of his mathematical mind, Cristiano found himself wondering what Lydia would be wearing. A split second later he sprang upright, called a break, and strode out of the boardroom into the adjoining office.

Sunlight glistening over her silvery fair hair, which she had confined with a clip, Lydia turned from the window that stretched the entire length of one wall. Her face, with its wide cheekbones and ripe pink mouth, was dominated by eyes as bright a blue as a midsummer sky. She focused on Cristiano's sudden entry, her heart thudding like crazy. Her tension rose as though a pressure gauge had been turned up too high. Beneath the current of apprehension lurked an edge of excitement that shocked her. When she had been seeing him, she had often found her responses to him so strong they scared her, and the reminder of that reality was unwelcome.

Sheathed in a stylish business suit that outlined his broad shoulders, narrow hips and long, lean legs in the finest mohair and silk blend wool, Cristiano looked spectacular. He was fantastically handsome, always superbly dressed and immaculate, always intimidating. His dark eyes glinted gold in the bright light. He really did have the most beautiful eyes, she acknowledged grudgingly, and a tiny pulse began to flicker below her collarbone.

The silence pounded and she couldn't bear it. Tossing back her head, so that a few silver-gilt strands of hair fell free of the clip, she lifted her chin. 'So here I am…as ordered.'

'Yes,' Cristiano rasped softly. 'It feels good to have you here.'

She had hoped to discomfit him with her comment, but he betrayed no unease whatsoever. Indeed, something in his rich, dark intonation sent the blood climbing below her fair skin. She had the horrendous suspicion that he was enjoying the situation. Furthermore, he was watching her with the incisive attention of a hunting hawk. When that narrowed golden gaze travelled over her, she was suddenly disturbingly aware of every pulse point in her body. Cupped in a fine cotton bra, her breasts stirred beneath her T-shirt, the tender peaks swelling.

'I can't believe you really mean to go through with this!' she told him breathlessly.

A sinfully attractive smile slashed his well-shaped masculine mouth. 'Every time I look at you I *know* I'm going to go through with it.'

'But it doesn't make sense—'

'Makes perfect sense to me, *bella mia*,' Cristiano confided. 'I want you—'

'But I don't want you, or this, and I can't pretend otherwise!' she blistered back at him.

His shimmering gaze intent, Cristiano strolled closer. 'If I believed that, you wouldn't be here.'

'B-believe it!' she snapped, infuriated by the way she tripped over the word, standing her ground with difficulty, for her every defence mechanism was trying to drive her into retreat.

'Since I'm the only rescue option you've got, shouldn't you be trying to persuade me that you're exactly what I want and need?'

He was so glaringly right on that score that she was seized by a combustible mix of fear and annoyance. He *was* her only hope. Suppose he took offence? Suppose he changed his mind? Where would her mother be then?

'Lydia…'

'What…?'

Cristiano was so close that she could have stretched out an arm and touched him, so close that she was alarmingly conscious of his sheer height and breadth. Her concentration was gone. There was the faintest tang of some exotic masculine cologne in the air and her heart was beating so fast she could hardly breathe.

Cristiano caught her to him with strong hands and drew her unresisting body into his arms. 'This is why you're being rescued,' he intoned huskily.

The most delicious tension tautened her every muscle. She knew it was wicked, but when she studied his lean, darkly handsome face, something wild leapt through her and made nonsense of her resistance. He curved long brown fingers to her cheekbone and let his hungry mouth taste hers with a sweet, savouring sensuality that tantalised her. The hand at her hip pressed her into the hard, muscular embrace of his powerful masculine frame, and she gasped beneath the probing exploration of his tongue. A dam of hot dark pleasure overflowed and roared through her in response. Suddenly her legs were like jelly and her breathing was rapid, and she was hanging on to him to stay upright.

Cristiano lifted her off her feet and brought her down on top of his desk. He meshed long fingers into the tumbling hair he had already released to tip her head back and allow him access to her throat. He covered her lowered eyelids, her cheeks, with tiny teasing kisses that made her want to curve round him like a sinuous cat, begging for more. He let his teeth graze her neck and he tasted her smooth white skin with lips and tongue, lingering in sensitive places, forcing a driven moan from her. Bending her back with astonishing ease over his arm, he pushed the T-shirt out of his path and glided his fingers up over her taut and quivering ribcage to curve his hand to a tiny pouting white breast. Her spine arched and she jerked as if she had been electrified. The brush of his thumb over the swollen and sensitive tip was a source of seething pleasure. The sound of her own choked cry of response catapulted her back to renewed awareness of her surroundings.

'For goodness' sake…*no*!' she gasped, pulling away and throwing herself off the desk in such a panic that she overbalanced and went down on her knees on the carpet. He stretched down a hand to help her rise again, but she scrambled up under her own steam and backed away fast. She was in as much shock as if she had been in an accident and her body felt heavy and clumsy and achingly disappointed.

'*Per meraviglia*…you could have broken your ankle.' Cristiano surveyed her with smouldering intensity and a frown of reproof.

Lydia was all the more shaken by the subtle shift in his manner. All of a sudden his tone was more intimate, possessive. He had kissed her and touched her, and she had encouraged him, and now he was telling her off.

Cristiano elevated a dark brow. 'Why are you so skittish? What's the deal? If the nervous virgin act is supposed to be sexy, it's not working, so you can drop it now.'

'I'm not putting on an act!' Shame and mortification blazed through her slender length like a burning flame. In her mind it was one thing to submit, but quite another to enjoy being touched by him to such an extent that she had had to knot her fingers into fists by her sides. Desire was in her like a cruel enemy, eager to betray her. And she could not win such a battle, nor even wish in the circumstances that she could. Suddenly she felt as trapped as if she had been put in a dungeon behind a solid steel door.

Pale as milk, she shot him an appalled glance from vivid blue eyes. 'I can't do this…I can't!'

Cursing himself for moving too fast, even while he wondered what had unnerved her to such an extent, Cristiano settled a chair down beside her as if she had not spoken and invited her to sit down. Unwittingly guided back into the safer tracks of polite behaviour, Lydia sank down, closing out her agitated thoughts in a desperate effort to regain her composure.

Cristiano handed her a document. 'This is the co-habitation agreement that I would like you to sign.'

Her smooth brow furrowed. 'It's a…what?'

'A co-habitation agreement. I haven't lived with a woman before, and there must be no misunderstanding with regard to the nature of our relationship. It merely defines our arrangement in the simplest terms possible and gives it a business rather than a personal basis,' Cristiano proffered smoothly. 'In it, the money which I am to repay the charity on your behalf becomes your fee for assuming the role of my hostess for the next year. You're lucky that I'm not including the donation I gave as part of that debt.'

Ludicrously unprepared for what he was telling her, Lydia nodded very slowly. 'Your…hostess?'

'A convenient label—'

Her eyes were widening and her sense of unreality was increasing. 'You're giving me an employment contract?'

His lean, strong face was sardonic. 'Nobody working for me earns that much.'

Lydia flushed red, then white, and focused carefully on the third button on his jacket. 'I'm agreeing of my own free will to all your demands...surely it's not necessary to tie me down to an actual written contract, with rules and conditions?'

'I believe that it is. Trust is a definite issue here.'

Her throat closed over, making her voice a little hoarse as she fought back angry tears. 'I think you're determined to make this entire affair as humiliating as you possibly can.'

'That's not the case. I think it's important that you know exactly where you stand with me,' Cristiano spelt out. 'If you break the agreement, you will have to pay back the money.'

Lydia was aghast at that information. 'But that would be impossible! Do you think I'd be here now if I had an alternative?'

'I know,' Cristiano confirmed without remorse. 'But I want to be assured of your loyalty.'

'My...loyalty?' she queried uncertainly, clutching the thick document while she strove to work out exactly what he meant.

His brooding dark eyes took on a derisive light. 'Your track record on that score is abysmal. Tell me, out of interest,' he murmured, 'were you shagging Mort Stevens the entire time I was seeing you?'

Feverish pink stained her porcelain-pale complexion. 'How can you ask me that? Of course I wasn't... I mean, nothing happened—'

'Even as a kid, I didn't go for fairy stories,' Cristiano sliced back very drily, his attention welded to the soft fullness of her lower lip. 'We need to move on—and fast. I have to get back to work.'

She bit her lip painfully at that tone of dismissal.

'I've made an appointment for you to see a solicitor so that you can enjoy independent legal advice,' Cristiano continued. 'If you decide to sign the contract, do so before three this afternoon. You'll then be returned to the airport for your journey home by private plane. A limo is waiting now to take you to the solicitor. Any questions?'

She was intimidated by his inhuman detachment. 'You said something about a year. Is that how long you expect this arrangement to last?'

Cristiano shrugged with fluid ease of movement. 'A day, a week, a month… A year is your limit, not mine. If you're still with me then, and I doubt it, you'll be free at the end of that period to renegotiate your terms.'

Lydia could not credit what she was hearing. Even the use of that horrible word 'renegotiate' demeaned her. Was his opinion of her so low that he assumed she was content to accept money in return for her sexual favours? But taking off with Mort Stevens had given him that impression, and she had only herself to blame for that. Her conscience reminded her that while that might be true, it was never too late to speak up and tell the truth—even if she was only prepared to offer a part of the truth. 'Can I say just one thing? And will you listen?'

Recognising that a last-minute plea was about to come his way, Cristiano hardened his heart against her deceptive appeal. With that gorgeous face and lithe, shapely body, she was every guy's fantasy, he acknowledged with bleak conviction. Add to that an air of vulnerability that implied she was a deeply sensitive soul and she became lethal. This time around, however, he had no intention of swallowing her sweet bait and being played for a fool.

He consulted his watch. 'You have one minute.'

'I just think I should warn you that I'm not what you think I am…' Yet, now that she had the opportunity she had sought, Lydia was having difficulty finding the right words. 'You're expecting a woman with a lot more know-how than me. I doubt that I can be what you want—'

'You'll be exactly what I want, because you don't have a choice. Don't embarrass me with this bull, *gioia mia.*' Cristiano sent her a winging glance of scornful amusement that rubbed her raw as an acid bath. 'Next you'll be fluttering those phenomenal eye lashes and swearing that you're a virgin, untouched by human hand!'

Lydia was rigid, her eyes as bright a blue as a peacock feather against the hectic flush that had climbed her cheeks as he spoke. 'And what if I was?'

Cristiano threw back his arrogant dark head and laughed with sardonic appreciation. 'I can safely promise you that if you turn out to be a virgin I'll marry you!'

'Is that a fact? Well, I wouldn't have you for a husband if you were the last man alive on this earth!' she bit out fiercely as she stalked to the door. 'Do you hear me?'

'Don't forget your deadline.'

While Lydia waited for the lift, she was conscious of being watched by a bunch of male executives chatting in the hall. Did others already suspect that she might be Cristiano Andreotti's latest acquisition? Her lovely face heated all over again, and a hard knot of chagrin and misery formed in her tummy. She had thrown proud words with no substance behind them, because he had made her feel such an idiot when he laughed at her, but of course he would never marry her or even offer to do so. Men didn't marry women they could buy or women they despised. Yet when she had been seeing him she had dreamt of the impossible, and that lowering memory hurt almost as much as his derision.

In the limo, Lydia studied the contract. Some of it she understood, but most of it she found impenetrable. He was determined to ensure that she depended on him for everything, from the roof over her head to the clothes on her body and the very food she ate. She shuddered with distaste. He would own her body and soul. She would have no rights left to exercise, for he would have taken them all away. She would simply be Cristiano Andreotti's whore. That was the price she was about to pay for trying to save face and hit back at him for breaking her heart.

'This is a legal work of art.' The urbane lawyer, an older man with shrewd eyes, tapped the agreement in wry acknowledgement. 'There's even a seven-point confidentiality clause which prevents you from talking about the contract or your relationship with Mr Andreotti outside this office.'

Lydia swallowed slowly. 'What's your opinion?'

'If you don't need the money, *run*,' he advised ruefully. 'There is no equality in this contract. While you are required to meet a strict code of conduct, Mr Andreotti can dispense with your services at any time and without explanation. Furthermore, neither your duties nor your hours of employment are defined. Sign and you will be contractually bound to agree to whatever Mr Andreotti demands.'

Lydia nodded heavily.

'Should you breach the contract, however, two hundred and fifty thousand pounds will immediately become a debt that requires repayment. That threat will put considerable pressure on you to meet all expectations, reasonable or otherwise.'

'I know,' she muttered tautly.

'Mr Andreotti is, however, disposed to be extremely generous in other ways. He promises to ensure that you

enjoy every possible luxury and advantage while you remain with him.' His mouth quirked. 'He may be offering
you modern-day slavery, but at least it's slavery with solid
gold manacles.'

Having signed, she travelled to the airport. Already she
was frantically trying to work out what she would tell
Gwenna, for she could see no good reason to distress her
cousin with the sordid truth.

Forty-eight hours later a removal firm arrived at her
little terraced home to crate up her possessions. She had
already given notice to the rental agency. The following
day the police contacted her to say that the charges against
her and her mother had been withdrawn. A tide of relief
flooded Lydia, leaving her weak, and she wished that she
had some way of contacting her mother to assure her that
she was no longer at risk of arrest. Virginia had believed
it would be safer if her daughter did not know how to get
in touch with her, and had promised that she would phone
when the fuss was all over. Lydia texted Gwenna to share
her good news, and, as she had expected, her cousin called
in on her way home from school.

'Why is a removal van sitting outside?' the brunette
demanded, elevating a brow at the sight of the man
engaged in packing china in the kitchen.

'Come upstairs,' Lydia urged.

'Are you moving somewhere?' Gwenna pressed worriedly.

'I'm moving out.' Lydia bent over the suitcase lying
open on the bed to wedge a shoe in one corner. 'You
remember I told you that I'd broken up with someone
before I left London last year?'

'Well, you didn't spill many beans—only that the revolting rock star was a publicity stunt that went wrong,'

Gwenna reminded her wryly. 'You didn't tell me who the mysterious someone was.'

'Cristiano Andreotti…you probably haven't heard of him—'

'We do live on the same planet, and I read the same magazines you do. Did you really date that mega-rich womaniser? No wonder you got burned!'

Lydia mentally crossed her fingers, because she was about to lie. 'When Cristiano saw that story about the missing money in the paper, he came to see me. He wanted to help,' Lydia hurried on, determined to tell her story before she could be interrupted. 'He's paid back the money, the charges have been dropped and we're getting together again.'

Gwenna dealt her an astounded look. 'So that's why you want to return to London…'

'I'm moving in with him. No, don't say anything! I know you don't approve—'

'Of course I don't. What am I supposed to think? He stumps up two hundred and fifty grand and five minutes later you're agreeing to live with him?'

Lydia winced. She saw no point in upsetting her cousin with the truth, but it was not as easy as she had hoped to tell a convincing story. In desperation she reached for the old biscuit box by the bed, which contained keepsakes from her adolescence. Wrenching off its lid, she lifted out the photo that she was seeking.

'Who's that?' Gwenna questioned.

Her face uncomfortably hot, Lydia handed it over. 'I cut it out of a newspaper when I was fourteen.'

Gwenna fixed astonished eyes on her cousin. 'But this is him, isn't it? Cristiano Andreotti? You had a crush on him when you were that young?'

'Yes. He's the love of my life, and, to be frank, what he's offering me now is as good as it's likely to get,' Lydia contended tautly, accepting the return of the photo and thrusting it down on the windowsill as though the worn metal frame was red-hot. 'I really want to be with him. Please don't spoil it for me.'

Gwenna studied her unhappily, compressed her lips and said nothing more. Instead the cousins discussed practicalities, with Gwenna offering to receive and check Lydia's post.

A member of Cristiano's staff rang to inform Lydia of her travelling schedule for departure, and she wondered if Cristiano's use of a third party to pass on his orders was a taste of what life would be like with him. It made her feel very much like an employee. It also sent a shiver of apprehension travelling through her. What would her life be like with Cristiano running the whole show?

In actuality, her first destination in London turned out to be an exclusive beauty salon, where she discovered that she had been booked in for an incredible range of treatments. She found it humiliating that Cristiano was evidently not even prepared to see her until she had been groomed to within an inch of her life. The rest of the day passed while she moved from one room to the next, her skin glowing from a spa, a massage and a facial, her nails manicured, her mane of unruly waves conditioned and styled back into shape.

Cristiano phoned only when she was back in the limo that had come to collect her.

'Did you enjoy being pampered again?' His honeyed dark drawl skimmed down her spinal cord and she tensed and sat up, clutching the phone between taut fingers. His voice made her think about sex, and ensured that she was suddenly contemplating the shocking reality that she would be sharing a bed with him that night.

'Yes…yes, of course,' she fibbed, reasoning that there was no point in sharing her true feelings with him.

'I can't join you for dinner. Make yourself comfortable at the apartment,' he advised, breaking off momentarily to speak to someone and then returning to conclude the brief dialogue in a tone of preoccupation. 'I'll meet you at a club later.'

His apartment proved to be even vaster than she had appreciated on her only previous visit. A manservant, clearly following orders, showed her round a very long procession of cool, contemporary rooms hung with breathtaking art, before finally ushering her into a bedroom which mercifully bore no sign of male occupation. Lydia breathed again and walked across the floor to examine the sleek silver dress which awaited her there. A creation of the season's hottest designer, it was fashioned of fabric that shimmered when the light hit it. It would, however, be very short on her, Lydia acknowledged ruefully, because she had extremely long legs.

But what right did she have to protest? Hadn't she signed a contract in which she'd agreed to be treated more as an object than a person? Her body was Cristiano's sole source of interest, and, as such, was to be maintained and presented in a manner that pleased him. It was horribly humiliating.

That feeling of having lost control of her own life was heightened by the arrival of a make-up artist and a stylist, both of whom had been engaged to add the final polish to her appearance. It also meant that she had no time whatsoever in which to eat the evening meal she was offered.

A big bulky man climbed out of the limo and introduced himself as her security guard, Arnaldo. When the car drew up at an ultra-chic nightclub in Mayfair, it was Arnaldo who dealt with the bouncers barring entry to all but the chosen few. She was ushered past the long queue waiting hopefully and escorted to a private room. On the threshold, she was greeted by a familiar and unwelcome face.

'This is some comeback you're making, darling,' the stocky, powerfully built banker Philip Hazlett gibed, with a look that made her feel naked. 'You're looking very fit. I don't think I can blame Cristiano for succumbing to a re-run with you.'

Colouring, she said nothing. She had never liked Philip, but he was a childhood friend of Cristiano's, who had attended the same public school. Cristiano, surrounded by men wielding notebook computers and wearing anxious expressions, was talking on the phone. His arrogant dark head lifted as she came in. In a dark suit, striped shirt and blue silk tie, he was drop-dead gorgeous. She met glittering dark golden eyes, fringed by black lashes and semi-screened from her vision. Simultaneously all the oxygen in the atmosphere seemed to vanish, and she jerked to a sudden halt.

Cristiano allowed himself to stare. It was a given that all his male executives would gape at Lydia like schoolboys, he conceded, for she was dazzling. Her pale blonde hair tumbled in shining waves round her spectacularly beautiful face. A glistening swirl of silver fabric graced her delicate curves and skimmed her slender thighs. Desire took a rare back seat for Cristiano as he appreciated how revealing the dress was. Just as swiftly he noticed that he was not alone in relishing that view of her bare shoulders and back and her never-ending legs. He cursed his own lack of judgement, and the sensual line of his handsome mouth hardened when he noticed that Philip was guilty of ogling too. What had happened to respect for another man's woman?

Aggressive antennae bristling, he shot a knife-sharp glance of censure at the offending male and the guy paled.

Strolling forward, Cristiano curved an arm round Lydia and swept her straight back out of the room, his security men falling in behind him. She could sit by the dance floor and drink vintage champagne. That would keep her occupied and pretty much out of sight, for his table was in a private booth. He let his fingers dance down her spinal cord. Her skin felt like the softest silk. 'You look and feel sublime…'

The caressing brush of his hand sent a spasm of almost painful awareness reverberating through her slim length. Her breasts tingled, their delicate peaks tightening. The dark, hungry note in his accented drawl made her knees feel as bendy as twigs.

'If I wasn't in the middle of a deal that's hotting up, I'd take you home right now, *bambola poca*,' Cristiano breathed in husky addition.

All of a sudden Lydia's knees felt a little sturdier. It seemed that nothing had changed. Rich beyond avarice though he was, Cristiano still devoted his time and attention to getting richer, and the woman capable of distracting him from business and profit had yet to be born. He was a workaholic in denial.

'What did you call me?' she asked, seeking a translation as he settled her behind a table.

'Little doll…'

Her knees now felt like concrete, unassailably steady and dependable supports.

Cristiano skated a confident forefinger gently along the exposed expanse of her slim thigh and made her jump and shiver in startled response. 'That's what you remind me of in that dress. It's very, very sexy—but really not that appropriate in public.'

'You picked it,' Lydia pointed out between gritted teeth, only he didn't hear her.

As a brimming glass of champagne was poured for her, Cristiano vaulted back upright again.

'Where are you going?' she exclaimed, before she could think better of it.

'I can't make calls here…' Cristiano laughed, shrugging with the innate grace that accompanied all his movements and indicating the music. 'Enjoy yourself. I won't be long.'

'Don't worry about it…I'll soon find company!' Lydia heard herself declare.

His lean, darkly handsome face froze. 'Is that a joke?' he launched at her, loud enough for Arnaldo to frown in surprise from his position several feet away.

'I just meant…talking…dancing—'

'No, and no,' Cristiano riposted with icy force. 'No talking, no dancing, no flirting. One false move of that nature and you're in trouble. There will be no second chances. Don't let me catch you even *looking* at another guy!'

Astonished by that chilling warning, and the derision in his hard gaze, Lydia had to snatch in a sudden breath and hold it to keep her temper under control. Forced to breathe again or burst, she leant forward without conscious thought and said, 'You'd better tell Arnaldo to watch me!'

Cristiano sank back down beside her, his stunning gaze flashing flames of gold as he slowly and carefully laced long elegant fingers into the pale waves tumbling across her breast. 'Do you know what I really want to do now?' he murmured huskily. 'I want to take you back to the apartment, spread you across my bed and teach you some manners.'

Open-mouthed, she stared back at him, shock paralysing her while colour washed her cheeks. That graphic response ripped through her hurt pride and defiance to remind her of exactly what their relationship was.

Slowly, he got up again. She didn't watch him walk away. Thanks to that absurd fiasco with Mort Stevens, he honestly believed she couldn't be trusted around other men. In fact he thought she was a real *femme fatale*. Why wasn't she laughing at the idea?

Instead she drained her glass and grasped it again as soon as it was refilled. Fear of the unknown had seized her and she was fighting it off. *His bed?* Would he realise that she was totally inexperienced? She thought it unlikely. After all, he had dismissed her claim of innocence with contempt, and she had once read that most men couldn't tell the difference between a virgin and a sophisticate. Her chin came up, her fierce pride kicking in. Playing the *femme fatale* to the bitter end appealed to her. Surrendering to him would be a sacrifice, and she did not want a guy she hated to appreciate that. She wanted him to think that he couldn't get to her, that she didn't care what he did or how he behaved. Indifference would be her armour, she told herself feverishly.

Forty minutes later, Cristiano broke the habit of a lifetime and delegated his phone. He strode back to his table and sat down beside her. An arm anchored round her, he lounged back, tugging her into intimate connection with the long, powerful sprawl of his relaxed muscular body. Celebrity friends and acquaintances began to drift up, for he was always the centre of attention. Incredibly tense and nervous, Lydia avoided all eye contact. Cristiano inclined his handsome head in aloof acknowledgement, exchanged the occasional sally, but he made no attempt to introduce her to anyone. Nobody dared to breach his reserve.

'Why are you acting like I'm not here?'

'That you are with me is my business alone,' Cristiano asserted with immense cool, even while he wondered why she was so on edge.

'I hate being stared at,' she muttered, wondering if she had been recognised as the former model and thief exposed by the tabloids. She thought that it was unlikely, for she had never been half as famous as most of the people present. Even so, tension made her tremble against him like an animal being exhibited in a cage.

'Get used to it. You're beautiful enough to stop traffic and you're with me. Maintaining a low profile isn't an option.'

He had never remarked on her looks before, and before she could think better of it Lydia turned her head to whisper inquisitively, 'Do you really think I'm that beautiful?'

'Why else are you here?'

Her momentary pleasure evaporated at that caustic response and she shifted uncomfortably. 'Can't we dance or something?'

'I don't dance.'

An employee signalled him from the door of the private room and he released her and sprang up.

A bag of nerves without his presence, Lydia downed more champagne. He had bought her out of trouble on a whim—as an amusement, an ego trip. Now he was laying down rules much as he intended to lay her down. Angry rebellion snaked through her. She wasn't to dance or talk with anyone. He had stuck her in a booth and deserted her like an umbrella on a sunny day. But he had said nothing about her dancing on her own, had he? Why should she hide? Straightening her slim shoulders, she got up. Her head swam a little, and for a moment she had to clutch the table to steady herself. How much champagne had she drunk, for goodness' sake? Flinging her head back, she breathed in deep and headed out on to the floor.

Ten minutes later, Cristiano came to an arrested halt on his passage back to her side. His ebony brows drew together above incredulous dark eyes. Lydia was dancing alone and there was a spotlight on her. Lost in the music, she was spinning with her eyes closed, silver-gilt hair fanning out in a glittering curtain, her divine body twisting in time with the driving beat. She looked amazing. Every guy in the club was watching her with his tongue hanging out, and he didn't like it. He wanted to drag her off the floor and take her home, and that caveman instinct startled him.

When Lydia opened her eyes and saw him, her reaction was not at all what she had expected. Somehow the messy tangle of emotions he evoked coalesced inside her to produce a treacherous current of raw excitement. She had loved him once, a little inner voice whispered in persuasive reminder. Wouldn't it be wiser to make the best of a bad situation? In confusion she stilled, her body awash with physical awareness. The tiny snaking curl of heat tugging low in her pelvis made concentration well-nigh impossible.

Without even thinking about it, Cristiano strode on to the floor and claimed her, lean brown hands closing to the elegant curve of her hips to urge her momentarily close. Her head fell back, her full pink lips parting, excruciating tension gripping her. She wanted him to kiss her. Never in her whole life had she wanted anything as badly as she wanted that kiss. He flashed her a dangerous smile and freed her again in an effortless dance move that took her by surprise. Taut with disappointment, she mirrored his steps, but such precision demanded real effort from her, and she soon learned that her limbs were slow to do her bidding. In fact it was a relief when Cristiano finally closed a hand over hers to walk her off the floor.

'Time for us to leave, *bella mia*,' he murmured thickly, and her tummy gave a wild little flip of anticipation that destroyed her pride.

CHAPTER FOUR

STEPPING out into the cool night air made Lydia feel
dizzy—and concealing that reality was a challenge. The
barrage of cameras on the pavement outside the club
provided a welcome distraction, and Cristiano's security
team cleared a path to the limo.

Subsiding breathlessly into the opulent vehicle, Lydia
focused on Cristiano. His lean, darkly handsome features
were achingly familiar. He was still so gorgeous! A lump
formed in her throat because, for the space of a heartbeat,
she was the dreaming teenager who had fallen madly in
love with his photograph. She felt incredibly emotional
and wondered if the champagne was responsible, but her
reasoning processes were too muzzy to think it through.

'I'm sorry about tonight… Socially, it was a washout,'
Cristiano sighed, dense black lashes screening his gaze
and then flicking up to add sizzle to his charismatic smile.
'But I now own a controlling percentage of IFS and I'm
in the mood to celebrate.'

'IFS…how thrilling,' Lydia told him, without a clue
what IFS was.

'You are more of a thrill.' Burnished golden eyes connected with hers. His aura of power had never been more

in the ascendant, and the delicious tension she had experienced earlier that evening gripped her all over again. He closed a hand over hers and tugged her closer, turning her round to face him so that she was half-kneeling on the seat. Her heart felt as if it was beating at the base of her throat, and she was on such a high of expectation she could barely breathe.

He rested a fingertip on the pulse going crazy below her collarbone, moved on to smooth it over the pale alabaster expanse of her skin beneath. She quivered, her breasts lifting and stirring, the sensitive crowns pinching into painfully taut buds.

'I want you so much, *cara mia*,' he murmured in a dark deep voice full of intimate intent. 'But you know that. You've always known that.'

Her lashes dipped, her lovely face betraying no change of expression. She was accustomed to hiding her thoughts from others, fitting in for the sake of peace, soothing more demanding personalities. Briefly pain broke through the numbing effect of too much champagne. She had once naively believed that she meant more to him than her predecessors, and had soon discovered how very wrong she was.

'So secretive…' His dark drawl was one of silken censure.

Lydia snatched in a desperate breath to swell her lungs, loving his voice, revelling in his proximity, her mind controlled utterly by her physical senses. He cupped her cheekbone to hold her steady while he tasted her full pink mouth, using his tongue to dart a more erotic exploration between her readily parted lips. Primitive excitement roared through her. Her hands swept up to his shoulders to steady herself, and a split second later he tumbled her down into his lap to kiss her. Her eyes were starting to feel very heavy, and she left them closed.

'I'm so sleepy,' she shared when he pulled her back up into a sitting position as the limo had come to a halt.

Cristiano laughed huskily. 'Not tonight,' he teased, urging her to climb out of the car, for the door beside her had been opened without her noticing.

The combination of sudden movement and fresh air was too much for Lydia in the state she was in. Her legs crumpled and she had to seize the car door to stay upright. 'Oops!' she gasped.

Cristiano observed her across the roof of the car. 'Oops,' he said, very drily.

Mortification almost swallowed her alive, for, by the sound of it, he had guessed what was wrong with her. Inspiration struck her, however, when she glanced down and saw that the strap on her shoe had broken as she stumbled. Flipping off the high-heeled sandal, she dangled it by the busted strap and fought to speak with clarity. 'Lucky I didn't break an ankle!'

Cristiano ditched his icy demeanour and instead came to her assistance. 'Are you hurt?'

'I'll live,' she told him bravely, hobbling pitifully in the direction of the lift.

'I'm sorry…for a moment I thought you'd had too much to drink,' Cristiano admitted. 'Drunkenness offends me…'

Clutching the bar on the wall to stay steady, Lydia ducked her head down and nodded in vigorous agreement even while guilt assailed her. But it was true. She totally agreed with him. After all, she was not in the habit of over-indulging in alcohol, and there was no reason why he should ever find out if she was careful. It was a question of mind over matter, she told herself feverishly as they entered the huge hall of his apartment.

'Come here.' Cristiano turned her round in the circle of his arms.

Lydia almost rested her swimming head down on his shoulder. It took a mighty effort to resist the urge. 'I'll just go and…er…freshen up,' she framed carefully, plotting a line in the direction of the bedroom.

Freshen up into what? she wondered, striving to enter *femme-fatale* mode while smothering a huge yawn and swaying. Discarding her clothes, she trudged into the bathroom to remove her make-up. Every step was a terrible effort. She pulled down the white cotton wrap hanging on the back of the door and dug her arms clumsily into it. By that stage she was feeling so light-headed she was afraid she was going to faint. Absolutely miserable, and ashamed of her condition, she sank down on the floor, struggling to breathe in deep and get back in control of her own body again. She closed her eyes—just for a moment, she promised herself heavily…

Someone was talking in a foreign language and she frowned, reluctant to be dragged from sleep. Had that same someone shaken her shoulder? Or had that been part of a dream?

Her head was aching. Her lashes lifted on a sunlit room that made her blink. Even as her pupils adapted to the brightness she recognised that the huge contemporary bedroom was entirely strange to her. She jerked taut. Her head turned on the pillow to widen her field of vision and zeroed in on the male back view silhouetted against the window. Tall, broad of shoulder, narrow of hip, long powerful legs braced slightly apart in a typically masculine stance.

Shock grabbed her by the throat and shook her inside out, provoking a slight gasp from her lips. Cristiano, effortlessly stylish in a beautifully cut dark beige business suit, swung round to look at her. Still talking in liquid Italian on his phone, he strolled over to the bed and sank down beside her. With a disturbingly confident hand, he gently pushed her tumbled hair back from her cheekbone. She stopped breathing altogether, wildly aware that she was naked beneath the sheet.

This had to be his bedroom—the one room that had not been included on her official tour the day before, Lydia registered in a panic. She had slept with him and she didn't remember it! Shame and embarrassment and disorientation seized her all at once.

Flipping shut his phone, Cristiano surveyed her with steady incisive golden eyes.

'*Buon giorno, gioia mia,*' he drawled softly.

Her cheeks hot, Lydia made a strangled attempt to return the greeting.

'No...' With care Cristiano repeated the phrase, and urged her to try it again. He did not quit until she contrived to pronounce the unfamiliar syllables to his satisfaction. 'Excellent,' he pronounced with approval. 'I would like you to acquire the basics of my language, so I've arranged for you to have lessons in Italian.'

Although she was utterly taken aback by that announcement, she said nothing while her strained gaze sidled uneasily to the dented pillow beside her own, and her heartbeat raced at that confirmation of fact. She had definitely been with Cristiano all night, and she did not even recall getting into his bed, never mind what they had done there! She was appalled at the blankness of her memory, and deeply ashamed.

'Even this early in the day, you look enchanting.' Seemingly impervious to the tense atmosphere, Cristiano skimmed a lean brown forefinger along the soft rosy fullness of her lower lip with a devastating familiarity that sent little nervous tingles of heat zinging through Lydia's quivering length. 'I would very much like to get back into bed with you, but I have a meeting.'

Lydia nodded with as much natural cool as a robot. Wild horses could not have forced her to meet his gaze.

Cristiano pushed up her chin with his thumb, enforcing the eye contact that she would have denied him. A razor-edged smile tilted his beautifully shaped mouth. 'You were amazingly affectionate last night.'

Absorbing that assurance, Lydia flinched, her mind running riot on what she might have said or done. Oh, goodness, was it possible that she had told him she loved him, or something stupid like that? How could she tell what she might have said under the influence of too much alcohol? Suddenly she wanted to die a thousand deaths.

His stunning dark eyes looked down into hers, the fringe of his lush black lashes simply adding to their dramatic effect. 'I liked it…I liked it very much, *carissima*. I also particularly enjoyed the exotic dance you performed—'

Hauling herself up against the pillows, her shadowed blue eyes luminous as sapphires, Lydia gasped in horror. 'Exotic dance?'

Cristiano shook his handsome dark head slowly and sighed with regret. 'You don't remember anything, do you?'

She shook her head in stricken acknowledgement.

'So I could tell you whatever I liked and you would know no different,' Cristiano pointed out without pity. 'That is why a woman should never get that drunk and out of control.'

Her slender hands knotted into fierce fists and she swallowed convulsively. Her pride was stung almost beyond bearing, but logic made it impossible for her to argue with that statement.

'I was concerned about you last night. I ended up smashing down the bathroom door in your suite. There I found you passed out on the floor,' he revealed drily. 'I brought you back into my room only so that I could take care of you. Nothing of a sexual nature occurred between us. It offends me that you could have assumed otherwise. I like my partners fully awake and aware, not in an inebriated stupor.'

Pale as death, Lydia compressed her lips and focused on the bedspread with hot prickly eyes. She hated him for owning the moral high ground, for having done the right and decent thing. Even though she knew that it was irrational, that was how she felt. Even so, she knew that in the circumstances he had the right to criticise her behaviour. 'Okay…I was in the wrong. But I don't do stuff like that normally—'

'It was dangerous. Some guys would have taken advantage,' he spelt out. 'I didn't, and I wouldn't.'

'I get the message,' she said tightly.

'You have a wilful streak,' Cristiano told her huskily. 'It infuriates me, but it also gives me a kick.'

Lydia shot him a startled glance and hugged the sheet to her breasts, for there was a light in his gleaming gaze that made her staggeringly conscious of her lack of clothing. 'You said you had a meeting,' she reminded him in desperation.

Checking his Rolex, Cristiano frowned and vaulted upright. 'You also have a busy morning ahead.'

'I…do?'

'Don't worry about it. Your staff will keep you on target.'

'My staff?' she whispered incredulously.

'Arnaldo, your stylist…You've met some of your support staff already. You also have a very efficient PA to organise your appointments and remind you of them. I don't want you so busy that you can't devote your time to me,' Cristiano confided silkily. 'You're flying to Tuscany at ten. We'll be staying at my *palazzo* for a few days. I'll meet you there.'

'Oh…' was all she could say, belatedly grasping why he might wish her to acquire a working knowledge of Italian. Support staff? He had actually hired people on a day-to-day basis to look after her? She could hardly get her head round the idea.

'I have a small gift for you…' He set a slim, shallow jewel case down on her lap.

Dry-mouthed, she flipped up the lid on a breathtaking sapphire and diamond pendant. 'I can't accept something this valuable from you…'

'Of course you can.' Cristiano removed the necklace from the case, turned her round and pushed her hair gently out of his way so that he could attach the clasp.

The superb jewel was cold against the tender skin in the shallow valley between her breasts. She was maddeningly conscious of his appraisal.

'Yes, I like it…don't take it off, *gioia mia.*' He bent down and captured her mouth with a hungry masculine brevity that made her tremble, then he strode to the door.

Her face burning, she refused to look after him.

'By the way, I want you to see a dietician in Italy.'

Her head flew up, blue eyes bright. 'Will you stop ordering me around?' she launched furiously at him.

'Don't hold your breath. I'm a bossy guy.' In the face of her anger, Cristiano lifted and dropped a broad shoulder in a studied gesture of untarnished cool. 'I promised to take care of you and I will. You look too thin to be healthy, so at my request you will take professional advice.'

Ten minutes later, with a lump of impotent rage still sitting like a rock inside her, Lydia surveyed herself in the mirror in his magnificent bathroom. Too thin to be healthy? She had always been skinny as a rake. Perhaps he meant she was too thin to be tempting? She squinted down at her very small breasts and reddened. Was he hoping to fatten her up like a Christmas turkey? She touched the sapphire and diamond pendant gleaming at her throat with an unsteady hand. It was so beautiful, but he had made it feel like the luxury equivalent of a ball and chain. Wasn't owning her body and soul by contract enough for him? Perhaps he was scared she might forget the fact? It was time that she showed him that she could not be controlled in every way.

Later that morning, Lydia boarded Cristiano's private jet. To Arnaldo's dismay, his charge had attracted a most unwelcome degree of attention on their passage through the airport. The perilously high red stiletto boots were out of season, and extraordinarily conspicuous on Lydia's long stunning legs. Her low-slung denim skirt was so short and tight it was a challenge to walk in it, and her lime-green top exposed a slender midriff adorned with a colourful fake tattoo above her navel. The make-up artist had revelled in fulfilling that special request.

During the flight Lydia ate a meal and tried to watch a film, but she couldn't concentrate on anything. She couldn't wait for the moment when Cristiano would see her. In fact she just couldn't wait to see Cristiano again.

Although she had visited Rome twice before, when she was modelling, she had never moved beyond the city limits or had the chance to go sightseeing. As she was driven through the Tuscan countryside she was enchanted by the scenery. In the somnolent heat of afternoon, the rolling landscape of verdant hills studded with ancient earth-coloured buildings and olive groves was ravishingly beautiful.

The limousine turned into a drive shaded by a long procession of splendid arrow-shaped cypresses. She sat forward to get a better look at the house ahead. The *palazzo* was very grand and very large, and the sweep of gravelled carriageway up to the front doors was adorned by formal topiary and playing fountains. The building looked as though it had sat there for centuries.

Nerves formed a tight little knot in Lydia's tummy and she climbed out into the hot sunlight to walk towards the imposing entrance. She could already see Cristiano, pacing in the shadowed hall, and she found herself smiling. Then she saw that he was talking on the phone again and sudden fury ripped through her. She wanted to race up to him, snatch the phone and stamp on it until it smashed into a hundred broken pieces. Bemused and dismayed as she was by that strange prompting, she slowed her steps.

As she approached, Cristiano fell still and stared, his frown induced by the particularly frustrating discussion that was unfolding into his ear. His scorching golden eyes locked to her slender figure like a heat-seeking missile and raked over her fabulous face and the glorious curtain of her platinum fair hair. He inhaled before letting his deeply appreciative scrutiny travel further south, to absorb her tiny waist and her spectacular legs accentuated by the ridiculously sexy scarlet boots. It did briefly occur to him on some inattentive level that the outfit was a touch off the wall, but what she was wearing was a great deal less important to him than the explosive effect she was having on his hormones. Without a word he cut the call and switched off his phone.

Feeling ridiculously self-conscious for a woman who had set out to fight fire with a visual putdown calculated to cause annoyance and embarrassment, Lydia flung her head back. 'I bet you don't like seeing me dressed like this…'

'*Per meraviglia*…where did you get that idea?' Cristiano dragged his attention from the ripe rosy pout of her mouth to let his gaze roam down to her slim pale midriff, which he now realised was adorned by bright letters in script. She had a word etched on her skin? 'Is that a tattoo?'

Lydia perked up at the look of astonishment that had drawn his ebony brows together. 'Not quite your style?' she prompted, sweetly acidic.

Having got closer to check out his suspicions, and noted that the word was actually a name—and, moreover, his own—Cristiano surveyed her with sudden vibrant amusement. 'Sorry to disappoint you. You've got my name written on you, and I don't mind that at all. It's good joke, but it also appeals to the caveman in me, *gioia mia*.'

Lydia breathed in so deep she felt dizzy, but it was insufficient to contain her aggravation at this far from satisfactory response. 'I was trying to embarrass you…with this cheap outfit, with the stupid fake tattoo!'

Cristiano curved a light hand to her taut spine to walk her into the vast and magnificent hall. 'Obviously, your beauty outshone the trappings—'

'For goodness' sake, I'm dressed like a hooker!' she hissed at him.

'*Dio mio,* let's not make a production out of the fact that, in common with most of the male sex, I like looking at a woman in high heels and a short skirt—especially when she is *my* woman.' Laughter curled along the edges of every syllable Cristiano voiced in his rich dark drawl. 'Yes, I know. It's tacky, predictable, even sexist. But at least I'm honest about what I enjoy—'

'I don't want to hear any more!' Lydia sliced back at him between gritted teeth. It had been bad enough that he had not been discomfited by the challenging message writ large in her attire, but to suggest that her appearance was something in the nature of a sexual treat outraged her even more.

'At the same time I should mention that, while I'm happy for you to dress in this manner within the privacy of my home, I would prefer you not to be seen out in public in such provocative apparel.'

Lydia dealt him a seething glance. 'Why? Are you scared it might give the wrong impression?'

'No. I don't want anyone else enjoying the same view!'

'Watch out…you sound possessive! It doesn't go with the Mr Cool image!' Lydia slung, furious that he was refusing to take her seriously.

'I don't think so…' Glittering golden eyes assailed hers with an almost physical force that shook her. 'You might let someone else enjoy *more* than the view. You were quick enough to play the slut with Stevens!'

The silence hummed like a buzz saw. Lydia flinched back in consternation and hurt at that derisive crack, and then swung up her hand. He caught her wrist before the slap could connect, and held on fast to her when she tried to pull violently free of his hold. 'Let me go!' she gasped.

Cristiano expelled his breath in a hiss. 'Not until you calm down, *cara mia*. I was out of line. But didn't I finally give you what you wanted? A sincere and honest reaction?

Congratulations—it's been a long time since a woman made me lose my temper!'

Lydia stopped struggling and lost colour. She dropped her head, determined not to betray her conflicting feelings. Yet at last she had the proof that her supposed preference for Mort Stevens had got to Cristiano and drawn real blood. He was human, after all. And if he thought she was a slut, could she blame him? Hadn't she ended their former relationship in a very public manner calculated to cause offence and invite the attention of the newspapers? But he had deserved that rough treatment, Lydia reasoned fiercely. A guy who pursued a woman purely to score and win a loathsome bet laid with his equally hateful friends had no right to have his finer feelings considered. *What* finer feelings?

'I apologise,' Cristiano breathed in the rushing silence.

Lydia jerked up a slender shoulder and continued to study the worn marble beneath her feet. It was not enough. It might be his first apology, but she really would have liked him on his knees and begging; anything short of that could only be a disappointment.

'Next time I'll let you slap me,' Cristiano promised.

A reluctant gurgle of laughter was wrenched from Lydia and she glanced up, her anger draining away. 'I'd have liked that better,' she admitted. 'There are times you make me so mad I could scream. You're the only person who does that to me.'

They walked through the hall, which was furnished with huge gilded mirrors and marble statues. Cristiano directed her towards the double doors lying open at the foot. 'I never realised how fiery you were, *bella mia*.'

'Why should you have?' Lydia worked hard at keeping the edge of bitterness out of her voice. When she had been head over heels in love with him, she had been blissfully happy and had had no reason to fight with him. True, she had wished he would understand her reluctance to sleep with him after only a handful of meetings. But, all too well aware that many of her acquaintances engaged in sex on the first date, she had been reluctant to blame him for his lack of comprehension.

'Are you in the mood to choose a new wardrobe?' Cristiano enquired huskily.

'Sorry?'

In the huge elegant reception room, Cristiano settled her down on a sofa and nodded at the hovering manservant. 'That's what you're about to do. I thought you would enjoy being the client for a change.'

A door to the right opened, and his meaning was clarified by the entrance of a model wearing a houndstooth check coat which she slid back to display the silk dress beneath.

'I like that…' Cristiano confided.

'Stuffy,' Lydia told him, wrinkling her nose.

'Sometimes I entertain stuffy people and go to stuffy places—'

Lydia sighed. 'It's a shame you were never given a dress-up doll as a child.'

'What sort of a response is that from a woman who has my name written across her stomach?' he quipped.

'I should've known you'd make a meal of that.'

A brilliant smile slashed his lean bronzed features and her heart lurched from the surprise and effect of it. In the interim, he shed his jacket and tie and dropped down into the seat beside her. Sliding an arm below her spine, he eased her close to the long relaxed sprawl of his lean body. She stiffened, and then gave way, enjoying that physical closeness, refusing to think about the fact. Cappuccino coffee was served with tiny sweet biscuits that melted on her tongue, and the fashion show continued throughout.

'I've got to see you in that, *cara mia,*' Cristiano decreed when he saw a striking blue evening dress, and three out of the next four outfits elicited the same response from him.

His determination to buy her an extensive selection of designer garments, every one of which cost thousands of pounds, filled her with deep mortified unease.

'I can't feel comfortable at the idea of you buying me clothes,' she was finally moved to admit. 'I put all that stuff out of my life when I quit modelling.'

'Why?'

'It seemed so vain and meaningless. I was just a clothes horse. I donated all my party clothes to charity shops.'

'How very noble and self-denying. I wonder why you felt the need to shed the trappings of your former lifestyle so completely,' he mused softly above her head, and she coloured, knowing that he had to be thinking with scorn of the money he believed she had stolen. 'So you then donned a pair of Wellington boots and signed up for a gardening course. I'm afraid I don't see the attraction.'

'I like the knowledge that I'm creating something. I love working outdoors.'

Curling her even closer beneath one powerful arm, Cristiano murmured in a tone of unmistakable finality, 'But now you're with me.'

'Probably not for long, though,' she dared.

'Don't get your hopes up, *gioia mia*. The more you play it cool, the more I want you.'

Silence fell, and the procession of models continued. When the showing was over Cristiano curled her round to face him and bent his dark head to claim her sultry mouth in a slow-burning kiss that lit a flame deep down inside her. 'If you don't go and try on those clothes,' he breathed thickly, 'We'll end up making love here.'

Her pupils dilated, she stared up at him, mesmerised by the high-voltage charge of his sexuality. Finally, in an almost clumsy movement, she pulled away from him and left the room. What happened to her when he touched her? All the anger and the hatred ebbed and she felt dislocated from planet earth.

Two svelte women were waiting for her to choose from the garments hung in readiness for her appraisal, and then to help her to dress.

Her expression now reflecting the haughty indifference of a fashion model, she strolled back into Cristiano's presence wearing raspberry-coloured separates. In absolute silence he watched her every move, and she was maddeningly conscious of it. As she spun round to walk back past him, she was awesomely conscious of the piquant little frisson of pleasure that shivered through her when she felt the onslaught of his glittering eyes on her. It really shocked her that his desire should thrill her to such an extent. How could she enjoy that attention and yet complain about it? Yet as she modelled outfit after outfit she felt more and more like a wildly sexy lady, and it gave her confidence an incredible boost. It was as though they were engaged in a tantalising and very private game.

When she sashayed in, clad in a white organza dress, Cristiano sprang upright and strode towards her. 'The show's over, *cara mia,*' he breathed in a driven undertone, closing a lean brown hand over hers...

CHAPTER FIVE

CRISTIANO walked her straight out of the room and across the hall.

Lydia was disconcerted, for she had inhabited a dream-world of her own while she paraded back and forth in front of him. 'Okay… So…?'

Cristiano led her up the superb staircase. 'I've told my staff that we'll retain the clothes until tomorrow. You can make your choices then.'

Lydia hesitated. 'I have to get changed out of this.'

'No need. You look like a perfect madonna lily in white. I'll buy it.' As they reached the magnificent landing, Cristiano shot her a glance from heavily lidded dark golden eyes. 'I must confess that I've never been so excited by a woman…and we haven't even hit the bedroom yet.'

'Oh…' His words were a reality check, a wake-up call that catapulted her out of her pensive mood.

'But we're about to.' Scooping her up off her feet, laughing at her startled intake of breath, Cristiano swung her up into his arms with easy strength and strode into his bedroom with her. He could not remember when he had last experienced such intense arousal, and he was on a high. If this was a taste of how she could make him feel, she was worth her weight in gold and more. Lowering her with scrupulous care down on to his bed, he decided that he was very satisfied with the deal he had made.

Having let her shoes slide off in a rather awkward manoeuvre, Lydia sat up, hugging her knees.

Cristiano studied her while he unbuttoned his shirt. He liked the way the light from the window fell across her face. Her blue eyes were as luminous as stars against the pale purity of her skin. Even so, he frowned, because she looked so young. He assumed it was the effect of the white unadorned dress, but he had discovered an unexpected gap in his knowledge of her. 'What age are you?'

'Twenty-two.'

Cristiano was disconcerted, for it had never once occurred to him that she could be that much younger than he was.

'I know…' Lydia, grateful to have something safe to talk about, added in a rush, 'I look at least twenty-five. I don't know why. I've always looked older. When I was thirteen I could've passed for eighteen. I'll have to hope at some point that the clock starts running the other way.'

'What age were you when you became a model?'

'Fourteen…'

Long enough to acquire a deceptively mature air of sophistication, Cristiano reckoned wryly. But she could have been only months out of her teens when he had first met her in Paris. He almost winced, for she had been more of a girl than a woman. Rare misgivings stirred. Simultaneously his attention locked to her flawless oval face. It was very far from the first time that he had tried to pinpoint exactly what it was that made Lydia Powell so unforgettable. Her wide cheekbones? The clarity of her crystalline blue eyes? That ripe peach-soft mouth that opened with such delectable eagerness beneath his?

Just as swiftly, Cristiano wasn't thinking any more. He was reacting on a purely physical plane and moving back to the bed.

'I held you all last night in my arms and I couldn't touch you,' he told her hungrily as he came down beside her. 'Every time I moved away you sidled back, like a homing pigeon.'

Chagrined colour warmed her cheeks. Evidently he had not been joking earlier, when he had teased her about being amazingly affectionate the night before. 'That must have been a pain.'

'I had a cold shower in the middle of the night. I'm not used to them…except around you, *cara mia,*' he qualified with subdued mockery, tugging her round with great care so that she was facing away from him.

He ran down the zip on her dress. She felt the edges of the fabric part at her spine and she tensed, for she wasn't wearing a bra. He pressed his lips to the hollow in her slender shoulder and she shivered in response, not even noticing the instant when the sleeves of her dress slid down to her wrists. But her entire body jerked in sensual shock when he raised his hands to explore the pouting curves of her small breasts and their tender peaks. She shut her eyes tight and swallowed a startled gasp of response.

'Let me look at you…' Disentangling her from the organza still clinging to her hips, Cristiano lifted her back against the pillows and began to trace the pale delicate swells crowned by lush pink nipples with caressing fingers. 'You are so very beautiful.'

Lydia fought a self-conscious urge to cover herself. But tension was rippling through her in waves, and her hands coiled tight by her sides. She collided with smouldering golden eyes. Famed though he was for his cool reserve, he could not hide his desire. His hungry, masculine appraisal made an answering warmth pool in her belly. When he bent his arrogant dark head and captured a rosy distended bud, teasing and tasting with his tongue and his even white teeth, she trembled. She had not known she would be so sensitive there, and he knew exactly what he was doing. Her fingers delved into his black luxuriant hair and curled. A whimper of sound was impelled from her throat, and then another. Wonderful sensation seduced her, until she twisted and turned, desperate to sate the longing that he had awakened.

Cristiano lifted his head again, sensuous golden eyes inspecting her. He curved long lean fingers to her fine jawbone and held her fast while he kissed her with passionate thoroughness, ravishing the moist interior of her mouth with his tongue.

'I've waited an incredibly long time for you,' he confided in a roughened undertone.

'It didn't do you any harm.' Her response was breathless, abstracted, because even while she was fighting to hold back her response to him she was simultaneously angling her head to extend her long elegant neck for his attentions. When he pressed his lips with practised expertise to a pulse-point below one small ear, tiny unmistakable tremors raked her slender length.

'You want me,' he growled with unashamed satisfaction as he levered back from her to strip off his silk shirt.

'It's possible…' Her mouth was running dry. He looked all dominant male and impossibly sexy. Pure muscle rippled below his smooth bronzed skin, accentuating the solid wall of his chest and the hard contours of his flat abdomen. His athletic lifestyle was etched in the sleek, powerful lines of his magnificent body.

'I think it's a certainty, *gioia mia*.' As Cristiano vaulted off the bed to remove his trousers she was still watching him, as though a spell had been cast over her. Sleek black boxers delineated the noticeable thrust of his rampant arousal, and the heat of intense embarrassment and curiosity swept her from outside in.

Immediately Lydia averted her attention from him, terrified that her expression might somehow betray her as a fake in the *femme-fatale* stakes. If Cristiano was to guess that he was about to become the first man she had ever slept with he would surely think it was hilarious. Furthermore, he would also realise that her supposed fling with Mort Stevens had been one big, fat pretence!

'Why should you have a problem with wanting me?' Cristiano asked silkily, sinking back down on the bed and reaching for her, his every instinct challenged by the aura of constraint and distance that now enclosed her.

'I don't have a problem in that line.' And Lydia was determined that it should be that way, that she should accept what she could not change but somehow remain above it, detached and safe from experiencing any real feeling.

'Liar,' he whispered thickly against her full lower lip, piercing gold arrowing down into dense blue in resolute probing enquiry. 'You fight everything I make you feel. You always did.'

'It's called self-control, Cristiano.' But her voice was distinctly uneven, for she was in his arms, the quivering tips of her breasts grazed by the black curling hair that dusted his pectoral muscles. Her body was already betraying her wishes, as she was painfully aware of the wanton dampness between her thighs.

'Lose it for me…' He nipped at her full lower lip and let his tongue delve deep in her mouth in an erotic foray while he skimmed off her panties with sure hands.

She shivered as if she was in a snowstorm. 'I *can't*—'

'For me...yes, you can. And you will,' Cristiano intoned in husky disagreement. 'You'll enjoy what we share much more.'

Scrambling free from his loosened hold, Lydia slid into bed, tugging the sheet over her. She made no answer because she was intimidated by the subject.

At her sudden retreat, Cristiano elevated a sleek ebony brow. 'Are you cold?'

Pink flushing her lovely face, she jerked a shoulder.

A wicked grin curved his beautiful sensual mouth. 'You were such a tease downstairs.'

Affronted by that assurance, Lydia sat up again. 'I was *not* teasing you!'

Tossing back the sheet, Cristiano drew her to him with easy strength. 'Nobody ever did it better,' he intoned, surveying her with grudging appreciation. 'You have this touch-me-not look, and it drives me crazy. I can feel the cheeky invitation behind it—'

'I don't do cheeky—'

'But you *do* do passion,' he claimed, bending over her to lash a lush rosy nipple to straining prominence with his tongue, and lingering to punish her tender flesh with a carnal skill she could not resist.

Her spine arched and she shut her eyes tight. He explored the soft swell of her tummy, skimming through the pale curls that crowned her feminine mound to the damp swollen softness beneath. A whimper erupted from her when he found the most sensitive spot. When a tormentingly sweet surge of pleasure engulfed her she lifted against him in bemused surprise, the breath rasping in her throat. Sensation piled on sensation and she writhed, her hands smoothing and clutching at the satin hard strength of his shoulders and his back. Wanton heat burned through her nerve-endings, filling her with restive energy, and her longing rose to an intolerable pitch.

Cristiano spread her out beneath him, long brown fingers momentarily clinging to hers. 'You're as hot as I am…'

'Don't talk…' she urged, passion-glazed sapphire-blue eyes meeting his in a brief collision as she pushed her mouth almost blindly up to his, a shaft of inner fear making her avoid words that might be dangerous.

In answer Cristiano drove her reddened lips apart in an explosive kiss, his hands fiercely linked to hers above her head as he slid his lean hips between her parted thighs. She felt his hard sex brush her stomach with a sense of wonder. She wanted his weight on her. She wanted to be so close that she did not know where he began or she ended. She squirmed up to him, tilting in a desperate effort to ease the dull ache at the centre of her. She wanted everything, too much at once, and her frustration tortured her.

'Cristiano…' she gasped strickenly.

'You're amazing.' He released her hands to press her thighs back and plunge hotly into the slick wet heat of her.

The stab of pain that accompanied that passionate on-slaught provoked a cry from Lydia. Immediately Cristiano stilled. Torn from the hold of the sensual world he had in-troduced her to, Lydia looked up at him in mortified dis-may, for it had not once crossed her mind that any degree of discomfort would accompany her initiation.

His incisive dark golden eyes narrowed and slammed down into hers, to hold her suddenly evasive gaze fiercely entrapped. '*Accidenti!* I don't believe it…'

Severe embarrassment clawed at Lydia. He knew he had discovered her deepest secret and she could not bear it.

'You're a virgin… *Dio mio,* there has been no one else.' His shock unconcealed, Cristiano stared down at her and slowly shook his proud dark head. 'No—don't even think of trying to deny it, *gioia mia.*'

Lydia felt her skin prickle and flush pink, from her chest up over her throat to her face. Chagrin was eating her alive, but at the same time tiny sensual aftershocks were still gripping her—and not unpleasantly. Ready to do anything to escape dialogue on the subject of her total inexperience, she closed her eyes and shifted her hips experimentally. She felt amazing. He felt amazing. The pain was gone as though it had never been. On a level where neither pride nor conscience could influence her she was still shamefully eager to explore the pleasure that had beckoned only to be so cruelly snatched away.

'Be still…' Cristiano grated. 'I'm trying not to hurt you.'

She looked up at him from below her lashes, thinking how handsome his lean bronzed features were and how much she ached for him, hating that enslavement but equally trapped by it. 'You won't hurt me.'

'I already have.'

'But please don't stop.'

A sudden vibrant smile curved his sculpted mouth, and with a raw groan of capitulation he sank deeper into her yielding warmth. She caught her breath at the intensity of sensation and trembled. He lifted her to him and moved with fluid insistent rhythm. She gasped out loud, for it was bliss, sheer bliss, to every newly awakened sense. Her heartbeat raced, her excitement was unleashed and control abandoned. It was everything she had ever secretly dreamt of, and she cried out loud as the spiralling charge of dark sweet pleasure forced her to a wild summit of rapture.

Cocooned in the aftermath of that surfeit of physical pleasure, she felt joyful and amazingly alive. She inhaled the achingly familiar scent of his skin and smiled dizzily. He kissed her with languorous gentleness and she lay contented in the circle of his arms. She adored the silence, the intimate feel of his long, hot damp body entwined with hers. For the first time in many weeks she was at peace.

He freed her of his weight but continued to study her with intent golden eyes that revealed no trace of emotion. Likewise, his expression betrayed nothing of his thoughts. Yet the electric tension that had entered the atmosphere was a powerful indicator of his true frame of mind. Her relaxation and her mood took a swift downturn in response.

'It seems,' Cristiano drawled, his melodic Italian accent unusually thick, 'that we have a lot of talking to do, *cara mia*. I'm not very good at that with women. You'll have to make allowances. But I need a shower first.'

Lydia was as still as a statue in the giant bed. So that was sex, she thought, her strained eyes feeling prickly, her throat tight and dry. She had finally found out what all the fuss was about and had not even been disappointed, as she had vaguely expected. In fact just minutes ago, after their passion, she had been feeling incredibly happy. That lowering recollection made her squirm. Even the slightest movement made her aware of a host of little aches and tender places that she would sooner not have been reminded about. She had not expected the stab of pain that had betrayed her inexperience. She had been even less prepared for Cristiano to realise that she was a total fraud in the sexual sophisticate stakes. He had been astonished, but he had not laughed, she reminded herself dully. Was that a plus?

Her brow indented. What did it matter what *he* thought? Why was she even wasting time wondering what *he* might think? Of what interest or relevance was that to her? There was nothing personal in their arrangement. That horrible contract said all there was to say. There had been no need for Cristiano to warn her that he didn't make a habit of talking to the women in his life. His lawyers had created a fifty-page contract expressly to enable their fabulously wealthy client to avoid that challenging necessity. She was just bedroom entertainment, and if he was displeased by her sad lack of exciting expertise between the sheets he could dump her right now, no questions asked, no apologies required. Suddenly it was as though a giant black hole yawned beneath her feet.

No longer able to stand being still, she scrambled out of bed. Terribly aware of her nakedness, she wondered where her own clothes were. Stowed away by efficient staff in some other bedroom set aside for her use, she guessed. For it had been obvious back in London that Cristiano preferred to preserve his own space. Her eyes aching, she snatched up his shirt and pulled it on. She felt as if she was falling apart inside, and that maybe only her skin was still holding her together. She rolled up the sleeves once, twice, and noticed that her hands were shaking.

What was the matter with her? What the heck was the matter with her?

Couldn't she live with the fact that she had been born to be Cristiano Andreotti's whore? Hadn't she just willingly given him what she had so effortlessly denied other men? Desperate for fresh air, she opened the door on to the stone balcony beyond the windows.

Her memory was serving up an excruciatingly accurate

picture of her behaviour while she had modelled the clothes for Cristiano. She pressed her palms to her burning cheeks in an effort to cool them. He had called her a tease, and she might not like the label but he had been right on target with that charge. She had gloried in his attention and revelled in every minute of being watched by him. The suggestive buzz in the atmosphere had thrilled her to death.

But, in the aftermath, she felt sick with shame and bewilderment. With him she was another person—a woman she didn't know and didn't want to know. She didn't like the way she behaved with him. She hated Cristiano Andreotti, she absolutely hated him, but when she looked at him, when he touched her, when he smiled in a certain way, this horrible cringe-making weakness could still surface inside her. She had not known that sexual attraction could be so powerful that it would totally overwhelm her loathing for him. How could that happen? Especially when she knew exactly what sort of a guy he was. Arrogant, heartless, notorious for his lack of emotion. It took a real bastard to give a woman white roses with one hand while with the other he bet fifty grand with his friends on the certainty of bedding her!

Desperate to punish herself for her behaviour, Lydia made herself relive that moment over a year back, when she had appreciated that the guy she had fallen hopelessly in love with was an unspeakable four-letter-word in the truth, trust and decency stakes.

Her insistence on a separate bedroom that weekend at his country house had exasperated Cristiano. 'I'm not into celibacy, and I don't see sex as a reward you give me either. We're both adults,' he had told her with a silken derision that had cut her to ribbons. 'So perhaps you should think about whether or not you want to be with me.'

Had he known what it would do to her nerves when he said that? That threat had cast her into despair when she was already feeling unsure of herself. Going to bed with him had felt like an enormous step to her, and she had needed to believe that if she slept with him it would actually mean something to him. Although she'd been very much in love with Cristiano they had still only managed to get together five times in almost two months. He worked impossibly long hours, travelled the globe, and was a stranger to compromise. Accustomed to others eager to accommodate *his* needs and wishes, Cristiano had been inclined to blame her for the infrequency of their dates.

Even so, she had been terrified of losing him that weekend, and had soon crumbled beneath the pressure. At pathetic speed she had decided that it was time to shelve her sexual insecurities and misgivings and capitulate. Ready to share that change of heart with him, she'd tracked him down to the billiards room, where he'd been playing a game with his society friends. Knowing that he would hardly thank her for interrupting that all-male gathering, she'd been about to walk away again unseen when she'd heard her name mentioned.

'So, let's talk about Lia Powell,' she had heard Philip Hazlett suggest, and her tummy had lurched in dismay.

'What about her?' Cristiano countered calmly.

'Don't keep us in suspense. Here we are together again, and you can tell all—omitting no sordid detail. There's fifty grand riding on this, and it's not the money, it's the principle.'

'Yes. Has the icicle finally put out? I can't believe you've strung her along for two months for nothing!' another voice commented.

'The gossip says the frozen lady is besotted, so the odds are that Cristiano is already shagging her senseless.' Philip Hazlett had loosed a coarse laugh. 'Betting against the Andreotti ability to score even against such odds wasn't our cleverest move!'

That cruel hilarity echoing in her ears, Lydia ran. Her world of dreams was shattered. It was demeaning to accept that she had been on the very brink of winning his bet for him by sharing his bed that same night. At first she planned to confront him, but deeper reflection persuaded her that she wasn't tough enough to conceal how devastated she was. The discovery that she was the pitifully naive target of a sexual bet laid by rich bored men in need of amusement had almost destroyed her already fragile self-esteem.

Afraid that Cristiano might seek her out in her bedroom, she took refuge out in the stone summerhouse in the grounds while an endless party continued through the night in the huge house. It was there that Mort Stevens found her, red-eyed and wretched and cold, at four in the morning. He was amazingly kind and understanding.

'You want to save face, and I could do with some raunchy headlines to remind my fans that I'm not dead yet as a sex symbol,' Mort admitted cheerfully. 'So why don't we walk out of here together and enjoy the bloody big scandal it will create? It'll infuriate Andreotti...and what's more he's certain to lose his bet!'

She wanted so badly to hit back at Cristiano, and since he didn't given a damn about her, taking off with Mort was her only option. It also made it unnecessary for her to see Cristiano again.

Unhappily, Mort was arrested at the airport for possession of drugs, and she was arrested with him. Her most important client dropped her from their advertising campaign and the ironic rumour that Cristiano had dumped her for drug abuse began to do the rounds. By the time her name was finally cleared, her career was dead in the water and she was yesterday's news.

Drifting back to the present, Lydia shivered, a slim fragile figure sheathed in a blue silk shirt that acted as a wonderfully understated foil for her natural beauty. She should have learned her lesson then, she reflected painfully. When she tangled with Cristiano Andreotti she always got badly hurt...

CHAPTER SIX

IN THE shower, Cristiano punched the cold button and stoically withstood the icy jets pounding his hot damp skin. Raking wet black hair from his brow, he switched on the heat and leant back against the marble wall.

A virgin! She had told him so and he hadn't believed her, he conceded, his even white teeth gritting on that acknowledgement. Revenge had hit a roadblock, a tripwire that led straight to a stick of dynamite capable of blowing his whole life apart. He was in deep shock. Even while he looked for someone to blame he knew that his own bone-deep aggression and arrogance had brought him down. And just when everything had seemed so perfect that he could taste it. For she challenged and amused him in a way that no other woman had ever contrived to do.

It should have been ideal—a relationship with a business basis that was on his terms. Black and white, simple and straightforward, with no room for misunderstandings or emotional scenes. He had liked that. He had really liked that. It hadn't mattered that she was mercenary and untrustworthy. A hunger for money had been the fatal flaw that had led to her downfall, and with the background he came from he understood avarice better than most. He had been happy to feed her addiction with money and jewellery and luxury beyond her wildest dreams. He had learnt very young what women expected from him. But now all bets were off on every score, because Lydia Powell was not the woman he had believed she was. How could she be? His image of her had been turned on its head and blurred out of recognition by one inescapable truth…

Eighteen months ago, without the slightest suspicion of the fact, he had been trying to railroad a virgin into his bed. Women had always eased his hunger so readily, so immediately, that he had been impatient at her reluctance. He grimaced. It was not a pretty picture. But even less could he comprehend her dawn elopement with Mort Stevens. Unless, he mused, he put those two facts together and read the message that had escaped him at the time, when he had still lacked the most important piece of the puzzle. *Per Dio,* how could he have been so slow to make the obvious connection that he now saw? A rush of rare anger energised Cristiano, and he snatched up a towel.

Lydia gave a nervous jerk when Cristiano reappeared in the bedroom. His black hair was still spattered with crystalline drops of water. He had paused only long enough to pull on jeans and a black shirt which hung unbuttoned to reveal a hair-roughened brown wedge of lean muscular chest. She had never seen him so casually dressed before, and it unsettled her.

'I've finally worked out what you were up to eighteen months ago,' Cristiano delivered with icy clarity.

A bemused expression stamped her lovely face, and she threaded an uncertain hand through the pale tangle of blonde waves tumbling across her brow, her frown deepening. His reference to the time when they had been dating completely disconcerted her. 'What I was…*up to*? I don't understand.'

Diamond-hard dark eyes gleamed with scorn. 'You were upping the ante. You decided to play a stupid childish game with me, and if you got badly burned you have only yourself to blame for it!'

Her soft full mouth fell wide. 'What on earth are you talking about?'

'Your sudden extraordinary flit from my country home with that ancient creaking rock legend Mort Stevens!' Cristiano derided with a sardonic smile. 'Obviously you were trying to make me jealous.'

Hot chagrined colour flushing her creamy complexion, Lydia went rigid, angry astonishment holding her still. 'I don't believe I'm hearing this. Trying to make you jealous?' she repeated with ringing distaste. 'Where do you get that crazy idea from?'

'It's the only explanation that makes sense—'

'Well, it's the wrong one!'

'*Dio mio*, what else could you have been doing with him? I now know that you didn't sleep with Stevens. There *was* no secret affair. The entire exercise was a manipulative infantile ploy.'

Lydia was getting so mad that she could hardly think straight. 'There is such a thing as an affair without sex!' she launched back, determined not to back down and admit that he had guessed any part of the truth.

'Is there?' Cristiano vented a caustic laugh of disagreement. 'It was all a fake. You holed up in his apartment for a few hours and then he took you to the airport to see him off and to introduce you to the press as his future fiancée. It was to boost his image and his album sales. It's so obvious now. I don't know why I didn't see it at the time—'

'You didn't see it because that's not how it was!'

'At one in the morning you rang my mobile, hung up before I could answer and switched off your own phone,' Cristiano recalled. 'That was your opening move and it was supposed to bring me to you. When it didn't, you had a note delivered to me saying that as things didn't appear to be shaping up between us you thought it was time for you to move on. That was the real bait—your threat to walk out of my house, my moment to appreciate that I was losing you—'

'You had *already* lost me!' Her luminous blue eyes were bright with fury at his scathing recital of events that night. 'And I did *not* have the note delivered to you. I left it sitting in my room.'

Cristiano looked unimpressed. 'You were still in the house when that note was delivered—but I don't react to that kind of pressure. I decided that if you were that keen to go home and sulk, I would let you do it.'

Loathing leapt up so high inside Lydia she was dimly surprised that she did not burst into spontaneous flames. 'So far you have called me stupid, childish and manipulative—'

'*Si, bella mia.* I'm being very restrained in my choice of words.' As Cristiano spoke, he was watching the sunlight lend translucence to his shirt and reveal the provocative outline of her delicate rose-coloured areolae. Almost imperceptibly he tensed, striving to cool the instinctive surge of desire that she aroused. 'Perhaps that's because in retrospect there is something rather pathetic about the little charade you were so determined to play out for my benefit.'

Her hands planted on her slim hips, Lydia slung him an

irate glance. 'Listen to me—there was no charade, no attempt to make you jealous!'

Cristiano groaned out loud. 'Mort used you for a publicity stunt, and you used him to try and wind me up into offering more than a casual fling. Do you really think you're the only woman ever to try that on me? Of course I was supposed to chase after you and snatch you back out of his wizened old arms, wasn't I?'

Her face burning hotter than hellfire, Lydia snatched up a silver-backed hairbrush lying on the dresser and flung at him. 'He's a much nicer guy than you are!'

Cristiano sidestepped the flying missile with offensive cool. 'But it's me you shagged.'

'Because—'

Glittering dark golden eyes pinned to her, Cristiano took a step closer. He just wanted to drag her into his arms and sink deep into her beautiful pale body again. He had never been so hot for a woman. '*Because*...you want me.'

'Because we have a contract,' she hissed back, colliding with his smouldering gaze. Her heartbeat started to race.

'The enthusiasm with which you're fulfilling my expectations is almost more than I dared to hope for, *gioia mia*,' Cristiano murmured huskily.

He was so close she trembled, and she attempted to break the spell with words, wanting to fight with him to keep temptation at bay. 'Why can't you appreciate how much I hate you?'

Cristiano closed long fingers to her elbows and drew her up against him. She jerked taut, but her eyes were as radiant as stars. As his hand splayed to her hip, to gather her closer, he could feel the tiny little vibrations passing through her slight figure and it gave him a high. 'Hatred could never taste as sweet as this…' he swore, and he crushed her soft pink mouth under his.

Without hesitation he stooped to curve a powerful arm below her hips and swept her up into his arms to carry her back to the bed.

'We can't… I'm not speaking to you!' Lydia protested frantically when he let her come up for air again.

'So?' Cristiano swooped down on the fingers she had raised in uncertain protest, engulfed them in his mouth and laved them with his tongue.

A frisson of heat twisted low in her pelvis, her tummy muscles tensing in response. She snatched in air audibly and the silence pounded. Her body was deliciously poised on the edge of wild anticipation. 'Don't…'

'But you like it, *cara mia.*' he breathed softly, his intent gaze narrowed to gleaming chips of sinful gold below ebony lashes.

Her very bones were ready to melt into the mattress beneath her. She studied him, helplessly admiring the strong slash of his nose, the smooth hard masculine planes of his lean strong face, and the beautiful passionate curve of his sensual lips. He was breathtaking. In a sudden movement that seemed to her to be quite unrelated to any process of thought on her part, her fingers slid from his shoulder up into the springy depths of his black hair.

'I don't like you…I really don't like you,' she whispered shakily. 'But somehow I find you…'

His shimmering gaze entrapped hers. 'The word you're searching for is…irresistible.'

'Dream on…' But the stormy hunger assailing her made her tug him down to her level so that she could claim his mouth for herself.

Breathing raggedly, Cristiano leant back from her to rip off his shirt and dispose of his jeans. There was nothing cool or practised about that process. She spread her fingers on the warm bronzed expanse of his chest, let her hand sink lower to the taut musculature of his abdomen, felt him shudder beneath her touch. She looked up at him in surprise. His eyes devoured her. In an almost clumsy gesture he cupped her face and kissed her with a breathless driving desire that sent a liquid tightening sensation shimmying through her.

'You burn me alive, *cara mia*,' he confided, unbuttoning the shirt she wore with scant ceremony, bending over her with predatory intent etched in every line of his magnificent length.

She trembled, and her eyes slid dreamily closed in silent welcome. He kneaded the lush distended buds of her nipples with skilful fingers and her spine arched, She moaned low in her throat. All thought had gone, to be replaced by a fiery elemental need that she was no longer able to fight.

'The very scent of your skin tells me that you belong to me,' Cristiano breathed erotically against her throat, when her entire body was taut and thrumming like a piano played by a master.

She shifted against him, thighs parting for him, the hunger already too great to be denied. 'Cristiano…'

He traced the damp delicate softness below her mound and she gasped and writhed, tiny cries escaping her, muffled in his strong shoulder as he toyed with the most sensitive spot of all. The pleasure was so intense she couldn't bear it. He came over her and she arched up to him, urging him on, frantic and out of control, wanting, needing, striving with every fibre of her being to sate her own longing for him.

'*Dio mio*...you match my passion.' One hand knotting into her tumbled silvery fair hair, he kissed her with sensual savagery. He slid provocatively against the moist heart of her, teasing her with the hot hard shaft of his sex. Sizzling golden eyes held hers with fierce desire. 'I like the fact that I am the first, the *only* lover you have ever had. I was shocked, but it is the most erotic discovery I have ever made, *carissima*.'

She said nothing, for she was beyond words, her whole being centred on sensation. He entered her in a single deep thrust and she cried out in urgent response. There was nothing for her but him and what he was making her feel. He had taught her this raw, insistent need that had driven her past the boundaries of control. He slammed into her faster and faster. Wildly excited, she moved against him in a frenzy of abandonment, grasping for the ecstasy she could sense lying just out of reach. In an instant she went from torment to a crescendo of glorious pleasure and plunged over the edge, quivering in shock as the ripples of ecstasy continued to tug at her. Nothing had ever been that intense for her. As he groaned and shuddered in satisfaction, her eyes were overflowing with tears. Dizzy with warmth and delight, she lay there, just holding him to her.

Perhaps it was unfortunate that just at that instant she should have caught an accidental glimpse of herself in the tall looking-glass on the wall by the door. She was wrapped round him like an adoring lover. She blinked and then stared, the mists of passion and misplaced affection dissipating faster than the speed of light. *Slut*, she mouthed at her image, hating herself with all the strength of character she possessed. At that same moment she recalled his last words on the score of her virginity, and such a flood of self-loathing filled her that she was surprised that her temper did not erupt like a volcano.

Cristiano lifted his dishevelled dark head to look down at her. 'That was amazing, astonishing…' He touched a wondering fingertip to the moisture sparkling on her cheeks and let his handsome mouth glide over her damp skin in a caressing benediction. 'We have something special here.'

'Time will tell. I was thinking about something else,' she admitted in a soft tone that gave no hint of what was to come. 'Isn't it a shame that you didn't know I was a virgin when you laid that bet with your friends?'

Stunned by the pure shock value of that controversial question, Cristiano jerked taut and rolled back from her.

Smiling stonily, she continued, 'After all, if you'd known that your target was a virgin, I imagine the stakes would have been even higher.'

For a timeless moment Cristiano shut his eyes and thought of every swear word he had ever known. That pointless pursuit was followed by a ferocious desire to smash his fist into the wall.

'Don't even *think* about denying it,' she warned him.

Brilliant dark golden eyes met hers with a lack of expression that infuriated Lydia. She wanted blood, and she wanted to discomfit and embarrass him. 'Your sense of timing is an art form,' he told her flatly.

'Is that all you've got to say?' Lydia gasped as he sprang out of bed.

'When…*how* did you find out?' he breathed, hauling on his boxers.

She sat up in bed. 'The party at your house.'

'That last night we were together?' he shot at her in astonishment.

'I went looking for you. You were playing billiards and the door wasn't shut. I heard you and Philip and some other guy talking,' she recited, bitter anger beginning to rise in her as she recalled that painful experience.

He pulled up his jeans. 'You were listening outside the door?'

'It was an accident!' she slung at him.

'And I never saw you again until I went looking for you last week,' Cristiano mused, darker colour demarcating his fabulous cheekbones.

'Are you surprised?' Lydia flung bitterly.

'No...' In an uneasy movement, he raked long brown fingers through his black cropped hair. 'But if you listened, surely you heard me offering to pay up because I wanted out of the bet?'

'Did you?' Lydia lifted and dropped a slight shoulder in dismissal of that plea. 'Really? Why would you have done that? And—even if you did—well, I'd evidently walked off by that stage, and didn't hear you say it.'

Cristiano expelled his breath on a hiss. 'I don't expect you to understand this—'

'Why? Why wouldn't I understand?'

'Because you're a woman,' Cristiano growled. 'That asinine bet was suggested a few hours after I was seen talking to you in Paris. It was the day we first met—'

'Gosh, that's so romantic,' Lydia told him, listening with an earnest air, her arms clasped round her raised knees.

Her sarcasm made Cristiano throw up his hands in a gesture of rueful acceptance. It was very charming, beautifully executed, and the effect was enhanced rather than spoilt by the fact that he was barefoot and bare-chested, with his jeans still unzipped. 'I had had too much to drink...we all had. I should have said no then.'

She tilted her head to one side, wildly tousled platinum-pale waves tumbling back from her pink cheeks. 'To me… or the bet?'

'The bet…*naturalamente*,' Cristiano declared. 'But a guy doesn't say no to something like that. It's all to do with—'

'Being a cool macho bastard who keeps his brains in his boxers?' Lydia asked bitterly. 'Don't you dare try to make excuses! It was disgusting—'

His strong shadowed jawline clenched. 'I know it was, and it wasn't my style, believe me.'

Her look was disbelieving.

'I didn't see those guys again until the weekend party at my house. By then I had forgotten all about the stupid bet. When the issue was raised—'

'Listen, don't use nice, clean businesslike words like "issue" to describe what I overheard. I heard those men talking about me in a manner that you should have objected to!'

'I *did* object…why did you have to walk away before you heard me doing exactly that?' Cristiano demanded in a driven undertone, a raw light in his dark golden eyes that lent them an unusual degree of clarity. 'Philip was drunk. I stopped the locker room discussion and I dropped the bet.'

The silence lingered while she considered that explanation. She had never known him to lie. Did he deserve the benefit of the doubt? Although she did not wish to give it to him, his patent sincerity was his most convincing defence.

'Will you accept that?' Cristiano prompted.

Lydia gave him a grudging nod, for she had enjoyed his discomfiture, that rare chance to see him shorn of a little of his glossy patina of aloof indifference. 'But don't ever expect me to forgive you for it,' she warned him.

'The bet is why you took off with Mort Stevens, isn't it?'

Again, Lydia nodded in confirmation.

'Why am I only finding out about this now? Why the hell didn't you talk to me about this when it happened?' Cristiano shot at her with a suddenness that disconcerted her.

'Why would I have?' she flung back at him, anger licking at her afresh. 'We'd only had a few dates, and it wasn't going very well for us that particular day, was it?'

'I had no idea you were a virgin. If I had known you were that inexperienced, if I had had the slightest suspicion, I would have had a totally different attitude. You should have told me.'

'It's so easy for you to say all this stuff now!' she condemned. 'Have you any idea how I felt after I found out about that bet?'

Cristiano tensed. 'I can imagine.'

'How could you possibly? I felt betrayed and humiliated. It was obvious that you were only with me because of a horrible bet, and that all you were interested in was sex.'

Cristiano sank down on the edge of the bed. 'It wasn't like that...'

'How was it?' she challenged.

The silence pulsed with undertones.

His lean, darkly handsome features were taut, his glittering gaze hooded. 'It's insane for you to believe that I was only with you because of a bet. That I utterly refute. I saw you; I wanted to get to know you. There was a very strong sexual attraction and I'm not ashamed to acknowledge that. The bet was a piece of foolishness between young men, all of whom should have known better. It was inexcusable and offensive and I apologise without reserve.'

'Yeah…right.' Lydia was lacing and relacing the fingers she had clasped round her knees. He had not denied her contention that his sole motivation had been sex, and that hurt. She questioned her own over-sensitivity. So she had loved and he had lusted? So it had been since time began. It was not the stuff of Greek tragedy, so why did she feel as though it was? Hadn't she always known that she was just another in a long line of fanciable bed partners in his fast-moving life?

In an unexpected move that disconcerted her, Cristiano tried to tug her back into his arms. Her emotions were already very shaken up, and in the grip of that inner turmoil she felt neither gracious nor forgiving. In fact, when she realised that he was attempting to assume a comforting role, her pride rebelled furiously. Rejecting him with positive violence, and pushing him away, she retreated to the far side of the bed. 'Leave me alone!'

Cristiano vaulted back upright and spread fluid brown hands in an angrily defensive gesture. '*Per meraviglia*…I only wanted to hold you. That, at least, should not be treated like a crime.'

Her head was beginning to pound with tension, and she felt incredibly tired and sorry for herself. 'That depends on your outlook. Now, I want to get up and have a shower in a room of my own—but I don't know where that is yet. And I want clothes…but I don't have any within reach. I also want something to eat!' To her dismay her voice emerged with a shrill sharp edge that made her want to wince.

Cristiano strode across the room and cast open a door in the wall. 'Your suite is through here. I'll get you something to wear…'

Her eyes felt horribly hot and scratchy, and she bowed her weary head. She had never felt more alone in her life.

Cristiano returned and laid her shabby pale pink cotton wrap at her feet. He maintained a careful distance, as though she had an exclusion zone marked around her. A huge lump mushroomed in her throat. She fumbled her way into the wrap, shying away from his silent offer of assistance. Like a snail bereft of its shell, she wanted to retreat into hiding—fast. Sliding out of bed, she went rigid when she brushed against him.

Her blue eyes glimmered with a determined flame, for she felt weak but had no intention of parading that fact. 'So, now you know I wasn't trying to make you jealous when I walked out with Mort that weekend.'

'And that maybe you weren't exaggerating when you said you hated me,' Cristiano incised, without any expression at all.

'That hasn't bothered you too much up to now. Let's face it,' she sniped, hearing the tart words flowing from her own lips and disliking them, but quite unable to stop them leaping off her tongue, 'you're not exactly Mr Sensitive.'

Cristiano watched the door shut. He didn't like that door closed between them. He swore vehemently under his breath. A gigantic wave of unfamiliar frustration gripped him. He was in shock. He wasn't used to being taken by surprise or put in the wrong. It was unnerving to suffer that experience twice in the same day. But much that had been obscure was now crystal-clear. She had an exquisite grasp of the concept of revenge. Mort Stevens had been a reprisal attack, a direct hit. To accept that he owed that experience to Philip and his own laddish refusal to admit his distaste for a stupid bet was infuriating!

His lean powerful face set into grim lines. He had to make amends. He had misjudged her and she had paid a high price.

A kindly older woman, who introduced herself in careful English as the housekeeper, brought Lydia a menu and talked her through it. Having made her selections, Lydia went for a soak in the sunken bath and scrubbed her tummy crimson to remove the fake tattoo. Not one of her cleverest ideas, she conceded, stifling the memory of Cristiano pressing his mouth there.

Clad in a pair of short pyjamas, she checked her phone for messages. She had been hoping to hear from her mother, for she was eager for the chance to tell Virginia that she was now safe from any threat of prosecution. She reminded herself that the older woman had been so scared that it might well be a few weeks before she had the courage to make contact with her daughter. After all, Virginia had anxiously mentioned the fact that mobile phone records could be checked.

Dinner was served at a beautifully set table in the opulent reception room that linked with hers. But she ate sitting cross-legged on the bed next door, and endeavoured to watch a gardening programme on the plasma screen she found concealed with other technology behind electronic sliding doors. Replete with food, she crawled into bed. She did not think she had ever been so exhausted. It was both emotional and physical. Yet, even though she tried to bar Cristiano from her thoughts, she fell asleep with his vibrant darkly handsome image in her mind's eye.

She did not awaken until mid-morning, when a maid opened the curtains and brought her a cup of tea. Emerging from the bathroom enveloped in a towel, she went into the attached dressing room and was astonished to discover that virtually all the outfits she had tried on the night before now hung in colour-coordinated rows in the fitted closets.

She glanced at the functional garments she had already taken out, and then slowly tidied them away again.

If Cristiano wanted her to dress in the latest and most expensive fashion, was it really worth the aggro of saying no? She snatched in a sustaining breath and compressed her soft lips. It was time to deal with life as it was, not life as she would have liked it to be. Shielding her mother and escaping a likely prison sentence came at a cost that she had agreed to pay. Nobody had twisted her arm, nobody had forced her to sign that contract, she reminded herself doggedly. She was a mistress. She was an accessory, arm-candy, a trophy to be put on display. And, whether she liked it or not, presentation was everything when only her face and her body counted in the balance.

A little while later, Cristiano phoned to ask her to join him for lunch on the terrace. As if she had a choice, she thought fiercely, her pride still stinging at the awareness of how much she was in his power. In his country, in his house, in the very clothes he had chosen, and with an intimate ache at the heart of her to remind her, if she needed a reminder, of his passionate possession.

'Of course…'

'Did you sleep well?' he enquired huskily.

His dark sexy drawl made her tingle as much as though he had trailed his fingers down her slender spine. Soft pink burnished her cheeks. 'Very well.'

'You didn't even stir when I checked on you around midnight.'

Lydia stiffened and her chin tilted. 'Why did you feel the need to check on me?'

'You were upset. I wanted to be sure that you were all right—'

'Well, there was no need. I wasn't upset, just tired!'

'Okay…' Cristiano dragged the word out with amazing expressiveness.

'I'm not being unreasonable!' Lydia snapped defensively.

'I didn't say anything.'

'It was the way you said, "Okay",' she mumbled in the silence that he allowed to stretch until she was forced to make a response. 'It sounded long-suffering.'

'Why would I sound like that?' Cristiano chided silkily, and she almost threw the phone across the room.

He made her so angry—yet she had never before had a problem with her temper. At least not until she had loved and lost Cristiano Andreotti. Until he had yanked her back to him, handcuffed to a contract that made self-respect a desperate challenge. Nonetheless, yesterday she had acted the part of mistress to the manner born.

Worrying at the underside of her lower lip, she glanced in the mirror. The blue silk organza dress hung like the exclusive garment it was, clinging to her slender figure where it should, skimming where it should not.

She saw the view from the terrace before she saw Cristiano, and it was so spectacular that she walked straight over to the stone wall to gaze in wonder. Low-lying clouds wreathed a village on the far side of the valley with a misty haze that lent the ancient ring of stone medieval buildings on the hill a fairytale quality.

'It's so beautiful,' she murmured when she heard steps behind her.

'Not quite as beautiful as you, *bella mia*,' Cristiano remarked, for she looked dazzling, in a dress that reflected the sapphire-blue of her eyes, with her abundant hair simply styled to fall round her shoulders. After the restive night he had passed, striving to come to terms with the concept of giving up his freedom, he was finally willing to acknowledge that there would be one very obvious reward.

Lydia spun round and momentarily allowed herself to take her visual fill of his extreme impact in a formal dark suit. Even that elongated glance proved to be a mistake. As she looked her fingertips tingled with the memory of the warmth of his bronzed skin and the silky feel of his hair. Ready colour rose in her cheeks and she moved hurriedly towards the table that sat in the cool shade of towering chestnut trees.

Wine was poured and *antipasto* was served. The golden liquid was dry on her tongue. She didn't much like wine but, having recognised the world-famous label on the bottle, she persevered. The first course arrived, and she asked Cristiano how long he had owned the *palazzo*.

'It's been in the family for a while,' Cristiano revealed.

Lydia gave her wine another valiant tasting. 'How long is a while?'

'A couple of hundred years.' His tiny shrug dismissed the subject as of no import, and he signalled the hovering manservant to pass on some instruction.

'I really know next to nothing about your background. You're an only child, aren't you?' she pressed, determined to keep the dialogue on lines that she could handle.

'My parents didn't live together for long.' His intonation was cool, discouraging, his reserve patent in his response.

A fresh glass was set in front of her and another bottle uncorked with Italian ceremony.

'What's this?' she asked.

Cristiano laughed. 'You're drinking what you've got as though it's cough medicine. I requested something sweeter.'

His acute observation powers mortified her, but he

made light conversation with enviable ease and the food
was fabulous. Slowly, she began to relax.

'I have something important to say to you,' he murmured gravely at the end of the meal.

Her blood ran cold. 'You've had enough of me already
and you're sending me home?'

'No, I don't want to let you go,' Cristiano confessed
without apology.

She felt almost light-headed at that news, and the realisation shook her. Was that *relief* she was feeling? Surely
not? Bewilderment and shame threatened her composure,
for she was finding it increasingly hard to comprehend her
own reactions around Cristiano.

His crystal glass casually cupped in one lean brown
hand, Cristiano rose and strolled across the terrace into the
hot sunlight, before looking back at her. 'I reached certain
conclusions last night,' he admitted flatly. 'I have treated
you in a way I have treated no other woman.'

'How nice to be singled out as unique!' But although
she tried to sound insouciant, she was dry-mouthed with
stress at the prospect of what he might be about to say next.

His stunning eyes were pure lethal gold. 'It's not a joking matter. I will be frank...from the hour you took off
with Stevens, I thought of you as a total slapper.'

That was frank indeed, and she reddened.

'And I was wrong. You're the exact opposite. You, on
the other hand, thought I was real bastard, and you were
right to think that,' he spelt out with sardonic cool. 'The
business with the bet was indefensible, and the contract
was designed to entrap and demean.'

She gripped her fine porcelain coffee cup so hard she was
surprised that the handle didn't break off. She stared at the
immaculate white linen tablecloth, her heart beating very fast.

'I owe you...I owe you big-time.' Cristiano breathed hard and low, as if the very words were being forced from him.

Lydia glanced up in surprise.

His lean strong face was sombre. 'I do have honour. I do have standards. I can't change the past, though. It seems that you've won this round hands down...I'm willing to marry you.'

CHAPTER SEVEN

LYDIA stared at Cristiano, unable to credit what he had said and scarcely daring to breathe in the hot still air. 'M-marry me?' she stammered shakily. 'You're *willing* to marry me?'

Cristiano tossed back the contents of his wine glass with seemingly little appreciation for the vintage. 'There will be some consolations. I find you incredibly desirable, *gioia mia.*'

'I'm thrilled.' Lydia cast her throwaway comment while very different emotions assailed her. Hurt pride, disappointment and pain combined inside her in a volatile mix. Once a proposal of marriage from Cristiano would have been her every dream come true. But his ambivalence, his reluctance to marry her, was almost comically obvious. Dully, she wondered why she wasn't laughing.

Cristiano dealt her a brooding look of dark cynicism. 'Of course you are.'

She wanted to hit him. He knew what a rich prize he was in terms of looks, status and wealth. It did not seem to occur to him that a woman might expect something more than those superficial attributes from him. Or that he might meet with a refusal.

'How do you feel about me?'

Cristiano shot her a frowning appraisal, his stubborn jawline clenching. 'What's that supposed to mean?'

Lydia was as pale as death, her fingers knotted below the level of the table and then frantically crossing for luck. 'You're not stupid. You know.'

'I don't do love—just sex,' he asserted very drily.

'I'm not cheap. I'll only marry for love!' She managed to force a laugh that was convincing enough at least not to shatter the glass in her vicinity, but deep down inside she felt as if a steamroller had gone over her vital organs. The crazy wheeling and dipping of her thoughts bewildered her as much as the distinct downward plunge of her spirits.

Cristiano rested unamused night-dark eyes on her. 'I appreciate that I've taken you very much by surprise.'

A tremor ran through her taut length. She was in a state of shock, and almost pointed out that an announcement of his nuptial plans would make headlines round the world. 'Yes, you have—'

'But I don't like your attitude,' he said bluntly.

Every scrap of colour ebbed from her lovely face and she bent her head, fighting for the control not to snap back at him. Her first marriage proposal and it was an insult. He knew his own worth too well. He saw no reason why he should dress up the degrading reality that all he wanted was her body on tap. He regarded her as a lesser being, whom he would be honouring with his name and his riches. Her role was to be a grateful recipient, scarcely able to believe her good fortune. Unfortunately torture could not have dragged such a humble response from her at that moment. How dared he think that she would take him on such terms? How dared he tell her to her face that sex was all she had to offer him? She hated him. That was all she was sure of just then. Hatred and pain were like a twisting knife inside her and she couldn't think beyond that.

'I'm sorry you don't like my attitude,' she said woodenly, staring a hole in the tablecloth. 'But I wouldn't want to marry someone like you.'

The tension was appalling. She was so stiff she was afraid a sudden movement would shatter her into tiny pieces, and the silence seethed around her like a menacing storm. She had offended him, and his displeasure chilled the atmosphere.

'Look at me…'

And she looked, even though she didn't want to look, for the habit of command was so engrained in him that she could not resist its powerful pull. He surveyed her with impassive dark eyes and she shivered.

'You're saying no?'

Like a marionette on strings, she nodded, hardly daring to credit her own nerve. Yet the more his formidable assurance and presence intimidated her, the harder she fought to remain untouched and unaffected.

Pure outrage leapt in Cristiano. He could not believe it. Unless there was someone else she cared about. But how likely was that when she had been a virgin? A celibate, very moral someone else? Some dead guy? He suppressed that unusually imaginative train of thought with icy distaste. Could she dislike him so much? He rammed that reflection back down into his subconscious while mercilessly crushing that disturbing sense of outrage stone-dead. He had made the offer. If she was too foolish to appreciate the advantages of becoming his wife, honour at least had been satisfied. She had done him a favour. For the first time he reminded himself that she was a thief, and just as quickly he was marvelling that he had ever contrived to overlook that reality and even considered marrying her.

While Lydia watched, Cristiano checked the time and murmured without expression, 'We're flying to London early tomorrow morning.'

Her spine was so rigid it ached. 'Are we? But we only got here yesterday.'

'This is how my life is. I have a board meeting at the UK office.'

'Right,' Lydia muttered, her entire focus locked to him in bemusement. Was that it? Was that really it? Was there to be no further discussion of that staggering proposal? It seemed not. The savage tension had already vanished as though it had never been. He appeared cool, indifferent.

'And you have an appointment to keep with the Happy Holidays charity.'

Her eyes opened very wide, and even though she assumed she had misheard him, she lost colour. 'I beg your pardon…?'

'I'm afraid that, regardless of how you feel, you will have to bite the bullet and smile throughout the proceedings.'

'What proceedings?'

'My staff have organised a photo opportunity and reception to which the press have been invited. You will officially hand over a cheque for the money you were accused of stealing,' Cristiano explained with unnerving calm.

Her stomach executed a nervous somersault. 'You're joking!'

'No. I have never regarded theft as a laughing matter. You do not have a choice on this one.'

Even though she had not been responsible for stealing the money in the first place, Lydia still cringed at the threat of being forced to meet the charity personnel again. 'I won't do it!'

'You *will* do it. The charity has agreed. It's a PR exercise. You're part of my life now, and your reputation must be rehabilitated,' Cristiano advanced without apology.

'But everybody's going to know it's your money I'm handing over!' she protested, rising from her seat in her distress. 'What's the point?'

'People may well wonder if it's my money, but they will no longer feel so certain of your guilt. Doubts will be aired. And if, in a couple of months, you are seen to perform another act of goodwill for the same charity, you will look even more like an innocent. Most will assume that the recent…unpleasantness…' he selected that word with acerbic bite '…was a storm in a teacup.'

'I won't do it,' she mumbled again, but it was like talking to a brick wall. 'I mean it, Cristiano.'

'Think of it as your penance.'

'I thought *you* were that!' she returned bitterly.

'Would you really prefer to carry the label of thief for the rest of your life?'

That derisive question cut through her defences and she swallowed hard. Years from now, who knew what her life might be? Her supposed theft might well come back to haunt her when she least expected it. His argument was unanswerable. She supposed it was best if the whole shameful episode could be decently buried with a show for the sake of appearances. But the very thought of having to face the Happy Holidays fundraising team again filled Lydia with dread.

'I thought not,' Cristiano murmured drily.

'I can't believe you asked me to marry you...' Lydia heard herself say with an abruptness that startled her. She flushed to the roots of her hair. She had truly not meant to voice that tactless reminder, but the thought had raced straight into reckless speech.

Cristiano was more than equal to that sudden diplomatic challenge. Angling brilliant dark golden eyes over her, he drawled with unblemished cool, 'Fact is often stranger than fiction.'

A manservant came to a tactful halt at the other end of the terrace and Cristiano spoke to him. 'Your Italian teacher has arrived for your first lesson,' he told her.

Her face was perplexed. 'You never did explain why you want me to learn Italian.'

He raised a sardonic brow. 'You will be a more useful hostess with it than without.'

A cheerful little man in his early sixties greeted them both in excellent English. After chatting for a few minutes, Cristiano left them. The teacher informed her that he would be concentrating on her ability to use conversational Italian. She listened with a fixed smile but she was a thousand miles away, thinking about Cristiano and wondering if she would ever understand him.

Why had he offered marriage when he so clearly didn't want to marry her? But perhaps being a wife would have been preferable to being a mistress...? That thought crept up on her and lingered even when she tried to shut it out. Well, it was too late for a change of heart now, wasn't it? In any case, she didn't want to be married to a guy who felt nothing for her, and she wouldn't marry him for the lifestyle he could give her. At least she was hanging on to a modicum of self-respect that way.

She dined alone that evening, and wandered through the

beautiful gardens, which were kept in immaculate order. She did not see Cristiano before she finally went up to bed, and although she lay tense as a bowstring while she waited, wondering if he would come to her, she was left undisturbed.

She couldn't sleep. She tossed and turned, wrestling with her seesawing emotions, until she finally shame-facedly acknowledged disappointment.

Cristiano went through a couple of reports with his staff on the flight to London, while Lydia slumbered, curled up in an unselfconscious heap like a child. He covered her with a blanket.

While he worked, every so often he would raise his head and his keen gaze would rest with cool probing force on her delicate sleep-flushed profile. It was rare for anyone to surprise him, but she managed that feat on a regular basis. She fought with him. She melted into his arms and then told him she hated him. He had a Byzantine mind of surpassing shrewdness. He liked things to add up, and her behaviour didn't. If there was another guy, dead or alive, he wanted to know about him. This was a live-in relationship, the most serious thing he had ever got into with a woman. It would probably only last a couple of months, but it would only be sensible to find out everything there was to know about her. He would have her checked out by a private detective agency.

'What time is this photo opportunity with the Happy Holidays crew kicking off?' Lydia asked tautly in the limo that was ferrying them through the London traffic.

'Two this afternoon.' He skimmed a glance over her pale tight profile. 'I don't know what you're worried about. Nobody in the charity team will dare to be unkind. My patronage is worth too much to them. As for the press, you'll just have to keep your smile pinned on and take what you get thrown at you.'

Having proffered that dollop of cold comfort in a bracing tone, Cristiano told her that he would see her later. The limo nosed in by the kerb, his bodyguards leapt out, and he vacated the limo and strode into the Andreotti building. She breathed in slow and deep. She promised herself that she would get through the day by dealing with it in small manageable bites.

Only then did it occur to her that her mother might well see a newspaper photo of her daughter handing over a cheque to the charity. Her eyes brightened. That would certainly signal the all-clear for her parent to get back in touch again. That cheering prospect made the coming ordeal seem well worthwhile.

Having pushed through his own agenda as usual, and been listened to in hushed silence by his awe-inspired board members, Cristiano emerged from the meeting in good form. His most senior PA approached him, wearing a curious air of anxiety.

'Problems?' Cristiano enquired with a raised brow.

'A Gwenna Powell has requested a meeting with you, and she's a very insistent woman.'

Cristiano frowned. 'Gwenna...*Powell*?'

The PA cleared his throat. 'I understand that she's related to Lydia Powell.'

Intrigued, Cristiano gave instructions for the lady to be shown into his office. Minutes later, a small brunette wearing a belligerent expression arrived.

'I'm Lydia's cousin,' she announced.

Cristiano was amused. He strolled forward, introduced

himself with unassailable cool, and suggested she sit down. 'What can I do for you?'

Gwenna Powell ignored the seat set out for her and dug into her capacious satchel bag instead. From it she withdrew a document which she tossed down on his desk like a challenge. Cristiano did not need to lift it to identify it as a copy of the contract that both he and Lydia had signed.

'Lydia asked me to check her post and open anything that seemed important. Imagine my horror when I discovered that she had been asked to sign *that* horrendous legal agreement!'

'My relationship with Lydia is of a private nature.' Cristiano was noting that, though there might be no physical likeness between the cousins, Lydia was also impulsive, spirited and quick-tempered. The melodic lilt of the brunette's accent was equally familiar.

In censorious unimpressed silence, Gwenna Powell removed a photoframe from her bag and extended it to him.

His ebony brows drawing together, Cristiano accepted the item. He studied the faded snapshot in considerable surprise. 'But this is an old photo of me...taken from a newspaper?'

'Yes, Mr Andreotti. You were Lydia's idol long before she ever met you. She was a schoolgirl of fourteen years of age when she framed that and you became her pin-up...'

'*Pin-up...*' Cristiano repeated huskily, surveying his own image while he absorbed this new and fabulously fascinating fact. He was attempting to imagine Lydia at that tender age, snipping his photograph out of a newspaper. She had been modelling by then, he recalled with a frown. She would have been very tall and skinny, and very beautiful, but still indisputably a child in his eyes. A whole new dimension had just been added to his knowledge of her. It was like being handed the key to a secret drawer that he couldn't wait to open.

'I want you to feel thoroughly ashamed of yourself,' Gwenna informed him. 'Lydia deserves a decent man, who respects her.'

'I asked her to marry me and she wouldn't have me,' Cristiano admitted, taking the wind from his visitor's sails in a spectacular feat of one-upmanship. 'Perhaps I failed to live up to that teenage fantasy.'

Gwenna Powell goggled at him.

Cristiano set the photo with the contract and carefully stowed both items away. His, 'May I keep this?' was purely rhetorical. He offered tea and was equally politely refused. His diminutive visitor appeared to have taken fright at his mention of a proposal, and was eager to take her leave.

'Will you tell Lydia that I came to see you?' she asked worriedly before she departed.

'No,' Cristiano asserted, without a second of hesitation.

When his PA came in with some figures that had been requested, he found Cristiano in a curiously abstracted mood. Thirty minutes later, his employer made several rapid phone calls and announced that he was finishing early.

Impervious to the effect of such a declaration voiced by a male who routinely put in eighteen-hour days, Cristiano left the office.

A rather domineering young woman from a PR firm accompanied Lydia to the exclusive hotel chosen for the event. Her nerves were like jumping beans. Back at the apartment, she had agonised about what to wear before finally choosing a black and grey fitted jacket and pencil skirt that Cristiano had picked to meet the requirements of the 'stuffy' sections of his social life.

When she entered the function room, her companion took her straight over to the charitable team, and a rather uncomfortable conversation ensued in which everyone talked too much and smiled too often. The three models whom Lydia had persuaded to volunteer for the fashion show four months earlier arrived together. As all but one had made angry phone calls to her when the story of the cheques that had bounced first hit the newspapers, Lydia had once again to rise above her embarrassment.

'I'm relieved that you got the mess sorted out,' one of the girls remarked with a reproving sniff.

'Yes, being associated with all those nasty rumours flying around didn't do much for my image.'

'I know. I'm really glad you could all be here today, and I'm sorry about all the fuss there's been,' Lydia said with genuine gratitude.

The third model was a staggeringly lovely Russian redhead called Helenka. Her sinuous curves and languorous appeal were showcased in a revealing short white dress. A rising superstar, with a firm sense of her superiority, Helenka flashed Lydia a scornful look. 'We've agreed that we don't want to feature in any photos with you.'

Lydia reddened as if she had been slapped. The PR woman at her elbow waded in to protest that that was unworkable, and moved away several feet to employ her mobile phone. Members of the press were already arriving. Lydia was uneasily aware that any sign of a rift between her and the other models would swiftly be seized on to make a better story.

In the midst of the discussion, Helenka vented an exclamation and pushed rudely past Lydia. 'I see a friend...'

As a whisper of comment ran round the room like an electric current, Lydia began to turn her head.

'It's Cristiano Andreotti... Oh, my word. Is he gorgeous? Or is he gorgeous?' one of the models gasped ecstatically.

A sense of relief surging through her tense body, Lydia spun round. He could only have come to support her. The tingle of awareness that his presence always caused danced through her nerve-endings like a wake-up call.

'All that, and oodles and oodles of cash into the bargain...this close to a billionaire I feel faint!' her friend proclaimed.

In the act of moving in Cristiano's direction, Lydia froze. Helenka already had a confident hand on Cristiano's arm and she was chattering to him with pointed familiarity. He glanced over at Lydia so briefly that she wasn't quite sure it had really happened, and then he laughed at something the redhead said.

Lydia was directed to the front to pose with the dummy cheque while the Happy Holidays director said a few words. All Lydia was conscious of was that Cristiano was smiling down at Helenka and having wine brought to her. Lydia's tummy churned, a lump forming in her tight throat. She knew the buzz of grabbing Cristiano's full attention, and the Russian girl was flirting like mad with him. Lydia hovered, waiting for him to acknowledge her, but it didn't happen. Press interest was now firmly focused on the couple. A few minutes later, Helenka strolled like a queen over to a gilded chaise longue and reclined there. Lydia and the other models were urged to join her for a group photo. There were no objections to Lydia's inclusion because Helenka was much too busy directing sultry smiles at Cristiano. Afterwards, Helenka surged back to Cristiano's side, and delighted in the cameras taking note of the fact.

Arnaldo approached Lydia. 'Miss Powell? The car's ready when you are.'

Lydia blinked. 'Did your boss tell you to take me home?'

For all his size, Arnaldo looked as if he very much wanted to run when faced with that awkward question.

'Never mind…' Mustering as much dignity as she could, Lydia would not let herself glance back in Cristiano's direction.

They left the hotel by a discreet side entrance. Her legs were all wobbly. She felt sick, frightened, shocked beyond belief. Cristiano had ignored her as though she didn't exist. She would not have believed it had it not happened before her own eyes. He had acted as if she was of no more account to him than a stranger.

But evidently Helenka amused him, and he had chosen to be with the sultry Russian and send Lydia away. Was she supposed to accept that rejection with grace and indifference? Why did she feel so absolutely gutted that she couldn't think straight? Shouldn't she be rejoicing at the possibility that Cristiano might already be planning to replace her with a more exciting lover? After all, she would then get her freedom back. She would be able to return to her own life. But could a guy who had only asked her to marry him a day earlier cool off that fast?

There had been nothing emotional about Cristiano's proposal. He had, however, found her response offensive. No doubt he had swiftly regretted the sense of honour and conscience that had prompted that proposal in the first place. Certainly, he had been very cold with her afterwards. He had kept his distance the previous night as well. Helenka was stunning, and much more sophisticated. Lydia's eyes misted over with tears. What was the matter with her? The tears rolled down her cheeks. She felt…she *felt*… Gritting her teeth, she wiped her face with the back of her hand. It was only when she was fumbling through her bag in search of a tissue that she finally noticed that there was a package on the seat beside her.

The gift tag carried her name. She lifted the parcel and tore the paper off to expose a jewel case. It bore the gold logo of an internationally renowned jeweller. An incredibly sparkly diamond bracelet nestled in a cushion of blue silk. Her mouth wobbled. She was being dumped, and she should be pleased. This was her freedom: the right to her own bed and diamonds into the bargain!

The car door opened and she climbed out. Disorientated by the discovery that the driver had ferried her to an airfield, she stared at the second limo that was disgorging Cristiano only ten yards away. In bewilderment she froze to the spot and stared. He was so breathtakingly handsome that it almost hurt her to look at him.

'You can keep that stupid bracelet!' she screeched at him, without even knowing that she was going to say that.

Cristiano studied her in polite astonishment. 'What's the matter with you?'

'I saw you with Helenka—'

'Talking.'

'You were smiling, flirting—'

'And you were jealous,' Cristiano slotted in, smooth as glass.

Her mouth opened and shut again. Fuming with rage at that accusation, she snatched in a ragged breath and blasted back at him, full volume. 'I've never heard anything so ridiculous…I was *not* jealous!'

A wicked smile that was pure provocation curved Cristiano's wide sensual mouth. The silence simmered. He said nothing.

'I was *not* jealous!' Lydia launched back at him again. 'You're famous for being a womanising rat, but I won't put up with that kind of behaviour! I'm delighted that we're breaking up!'

'But we're not breaking up, *gioia mia*. We're flying down to Southampton to board *Lestara*.'

With no grasp whatsoever of what he was talking about, Lydia could not hide her confusion. 'But I thought the bracelet in the car was a goodbye present…'

'I'm not that tacky. When it's over, I'll tell you.'

She raised an uncertain hand to her pounding brow. 'But you didn't speak to me at the hotel. You let me leave the reception alone—'

'The press can find out we're together at some other occasion. I like my privacy. I didn't want our relationship to overshadow the whole purpose of the photo session, which was to re-establish your reputation,' Cristiano murmured, walking gracefully closer to her rigid figure. 'The PR firm called to warn me that Helenka was playing up, so I set out to distract her—'

Her lips felt clumsy as she parted them. 'You distracted her…'

'It averted the attention of the press from you as well. The journalists were more interested in the idea that I might have something going with Helenka than in asking you about your time in police custody,' Cristiano pointed out. 'It also worked a treat with Helenka, who chose not to act the diva in my presence and submitted to the photos.'

Those ramifications were too much for Lydia to take in just then. The source of her deepest misgivings was still his manner towards the beautiful Russian model. 'It was obvious that you already *knew* Helenka very well!'

'She did a series of television ads for a company of mine last year. Didn't you know that?'

She shook her head. She was out of touch with the modelling world and rarely watched television. She could not bring herself to ask if the acquaintance had been an intimate one. She swallowed with difficulty and said tightly, 'She wants you…'

'But I want you, *cara mia.*'

That husky assurance set up a chain reaction through Lydia's unbearably tense body. She was shaking, and her knees were threatening to fold beneath her. She wanted to cry. Even though that horrendous sense of humiliation had evaporated, she still wanted to cry. A storm of emotion had sent her out of control, and now she was struggling to accept that it had only been a simple misunderstanding.

He had not betrayed her or rejected her. He had not preferred Helenka. Their affair, so recently begun, was not yet over. Regardless, she had made a horrible jealous scene—and a total fool of herself. How could she be jealous of him? How could she possibly be possessive of a guy she professed to hate? But she *had* been jealous, bitterly jealous, when she'd seen him laughing and smiling with Helenka. It took great courage for her to make that inner admission, and in doing so she was confronted by a much worse fear. Had she been weak enough to fall in love with him again?

Cristiano curved steadying hands to her waist and gazed down at her strained face. He wondered why that stupid scene had not made him angry, for he had little tolerance for such displays in public places. His security team had retreated behind the limos in an effort to hide their amusement. But he could see that she was not aware of their surroundings or their audience. She was still very worked up. He looked down at her, and suddenly he wanted her so badly that if there had been a hotel within reach he would have rushed her there. Disconcerted by an urge that lacked his trademark self-discipline, he tensed.

A sob was locked in Lydia's throat. She met his smouldering dark golden eyes and it was like shock therapy, for all thought of tears vanished as though it had never been. That devouring appraisal sent a frisson of helpless excitement rippling through her slight taut frame.

'Our luggage should be on the helicopter by now. We should board,' Cristiano murmured thickly, and even though he knew he should not he cupped the soft swell of her hips to bring her into closer contact with his long powerful thighs. It was an act of pure sexual provocation.

A tiny little whimper of sound, only loud enough to be heard by him, was wrested from her as she felt the hard hungry swell of his arousal against her tummy. She tilted forward into his big powerful frame, suddenly boneless with need. With a ragged laugh, he turned her round with sure confident hands and headed her in the direction of the waiting helicopter.

CHAPTER EIGHT

LYDIA was in a daze. Mercifully the racket of the helicopter rotors made speech impossible during the flight, and she sat back in her comfortable seat to recoup her energies.

She had no idea where Cristiano was taking her, and she didn't much care either. Although she thought he had mentioned Southampton she wasn't sure, and she believed she must have been mistaken—for, on reflection, it did not strike her as an exotic enough destination for Cristiano. Whatever, she had lived on her nerves all day, and felt that she had more important things to worry about.

First and foremost, she refused to credit that she could be developing any form of emotional attachment to Cristiano Andreotti. Sex was the only hold he had on her, she told herself vehemently. It was shameful and disgusting, and it made her hate herself, but at least it wasn't love. Only an absolute dimwit would fall for a man in such circumstances, and she was not one. Nor had she any plans to become one.

Cristiano set the jewel case she had abandoned in the limo on her lap.

Lydia passed it back like a hot potato that might burn her fingers.

Out of the corner of her eye, she watched him flip up the lid and remove the bracelet. It lay across his lean brown fingers like a white river of glittering fire. He caught her hand in his and attached the bracelet to her wrist. Angrily she turned her head. He was only inches from her, brilliant golden eyes challenging. Her breath caught in her throat. He meshed his fingers into the silvery fair fall of her hair and took her soft pink mouth in a savagely intoxicating kiss that made the blood drum through her veins at an insane rate.

'Why are you so stubborn?' he demanded in stark reproof.

Lips tingling from that deeply sensual assault, Lydia turned away to gaze into space and sink deeper into her thoughts. If she didn't fight his power over her at every opportunity, where would she be? His charismatic strength and assurance were traits that she found dangerously attractive and exciting. But that did not mean that total surrender was an option for her. On her wrist the bracelet glinted and gleamed like a mocking reminder of her exact boundaries.

As the helicopter settled down on a landing pad, Lydia surfaced from her reverie and unclipped her seat belt. She caught a glimpse of the view through the front windscreen and saw some sort of a giant pulley, and beyond that rails and industrial buildings that looked like warehouses. Maybe Cristiano was coming here on business, she reflected, submitting to the necessity of letting him lift her out of the craft because he was too impatient to wait for steps. A vaguely familiar smell made her nostrils flare and she stiffened when she identified it. It was the salty fresh scent of the seaside, and her tummy immediately knotted into a little cramp of alarm.

Cristiano was guiding her towards an open door. But she was hesitating, seeking to identify her surroundings. Horror was nudging at the back of her mind and she was striving rigorously to control it. She was walking on a metal-surfaced floor, and several feet away were the polished railings that reminded her very much of a documentary about the wreck of the *Titanic*. She sucked in a rasping breath, yanked her hand free of his and moved towards the railings.

'Lydia…?' Cristiano turned back, wondering why she was being so quiet.

'This is…this is a ship,' she breathed, in what he took to be a tone of excitement.

'A boat—my yacht *Lestara*.' For the very first time Cristiano was proud of his floating palace. They would cruise in total peace and privacy. He would choose some places that she would enjoy seeing, and the yacht would dock there for them to go ashore. There would be no set itinerary. The paparazzi would never be able to track them. She would love that freedom. She would relax and unwind and stop talking nonsense about hating him. His veiled gaze gleamed with satisfaction.

Lydia forced herself inch by inch closer and peered sickly through the terrifying gaps in the rails. It was a long, long way down, but there it was, the substance of her worst nightmares: water in perpetual motion, and beneath its surface the terrifying churning dark depths that had claimed the lives of her father and her brother. Her skin was turning clammy, perspiration breaking out on her brow.

'I don't like boats,' she whispered chokily.

Cristiano laughed. 'It's a very big boat, Lydia.'

'I feel sick…'

'You couldn't possibly be feeling seasick,' he told her wryly. 'We haven't even sailed yet.'

While Cristiano watched in frank disbelief, Lydia threw up over the side of the yacht. He went immediately to her assistance, pressing an immaculate handkerchief on her and urging her away from the railings. 'Let's get you inside…'

But Lydia didn't want to go inside. All she wanted was to be off the boat and back on to dry land again. She was attempting to withstand a hysterical desire to throw herself back into his helicopter.

'I don't like the sea,' she confided tautly.

'Then don't look at it,' Cristiano countered, as if he was dealing with a fractious child. 'You must have eaten something that disagreed with you. I'll ask the doctor to check you over.'

'I don't need a doctor.' When he wasn't looking at her, Lydia crammed a fist against her wobbling mouth, tears standing out in her eyes.

Cristiano took her straight to a huge and opulent state room, but she was only interested in the washing facilities. From a window she saw the sea, seemingly so tranquil, with the summer sunlight shining on the water, and she was sick again.

'Go away,' she told him wretchedly, her teeth chattering together with misery.

Ignoring her feeble remonstrations, Cristiano carried her out of the superb marble bathroom across to the wide bed, where he rested her down and pressed a cool cloth to her pounding brow. 'The doctor will arrive at any moment, *cara mia.*'

'Don't you understand? I'll be fine if you take me off this boat!'

'When did you last eat? You slept through breakfast on the flight from Italy. Did you have any lunch?'

'I'm just sick with fear!' she gasped strickenly.

'But there's nothing to be afraid of...'

Suddenly it was all too much, and she burst into floods of tears, sobs racking her slight body where she lay on the bed. He cradled her in his arms and pulled her against him, urging her to calm down. He didn't understand, and she knew he didn't. Running away, surrendering to fear, was anathema to him. He could not comprehend her irrational terror. She fought that suffocating darkness in her mind long enough to say, 'My father and my brother drowned...'

Cristiano was suddenly still. He looked down at her pale tormented face and read the truth of those desperate words in her haunted eyes. *I don't like boats...I don't like the sea.* He wrapped his arms tightly round her.

'I'm sorry...I'm very sorry,' he intoned half under his breath. 'We'll leave as soon as the doctor has seen you.'

A knock on the door announced the doctor's arrival. The two men spoke in low voices and Cristiano returned to her side. 'Will you accept an injection to ease the sickness?'

'And then we'll leave...immediately?' she pressed frantically.

'I promise.' He gripped her hand.

She was so overwrought that she was supersensitive to everything, and she flinched from the tiny prick of the injection in her arm. A miasma of drowsiness crept over her. Her sense of time ebbed. Her frantic thoughts were dulled, her limbs increasingly heavy. She pressed her cheek into Cristiano's jacket, the achingly familiar scent of him washing over her like a soothing balm, and fell asleep.

* * *

Lydia dreamt that she was trapped deep under water. Her lungs burning, she struggled frantically to break free and find her little brother. She was calling his name and only bubbles were coming out.

'Lydia…'

Her terrified eyes flew wide on a softly lit room. She was sobbing for breath, hopelessly disorientated, her skin damp.

'That was some bad dream.' Cristiano was hunkered down by the side of the bed so that their eyes were level. 'I could hear you yelling from next door.'

'It's always the same dream,' she whispered shakily. 'I hate it!'

'You need something to eat.' Vaulting upright, he picked up the phone by the bed.

She pulled herself up against the pillows. Registering that she was naked, she anchored the sheet below her arms. Her eyes had adjusted to the dim light and she knew where she was: back in the master bedroom of the penthouse apartment in London. She reached for his hand and turned his wrist to check the time on his watch. 'For goodness' sake,' she exclaimed, when she realised it was one in the morning.

'That injection really knocked you out, but you needed the rest,' Cristiano contended.

'I don't remember flying back—'

'We travelled by limo. With you fast asleep, it made more sense.' He was wearing cream chinos that sat low on his lean hips, and a black shirt. Even though it was the middle of the night, and he was badly in need of a shave, he still looked drop-dead gorgeous.

'I'm sorry…you must've thought I'd gone off my head or something,' she muttered in a mortified rush. 'But I haven't been on a boat since…well, since the accident. I suppose that's pretty gutless of me, but until today I was always able to avoid it.'

'You were with your father and brother when they died?' Cristiano queried in surprise. 'What age were you?'

'Ten. Robert was only six,' she framed unevenly. 'We were on holiday in Mallorca. Dad used to take us down to the beach to watch the motor boats racing about. I asked him to take us out on one, and we went on the last day. He took us round the headland because the bay was so busy. He said it would be safer, but it meant we couldn't be seen from the beach. And before you ask, no, we weren't wearing lifejackets…'

'What happened, *cara mia*?' Cristiano used the question to break the heavy silence that had fallen.

'A couple of other boats passed us, and then this big wave came over the edge of the boat and water came in. It happened so fast I couldn't believe it. Robert was screaming, Dad was panicking, and the boat capsized. Apparently Dad hit his head on something and was knocked out. All I know is that I n-never saw him alive again.'

Cristiano closed both hands round the fingers she had tightly knotted together. 'You…? Your little brother…?'

'I was thrown clear…but he was caught under the boat. I was a good swimmer…I went underwater but I couldn't find him. It was so dark, and there was a strong current. A fishing boat came, and they got Robert out, but it was too late.'

'It's a miracle you survived.'

A sob was wrested from her and she pulled her fingers free of his to cover her face, for the recollection of that tragic day still haunted her. 'It was my fault… If I hadn't begged, we'd never have been in that boat.'

'That's nonsense. You were a child. It was an accident.

Nobody should be allowed to go sailing without life pre-servers. What was your nightmare about?'

And she told him. It had been a very long time since she had talked about that day, or its repercussions, and he was a surprisingly good listener. So she told him about how her mother had gone to pieces after the boating accident, and how her father's business had gone belly-up within months.

When it had all been aired, she felt a surprising sense of relief, and the past settled back into the recesses of her memory. Only then did she put a hand up to brush her hair from her brow and register that, after hours of sleep, it was a tangle of tousled waves and she probably looked a real mess.

'I could do with a shower.' Forgetting that she was naked as the day she was born, she pushed back the sheet and scrambled out of bed. With a moan of embarrassment, she raced for the bathroom to the sound of his laughter.

'You have five minutes before we eat,' he warned her cheerfully.

Wrapped in a big towel, her wet hair slicked back from her brow, she emerged again, thoroughly scrubbed, squeaky clean and breathless. He was lounging back on the bed, watching the business news.

A trolley of food awaited them in the room next door.

Hurriedly tucking in the end of her towel as it pulled free, Lydia muttered, 'I should get dressed.'

'I forbid it, *bella mia.*' Pulling out a chair for her oc-cupation, Cristiano dealt her a slow-burning smile of sensual appreciation. 'Why put on clothes that I'm only going to take off again?'

She blushed, while a tiny wicked twist of anticipation leapt low in her pelvis. Once again her own sensuality took her by surprise and filled her with chagrin. He only had to look at her in a certain way and she was gripped by a fever of wanton longing. He knew it too. That awareness made her cringe, and she focused her attention on her meal and ate with appetite.

'Aren't you having anything?'

'I dined earlier.' He cradled a glass of red wine in one lean hand. 'I'm relieved to see that you can eat a healthy meal…you skip too many.'

'The last few months have been stressful. But let's not talk about that,' she said hastily, for she was reluctant to drag up anything controversial that might spoil the relaxed mood between them. 'Now you know all about me, isn't it time for you to talk about *you*?'

'Me…?' Taken aback, Cristiano frowned.

'Your mum…your dad—just that sort of basic stuff.' Lydia pushed her empty plate away. 'Who were they? Are they still alive?

Cristiano groaned and sprang upright. 'They're both dead. That's all a matter of public record.'

'Well, I don't know it…please,' she pressed, rising from her seat as well.

Cristiano closed a hand over hers and walked her back into the bedroom with a distinct air of masculine purpose. 'Do you want me to start, "Once upon a time"?'

'Was your childhood like a fairytale?'

Cristiano settled her down against the pillows and stepped back as though to admire the picture she made. 'Not at all—although the *palazzo* is the family castle and money was always plentiful. My mother was an heiress, very rich and very spoilt.'

Lydia was hungry for detail. 'Did she look like you? Was she beautiful?'

'I believe she was considered so.' His lean dark face had

a bleak light as he undid his shirt and stretched out beside her. Even though she tried to resist the urge, his long, lithe powerful physique drew her gaze. 'She wasn't the maternal type. I was an accident, and my nannies knew me better than she ever did. She liked to be amused, and I wasn't an amusing kid.'

'What about your father?'

'An entrepreneur of great brilliance and very success-ful—but he was my mother's slave.' Cristiano could not hide his distaste. 'She had endless affairs. She dragged his name in the dirt, slept around, and laughed in his face. He couldn't live with her and he couldn't live without her. When I was eighteen he found her in bed with one of my friends, and that night he shot himself...she didn't even attend the funeral.'

Lydia flinched, appalled by that flat recitation of the distressing facts and the horrendous scandal that must have marred his youth. She leant over him, sapphire-blue eyes bright with sympathy. 'I don't know what to say...'

He wound two fingers slowly, enticingly, into her hair, and used the silky waves to draw her down to him. Hot dark golden eyes entrapped hers. 'Then show me, *gioia mia.*'

Her eyes drifted shut when he kissed her, her heart thudding very hard against her breastbone, anticipation running like a fiery river of molten lava through her. 'Cristiano...' she whispered, feeling the sensitive peaks of her breasts tighten and throb below the rough towelling.

He pulled back from her again, and reached up with a leisurely hand to tug loose the towel. He made a ragged sound of appreciation low in his throat when he had bared the pouting swells of her breasts. 'I love your body...I love what it does for mine.'

To steady herself, her fingers spread like a starfish on his hard muscular thigh. He stroked a tender candy-pink nipple with skilful fingers that knew a woman's body as well as his own. He listened to her breath catch, watched her tremble. His scrutiny was so intense that she muttered anxiously, 'What?'

'You want me so much and you can't hide it. I like that,' he confided thickly. 'You excite me.'

She was mesmerised by his compelling gaze. 'Do I?'

'Sex has never been this hot for me. If you tried to walk away from me now, I'd lock you up,' he swore.

'I'm not going anywhere.'

'Anywhere that I don't, *cara mia,*' Cristiano affixed with husky satisfaction, tumbling her down to him to taste her reddened mouth with an erotic intimacy that made her tummy perform a somersault.

'That's romantic…'

Cristiano tensed. 'There are more of my mother's genes in me than I like to admit. I won't be unfaithful to you, but I don't do the romantic stuff.'

'I only said that because it sounded better than admitting that the only thing I like about you is how you make me feel in bed!' Lydia snapped back at him in a defensive surge.

Cristiano laughed, tipping up her chin, pinning her under him so that he could kiss her again with slow, sensual deliberation. 'You're such a liar…such a gorgeous, sexy liar. You have so much to learn, and I will very much enjoy teaching you.'

Lydia was embarrassed and uneasy, wondering why he had so smoothly brushed off her declaration of indifference to him. 'Teaching me what?'

'How to enslave me between the sheets,' he teased,

sliding off the bed to skim away his shirt and remove his chinos. 'Methods, techniques, timing.'

'I don't want to be taught that sort of thing.' Watching him, she felt her mouth run dry. She felt as though a pool of honey was dissolving inside her, and the charge of that languorous heat made her quiver.

'Yes, you do, *gioia mia*.' Cristiano came down to her again, smoothing caressing hands over the pale skin of her narrow shoulders, leaving an invisible trail of fire where he touched her. 'Although it would take a lot of patience and discipline on my part, and right at this moment those qualities are in very short supply.'

His brilliant golden eyes were raking over her small white breasts and rosy nipples with unashamed hunger. Her face was burning, and her body was equally heated. She was breathing in short rapid spurts. Desire was in her and she couldn't suppress it. He raised her up on her knees and toyed with the tender buds until she moaned, and then he kissed her with roughened masculine need. He traced the delicate flesh between her thighs and she shivered, wanting him, needing him. It was as though her bones were melting below her super-sensitive skin. When he stroked the most tender spot of all she gasped, whimpered, momentarily losing herself within that surging tide of drowningly sweet pleasure.

'I can't bear it,' she finally cried, rising up against him, rebelling against the tormenting ache of need that drove her.

He took her without words in a storm of passion that sent response hurtling through her in a fireball of energy. Answering her wildness, he cast aside his smooth self-control and plunged into her with hard, sensual force. Frenzied excitement seized her. She had never been so attuned to him. She was stunned that he could know so exactly what she craved.

She wasn't prepared when he pulled out of her and re-arranged her almost roughly on her knees. In shock and arousal, she gasped his name.

'Trust me,' he urged raggedly.

Without hesitation he hungrily repossessed her willing body with a primal savagery that drove her out of her mind with pleasure. When her world erupted in a dazzling rush of ecstatic sensation she went with it in mindless acceptance. Convulsive waves of delight quivered through her while he vented an uninhibited growl of satisfaction and shuddered with release.

'Hmm…' Having tipped her over and drawn her back into his arms, with a hair-roughened thigh hooked over hers to hold her in place, Cristiano nuzzled her brow and sighed, 'You're sensational, *bella mia.*'

'So we can skip the lessons?' she dared, languorous with the sense of joy and contentment that always followed their passion.

Husky laughter shifted him in the circle of her arms. 'No. You can tell me why you were still a virgin when I had my wicked way with you.'

Lydia tensed, her fingers absently stroking over the satin smooth damp skin of his back. 'I was very wary, and not very interested when I was younger. Maybe I took longer to grow up than other girls. My mother had a boy-friend who tried to get into bed with me once. Nothing happened, because I screamed the place down, but he really scared me and made me feel bad about myself,' she shared. 'Mum said I must've encouraged him—'

Cristiano raised his head, his beautiful dark eyes narrowed to gleaming pinpoints of steel. 'You're kidding me? What age were you?'

'Thirteen. He'd been living with us a couple of months

when it happened.' She grimaced. 'Something about him gave me the creeps, but I could never work out what it was. Then one night, when Mum was out, he started coming on to me and I went up to bed to get away. If Mum hadn't come back early and found him in my room, I don't know what would've happened.'

'I do—and if you'd been raped I imagine your mother would've found some way to blame you for that too!' Cristiano cut in with contempt.

Lydia winced. 'Don't say that. You've got to understand how upset she was! She was hoping to marry him.'

'Her first loyalty should still have been to you.' Cristiano smoothed a surprisingly gentle forefinger down over her cheekbone and studied her. 'No wonder you were still a virgin, after that frightening introduction to the adult world of sex! I was an insensitive bastard as well. I was so hot for you I had no patience.'

'It just all feels different with you,' she muttered, unable to find the words to describe how that was when she didn't understand it herself.

'I want to hear that it feels earth-shattering with me, *gioia mia,*' he breathed in a low pitched undertone that skimmed her spine like a caress.

As she was smiling helplessly at that shameless invitation to boost an ego that required no such encouragement, Cristiano flipped back from her without warning, his lean, darkly handsome features set taut. He swore rawly in his own language.

'What's wrong?' Lydia demanded anxiously.

Cristiano stared at her with bemused golden eyes. 'I didn't use a condom. For the first time in my life, I forgot!'

Lydia tensed. 'I'm not taking anything…'

Still evidently dumbstruck by his oversight in the contraceptive stakes, Cristiano squared his aggressive jawline. 'When will we know whether or not you're pregnant?'

She reddened, and shut her eyes to recall dates and count. 'In about two weeks.'

'So right now you're at your most fertile?' he deduced. 'How do you feel about babies?'

'Never thought about them.'

'Neither have I,' Cristiano admitted, still deep in shock at his own carelessness. 'But if we're unlucky—'

'Isn't it funny how a single word can say so much? *Unlucky...*' Lydia was pale.

'All I meant to say was that I'll look after you...and the baby,' he tacked on, his accent very thick. 'So you don't need to worry about that angle.'

'I'm not worrying,' she lied, thinking how dreadful it would be to end up unintentionally pregnant by a guy whose sole source of interest in her was her ability to amuse him in bed. 'But I could go to the doctor and ask for the morning-after pill.'

'No.' Cristiano's rejection of that suggestion was immediate, and it surprised him as much as it surprised her. 'I don't want that. That wouldn't sit well with me. We'll wait and see.'

Cristiano settled back against the pillows, scrutinised her taut profile, and then eased an arm round her to pull her up against him again. 'Get some sleep and stop worrying,' he instructed huskily. 'We're heading back to Italy tomorrow.'

'I wish I qualified for air miles.'

He laughed in surprise and appreciation and doused the lights.

She snuggled in to him, imagining herself with a buggy. She really quite liked the idea, and blinked in confusion in the darkness. It would be a disaster if she *had* conceived, she reminded herself in consternation. She couldn't act like a silly kid and daydream about motherhood without considering the realities. What was happening to her? Furthermore, what had happened to that hatred she had been so certain she felt? That terrible bitterness had ebbed, although the same fear of hurt lived on inside her, she acknowledged ruefully. Was she falling for him again?

Cristiano ran a possessive hand down over a slender hip. 'How tired are you?'

'Not that tired,' she whispered breathlessly, excitement licking at her between one breath and the next, and all serious thought suspended.

A wonderful pair of stylish diamond earrings sparkled up at Lydia. She paled and, pushing the case back across the table, spun away. 'I can't accept these…I can't!'

Cristiano gave her an exasperated appraisal. 'What's the matter with you? It's a gift…you can't refuse it!'

'You've given me a necklace, a bracelet, a watch…now these. And I bet they're worth a fortune!'

'So I'm not cheap, *bella mia*. I'm generous. It's a character trait, and it's supposed to be plus in my favour.' Cristiano closed his hands over her slender wrists and tugged her inexorably closer.

Lydia resisted the temptation to point out that he needed no more pluses in his favour. She was hugely uncomfortable with the outrageous number of extravagant presents he was giving her. Did he think she expected such riches? Did he feel he had to pay for her services? Wasn't the vast sum he had paid out to the Happy Holidays charity sufficient? Whatever, her jewel box—an extremely expensive miniature antique trunk that had also been a gift—was full to overflowing with dazzling diamonds and sapphires!

'Maybe it makes me *feel* cheap,' she muttered accusingly. 'Some people would call those diamonds the wages of sin!'

Cristiano groaned in disbelief. 'You can be such a drama queen.'

'Who made me sign that horrible contract?'

Cristiano did not want to think about the contract. He locked her to him and claimed her soft pink lips with a devastating hunger that had not abated, even though they had been together without a break for weeks. 'I like structure and rules. I misjudged you. There's much more than a legal agreement operating between us now.'

Lydia wanted so badly to believe him.

The phone rang and he set her free to answer it. Strolling over to the boundary wall of the terrace, she sat down. The golden sunlight was wonderfully warm on her skin. The same glorious, timeless view of the green valley of fields and vineyards had greeted her every morning and evening for almost three weeks. She could hardly believe that she had been in Tuscany with Cristiano for so long. The days had flown, when she would have preferred every moment to pass by at a snail's pace because she was so incredibly happy.

No longer was she trying to convince herself of her undying hatred for him. She had accepted that she loved him and she wasn't ashamed of her feelings any more. When he walked into a room it was as if the sun came out inside her. When he smiled it gave her a floaty feeling. When she wakened in his arms in the morning she felt safe and contented. When he touched her, emotion and sensation came together so powerfully she had felt tears sting her eyes more than once.

It was his fault she had fallen for him, she reflected ruefully. He had been so incredibly attentive, affectionate and romantic. He might not do love, but he did do candle-lit dinners, moonlight walks through the gardens, picnics in secret glades in the forest. They had walked hand in hand through medieval hill towns, sat in sleepy restaurants talking for hours. He had taken her to see a dietician and had had to grudgingly accept that, while a few extra pounds of weight would do her no harm, she was naturally thin. He had patiently helped her with her Italian lessons. He had flown her to Paris for a concert given by her favourite singer and taken her to view the two famous gardens in the vicinity.

Was it any wonder that once or twice she had wondered if he was the same guy she had first met? After all, when they had dated he had been an incurable workaholic who would not spare the time to get to know her. But now he was continually cutting short his working hours to be with her. The change in his attitude meant a lot to her. She had decided that since she was happy, and happiness was not that easy to find, she should live for the moment and strive to forget their relationship's questionable beginnings.

Just two clouds marred her contentment. The apprehension that Cristiano's moment of forgetfulness in bed might have fertile consequences *did* worry her. She had tried not to worry too much, for she had persuaded herself that there was only a very small risk of such a development. Even so, she was firmly convinced that an unplanned pregnancy would destroy their relationship, for no male appreciated his freedom more than Cristiano.

Her greatest concern, however, related to her mother, who had still to get back in touch with her. Lydia had phoned everyone with a connection to the older woman, and had been surprised that so many of those people had told her that they hadn't seen or spoken to Virginia in months or even years. Her failure to establish a single lead to her mother's whereabouts had left Lydia feeling that she didn't know the older woman as well as she had believed. Surely her mother could not have intended to disappear from her daughter's life so completely?

'Okay…' Cristiano breathed. 'Tell me what's up.'

She sighed. 'I'm worried about my mum. I'm starting to think that she's disappeared off the face of this earth!'

'Since when?'

'Since just before I was arrested. She was afraid she'd be accused with me, and got in a panic.'

'Why? Was she involved in the fashion show as well?' Cristiano directed a look of polite enquiry at her, and she relaxed a little and advanced further details in answer to his questions. 'Would you like me to see if I can find out anything for you?'

'Yes…but I don't see how.'

'I have great resources.' Cristiano thought it likely that the results of the checks he had ordered on Lydia might well contain some useful leads. He had left that report sitting unopened and unread in London, because investigating Lydia without her knowledge had belatedly struck him as unethical. He would have it forwarded.

'I'd be really grateful. I'm worried sick about her,' Lydia admitted honestly. 'Her marriage broke up shortly before she went away, so goodness knows what sort of state of mind she might be in.'

'I'll find her for you, *cara mia.*' Cristiano consulted his watch, slanting ebony brows drawing together. 'But right now we have an appointment to keep, and we should make a move.'

Lydia gave him a puzzled glance. 'What appointment?'

Cristiano shrugged with a shade less cool than was usual. 'I think it makes sense for you to have a pregnancy test done by a doctor, so I've gone ahead and organised it.'

Lydia was truly taken aback. 'But that's crazy...I can easily buy a test.'

'A test you perform yourself might give a false result.'

Lydia flushed and lowered her lashes. Obviously he was really worried that she might have conceived. He had hidden the fact well, only casually alluding to the possibility on a couple of occasions since that night. But now it was clear that he was not prepared to wait even another couple of days to see if there was cause for a test to be done.

'If you prefer this way of going about things...that's fine,' she muttered uncomfortably.

'It's something we should share,' Cristiano decreed with assurance.

The appointment was at a private clinic. The doctor, a suave gynaecologist, left them in his smart office and re-appeared with a grave expression. 'The test was negative. You're not pregnant, Miss Powell.'

Lydia was quite unprepared for the sharp stab of disappointment that afflicted her in response to that news.

Cristiano was stunned. He had firmly believed that she would be pregnant. They were both young and healthy. For fifteen years he had assiduously guarded against any possibility of conception. He had never taken a risk, made a mistake or had an accident. Was it any wonder that he had been fully convinced that one contraceptive oversight would infallibly lead to the creation of a baby? All that said, however, he reasoned, in a bewilderment that was new to him, it should still be a huge *relief* to receive the news that he was not to become a father.

Lydia was struggling to feel equally relieved. It occurred to her that in recent weeks Mother Nature had been playing games with her subconscious mind. While on the surface she had maintained a sensible attitude to the concept of an unplanned pregnancy, little daydreams, doubtless fuelled by sneaky female hormones, had made her consider the possibility of motherhood for the very first time. And the truth was that she had really warmed to the idea of having a baby.

'I'm sure you must be pleased that we don't have anything to worry about any more,' she muttered tautly when they were back in the limo.

Cristiano said nothing in response to that leading question. Lean, strong face impassive, he was deep in thought.

Her eyes were stinging. She was seriously embarrassed, and terrified he would notice that she was upset. A lump formed in her throat and she tried and failed to swallow. She blinked back tears furiously.

'Perhaps it is human nature to want what has been denied,' Cristiano commented. 'You're disappointed, aren't you?'

'No, I'm not!' she gasped chokily, rifling through all his pockets to find a hanky and then burying her face in it. 'It's just the tension, that's all…and now I'm feeling a little tearful.'

'I'd like to have a baby with you, *gioia mia*,' Cristiano told her, as though it was the most natural thing in the world.

CHAPTER NINE

THE hanky dropped from Lydia's nerveless fingers. Her tear-drenched blue eyes locked to his lean, darkly handsome features with dazed uncertainty, for she was unable to credit that he meant what he had said. 'Are you teasing me?'

'It's not a joking matter. I am very much in earnest,' Cristiano asserted in his dark deep drawl. 'I've realised that I would like a child.'

'Oh...' It was all she could think of to say. The thought of having a baby with Cristiano was making nonsense of all rational thought, for at that moment he was offering her what she most wanted on earth. Indeed, it shook her that her desire for a child could have gone so deep.

'I suppose it is natural.' Cristiano shifted a lean brown hand in a graceful gesture of acceptance. 'I've reached a stage in life where I'm ready to be a father. This little drama of ours has simply brought that truth home to me. I, too, was disappointed when we learned that there was not to be a child.'

'I honestly didn't know I'd feel like that,' she admitted in a rush, attempting to put her thoughts in order. 'I just can't believe that you feel the same way.'

Enquiring golden eyes rested on hers. 'Why not?'

She could've told him fifty reasons why not. Babies weren't cool lifestyle choices. Babies didn't travel well and he never stopped. But, most of all, babies deserved two parents. Although that wasn't always possible, it was definitely an objective that required serious consideration. Her thoughts were spinning like whirling dervishes, leaving her dizzy. 'I don't fancy being a single parent,' she admitted abruptly.

The silence simmered and bubbled like a witch's cauldron on the boil.

Cristiano surveyed her with inhuman calm. 'So…you have a point to make?'

Lydia went very pink and studied her linked hands. Just weeks ago he had proposed. She had shouted *no* on principle, and that had been that. She had let pride and bitterness do her talking for her. It had since occurred to her that she might have been more than a little hasty in giving him that spirited negative response. Yes, she would love to be valued for something more than her ability to entertain him in bed several times a day. On the other hand, it would be grossly unjust of her not to acknowledge that she was pleasing herself there too. Everything in the bedroom department was absolutely amazing, and she had no complaints whatsoever. In fact, on every level, life with Cristiano was wildly exceeding her expectations. He treated her so well. He made her feel incredibly happy. But she could not rely on that. He didn't love her, and inevitably their affair would run its course and come to an end.

'Lydia…?'

'Shush…I'm thinking very hard here.' She sighed, thinking worriedly that it would be very wrong to even consider having a baby in such an insecure relationship.

It didn't matter that she believed that a child would be a comfort to her when he had gone from her life. That would be a very selfish way to look at parenting, she decided shamefacedly. She had to act like a responsible adult. She might love him and want his baby but only the commitment of marriage would give them both security. How much did he want to be a father? Enough to marry her?

'Can I help?' Cristiano enquired gently.

Before she could lose her nerve, Lydia breathed in very deep, and just fired the words at him. 'I'll be happy to have a baby with you. But there's a condition.'

'No pain, no gain,' Cristiano quipped, lush black lashes low over smouldering golden eyes as he let a caressing masculine fingertip slowly skate a provocative trail down over her slender thigh, smiling when she shivered. 'But we could shelve the negotiation until sunset, and spend the afternoon working on the project, *carissima*.'

Her heart skipped a beat, and then raced with a sad lack of self-control. She shot him a sidewise glance, tummy flipping when she met his stunning eyes. 'I'm trying to have a serious talk here... What I want to say is that I'll have a baby if you marry me...'

Cristiano elevated a sleek ebony brow in apparent surprise. 'So what happened to love?'

Lydia blinked. 'I beg your pardon?'

'You said you would only marry for love,' he reminded her smoothly.

Lydia blushed to the roots of her hair and shifted uneasily on her seat. 'Well, perhaps that was a bit...er...fanciful,' she selected in desperation.

'You also said that you wouldn't marry..."someone like me" I believe was the term you used.'

She winced, and then up came her chin. 'So I changed my mind? It would be better if you could just forget some of the stuff I said that morning.'

'I have a photographic memory. To recap—marriage is your condition?'

'Gosh, did it sound like I was pointing a loaded shotgun at you?'

Not a flicker of expression revealed Cristiano's opinion on that score. 'It's my first proposal. I have no basis for comparison.'

Mortification was welling up through her like a fountain. 'You are obviously trying to avoid saying no. That's okay—don't worry about it. I'm really not bothered,' she framed as jaggedly as broken glass.

Cristiano cleared his throat.

It belatedly dawned on Lydia that the chauffeur had opened the door for her to alight. She scrambled out and headed at a speedy rate of knots into the *palazzo*. She was so embarrassed she wanted to curl up and die. She had asked him to marry her! How could she have done that? All right, so she had regretted turning him down outright. She'd known that even the direst torture would not persuade him to mention the idea again. But she should've been more subtle. Tears of hurt and anger were stinging her eyes.

Abruptly she spun back to him in the hall. 'It's because you think I'm a thief, isn't it? Well, maybe that's not as cut and dried as you believe. I mean…maybe I *didn't* take the money! Has that idea ever occurred to you? Did you ever wonder what I did with two hundred and fifty grand when I was renting a house that would fit under your stairs?'

'On several occasions,' Cristiano admitted. 'You have

no decent jewellery, no expensive possessions, and from what I have so far seen no extravagant habits. But you could have been in serious debt.'

Lydia had fallen silent. She worried at the soft underside of her full lower lip. She hated him thinking that she was dishonest. At the outset of their relationship she had been too desperate for help to worry, and too bitter to care about his opinion of her. But now Cristiano's view of her mattered a great deal, and she really did want to tell him the truth. After all, now the missing funds had been replaced, she reasoned anxiously, did she need to continue the pretence that she had stolen the charity money?

Just as quickly as she thought that, she realised that she still had good reason for keeping quiet on that score. Cristiano could be very black and white in his outlook, unforgiving and intolerant of shades of grey. Suppose she admitted the truth and he decided to report her mother to the police? Was that still possible? She had no idea. But she did suspect that Cristiano would react badly to the news. Trusting him with too much information might compromise everything she had so far done to protect Virginia. Right now, Cristiano was not only keen to help her find her mother, but he also had the resources to do so. If she admitted that Virginia was the guilty party who had helped herself to charitable funds, would he still be so willing? It was certain to affect his attitude. At the very least he would be furious that she had let him credit a lie.

Cristiano pressed a firm hand to her slender spine and urged her into the grand drawing room. He leant back against the door, his shrewd gaze intent on her troubled face. 'You're wondering whether or not to tell me something, *bella mia*. Let me make that decision for you. Now that I know that there's a secret, there will be no peace on this earth for you until you tell all.'

'There's no secret…' Suddenly the very last thing Lydia wanted to do was open a controversial subject that would annoy him.

'You can tell me anything.'

'There's nothing to tell.'

'It's a very bad idea to lie to me,' Cristiano warned her with chilling softness, dark eyes shorn of gold enticement. 'You're not a good liar either.'

Her colour fluctuated, a tight knot of alarm forming in her tummy. The atmosphere had dropped several degrees in the blink of an eye. 'It's not something that would hurt you.'

'Perhaps I'm not prepared to let you make that judgement call.'

'Please…it's not important,' she protested.

'If I'm going to marry you, I need to know I can trust you. So you think about that angle, and work out whether or not you have something you want to share with me,' Cristiano advised with devastating cool as he walked over to the tall window and swung back round to face her.

'That's blackmail!' Lydia condemned in consternation.

Cristiano shrugged with magnificent disregard of the effect that it would have on restoring peaceful relations. 'It is me telling you like it is.'

'I don't want to marry you anyway!' she launched back at him in angry frustration.

Cristiano released a weary groan. '*Dio mio,* please don't start that refrain again.'

'Why? Do you find it so hard to believe that I wouldn't want to marry you?'

Brilliant golden eyes struck literal sparks off her challenging blue gaze. 'I have my reasons.'

'Explain those reasons.'

'I don't want to.'

'I don't like secrets either.'

'Let's wind this down,' Cristiano breathed with sudden impatience. 'This is not a conversation we need to have—'

'Yes, it is. I want to know why you are so certain that I want to marry you!'

Cristiano shifted lean brown hands in a silencing gesture. 'This is getting very childish.'

If anything, that comment only made Lydia even angrier. 'You shouldn't say things that you can't justify.'

Cristiano shot her a glittering glance, strode over to the desk, extracted something from a drawer and set it out. 'You shouldn't challenge me…'

Lydia stared at the familiar photo, which she had last seen when she was packing up her possessions in Wales. Immediately she realised that she must have overlooked it and left it lying on the windowsill. Confronted with it in Italy, however, she could not credit her eyesight and was literally struck dumb. Where had he got it from?

Cristiano watched every scrap of colour ebb from beneath her translucent skin and cursed his competitive instincts and his temper. He wondered why his cool logic always let him down around her. As he approached her she sidestepped him in an abrupt movement, snatched up the old photo frame and clasped it in front of her.

'I shouldn't have shown you,' he said flatly.

'How did you get hold of this? I think you owe me an explanation for that at least.'

He told her about Gwenna's visit to his office.

She swallowed hard, imagining how shocked her cousin would have been by that contract. Gwenna certainly wouldn't have intended to embarrass her. But that Cristiano should have seen that photograph stripped Lydia of all pride. Her biggest secret, and Cristiano now knew that he had been her idol when she was a brainless little teenager, with nothing better to do than mope over a guy she'd never met. Her sense of humiliation knew no bounds. For goodness' sake, had her cousin also let drop that Lydia had referred to Cristiano as the love of her life?

Feeling literally sick with mortification, she yanked open the door.

'Lydia…' Cristiano breathed. 'Where are you going?'

'I need fresh air!' She raced down the hall, pausing only to scoop up the keys of the sports car he had said she was free to use.

'I don't want you driving in the mood you're in!'

Nothing could have made Lydia more determined to get into a car.

The sleek little Lamborghini gunned down the long drive at a satisfying pace—fast enough to give him pause for thought—but she slowed right down the minute she rounded a corner and was no longer within sight. That wretched juvenile picture of him! Why had she ever kept it? Her teeth gritted. She headed up the steep twisting road to the little fortified hill town at the top.

Parking the car beside a medieval church, she walked down a flight of worn steps to the sunny *piazza*. She ordered a soft drink at the wine bar where she had sat with Cristiano one evening a week earlier. Everyone who'd walked by had known him. The local priest had joined them for a glass of wine. There had been a constant procession of people wandering up to exchange news with Cristiano. She had noticed that here in the town he had known since childhood he was very relaxed.

She loved him, she conceded ruefully. So what if he

suspected that? Was her pride more important to her than her happiness? And hadn't he been right to say that if they were going to marry they should have no secrets from each other? Now that her angry mortification had had a chance to cool, she was willing to admit that she liked that idea. That was a good solid principle on which to base a relationship—so why was she refusing to trust him with the truth about the Happy Holidays money?

Cristiano brought his Ferrari to a far from cool halt beside the Lamborghini and leapt out. He could not understand why he had shown her that photo. It had been a bloody insensitive thing to do! But why had she taken off like that? Where was she? He glanced inside the church. He strode over to the low wall which warned the unwary of the sheer terrifying drop into the valley far below. If anything had happened to her, he would never forgive himself.

A wolf-whistle sounded in the hot still air and he swung round to see where it had come from. He saw her from the top of the steps. She was an exquisitely feminine vision in a mint skirt and a sleeveless top. His heartbeat steadied again. The kid who had whistled waved at him from the *piazza* and ran off laughing.

When she saw Cristiano crossing the *piazza*, her mouth ran dry. He was so very Italian, in his elegant, beautifully cut white shirt and cream chinos, and looked absolutely gorgeous with sunshine gilding his ebony hair and superb bone structure.

'May I sit down?'

'Well, you've chased off the competition…that little boy will go far.'

'He knew you were already taken, *gioia mia.*'

Her sapphire-blue eyes glimmered. 'Is that a fact?'

'I'm sorry I upset you,' he breathed tautly. 'But I

thought it was really sweet that you had a photo of me at that age. I was honoured, and very touched.'

Her cheeks warmed, for his words still stung. He had probably guessed that she loved him. Why else would he be honoured and touched? A guy notorious for his lack of heart? *Sweet*? He felt sorry for her, didn't he? Here she was, she had fallen like a ton of bricks for him before she even met him, and after all this time he was still the only man she had ever cared about! She decided that a change of subject would be her wisest move.

'I've got something to tell you,' she announced once the barman had poured their wine and returned to reading his newspaper in the sunshine. 'It wasn't me who took the charity money. It was my mum…'

Cristiano studied her with frowning force, not a muscle moving in his bold bronzed features. For a split second he closed his eyes, and then he released his breath in a slow ragged exhalation.

'My stepfather, Dennis, left her with a lot of debt, and she borrowed from the charity account. Of course she didn't think through the reality—that once she'd settled bills with the money she had no way of replacing it.'

His bronzed complexion had developed a pale cast. 'But why didn't you tell me this weeks ago?'

'I would've told you eventually, but at the start I couldn't imagine us being together even this long,' she confessed. 'I didn't really care what you thought of me either. I was worried sick about Mum. I only accepted your financial help when I realised that the police intended to track her down and question her.'

Cristiano looked grave. 'You could have told me the truth.'

'I didn't actually think you would be that interested in whether or not I was guilty.'

His lean powerful face tightened at that admission.

'And I didn't trust you,' Lydia admitted ruefully. 'How did I know how you would react? You might have gone and told all to the police just on principle. I kept it secret to protect my mother. And even now I feel bad about telling you. I don't want you to think badly of her.'

'I can't imagine why I would do that,' Cristiano murmured stonily, pushing his empty glass away. 'Why would I think badly of a woman who stole a quarter of a million from underprivileged children and left her daughter to face the music?'

Lydia directed a look of reproach at him and watched him pay for the wine. They mounted the steps from the *piazza* together. 'I've never been anything but bad luck for my mother, and I was more than willing to do whatever it took to help her when she needed me,' she admitted tautly. 'Please try to understand that it was my choice.'

'Including making the ultimate sacrifice in my bed?' Cristiano vented an unamused laugh and raked a rough hand through his cropped black hair, his lean, vibrantly handsome face bleak. 'When I said I owed you, a few weeks ago, I had no idea how much.'

'You don't owe me anything. I chose to mislead you. And if you find out where my mother is now, I'll be forever grateful.'

'That's the least of what I can do. Get in the Ferrari. Arnaldo can bring the Lamborghini back.'

Lydia climbed into the passenger seat of his car. 'Does it ever occur to you that, as sacrifices go, I'm a reasonably happy one?'

Brooding dark golden eyes met hers levelly. 'I wanted you at any price, *bella mia*. Honour and decency didn't come into it until it was too late to change anything. I'll always regret that.' He drove the powerful car down the hill at a speed that she would not have dared on a straight road, never mind a twisting one. 'But I promise that no matter what it takes I'll find your mother for you.'

Her wide warm smile began to blossom. 'And you won't report her to the police or anything?'

'I doubt that they'd be interested when there's no charge left to answer.'

Back at the *palazzo*, Lydia hovered several inches from him, helpfully within reach. She wanted him to haul her into his arms and drag her off to bed, or make mad passionate love to her on the spot. He didn't usually require encouragement. She felt slightly foolish when he said that he had some phone calls to make.

She dined alone that evening, and went to bed early, on the principle that he deserved to have to come looking for her.

She rose early the next morning, distinctly troubled by Cristiano's failure to put in an appearance. She went for a stroll in the dappled shade of the trees. At that hour the gardens were cool and silent. She was relieved when she emerged from a tranquil green arbour of vines and saw Cristiano striding towards her.

He came to a halt several feet away. 'I have an address for your mother!'

Lydia was astonished. 'My word—how did you manage to find that out so soon?'

Cristiano told her about the report he had ordered several weeks earlier. She nodded, not particularly concerned, because she was much more interested in learning Virginia's whereabouts. The report had contained a lead that he had had followed up. 'France?' she repeated. 'Okay—so…'

'The jet's on standby. We'll leave at noon, *cara mia.*'

A huge smile curved her soft full mouth. 'How am I ever going to thank you for this?'

It seemed to her that his lean dark features shadowed, but when he closed his hands over hers and tugged her into his arms she believed she must have been mistaken. He gazed down at her, stunning dark golden eyes very serious. 'You can say thank you by marrying me, *carissima*.'

'Yes…oh, yes,' she said immediately, and she thought he might laugh at the speed of her response but he didn't.

'I want to do it all by the book. We'll throw a massive engagement party so that I can show you off to all my friends.'

Misgivings stirred, in spite of her attempt to stay totally positive. Was he only marrying her because he felt he owed it to her?

Signing her up to a contract had definitely given him the chance to get in touch with his conscience, she reflected worriedly. Here she was, like Faithful Penelope in the legend, not quite growing old waiting for him, but certainly in the dogged and devoted category. But why shouldn't he like that? And when he had decided he'd like to be a father, why not choose her? After all, as he had so freely admitted, he didn't do love.

He eased her into the shelter of his lean powerful body and showed her what he *did* do. It wasn't love, she acknowledged, but even before he savoured her ripe mouth she literally couldn't breathe for excitement.

'Don't stop,' she mumbled between frantic kisses, backing up against the trunk of a tree, every inch of her exuding weak, wanton invitation.

'We must,' Cristiano sighed. 'I've invited a friend in the jewellery trade to call with a selection of rings.'

The speed with which everything was happening continued to surprise Lydia. Cristiano was usually a cautious guy. Now he was suggesting that the engagement party be staged within a fortnight and the wedding date be set immediately. In a magnificent reception room in the *palazzo*, she agonised with immense enjoyment over a gorgeous choice of rings, before finally choosing a ravishing diamond cluster that she adored.

Lydia was so excited at the prospect of seeing her mother again and introducing Cristiano to her that she couldn't settle during the flight. She flicked through magazines and picked at her lunch.

Cristiano was very quiet, and when she finally noticed that it bothered her.

'Is there something the matter?' Lydia asked in the limo that picked them up at the airport.

'I think you may be in for a few surprises when you see your mother.'

She tensed. 'What sort of surprises?'

'She would appear to be living with your stepfather—Dennis.'

'Oh, my word—have they got back together again? That's wonderful…she'll be over the moon!' Lydia declared with satisfaction.

Cristiano reached for her hand. 'I can't let you walk into this unprepared—'

'Unprepared for what?'

'I believe that you've been the victim of some very cruel scams. I've checked out certain facts. That nightclub in which you invested did not go bust to the tune of anything like the amount of money you lost. I think your stepfather used the club venture to strip you of your savings.'

Lydia studied him in horror. 'Are you serious? You honestly believe Dennis is a crook?'

'He's a conman with a criminal record for petty theft.'

'But he's an accountant—'

'He has no professional qualifications. I'm afraid I also suspect that Dennis did not work alone. I know you don't want to hear this,' Cristiano imparted grimly. 'But all the evidence that I've seen indicates that your mother was fully involved at every level—'

'Stop it—you're right, I don't want to hear it!' Lydia told him, more in dismay than anger. 'You're a terribly cynical person, Cristiano. I'm willing to believe that Dennis is dishonest, but not my mother too.'

The limo had come to a halt while a member of Cristiano's security team spoke into the intercom beside a tall wooden gate. Beyond it she could see the roofline of a substantial villa.

'But this can't be where they're living,' she reasoned when the gate opened and the car moved forward again. 'The police had got hold of some mad rumour about a big house in France as well. I think we're on a wild-goose chase.'

'It wasn't a rumour. Dennis and Virginia had to disappear to enjoy their ill-gotten gains,' Cristiano advanced harshly. 'They go by the names of Janette and Brian Carson here. Your stepfather has set up as a property developer.'

'This can't possibly be my mother's home. It's a case of mistaken identity…it's got to be! If Virginia had this kind of money, why would she have taken the Happy Holidays funds? How could she have been in debt? Why would she have begged me to tell the police that *I* took the missing cash?'

'Greed. A last little sting before they embarked on their new life as well-heeled ex-pats. You'd never have heard from them again.'

'You are wrong…' Lydia almost fell out of the car in her haste to vacate it.

A middle-aged maid answered the door. Behind her, Lydia saw her mother, clad in a sunhat and a stylish shift dress.

'Lydia?' Virginia studied her daughter in horror. 'I thought it was a furniture delivery! How did you get in? How did you find us?'

CHAPTER TEN

LYDIA was trembling. She was afraid to look at her mother, and found it easier at that moment to appraise her surroundings instead. What she saw shattered her hope that there might be an acceptable explanation. This was definitely Virginia's home. The paintings, sculptures and luxurious furniture were all recognisably in her parent's theatrical decorative taste.

'Did Dennis ever walk out on you? Or was that just part of the sob story you fed me?' Lydia enquired tightly.

'We've just reconciled,' Virginia said shrilly.

Unimpressed by that claim, Lydia walked past the older woman into a spacious reception room. Her stepfather, wearing shorts that did not flatter his rotund dimensions, was watching football there, on a giant plasma screen. When he saw his stepdaughter his jaw dropped.

'Where did you get the money for all this?' Lydia asked her mother painfully.

Cristiano appeared in the doorway.

'Who on earth have you brought with you?' Virginia lit a cigarette with a bold flourish.

'Never mind who he is. You told me you were in debt

and broke, but that was obviously untrue,' Lydia continued tightly. 'For how long have you owned this villa?'

'We're only minding this house,' the older woman told her.

'The villa is in your mother's name. She bought it with cash a couple of years ago,' Cristiano contradicted drily. 'You were a very generous daughter, but they wanted everything you had. They siphoned off thousands from your bank accounts.'

'That's a dirty lie!' Her stepfather's heavy face was brick-red.

Cristiano dealt him a look of derision. 'You left a paper trail of evidence any good accountant could follow. Moderate your tone and your attitude. Lydia has enough documentary proof to put both of you in prison for fraud for a good few years.'

'But she won't do it,' Virginia declared, with a complacent smile of challenge. 'I'm her mother, and what was hers is mine. Didn't you often tell me that, Lydia?'

Lydia found that she was both hurt and shamed by her mother's behaviour. Clearly the older couple had been stealing from her for a very long time, but Virginia's blue eyes, which were so eerily like her own, remained hard and defiant. There was no apology, no regret there.

'Didn't you care that I might go to prison for your crime?' Lydia could not help whispering.

The blonde woman made no answer.

Lydia could feel tears welling up, and she fought them with all her might. In that silence lay her answer. Gwenna had once called her the family cash cow, and now she saw the truth of that wounding label. She had been valued only for the money she could bring home. Recalling how much

Virginia and Dennis had resented her decision to retire from modelling, she almost shuddered. When the cash cow had run dry they had had to devise new ways of stripping her of her savings.

With as much dignity as she could muster, Lydia walked straight-backed out of the villa and climbed into the limo. It moved off, and she stared out of the window with blank eyes. Fierce emotion was warring within her. Then, without a word, she scrambled along the seat and flung herself into Cristiano's arms. He said nothing, which was fortunate, for she believed that words of sympathy would make her break down completely. Her eyes burned but she didn't cry.

'She never loved me...and deep down inside I always knew it too,' she muttered chokily. 'But I used to try so hard to please her.'

'I won't let her hurt you ever again, *gioia mia*.'

He held her close and she shut her eyes tight, loving him with so much force and passion she quivered. Desperate to offer something back, she said, 'I'll try getting on your yacht again...okay?'

Above her head, Cristiano drew in a slow deep breath. He smoothed her tumbled hair in a soothing gesture. 'Maybe some time. It's really not important.'

The helicopter flew over the vast roof that distinguished Cristiano's country home in England. Welbrooke Park was a very beautiful country house, and as the helicopter landed Lydia was recalling her last fateful visit, which had concluded with her early-morning departure in Mort Stevens's ridiculously small sports car. She smiled ruefully

at that tragi-comic memory. The agony of pain and disillusionment she had suffered that weekend was far behind
her now. In a couple of hours she would be greeting the
guests invited to their engagement celebrations.

Cristiano, who had been in London on business for two
days, strode out of the drawing room to greet her. 'Come
and meet some of my friends,' he imparted, and then, half
under his breath, 'Sorry, I had hoped to have you to myself
for a while, but it's not to be.'

Preceding him into the room, she stiffened when she
saw Philip Hazlett, but relaxed when she was introduced
to his languid fiancée, Jodie.

'Quite the miracle-worker, aren't you?' Philip remarked
under cover of the general conversation. 'You went from
rank outsider to winner and took us all by surprise.'

'I'm not sure I understand.'

The thickset banker vented a suggestive laugh. 'Who
wouldn't be impressed? A bimbo with a beautiful body has
caught one of the world's richest men. I can only assume
that you're a real goer in the bedroom!'

Lydia reddened, realising in dismay that her unease in
Philip's radius eighteen months earlier had been well
founded. Some sixth sense had warned her that he was a
creep even before she'd heard him discussing that
infamous bet. 'Don't speak to me like that.'

'If I'd come along before Cristiano, you'd have been
singing a very different tune,' Philip asserted with unmistakable meaning.

'No...never in this lifetime.' Lydia could not hide her
look of revulsion, and she saw angry resentment harden
his florid face before she turned gratefully away.

So that, she thought with an inner shudder, was what she had sensed in Philip Hazlett. He had been attracted to her, and seeing her with Cristiano would've annoyed him—for Philip cherished a high opinion of himself. He was charm personified with women he accepted as his equals, but an ignorant swine with those he considered to be socially beneath him. What a shame that he should be such a close friend of Cristiano's, she reflected uncomfortably. She wasn't planning to tell tales. But Philip would have to get over his need to put her down.

Cristiano strode into the bedroom when she was fresh out of the shower. His dark golden eyes glittered and her tummy flipped, because she knew what that smouldering look meant.

'You smell wonderful,' he breathed, pulling her back against him with single-minded purpose.

'Soap.'

Laughing huskily, he brushed her glorious hair out of his path and pressed his sensual mouth to her neck. A little gasp broke from her lips and she trembled. After forty-eight hours without him, sudden contact made her feel shamelessly wanton. 'My hair and my make-up still have to be done,' she muttered, more than willing to be over-ruled.

'I know…and I won't make you late tonight, *cara mia.*' Cristiano set her back from him with a distinct air of self-denial. 'Maybe I'll drag you into a dark corner around midnight. I don't think I can restrain myself much longer than that. I missed you so much.'

Later, Gwenna came to keep Lydia company.

'So, tell me, what do you think of Cristiano?' Lydia asked almost shyly.

Gwenna pulled a comical face. 'He's a good sport. When I cornered him in his office, he kept his cool.'

'You like him?'

'What woman *wouldn't* like him? He spent fifteen minutes talking to me downstairs. I felt really important. He's a total babe!'

'Gwenna!' Lydia laughed.

'With that amount of charisma, he's definitely a catch.'

'His friend Philip would certainly agree with that. Unfortunately he sees me as a bimbo, who used sex to trap his mate into marriage,' Lydia confided with a grimace.

'Surely the dreadful man didn't dare to say that to your face?'

Lydia told her story, her wounded feelings soothed by Gwenna's annoyance on her behalf. Predictably, Gwenna thought she should tell Cristiano, but Lydia grimaced at the idea. She knew she was probably being silly, but she was scared that if she repeated Philip's comments Cristiano might start wondering whether there were any grains of truth in his friend's derisive opinion of his approaching nuptials. When men talked with other men about such things they could really be quite obnoxious, she thought worriedly, her memory dwelling on that ghastly betting business. Even Cristiano had not been proof against the masculine need to seem ultra-cool and callous. Did some sort of pack instinct come out in guys when they got together?

An hour later Lydia, stunning in a magnificent pale

green ball gown that bared her shoulders, descended the wonderful Georgian staircase. Diamonds sparkled like white fire at her ears, throat and wrist. The society photographer waiting to record her appearance took several shots and Cristiano, the very epitome of sleek male fashion, in a cutting-edge designer suit and open-necked black shirt, joined her for another few.

Philip Hazlett was in the crowd of guests watching the photo session, and she glimpsed his sour expression before hurriedly looking away, determined not to let anything spoil her engagement party.

Cristiano whirled her round the ballroom. 'You're on edge, and it's not like you.'

Lydia rested her brow against his shoulder. She was getting really annoyed with herself. It was a wonderful party, and their guests were having a terrific time. Only Philip had been rude. Why was she letting that bother her so much? Was she getting precious? Did she expect everyone to like and approve of her?

But she knew what was the matter with her, didn't she?

Being reminded that all she had to offer Cristiano was her body had been painful. He wasn't in love with her, and that made her feel insecure and vulnerable. Love was like a glue that could keep people together through rain and shine. Cristiano, however, was perfectly happy to settle for amazing sex. He had discovered that he wanted a child, and she had been in the right place at the right time when he decided that he would like to try settling down. That was why she had a dazzling diamond on her engagement finger. But with such a foundation wasn't he likely to get bored with her? And, when he did, what would they use for glue? *Her* love?

Around midnight, she noticed that Gwenna was still dancing with the same man and she smiled. Feeling warm, and wondering where Cristiano was, she walked through the house to the suite of offices he used. She was already deciding what she was going to say if she found him there working when he shouldn't be. The rooms, however, were in darkness. Beyond the windows the gardens had been transformed with glimmering fibre-optic lights. She was thinking how beautiful it looked, and grinning at the sight of the young man being chased by not one but two giggling girls across the lawn, when she heard a noise behind her.

'I thought I'd never get you on your own.'

Lydia spun round, her oval face taut.

Philip Hazlett was leering at her from the doorway. 'What will Cristiano think if he finds you've been down here with me? We've been friends all our lives. He trusts me like a brother. Who do you think he'll believe if I say you were flirting like mad and gagging for it?'

Cold apprehension clutched at Lydia. She could feel his menace. She could feel him savouring her fear. If she screamed it was unlikely anyone would hear her above the music emanating from the party. Philip was blocking the only exit, and he was built like a concrete cube of muscle.

'I'm meeting Cristiano here.'

Philip advanced. 'Don't waste your breath. He's in the main hall, talking business over a brandy.'

Lydia took a sidewise step, staying out of reach, her heart thumping so hard inside her chest that she felt sick. 'Stay away from me—'

'You'll be too scared to tell him I've had you. You have too much to lose,' he asserted smugly. 'It'll be our little secret for evermore…'

Lydia jerked as she saw movement behind Philip. Someone flipped him round and hit him so fast and hard that he crashed down like a felled tree. Trembling, she just stood there gaping as Philip leapt back up—only to be flattened a second time with an even harder punch.

'You filthy bastard!' Cristiano growled, only backing off to extend a strong supportive arm round Lydia, whose state of shock was patent. 'If you had laid one finger on her I'd have killed you for it! But you frightened her, and that's bad enough. I'm calling the police—'

'No—no police,' Lydia mumbled unevenly. 'He didn't touch me. Don't him let him spoil the party. Just get him out of here!'

Arnaldo gave her an approving nod and anchored a hand like a giant meat hook in Philip's jacket, to remove him from the scene.

Lydia was shaking like a leaf. 'How did you know I was here?'

'Arnaldo was keeping an eye on you and on Philip all evening. I suspected Philip had said something to you when you arrived. You went all quiet, and I noticed the freaky way he was watching you. It wasn't the first time I'd noticed his interest in you.' His strong jawline squared. 'He always wanted you, *bella mia.*'

'You *knew* that?'

Cristiano gave her a rueful look as he shepherded her out into the corridor. 'Look in the mirror. *All* my friends wanted you. I couldn't make it a hanging offence. I didn't think anything of it eighteen months ago. But this time around, with Philip engaged to Jodie, I found it offensive and rather disturbing.'

'I thought he was your best friend.'

'Did he tell you that? I've tolerated him because I do a lot of business with his father, who is everything the son is not. I have nothing in common with Philip now. What friendship we had left withered over that crass bet. Tonight...' Cristiano paused, his dark golden gaze gleaming over her pallor and hardening to cold steel. 'Tonight I could have killed him.'

'I was really scared—'

'Blame me for that. I had no idea that he might have an assault in mind,' Cristiano breathed with fierce regret. 'I thought he might be pestering you and making a nuisance of himself. I intended to put a stop to it. But you were never in any danger. Arnaldo would have intervened had I not arrived.'

'I suppose we should go back to our guests.'

But Cristiano directed her up a flight of service stairs. 'They don't need us present to party. You've had an unpleasant experience and you need time to recover from that. If that bastard had managed to touch you—'

'But he *didn't*...' Stretching up on tiptoe on the landing, Lydia rested a placating finger against his parted lips. 'I'm unhurt and I'm okay—'

'No thanks to me. I can't even keep you safe from harm under my own roof,' Cristiano growled in a driven voice. 'I'll also have to tell Jodie about what happened. She's an old friend, and it would be wrong to keep it from her.'

'If she loves him, she may not want to know.'

'Thankfully, that's not our business.'

On the threshold of their bedroom, Cristiano scooped Lydia up into his arms and carried her over to the bed, where he laid her down with gentle hands. He studied her with brooding intensity, as if he still wasn't quite sure that she really was all right.

'Will you stop blaming yourself?' she sighed. 'I'm fine—right as rain—fighting fit!'

'Of course I'm blaming myself!' Cristiano fielded without hesitation. 'I didn't appreciate what a nutter Philip was. I seem to screw up everything with you!'

'No, you don't.'

Cristiano looked unconvinced. He moved away several feet, turned in a restless arc like a lion confined in too small a space. 'There are some things I need to tell you…'

Lydia sat up in readiness. Cristiano stared at her, then looked away again, almost imperceptible colour scoring his taut cheekbones.

'Yes…?' Lydia prompted.

'I haven't been straight with you or with myself. I fell in love with you almost two years ago. I saw you on that catwalk and then I heard your voice, saw the way you put your head to one side when you speak. There was just something so unbelievably appealing about you,' he confided, seemingly unaware that she was now studying him with a dropped jaw. 'But I didn't realise that what you made me feel was love, because I hated the trapped feeling it gave me.'

'The…trapped feeling?' Lydia echoed, thrust back down to earth again with a nasty bump. Had he really said what she thought he had? Or had her imagination taken a gigantic leap all on its own?

'I don't think I was ready for anything serious. You got inside my head and spooked me. *Dio mio,* I'd be in a meeting and then *bang*—out of nowhere I'd find that I was thinking about you!' he recalled with a shudder that spoke volumes. 'All my focus would be gone. It was a nightmare. So when I wanted to see you I would make myself wait longer. That way I stayed in control of events.'

'So I was right to blame you for not making more effort to see me.'

'I showed how interested I was in other ways,' Cristiano countered. 'I bought you roses. I even sent you a card on Valentine's Day.'

'It was a black and white picture of New York with your name in it and no message—'

Cristiano wasn't listening. 'I also phoned you all the time. That was serious new territory for me.'

'I'm surprised that fact didn't wake you up in the night in a cold sweat!'

'All that woke me up was the need for a cold shower, because you weren't there in my bed with me, *bella mia*.'

Lydia went pink. 'When I overheard Philip talking about that horrible bet, it wrecked everything.'

'That was all my fault.' His lean, darkly handsome face was bleak with recollection. 'I'm sorry you were hurt, but if it's any consolation it was a body-blow when you took off with Mort Stevens. I was gutted. Life lost all its flavour, and I didn't work out why until very recently. But I did have a recurring fantasy in which you came to me on your knees, begging to be taken back, *cara mia*.'

Lydia was perched on the side of the bed, her entire attention lodged on him. 'Is that why you turned fantasy into fact when you heard I was in trouble?'

'And the next time I got you in my sights I made sure there was no way you could leave me a second time.'

'The contract?' Now that its purpose had been fully explained, Lydia felt almost fond of that part of their history.

'I wanted you tied hand and foot to me, so that you couldn't walk away again.'

'Obviously somewhere along the line you got acclimatised to that trapped feeling,' Lydia remarked.

'Losing you to Stevens was a painful cure. Although I got you back into my life, I couldn't forget that you'd walked out on me…'

'The first time you proposed—?'

Cristiano vented a rueful laugh. 'It was a disaster. I was all over the place. I hadn't thought anything through. I felt so guilty, and I wanted to keep you with me. But I thought you hated me and that made me arrogant.'

Her nose wrinkled. 'I thought I hated you too.'

'When Gwenna showed me that photo you'd kept of me, it was like a shot of adrenalin. I was so low,' he confessed. 'I wasn't getting anywhere with you. But it seemed to me that if you'd felt that way about me once, there was still hope. When you got the wrong idea about that Russian model, I was delighted.'

Her eyes were radiant, for she was looking back and recognising how hard he had worked to win her trust and love. Sliding off the bed, she walked over to him and slid her hands up to his shoulders. 'When did you start *really* wanting to marry me?'

'Probably the moment you said no.' His stunning gold eyes rested intently on her lovely face. 'I need to know you're mine. I won't feel safe until you've signed our marriage certificate in triplicate in two weeks' time.'

'What if I asked you to sign a contract?' she teased.

His handsome dark head lowered, for he was mesmerised by the tantalising smile on her soft pink mouth. 'It would depend on the terms.'

'You have to love me as much as I love you.'

'*Do* you love me?' Cristiano searched her eyes with wondering appreciation. 'I thought I still had to work on that angle.'

'Actually, you didn't have to work half as hard as you deserved. That teenage crush of mine worked in your favour.' Lydia traced a high masculine cheekbone with loving appreciation, her fingers gentle. 'I told myself I hated you to protect myself from getting hurt again, and then I had to accept that I still loved you.'

'I'll never give you cause to regret it,' Cristiano swore, with a raw sincerity that touched her to the heart.

He claimed her mouth in a long, drugging kiss. The instant physical contact was renewed, their overwhelming need to express their love in passion drove every other consideration from their minds.

The host and hostess did not reappear downstairs until dawn was high in the sky.

Eighteen months later, Lydia gave her daughter, Bella, a last tender kiss and tucked her in for the night. Bella was two months old and her dark blue eyes were drowsy. Within minutes the gentle rocking of the cradle sent her to sleep. She was a very pretty baby, with black hair that lay like a silk cap on her pale skin, and a tiny serene face.

Standing with a glass of wine on the terrace an hour later, Lydia savoured the peace and the view across the Tuscan valley that now, more than any other place, felt like home to her.

Two weeks after their engagement party she and Cristiano

had exchanged rings and vows in the little candlelit church on the hill. It had been very much a private affair, hushed up to keep the paparazzi at bay and attended by only a chosen few. Gwenna had been her only attendant. Jodie, who had ditched Philip Hazlett, had attended with her latest boyfriend. Lydia had worn fluid white silk georgette, and the Andreotti diamond tiara had come out of the bank vault for the occasion. A single photo of the bride and groom on the church steps had been released to the press. The happy couple had spent their honeymoon on a private island in Greece, enjoying the feeling that they were getting back to nature while actually living in the lap of luxury.

The period since then had been one of great happiness for Lydia. In six weeks Gwenna was getting married to the businessman she had met at the engagement party. Cristiano had endowed the Happy Holidays charity with a house in Cornwall, and the funds to keep it running for the children. Lydia had presided over the official opening and had done sufficient fundraising to have long since forgotten her former embarrassment around the staff.

Of course there had been one or two more trying moments in their lives as well. In that category Lydia included Virginia's frantic appeal for the name of a good lawyer after she and Dennis were arrested by the French police and held in custody for dubious property deals. Everything the couple possessed had since been seized, and a prison sentence for them both looked unavoidable. Cristiano had made one or two pithy comments about justice being done.

There had also been the time that Lydia had snatched Cristiano's mobile phone from him and chucked it in the sea. She had got away with that because it had been the same day that he'd managed to persuade her to paddle in the surf. Since then she had reached the stage where she could fool about in the shallow end of a pool without suffering a panic attack, and she had been on *Lestara* twice for brief cruises. Bit by bit she was overcoming her fear, but she couldn't have come so far without Cristiano's support and patience.

A warm smile curved Lydia's lips when she heard the distant chop-chop of the helicopter approaching. It was Cristiano, flying back from a meeting in London. She heard his steps ringing across the tiled hall inside the house and her heartbeat picked up pace the way it always did when he was near.

When he appeared on the terrace, she flung herself into his arms without hesitation. Releasing a hungry groan, he held her to him and kissed her breathless.

'It's so uncool when we do this. Our friends would be shocked. No wonder we don't entertain much.' Closing a lean hand over hers, Cristiano took a long, appreciative look at her. 'How's Bella?'

'Fast asleep.'

'I guarantee she won't be at three in the morning,' her father forecast. 'Knowing that, I came home with all possible haste. We can have an early night and still be fresh for our darling daughter when she wakes up in the middle of the night.'

'But it's only eight o'clock.'

A provocative smile slashed his lean dark features. 'I know.'

She burst out laughing.

'London was a desert without you,' Cristiano confided.

'Every time I have to leave you I find out all over again how much I love you, *gioia mia.*'

Happiness lighting her face, Lydia glowed beneath the tender look in his stunning eyes. As she settled back into his arms she had not a care in the world—for she had found her place...

The Cozakis Bride

LYNNE GRAHAM

CHAPTER ONE

'YOU have ruined your life just as your mother did,' Spyros Manoulis condemned.

Olympia studied her Greek grandfather with shuttered eyes the colour of sea jade. She was sick with nerves but she had come on a begging mission. If venting his spleen put the older man into a better mood and made him look more sympathetically on her mother's plight, she could stand the heat of any attack.

Well-built and fit, for all his seventy-plus years, the white-haired older man paced the lounge of his luxurious London hotel suite, his lined features forbidding. 'Look at you, still single at the age of twenty-seven! No husband, no children,' he cited grimly. 'Ten years ago, I opened my home to you and I attempted to do my best for you...'

As he paused for a necessary breath, broad chest expanding, Olympia *knew* what was coming next. Beneath the mahogany hair she wore confined in a French plait, her pallor became pronounced.

'And how was my generosity repaid?' Spyros was working himself up into a rage at the memory. 'You brought dishonour on the family name. You disgraced me, destroyed your own reputation and offered unforgivable insult to the Cozakis family—'

'Yes...' Olympia was desperate enough to own up to murder itself if it calmed her grandfather down and gave her the chance to plead her mother's cause.

'Such a marriage as I arranged for you...and very grateful you were to have Nikos Cozakis at the time! You wept when he gave you your betrothal ring. I remember the occasion well!'

5

Olympia clenched her teeth together: a necessary self-restraint. Hot, cringing humiliation was eating into her self-discipline.

'Then you threw it all away in a wanton moment of madness,' Spyros Manoulis ground out with bitter anger. 'Shamed me, shamed yourself—'

Olympia whispered tautly, 'Ten years is a long time—'

'Not long enough to endow me with forgetfulness!' her grandfather countered harshly. 'I was curious to see you again. That's why I agreed to this meeting when you wrote asking for it. But let me tell you now without further waste of time that you will receive no financial assistance from me.'

Olympia reddened. 'I want nothing for me…but my mother, your daughter—'

Spyros interrupted her before she could mention her mother's name. 'Had my foolish daughter raised you to be a decent young woman, according to our Greek traditions, you would *never* have brought dishonour upon me!'

At that judgmental assurance, Olympia's heart sank. So her innocent parent was still to suffer for her daughter's sins. Squaring her slim shoulders, she lifted a chin every bit as determined as his own. '*Please* let me speak freely—'

'No, I will not hear you!' Spyros stalked over to the window. 'I want you to go home and think about what you have lost for you and your mother. *Had* you married Nik Cozakis—'

'I'd have castrated him!' Olympia's control over her temper slipped as the older man made it clear that their meeting was already at an end.

Her grandfather's beetling brows rose almost as high as his hairline.

Olympia coloured. 'I'm sorry—'

'At least Nik would have taught you to keep a still tongue when a man is speaking to you!'

Olympia sucked in a deep, steadying breath. He was as mad as fire now. She had done nothing but add fuel to the

flames. No doubt she ought to have arrived steeped in sack-
cloth and ashes and hung her head with anguished regret
when he referred to her broken engagement.

Spyros Manoulis moved his hand in a gesture of finality.
'You could only win my forgiveness by marrying Nik.'

Fierce disappointment filled Olympia to overflowing.
'Why don't you just throw in climbing Everest too?'

'I see you get the picture,' her grandfather said drily.

But there was a little red devil buzzing about now inside
Olympia's head. 'If I could get him to marry me, would I
still come dowered with the Manoulis empire?'

The older man dealt her a thunderous appraisal. 'What are
you suggesting? *Get* him to marry you? Nikos Cozakis,
whom you insulted beyond belief, who could have any young
woman he wanted—'

'Few young women come with as large a dowry as you
offered as a sweetener to the deal over me ten years ago.'

Spyros Manoulis was aghast at her bluntness. 'Have you
no shame?'

'When you tried to flog me off like one of your tankers, I
lost my illusions and my sensitivity,' his granddaughter asserted curtly. 'You still haven't answered my question.'

'But what is the point of a question that crazy?' The older
man flung both hands up in complete exasperation.

'I'd just like to know.'

'I would have signed control of Manoulis Industries over
to Nik on your wedding day...and I would *still* gladly do so,
were it possible!' Weary now, his big shoulders slumping,
Spyros vented an embittered laugh at what he saw as a total
impossibility. 'My only desire was to pass on the business I
spent a lifetime building into capable hands. Was that so
much to ask?'

Olympia's generous mouth compressed. The longevity of
his name in the business world meant so much more to her
grandfather than family ties. But then to be fair that was not
her gentle mother's view. Irini Manoulis might long to be

reconciled with her estranged father, but the older woman had never blamed him for turning his back on her. However, an increasing sense of despair was creeping over Olympia. Her grandfather was immovable. He had admitted to only seeing her out of curiosity. So why was she still hanging around where she wasn't welcome?

Olympia walked stiff-backed to the door and then decided to make one last attempt to be heard. 'My mother's health is failing—'

Spyros growled something at her in outraged Greek, his refusal to listen instantaneous.

Olympia spun back, sea-jade eyes flashing like gems. 'If she dies poor and miserable, as she is now, I hope your conscience haunts you to the grave and beyond, because that's what you'll deserve!'

For a second, Spyros Manoulis stared at her with expressionless dark eyes. Then he swung away, his broad back stiff as an iron bar.

Leaving her grandfather's suite, Olympia got into the lift before she slumped. Minutes later, having got herself back under control, she crossed the busy hotel foyer back out into the open air. Maybe she should run really insane and kidnap Nik Cozakis, she thought with enormous bitterness. If she'd had the money she could have hired hitmen to snatch him out of his stretch limo. And she could have personally starved and tortured Nik in some dark, dank cellar with a completely clear conscience. After all, she hated him. She really, really hated him.

Although already wealthy beyond avarice, greed had led Nik at the age of nineteen into getting engaged to a plain, overweight girl who'd had no attraction for him *but* her value as the promised Manoulis heiress. Nik Cozakis had broken her heart, dragged her pride in the dirt and ultimately ensured that there was no prospect of Spyros *ever* forgiving either her or her mother.

But then maybe her mother had been born under an unlucky star, Olympia conceded, wincing at the hardness of the pavement beneath shoe soles worn thin as paper with overuse. For the first twenty-one years of her life Irini had been cocooned in a world of wealth and privilege. Then she had made the fatal mistake of falling in love with an Englishman. Meeting with heavy paternal opposition, Irini had fled to London to be with her boyfriend. But the day before their wedding was to take place Olympia's father had crashed his motorbike and died.

Shortly afterwards, Irini had discovered that she was pregnant. From that point on there had been no turning back: she was expecting a child and she was unmarried. Her only talent a willingness to take any manual work available, Irini had raised Olympia alone. Throughout her childhood, Olympia could only recall her mother with a wan, exhausted face, for Irini Manoulis had never been strong. And the reality was that all those years of taxing physical labour had wrecked what health she did have and weakened her heart.

Once Olympia had been old enough to get a job of her own, matters had improved. For a few years, Olympia recalled with painful regret, they had been happy in a tiny flat which had seemed like a palace to them both. Then, eighteen months ago, the firm where Olympia had worked as a receptionist had gone bankrupt. Since then she had only managed to get temporary employment, and even that had been thin on the ground in recent months. They had had to give up the flat, and the savings which Olympia had painstakingly built up were long since gone.

The council had rehoused them in a tough inner city estate. Her mother was so terrified of the aggressive youths there that she no longer dared to venture out. Olympia had been forced to watch the mother she adored decline before her eyes, growing ever more thin and weak, her brave smiles of cheer pathetic to witness. It was as if Irini Manoulis had given up on life itself.

She was dying, Olympia reflected sickly, dying inch by

inch, always talking about the distant past now, because the
unlovely present was too much for her weakened spirit to
handle. A rundown apartment they couldn't afford to heat,
no telephone, no television, noisy, threatening neighbours
and surroundings bereft of all beauty. Nothing, nothing whatsoever to look forward to with the smallest anticipation.

If only Olympia had had the benefit of a crystal ball ten
years ago…*if only*! Would she have made the same decision
as she had made then? A despairing laugh was dredged from
Olympia. Guilt and all the regret her grandfather could ever
had wished on her washed over her now. She would have
been married to a billionaire! Long before her health had
failed her mother would once again have enjoyed security
and comfort. Now, with bitter, realistic hindsight, Olympia
knew that had she had the benefit of a crystal ball at the age
of seventeen she would have married a monster for her
mother's sake!

So what if Nik had been snogging the face off a gorgeous
Italian model not ten feet from her?

So what if Nik had confided in his second cousin, Katerina,
that Olympia was, 'Fat and stupid and sexless, but literally
worth her weight in gold!'?

So what if he would have been continually unfaithful
throughout their marriage and a total arrogant, loathsome pig
to live with?

So what if he had said to her face, without scruple, conscience or decency, the morning after that dreadful night,
'You're a slapper! And I, Nik Cozakis, refuse to marry another man's leavings!'?

Gripped by those painfully degrading recollections, Olympia hovered by a shop window. She knew that right now Nik
was sure to be over in London for the same reason as her
grandfather was. It had featured in the newspapers: a meeting
of powerful Greek tycoons with shared interests in British
business. And, unlike Spyros Manoulis, Nik had a massive

office headquarters in the City of London, where he very likely was this *very* minute…

What did she have to lose? He was still single. And Spyros Manoulis never joked about money. Spyros would happily pay millions and millions of pounds to marry her off to Nik Cozakis. Personalities didn't come into it: primarily it would be the linking of two enormous business empires. And with that size of a dowry still available, even a plain Jane slapper ought to have the gumption to put a late offer on the table! Was she crazy? No, she owed a huge debt to her mother. Irini Manoulis had sacrificed so much to bring her into the world and raise her to adulthood. What had *she* ever given back?

Olympia squinted at her reflection in the shop window. A dark-haired woman of five foot five inches, clad in a grey skirt and jacket shabby with age. Even on a restricted diet she was never going to be thin. Her shape was lush—horribly, embarrassingly lush. She must have inherited such generous curves from her father's side, because her mother was slim and slight. Well, she was worth her weight in gold, she reminded herself bracingly. And if there was one thing Nik Cozakis reputedly excelled at, it was ruthlessly exploiting any proposition likely to enrich his already overflowing coffers…

Nik was planning a major deal.

All calls were on hold, with only the direst emergency excuse for an interruption of any kind. So when even the softest of knocks sounded hesitantly on the door of his office his dark head came up, well-defined black brows rising in exasperated enquiry. His British PA, Gerry, hurried to the door, where a whispered exchange took place.

Gerry moved back to his powerful employer's side. 'I'm sorry, but there's a woman asking to see you urgently, sir.'

'No interruptions, particularly not of the female variety,' Nik cut in with harsh impatience.

'She says she's Spyros Manoulis's granddaughter, Olympia. But the receptionist isn't convinced of her identity. I gather the woman doesn't *look* like someone you would be acquainted with, sir.'

Olympia Manoulis? Arrested into tangible stillness, Nik Cozakis frowned in silent disbelief. Olympia Manoulis. Rooted deep in his subconscious lurked a tender spot still raw with a rage that had yet to dim. How dared that whore enter his office block and have the effrontery to ask to see him? He plunged upright, startling his staff so much that everybody jumped, and one unfortunate dropped several files.

Striding over to the tall tinted windows like a leopard on the prowl for fresh meat, Nik stilled again. Spyros had sworn he would never forgive her. Spyros was a man of his word. And Nik still pitied the older man, whose deep shame over his erring granddaughter's behaviour had been painful to witness. His only son had drowned in a yacht race and his daughter had become an unwed mother. Bad blood in that family, Nik's own father had decided, implying that his headstrong son had had a narrow escape.

Yet still Nik simmered like a boiling cauldron when he recalled the humiliation of being publicly confronted with the fact that *his* fiancée, *his* doe-eyed supposedly virginal bride-to-be, had gone out to *his* car with a drunken friend and had *sex* with him. It was disgusting; it was filthy. In fact, just thinking about that degrading, utterly inexcusable episode still had the power to make Nik regret that he had never had the opportunity to punish Olympia Manoulis as she had so definitely deserved.

The atmosphere was so explosive that the silence was absolute. His staff exchanged uncertain glances. Gerry Marsden waited, and then slowly breathed in. 'Sir…?'

Nik wheeled back. 'Let her wait…'

His PA concealed his surprise with difficulty. 'At what time will I tell your secretary that you will see her?'

'No time.' His eyes cold enough to light the way to Hades, Nik threw back his proud dark head. 'Let her *wait*.'

As the hours crept past into the lunch hour, and then on into the late afternoon, Olympia was conscious that quite a few people seemed to pass suspiciously slowly through the impressive reception area and steal a covert glance in her direction.

She held her head high, neck aching from that determined show of indifference. She had her foot in the door, she told herself bracingly. Nik hadn't had her escorted off the premises. Nik had not flatly refused to see her. And if he was very, very busy, that was only what she had expected, and she could not hope for any favours. Curiosity would eventually penetrate that arrogant, macho and bone-deep stubborn skull of his. Even Nik Cozakis had to be that human.

Despair was the mother of invention, she conceded. Nik Cozakis was literally her last hope. And why *should* her fierce pride hurt? No false pride had held her mother back from scrubbing other people's floors so that she could feed and clothe her daughter.

Just before five o'clock, the receptionist rose from behind her desk. 'Mr Cozakis has left the building, Miss Manoulis.'

Olympia paled to the colour of milk. Then she straightened her stiff shoulders and stood up. She stepped into the lift and let it carry her back down to the ground floor. She would be back tomorrow to keep the same vigil, she told herself doggedly. She would not be embarrassed into retreat by such tactics. But, even so, she was as badly shaken as if she had run into a hard brick wall.

As she stood on the bus that would eventually bring her within walking distance of home, she realised that she had read the situation wrong. Nik was no longer the teenager she had once been so pathetically infatuated with: impatient and hot-tempered, with not a lot in the way of self-control. The eldest son of two adoring parents, he had been the natural leader in his sophisticated social set of bored but gilded youth.

And so beautiful, so heartachingly, savagely beautiful that

it must have seemed like a crime to his unlovely friends that he should be matched with an unattractive, plump and charmless bride-to-be...

But now Nik was a fully grown adult male. A *Greek* male, subtly different from others of his sex. Like her grandfather, he saw no need to justify his own behaviour. There had been no quiet announcement that he was unavailable. He had *let* her wait and cherish hope. That had been cruel, but she should have been better prepared for that tack.

The scent of cooking greeted Olympia's return to the flat she shared with her mother. She hurried into the tiny kitchen and watched her mother gather her spare frame and turn with a determined smile to greet her. Her heart turned over sickly at the grey pallor of the older woman's worn face.

"I thought we agreed that *I* do all the cooking, Mum.'

'You've been out looking for a job all day. It's the least that I can do,' Irini Manoulis protested.

Later, as Olympia climbed into bed, she was consumed by guilt for the evasions she had utilised with her mother. But how could she have told the older woman what she had *really* been doing all day? Irini would have been upset by the knowledge that her daughter had secretly got in touch with her grandfather, but unsurprised by the outcome. However, an admission that Olympia had tried to see Nik Cozakis would have left her mother bereft of breath and a frank explanation of *why* her daughter had sought that meeting would have appalled her quiet and dignified parent.

But how much more shattered would her trusting mother have been had Olympia ever told her the whole dreadful truth of what had happened in Athens a decade earlier? Olympia had never told that story, and her awareness of that fact still disturbed her. Then, as now, Olympia had kept her own counsel to protect her mother from needless distress...

The next morning, Olympia took up position in the waiting area on the top floor of the Cozakis building three minutes after nine o'clock.

She made the same request to see Nik as she had made the day before. The receptionist avoided eye contact. Olympia wondered if *this* would be the day that Nik lost patience and had her thrown out of the building.

At ten minutes past nine, after a mutually mystified consultation with another senior member of staff, Gerry Marsden approached Nik, who had started work as usual at eight that morning. 'Miss Manoulis is here again today, sir.'

Almost imperceptibly the Greek tycoon tensed and the silence thickened.

'Have you the Tenco file?' Nik then enquired, as if the younger man hadn't spoken.

The day wore on, with Olympia praying that a pretence of quiet, uncomplaining humility would ultimately persuade Nik to spare her just five minutes of his time. By the end of that day, when the receptionist apologetically announced that Mr Cozakis had again left the building, Olympia experienced such a violent surge of bitter frustration that she could have screamed.

On the third day, Olympia felt hugely conspicuous as she stepped out of the lift on to the top floor.

Before leaving home she would have liked to have filled a vacuum flask and made herself some sandwiches, but to have done so would have roused her mother's suspicions and her concern. Since Olympia had yet to admit to her mother that their slender resources were now stretched unbearably tight. Irini fondly imagined that her daughter *bought* lunch for herself while she was out supposedly seeking employment.

However, at noon, when Olympia returned from a visit to the enviably luxurious cloakroom on the top floor, she found a cup of tea and three biscuits awaiting her. Her strained face softened with her smile. The receptionist gave her a decid-

edly conspiratorial glance in return. By then, Olympia was
convinced that just about every person of importance in the
building had traversed the reception area to take a peek at
her. Sympathy was now softening the discomfiture her initial
vigil had inspired. Not that it was going to do her much good,
she conceded heavily, when Nik obviously had an alternative
exit from his office.

At three that afternoon, when the last of her patience had
worn away, her desperation started to mount. Nik would soon
be on his way back to Greece and even more out of her reach.
Olympia reached a sudden decision and got up swiftly from
her seat. Hurrying past the reception desk that she had previously respected as a barrier, she started down the wide corridor that had to lead to Nik's inner sanctum.

'Miss Manoulis, you *can't* go down there!' the young receptionist exclaimed in dismay.

She would be a loser now whatever she did, Olympia reflected with despairing bitterness. Forcing a confrontation
with Nik was the wrong line to take. No Greek male appreciated an in-your-face female challenge. He would react like
a caveman, every aggressive primal cell outraged by such
boldness.

As she headed for the door at the foot of the corridor, a
set of male hands whipped round her forearms from behind
and stopped her dead in her tracks.

'I'm sorry, Miss Manoulis, but nobody goes in there without the boss's say-so,' an accented Greek voice spelt out
tautly.

'Damianos...' Even after ten years Olympia recognised
that gravelly voice, and her rigid shoulders bowed in defeat.
Nik's bodyguard, who was built like a tank. 'Couldn't you
have looked the other way just once?'

'For your grandfather's sake, go home,' Damianos urged
in a fierce undertone. '*Please* go home, before you are eaten
alive.'

Olympia trembled as the older man's fingers loosened their

hold. But that reluctance on his part to treat her like any other unwanted visitor was Damianos's mistake. Breaking free without hesitation, she literally flung herself the last ten feet and burst through that door.

There was a blur of movement from behind the desk: Nik rising with startled abruptness at so explosive an interruption.

In the split second that she knew was all she had at her disposal before Damianos intervened again, with greater effect, Olympia parted her lips and breathed rawly, 'Are you a man or a mouse that you won't face one woman?'

CHAPTER TWO

FROM behind Olympia, Damianos read Nik's face and avoided seeing the slight inclination of his employer's head which signified his own dismissal.

Out of breath, and expecting at any minute to be dragged out again, Olympia focused on Nik Cozakis for the first time in ten long years. Shock shrilled through her. He had got taller, his shoulders wider, and he had been tall and wide even to begin with. Well over six feet, he had towered over his relatives and friends. Now he cast a shadow like an intimidating stone monolith.

Olympia could feel his outrage like a physical entity churning up the heavy silence, beating down on her in suffocating waves. *Man or mouse?* A truly insane, derisive opening likely to push the average Greek male to violent response. She marvelled at his self-control, even as she winced at the loss of her own. Had she been a man, Nik would have knocked her through the wall for such an insult.

'I'm sorry,' Olympia said, though she wasn't one bit sorry.

'Damianos...' Nik murmured flatly.

The door behind her finally closed.

Olympia stared at him, couldn't help it. His sheer impact hit her and she reeled back an involuntary step, her tummy full of butterflies, her skin dampening. She took all of him in, all at once, in a single, almost greedy visualising burst. The devastating dark good looks, the raw, earthy force of his sexual aura, the contrasting formal severity of his beautifully cut dark suit. All male, nothing of the boy left but that aching beauty which had once entrapped her foolish heart. And those eyes, amber-gold as a jaguar cat, spectacularly noticeable in that lean, strong face.

18

'Why are you humiliating yourself in this way?' Nik enquired in a drawl as lazy as a hot summer afternoon.

Belatedly, Olympia recognised her disorientation for the weakness it was. Angry dismay trammelled through her. She dredged her dilated pupils from his and stilled a shiver. 'I haven't humiliated myself.'

'Have you not? Were it not for the respect I have for your grandfather, I would have had you forcibly ejected on the first day,' Nik shared in the same conversational tone.

That dark, deep drawl betrayed no anger, but still a reflexive quiver snaked down Olympia's taut spinal cord. Colour ran up over her cheekbones. She forced her head high, dared a second collision with those stunning eyes, but was now careful to blank them out. 'I have a proposition to put to you.'

'I'm not listening to any proposition,' Nik asserted drily.

But in spite of that cool intonation the atmosphere sizzled. She could feel goosebumps rising on her arms. She forgot to look through him without focusing and registered that those extraordinary eyes of his were now roaming over her with unconcealed derision. And instantly she became aware of her creased suit, the flyaway tendrils of hair that had dropped round her hot face, indeed of how very, very plain she was. In fact, just plain ugly next to him: Beauty and the Beast with a transfer of sexes.

And it was that harsh, long-accepted reality that hardened Olympia and gave her the backbone she had almost lost. Ten years ago it had broken her heart not to have even a smidgen of the beauty that might have attracted Nik to her. Now, that contemptuous look of his only reminded her of the pain he had caused her.

'How can you look me in the face?' Nik growled in sudden disgust.

'Easily…a clean conscience.' She flung her head back, challenging him.

'You're a little whore,' Nik contradicted with purring insolence.

Untouched by an accusation so far removed from the truth, Olympia was, however, quite amazed that he still felt a need to abuse her so long after the event. It struck her as almost hilariously ironic that she appeared to have made a bigger impression on Nik with her apparent infidelity than she had ever contrived to make on him as his fiancée.

As a rueful laugh fell from her lips, his darkly handsome features clenched hard. 'Call me what you like,' she advised with patent indifference. 'But I have genuinely come here with the offer of a business deal.'

'Spyros Manoulis would not employ you as his messenger,' Nikos derided.

'Well…in this particular case, of the three of us, it seems that only I have the indelicacy it requires to make this direct approach,' Olympia informed him in taut and partial apology for what she was about to spring on him. 'Can't you just take your mind off what happened ten years ago and listen to me?'

'No.'

Olympia frowned in honest surprise. 'Why not?'

Nik studied her with blazing golden eyes full of even greater incredulity.

Refusing to be discouraged, Olympia breathed in very deep. 'My grandfather still wants you to take over Manoulis Industries. Now, let's face it…that's all he ever wanted, and all your father ever wanted was to ensure that you *got* it. I was just the connecting link…I wasn't remotely important except as a sort of guarantee of family kinship and mutual trust.'

'What is this nonsense?' Nik demanded with raw distaste.

'I'm stripping matters back to their bones…OK?'

'No, it is not OK. Get out,' Nik said flatly.

'No…no, I am *not* getting out!' Olympia's hands trembled and she clenched them into fierce fists. 'You've had ten years of revenge already—'

'What the hell are you talking about?' he grated.

'If you marry me, I'll sign everything over to you...' Olympia told him shakily.

She really had Nik's attention now. His brilliant eyes rested on her with a quality of stunned stillness she had never seen etched there before.

'Not a proper or normal marriage...just whatever would satisfy my grandfather—and he doesn't give a damn about me either, so he really wouldn't be looking for much!' Olympia pointed out, frantically eager to state her case before Nik emerged from what had to be a rare state of paralysis. 'I'd stay on here in England...all I'd need is an allowance to live on, and in return you'd have the Manoulis empire all to yourself and not even the annoyance or embarrassment of me being around...'

A dark flush of red had now risen to accentuate the prominence of Nik's fabulous cheekbones. He grated something in guttural Greek.

'Nik...try to understand that I'm desperate or I wouldn't be suggesting this. I know you think—'

'How *dare* you approach me with such an offer?' Nik demanded thunderously.

'I—'

Striding forward, Nik Cozakis fastened powerful hands to her slim forearms before she could back away. 'Are you insane?' he questioned rawly. 'You must be out of your mind to come to me like this! How could you think for one moment that I would marry an avaricious, brazen little tramp like you?'

'Think business contract, not marriage.' Although Olympia was shaking like a leaf in his hold, she was determined not to be sidetracked by meaningless personal insults. After all, she didn't give two hoots what he thought of her.

His outraged amber-gold gaze raked her pale oval face. 'A woman who went out to a public car park to lift her skirt for one of my friends like a common prostitute picked up out of the street?'

Not having been prepared for Nik to get quite that graphic, Olympia jerked and lost every scrap of colour. She parted tremulous lips. 'Not that it matters now...but that never happened, Nik.'

He thrust her away from him in unconcealed disgust. 'It was witnessed. That you should offend me with such an offer—'

'Why should it be an offence?' Olympia demanded fiercely. 'If you could just turn your back on the past, you would see that this is exactly what you wanted ten years ago and *more*...because I'm not expecting to be your wife or live with you or interfere with you in any way.'

'Spyros would strike you dead where you stand for this...'

Olympia loosed a shaken laugh. 'Oh, he would cringe at my methods, but not three days ago he told me that the only way I would ever win his forgiveness would be to marry you...so it's not like I have a choice, is it?'

'You made your choice ten years ago in the car park.'

Studying the carpet, Olympia felt drained. She saw the pointlessness of protesting her innocence now when she had failed to do so at the time—when, indeed, silence had been so much a part of her revenge.

Warily, she glanced up again, and noticed in some surprise that his attention was welded to her chest. Lowering her own gaze, she saw that a button had worked loose on her blouse and exposed the full swelling upper curves of her breasts. With unsteady hands, her cheeks hot and flushed, she hastily redid the button. Nik slowly lifted his eyes, inky black spiky lashes low on a glimmer of smouldering gold that entrapped her eyes and burned through her like a blowtorch.

'I just wish I'd had you first...if I'd had you, you wouldn't have been desperate enough to go out to that car park.'

'Don't talk to me like that,' she muttered, seriously disconcerted both by that statement and the offensive manner in which Nik was looking her over.

A hard curve to his wide, sensual mouth, he watched her fumbling efforts to tug her jacket closed over her blouse with derisive amusement. 'I'll talk whatever way I want to you. Did you think you'd cornered the market on forthright speech?'

'No, but—'

Nik flung back his handsome head and laughed outright. 'You thought you could come here and ask me to marry you and get respect?'

'I thought you would respect what I could be worth to you in terms of financial profit,' Olympia framed doggedly.

A tiny muscle jerked tight at the corner of his unsmiling mouth. 'You play with fire and you don't even know it. How desperate are you, Olympia?'

Her knees were wobbling. Something had changed in Nik. She sensed that, but she couldn't see or understand what. The atmosphere was so tense, and yet he was now talking with smooth, calm control, and she couldn't believe that he was still angry. Perhaps he had finally let go of that anger, seeing how irrational it was to still rage about something which had only briefly touched his ego. After all, it wasn't as though he had cared one jot about her as a person.

'My mother's not been well—'

'Oh, not the sob story, *please*,' Nik cut in very drily. 'What sort of idiot do you take me for?'

Olympia's hands curled into tight, defensive fists by her sides. 'Maybe I'm just sick of being poor…what does it matter to you?'

'It doesn't.' Making that confirmation, Nik lounged back with innate poise and grace against the edge of his desk and surveyed her where she hovered tautly in the centre of his office carpet. 'However, one fact I will acknowledge. You have more nerve than any woman I've ever met.'

A little natural colour eased back into Olympia's drawn cheeks.

'You must indeed be desperate to approach *me* with a marriage proposal. I'll think it over,' Nik drawled with soft, silken cool.

The rush of hope she experienced left her light-headed.

'Giftwrapped with the Manoulis empire, you saw *no* reason why I shouldn't consider your proposition?' Nik questioned in smooth addition.

She frowned uncertainly. 'You're a businessman, like my grandfather. You would have nothing to lose by agreement, and so much to gain...'

'So much,' Nik Cozakis savoured, regarding her with veiled eyes that were nonetheless surprisingly intent on her.

But then he wasn't really seeing her, Olympia reckoned. He was thinking of the power he stood to gain. Yet the sizzle of unbearable tension still licked at her senses. Her breath shortened in her throat, her heart-rate speeding up. She collided head-on with his steady gaze and the most disturbing sense of dizziness almost overwhelmed her. It vaguely reminded her of the way she'd used to feel around Nik, electrified in all sorts of deeply embarrassing ways by his mere proximity in the same room. But now she put the reaction down to hunger, stress and sheer mental exhaustion, because she wasn't attracted by him any more. It had only been the initial shock of seeing him again which had discomfited her at the outset of their interview.

'So where do I contact you?' Nik enquired.

She stiffened. Her fierce pride was reasserting itself now. There had been nothing personal in the proposal she had made to him: that had been strictly business. But she really didn't want him to know that she couldn't even afford a telephone line. Indeed, she couldn't bear the idea of him finding out just how deep she had sunk into the poverty trap because that felt like a very personal failure. 'I'll give you a number but it's not my own…you can leave a message for me there.'

'Why the secrecy?'

Olympia ignored the question. After a moment, he extended a notepad and pen to her. She scrawled down the number of the only neighbour she and her mother had become friendly with. Mrs Scott was the middle-aged widow who lived opposite them.

'I'll go now, then…' she said, suddenly awkward again now that she had nothing more to say.

Nik shifted a careless shoulder, signifying his indifference. And she thought then that he wouldn't *ever* use that phone number. Her own shoulders downcurved. Without another word, she walked out of his big fancy office and closed the door with a quiet snap. Damianos was waiting outside, his broad features stiff and troubled.

'He didn't eat me alive,' Olympia announced with a weak but reassuring smile, for she had always liked the older man.

'He will…' The bodyguard muttered heavily. 'But that's none of my business, Miss Manoulis.'

She reached Reception before her head began to swim and her legs threatened to buckle. She dropped down into a seat and bowed her head, breathing in slow and deep, struggling to get a hold on herself again. It was as if she had used up every resource she possessed. Never had she felt so totally drained. But a minute later she got up, hit the lift button and raised her head high again. She had done what she had to do and she was not about to waste time regretting it.

Before she let herself into the flat she shared with her mother, Olympia called in on Mrs Scott to mention that she might be receiving a phone call. The older woman looked amused when Olympia added with palpable embarrassment that if a call did come, she would be grateful if any message was passed on to her personally, rather than to her mother.

But three days later Nik hadn't called.

*   *   *

Exactly a week after she had stood in Nik's office, Olympia was on the way back from posting yet another pile of job applications when she saw Mrs Scott waving to attract her attention from the other side of the road.

Olympia forced a smile onto her downcurved mouth and waited at the lights to cross. She had been thinking how easy it was to fall into the poverty trap and find it all but impossible to climb out again. Did prospective employers just take one look at her less than impressive address and bin her application, writing her off as a no-hoper? It had been ten months since she had even got as far as an interview for a permanent job.

'That call came this morning,' Mrs Scott delivered with lively curiosity in her eyes as Olympia drew level with her.

'What call? *Oh…*' Olympia just froze to the pavement.

'He didn't leave his name. He just asked me to tell you that he'd see you at eight tonight at his office.'

Olympia tried and failed to swallow, her mind rushing on from shock to register that she couldn't make any assumption on the basis of that brief a message. It was more than possible that Nik Cozakis simply wanted to watch her squirm while he turned her down flat. 'Thanks,' she said tautly, averting her eyes.

'Job interview?' the older woman prompted doubtfully.

'Something like that.'

'Shameless as it is of me, I was really hoping it was an illicit assignation! You could do with a little excitement in your life, Olympia.'

At that disconcerting statement of opinion, Olympia looked up in frank surprise.

'I'll sit with your mother tonight. I know she doesn't like to be on her own after dark,' Mrs Scott completed ruefully.

Excitement, Olympia later thought grimly as she teamed a long navy skirt with a loose, concealing cardigan jacket. Nik Cozakis had squashed her girlish dreams flat ten years back. Oh, it had been exciting to begin with, then agonising to sit

by on the sidelines and appreciate that, never mind her lack
of her looks, she was so colourless to someone like him that
he simply forgot she existed.

A fiancé who couldn't even be bothered making a pass at
her! She studied herself in the wardrobe mirror. She looked
sensible. She had *always* looked sensible. Once she had experimented with make-up and clothes and she had been proud
of her good skin and clear eyes. After all, who was perfect?
Only after that disastrous trip to Greece had Olympia lost
every ounce of her confidence...

Every year her mother had sent a Christmas card to her
father, Spyros, always enclosing a photograph of Olympia,
who had been named for her late grandmother. Her grandfather had not responded but Irini's diligence had ensured
that the older man always knew where they were living. Then
out of the blue, when Olympia was sixteen, had come the
first response—a terse three-line letter informing them of the
death of her mother's only sibling, Andreas. The following
spring an equally brief letter had arrived inviting Olympia
out to Greece to meet her grandfather.

'But he's not asking *you*...' Olympia had protested, deeply
hurt on her mother's behalf.

'Perhaps in time that may come.' Irini Manoulis had
smiled with quiet reassurance at her angry teenage daughter.
'It is enough that my father should want to meet you. That
makes me very happy.'

Olympia really hadn't wanted to go, but she had known
how much that invitation meant to her mother. And while
Irini Manoulis had often talked about how prosperous a businessman Olympia's grandfather was, Olympia had genuinely
not appreciated the kind of lifestyle her mother had once
enjoyed until a chauffeur-driven limousine had picked her up
at the airport and wafted her out to a magnificent villa on the
outskirts of Athens.

On first meeting, Olympia had sensed her grandfather's
disappointment with a granddaughter who had only a handful

of Greek words in her vocabulary. And although Spyros spoke fluent English he had been a stranger to her, a stiff and disagreeable stranger too, who had sternly asked her not to mention her mother in his presence. Indeed, within hours of arriving at her grandfather's home Olympia had wanted to turn tail and run back home again.

The very next day, Spyros had sent her out shopping with the wife of one of his business acquaintances.

'What a lucky girl you are to have such a generous grandfather!' she had been told.

Olympia had suppressed the sneaking suspicion that her grandfather was ashamed of her appearance. The acquisition of a large and expensive new wardrobe *had* been exciting, even if she hadn't been terribly fussed about the staid quality of those outfits. Nothing above the knee, nothing more than two inches below her throat. It hadn't occurred to Olympia that she was being carefully packaged to create the right impression.

The following day, Spyros had informed her that he had invited some young people to his home for the afternoon, so that she could have the opportunity to make friends her own age. While Olympia had been agonising over what to wear, a light knock had sounded on her bedroom door. A very pretty brunette with enormous brown eyes and a friendly smile had strolled in to introduce herself.

'I'm Katerina Pallas. My aunt took you shopping yesterday.'

Her aunt had seemed a pleasant woman, and Olympia had soon come to think of the other girl as her closest friend. She had been grateful for the sophisticated Katerina's advice on what to wear and how to behave. Katerina had never once so much as hinted that full skirts and swimsuits with horizontal stripes might be less than kind to Olympia's somewhat bountiful curves. For all her seeming pleasantness, Katerina's aunt had contrived to buy Olympia a remarkably *unflattering* wardrobe to wear that summer.

Looking back to those early days in Greece, and recalling how naive and trusting she had been, now chilled Olympia to the marrow. Wolves, who had worn smiles inside of snarls, had surrounded her. When friendship had been offered she had believed it was genuine, and she had accepted everything at face value. She hadn't known that Spyros was planning to make her his heir. She hadn't known that the possibility of her marrying Nik Cozakis had been discussed *long* before she'd even met him...or that others might find that possibility both a threat and a source of jealousy.

A security man let Olympia into the Cozakis building just before eight that evening.

She crossed the echoing empty foyer and entered the lift. After hours, with the lights dimmed, she found the massive office block kind of spooky. It felt strange to walk past the deserted reception desk on the top floor and head straight for Nik's office without any fuss or fanfare.

Her heartbeat feeling as if it was thudding at the foot of her throat, she raised her hand and knocked on the door before reaching for the handle with a not quite steady hand and entering.

Only the desk lamp was burning. The tall windows beyond were filled with a magnificent view of the City skyline at night. A million lights seemed to twinkle and sparkle, disorientating her. Then Nik Cozakis moved out of the shadows and strolled forward into view. His superb silver-grey suit lent him formidable elegance.

'Punctual and polite this evening, I note,' Nik remarked.

A wash of colour stained Olympia's cheeks. The balance of power *had* changed. A week ago she had been strengthened by the power of surprise and her own daring, sufficiently desperate not to care about anything but being heard. But all that was past now. She had come here tonight to hear Nik's answer *and* she had politely knocked on the door. He knew the difference as clearly as she now felt it. The whip-hand was his.

'Would you like a drink?'

Olympia nodded jerkily, suddenly keen for him to be otherwise occupied for a minute while she regained her composure.

A faintly amused look tinged Nik's vibrantly handsome features. 'What would you like?'

'Orange juice…anything.' She heard the tremulous note in her own response and almost winced, her full mouth tightening.

He strolled over to a cabinet, his long stride lithe and graceful. She remembered how clumsy she had once felt around him. Had that been nerves or over-excitement? Right at that moment she was *so* nervous she could feel a faint tremor in her knees. As he bent his well-shaped dark head over the cabinet the interior light gleamed over his blue-black hair and she relived how those springy strands had once felt beneath her palms. Flinching, she tried to drag her thoughts into order, but her attention only strayed to the bold line of his patrician nose, the taut slant of a clean-cut masculine cheekbone and the hard angle of his jaw.

'You were always fond of watching me,' Nik mused lazily as he crossed the carpet to extend a crystal tumbler to her. 'Like a little brown owl. Every time I caught you looking, you would blush like mad and look away.'

Embarrassed by that recollection, which was way too accurate for her to dare to question it, Olympia managed a jerky shrug. 'It was a long time ago.'

Nik sank down on the edge of his desk, his attitude one of total relaxation. He saluted her with his glass. 'You were a class act. I was a hundred per cent positive you were a virgin.'

Suddenly Olympia was feeling uncomfortably warm in her cardigan jacket, and although she wanted to meet his eyes with complete indifference, she was finding that her eyes were unwilling to go anywhere near him. She hadn't known what to expect from Nik tonight, but she definitely *hadn't* expected him to refer with such apparent calm to that long-ago summer.

'So...' Nik trailed the word out in his darkly sensual drawl. 'I have only one question to ask before we get down to business. It's like a trick question, Olympia—'

Confusion was starting to grip her. 'I don't want to hear it, then—'

'But you have to answer it with *real* honesty,' he continued with the same unnerving cool. 'It would not be in your best interests to lie. So don't give me the answer you *think* I want to hear because you might well end up regretting it.'

Her mouth was dry as a bone. She tipped her orange juice to her lips. Her hand was trembling and the rim of the glass rattled against her teeth. The tension was so thick she could taste it. But she couldn't think straight because Nik Cozakis now, tonight, was not behaving remotely as he had done a week earlier.

'That night at the club, you may have seen me with another girl...*Theos*, I hope I'm not embarrassing you with this rather adolescent walk down memory lane,' Nik murmured in a voice dark and smooth as black velvet as Olympia perceptibly jerked in shock at what he had thrown at her without warning.

'Why should you be embarrassing me?' she asked between gritted teeth.

'Then let me plunge right to the heart of the matter that engages my curiosity even now,' Nik continued softly. 'Did you go out to my car with Lukas because you were drunk and distressed by what you *may* have seen, and did he then take advantage of you in that state? *Or...*'

Olympia stared fixedly at the desk lamp, outraged resentment and sheer hatred clawing at her. She wanted to toss the remains of her drink in his arrogant face and then hit him so hard, he wouldn't pick himself up for a month. Ten years on, having been judged and found guilty for a sin she had not committed, why should she admit the agonies that he had put her through that night? Why should she further humiliate herself with that kind of honesty? Where did he get off asking her such questions? He darned well hadn't asked her them at the time! Nor had there been any reference to the possibility that she might have seen him carrying on with another girl!

'Or...*what*?' she prompted in a hissing undertone.

'Or...' Nik responded without the smallest audible hint of discomfiture. 'Did you go out to my car with him either because you thought you could get away with not being seen or *because*—'

'I went out to your car with him because I fancied him like mad!' Olympia suddenly erupted, provoked beyond bearing by his sardonic probing, her sea-jade eyes hot with defiance and loathing.

Dark eyes with a single light of gold held to her flushed and furious face. His outrageously long, lush lashes lowered, leaving only the dark glimmer of his gaze visible.

Her tummy clenched and she trembled, an odd coldness spreading inside her, as she met those dark, dark eyes. She spun away, shocked at the gross lie she had thrown at him, shocked that even ten years on her own desire for revenge could still burst back into being and send her off the edge into an insane response, for at the exact same moment she recalled exactly *why* she had come to Nik's office.

'You're just toying with me for your own amusement!' Olympia flung him an agitated glance of condemnation. 'You're going to say no, of course you're going to say no...I really don't know why I bothered coming here tonight!'

'You were desperate,' Nik reminded her with dulcet cool.

'Well, why don't you just *say* no?' Olympia was beyond all pretence now, and she didn't care that she sounded childish. He was winding her up and making a fool of her. She couldn't wait to get away from him.

Nik rose lithely upright. 'No need to get so rattled, Olympia,' he mocked. 'Why don't you take that baggy cardy off and sit down?'

Her hot face got even hotter. She was boiling alive in her jacket, but she folded her arms.

Nik laughed with a sudden amusement that she found even more unnerving.

'What's so funny?' she demanded sharply.

'You always seemed so quiet. I awarded you all these qualities that you never actually possessed.' His expressive mouth twisted with derision. 'But now I'm seeing the *real* Olympia Manoulis. Hot-tempered, stubborn and reckless to the point of self-destruction.'

'These are hardly normal circumstances. Don't presume to know anything about me...because you don't!' Olympia slung back at him defensively.

'But if you don't take the ugly cardy off, I'm going to rip it off,' Nik spelt out softly.

Olympia backed off a startled step. Only now was it dawning on her that she had never really known Nik Cozakis either. Clashing with brilliant dark eyes, she watched him extend a lean brown hand to receive the jacket, and suddenly it didn't seem worth arguing about any more. Tight-mouthed, she peeled it off and tossed it to him. 'You like throwing your weight around, don't you? I should've remembered that.'

Ignoring that comment, Nik cast the jacket on a nearby chair. 'Now sit down, so that you can hear *my* terms for marriage.'

Her eyes opened very wide and she froze.

'*Né*...yes. What you want is within reach, but you may yet choose not to pay the price.'

'The price...?' Thrown by that smooth acknowledgement that he was seriously considering her proposition, Olympia backed hurriedly down into the armchair closest.

'All good things come at a price...haven't you learnt that yet?' Nik murmured in a voice as smooth and rich as honey.

All of a sudden she couldn't concentrate. Having forgotten to keep Nik out of focus, she collided head-on with amber-gold eyes. It was like being suddenly dropped from a height. Such beautiful lying eyes, she thought helplessly, curling her taut fingers into the fabric of her skirt. A quivering, insidious warmth snaked up between her thighs, making her tense, jerk her lashes down and freeze, no longer under any illusion about what was happening to her. As she felt her breasts stir and swell, their soft peaks pinch into straining sensitivity, she was aghast. A tidal wave of embarrassment surged up over her. Already her heart was banging as if she had run a race.

'Olympia…?'

She crossed her arms and lifted her head again with pronounced reluctance. Nik was over by the window at a comfortable distance. He was planning to agree; he was going to marry her. She was home and dry, she reminded herself. What did it matter if her stupid body still reacted to him? He was really gorgeous, really, really gorgeous. It was a chemical response, nothing more. So she didn't like it, in fact she hated that out-of-control feeling, but it wasn't as if she would be seeing much of him in the future.

'You're in shock…I'm surprised,' Nik admitted. 'You seemed so confident last week that you could win my agreement.'

'You weren't very encouraging,' she pointed out unevenly, no longer looking anywhere near him. It might just be a chemical response but she didn't want to encourage it.

'I thought your proposition over at length. I feel I should warn you that I tend to be ruthless when I negotiate…'

'Tell me something I didn't expect.'

'I have certain conditions you would have to agree to. And there is no room for negotiation at all,' Nik imparted gently.

'Just tell me what you want,' Olympia urged.

'You sign a pre-nuptial contract—'

'Of course.'

'You sign over everything to me on our wedding day—'

'Apart from a small—'

'*Everything,*' Nik slotted in immovably. 'I'll give you an allowance.'

She glanced up in surprise and dismay. 'But that's not—'

'You'll just have to trust me.'

'I want to buy a house for my mother.'

'Naturally I will not see your mother suffer in any way. If you marry me, I promise you that she will live in comfort for the rest of her life,' Nik asserted. 'I will regard her as I would regard a member of my own family and I will treat her accordingly.'

It was a more than generous offer, and she was impressed and pleased that there was no lack of respect in the manner in which he referred to her mother.

'Your grandfather was born seventy-four years ago,' Nik pointed out, as if he could see what she was thinking. 'He's from a very different generation. Your birth outside the bonds of marriage was a source of enormous shame and grief to him.'

Fierce loyalty to her mother stiffened Olympia. 'I know that, but—'

'No, you *don't* know it, or even begin to understand it,' Nik incised with sudden grimness. 'Your mother brought you up to be British. She made no attempt to teach you what it was to be Greek. She stayed well away from the Greek community here in London. I am not judging her for that, but don't tell me that you understand our culture because you do not.'

Lips compressed, Olympia cloaked her unimpressed gaze.

'Greek men have always set great value on a woman's virtue—'

'We're getting off the subject,' Olympia said in curt interruption, tensing at the recollection of the names he had called her. In retrospect, she recognised that she now felt sensitive to his low opinion of her morals, and she wondered why on earth that should be.

Just as quickly, she marvelled at her stupidity in allowing him to demand, unchallenged, that she sign away any claim on the Manoulis empire and trustingly depend on his generosity. 'What you said about me signing away *everything*—'

'Non-negotiable,' Nik interrupted with gleaming dark eyes. 'Take it or leave it.'

Olympia breathed in deep. 'I don't care about the money—'

'If you don't care, why are you arguing?'

She didn't trust him. But she did nonetheless trust the promise he had made about her mother, and that was all that mattered, she reminded herself. After all, she would be living with her mother and looking after her. Why *had* she argued?

Nik shot her a sardonic appraisal. 'Do you think I would keep my wife in penury?'

She flushed. 'No.'

He glanced down at the slim gold watch on his wrist and then back at her. 'This is progressing very slowly, Olympia. May I move on?'

She nodded.

'Your belief that we could marry and separate immediately after the ceremony is ridiculous. Your grandfather would not accept a charade of that nature, and nor would I be prepared to deceive him in that way.'

She tensed. 'So what are you suggesting?'

'You will have to live in one of my homes…for a while, at least.'

She focused her mind on her mother's needs and gave him another reluctant nod.

'You give me a son and heir.'

Olympia blinked, lips falling slightly apart.

'Yes, you did hear that.' Nik surveyed her shocked face with cynical cool. 'I need a son and heir, and if I have to marry you, I might as well make the most of the opportunity.'

'You've got to be joking!' Olympia gasped, so taken aback by that calm announcement she could barely vocalise.

Nik elevated a black brow. 'The son and heir is also non-negotiable. And, unless I change my mind at some future date, a daughter will not be an acceptable substitute. Sorry if that sounds sexist, but there are still a lot of daughters out there who do *not* want to be leaders in industry!'

Olympia sat in the armchair staring at him as if he had taken leave of his wits. 'You hate me, you can't possibly *w-want* to—'

'Wouldn't faze me in the slightest, Olympia. You may be damaged goods, but I'm not over-sensitive when it comes to practicality,' Nik delivered, running slumbrous dark eyes over her as if he was already stripping off her clothes piece by piece. 'And as I have no respect for you whatsoever, conceiving a child should be fun.'

'You'd have to make me!' Olympia breathed in growing outrage.

Nik winced and regarded her with semi-screened eyes. 'Oh, I don't think so...I think you'll cling and beg me to stay with you like all my other women do. I'm a hell of a good lay, believe me. You'll enjoy yourself.'

Olympia jerked up out of her chair, so shattered by that speech she was at screaming point. 'You invited me here to try and humiliate me—'

'Trying doesn't come into it. Sit down, Olympia, because I haven't finished yet.'

Olympia threw him a look of fierce disgust. 'Get lost!'

She stalked over to the chair where he had tossed her jacket and snatched it up.

'If I were you, I wouldn't push me,' Nik drawled in a soft undertone that danced down her rigid spine like a gypsy's curse. 'I've got you where I want you.'

'No way!' she launched at him, in such a temper that if he had come any closer she would have swung a fist at him with pleasure.

'Does your mother know about the sordid little encounter

in the car park that concluded your visit to Greece ten years ago?'

Olympia's feet welded to the carpet. Her face drained of colour as if he had pulled a switch. So appalled was she by that question she just stared into space, her stomach knotting with instant nausea.

'Lesson one, Olympia,' Nik murmured with soft, sibilant clarity. 'When I say I've got you where I want you...*listen*!'

CHAPTER THREE

NIK COZAKIS strolled across his enormous office and gently eased the jacket from Olympia's loosened grasp to cast it aside again.

He closed his hand over hers and guided her back to the armchair. Positioning her in front of it, he gave her a gentle push downward, and her knees bent without her volition. She sank down in slow motion but settled heavily as a stone.

'You wouldn't...you *couldn't* approach my mother...'

Nik hunkered down in front of her with innate athletic grace. Level now with her, he scanned her ashen face and appalled eyes. 'Oh what a dark, dark day it was for you when you walked into my office, Olympia...' he murmured with silken satisfaction.

Olympia was now in so much shock she was shaking. 'You don't know what my mother knows—'

'What do you think I've spent the last week having done? I've had enquiries made,' Nik told her levelly. 'Your mother was very friendly with your next-door neighbour at your last address, and she was a *very* talkative woman.'

'Mrs Barnes wouldn't remember—I mean, you couldn't possibly...' Olympia was stammering helplessly now, so horrified by the threat he had made she could barely string two coherent thoughts together.

'Unfortunately for you, the lady remembered very well, for the simple reason that your *disappointment* that summer ten years ago has long been an ongoing source of regret to your mother, Irini, and a subject to which she often referred.'

'*No*—'

'You came home to loads of tea and sympathy, you little liar,' Nik framed with slashing scorn, his dark, deep drawl

39

flaming through her like a cutting steel knife. 'You lied your head off about why our engagement was broken!'

Transfixed, Olympia gasped strickenly. 'It wasn't all lies, j-just a few evasions…I mean, I never did what you thought I did in that car park anyway, so why would I mention it?'

Nik shook his arrogant dark head at that claim and sighed, 'You're getting just a little desperate here, and really there's no need.'

'No need? After what you just—?'

'If you do as you're told, you have nothing to be afraid of. I will take your sordid little secret to the grave with me,' Nik promised evenly. 'Hand on my heart, I would really *hate* to be a prime mover in distressing your mother.'

'Then don't!'

Nik vaulted fluidly upright again and spread lean brown hands wide. 'I'm afraid there's a problem there…'

'What problem?' Olympia rushed in to demand jerkily.

'I have a powerful personal need for revenge,' Nik admitted, without a shadow of discomfiture.

'*Revenge?*' Olympia stressed with incredulity.

'You dishonoured me ten years ago. *Philotimo*…or do you not even know what that word means?' he derided.

Olympia had turned even paler. *Philotimo* could not be translated into one simple English word. It stood for all the attributes that made a man feel like a real man in Greece. His pride, his honesty, his respect for himself and for others.

'I see that your mother educated you to some degree about our culture,' Nik noted. 'I wish to avenge my honour. You shamed me before my family and my friends.'

'Nik…I—'

'I could just about bear you surviving in misery somewhere in the world as long as I never had to see you or think about you,' Nik extended gently. 'Then you came into my office and asked me if I was a man or a mouse and I found out which…just as you're going to find out by the time I'm finished with you.'

'I apologised—'

'But you didn't mean it, Olympia.'

'I mean it *now*!'

Disconcertingly, Nik flung his handsome dark head back and laughed with reluctant appreciation at that qualification.

Olympia took strength from that sign of humanity. 'You're not serious about all this,' she told him urgently. 'You're angry with me and you want to shake me up, and I wish...I really do wish now that I had never come near you.'

Nick dealt her a hard, angry smile. 'I bet you do. Accept that you've brought this particular roof down on yourself!'

Olympia squared her aching shoulders. 'All I did—'

'*All* you did?' Nik rasped with seething force, his lean strong face hard as iron, his fierce anger blazing out at her in a scorching wave of intimidation. 'You dared to believe that you could *buy* me with your dowry!'

Olympia gulped. 'I—'

'Even worse, you dared to suggest that I, Nikos Cozakis, would sink to the level of *cheating* an elderly man whom I respect for the sake of profit. That elderly man is your grandfather...have you no decency whatsoever?' he roared at her in disgust.

Olympia was cringing, devastated by the manner in which he seemed to be twisting everything around and making her sound like a totally horrible person. 'It wasn't like that. I thought—'

'I'm not interested in hearing your thoughts...every time you open your mouth you say something more offensive than you last said. So if you have any wit at all, you'll keep it closed!' Nik advised with savage derision, a dark line of colour delineating his hard cheekbones. 'You *owe* debts, and through me you will settle those debts.'

'What are you t-talking about?'

'What you *did* ten years ago cost your poor mother any hope of reconciliation with her father. What you *did* ten years ago savaged your grandfather. And what you did to me, you can find out the hard way,' Nik concluded darkly.

Stabbed to the heart by that reminder about her mother, Olympia dropped her head, tears springing to her eyes. 'It wasn't my fault…what happened…I was set up—'

'You're embarrassing me,' Nik slotted in with contempt. 'Lies and fake shame are not going to protect you.'

'You're scaring me…' Olympia condemned tearfully. 'You are really scaring me!'

Nik bent down and closed his hands to hers and tugged her upright. 'You're getting too upset.'

'You can't mean all this stuff you've been saying…'

'I do…but I don't like seeing a woman cry.' Linking his arms round her, Nik stared down at her from his immensely superior height, dark eyes smouldering gold over her damp upturned face.

Olympia's breath tripped in her throat. Suddenly she could feel every individual nerve-ending in her trembling body coming alive. The effect was so immediate it made her head spin. The scent of him was in her nostrils. Warm, husky male with an intrinsic something extra which was somehow exotic and exciting and dizzily familiar. Her heart began to pound in her eardrums.

'Even crocodile tears can get a reaction from me.' Nik slid a big hand down over her hips and eased her so close to the muscular power of his thighs that she gasped, a sort of wild heat whipping over her entire skin surface, leaving every inch terrifyingly sensitive to the contact of his lean, hard physique.

'Nik…no—'

'Nik…*yes*, only you'll learn to say it in Greek and it will be your favourite word,' Nik husked, suddenly hauling her up to him and plunging his mouth down on hers with devouring force.

The hard, sensual shock of him engulfed her in a split second. She had never tasted passion like that before. The stab of his tongue inside the tender interior of her mouth hit her with such electrifying effect her whole body jerked and quivered, a low moan of response breaking deep in her throat. Instantly she was melting, burning, craving more. Her arms closed round him and an amount of hunger that blew her away erupted with the shuddering force of a dam breaking its banks within her.

Nik dragged his mouth free of hers and lowered her to the carpet again, a derision in his raking scrutiny that stabbed her to the heart. 'Hungry, aren't you?'

Devastated by what she had allowed to happen between them, and jolted by a sense of loss so strong it hurt, Olympia swung up her hand to strike him. Nik caught her wrist between firm fingers, the speed of his reaction shocking her. 'Those kinds of games don't excite me,' he warned her drily.

Olympia whirled away from him in a fever of confusion and distress. She couldn't believe that she had responded to him. She didn't want to believe it, any more than she could come to terms with the stormy surge of sexual need which had betrayed her. 'You *wouldn't* tell my mother—'

'Want to run that risk? And destroy the single character trait you have that I can admire?'

'And what's that?' she muttered shakily.

'You love your mother and you don't want her to know what you're really like.'

Olympia felt her jacket being draped round her slumped shoulders. 'You can't want to marry me—'

'Why not? I get the Manoulis empire and a son and heir. Spyros gets a great-grandson—a reward and consolation which he certainly deserves. I also get a wife who really knows how to behave herself, a wife who never, ever questions where I go or what I do because we have a business deal, *not* a marriage,' Nik enumerated lazily. 'A lot of men would envy me. Especially as I didn't even have to go looking for my bridal prize...she put herself on a plate for me.'

'I hate you...' Olympia whispered with real vehemence. 'I'll never marry you...do you hear me?'

'I hope you're not about to go all wimpy on me, Olympia,' Nik sighed. 'I'd find that very boring.'

'You bastard…you rotten bastard…what are you doing?' she demanded as he separated the fingers of her hand.

'Here is your engagement ring… No, *not* the family heirloom you flung back at me ten years ago…you don't qualify for a compliment like that.'

Olympia stared down mute and stunned at the diamond solitaire now adorning her engagement finger.

'Romantic touch. Your mother will appreciate it even if you can't.'

Nik walked her through a connecting door into another room and straight into a lift.

'You can't do this to me, Nik!' Olympia argued weakly.

'Damianos is waiting in the car park down below. He'll see you get driven home. Get some sleep. I'll see you tomorrow.' As Olympia's cardigan threatened to fall off, Nik wrapped it round her like a blanket. Then he punched the relevant button on the lift control panel for her.

The doors whirred shut. Olympia snatched in a shivering breath, suddenly appreciating that she had a dreadful pounding headache and that she had never felt so exhausted in her entire life. She tottered out of the lift into a well-lit basement car park. Damianos glanced at her waxen face and averted his attention again.

Nik's bodyguard had warned her that she would be eaten alive, she recalled dully. She hadn't listened, hadn't believed him, would not have credited in a million years that Nik Cozakis could run rings round her now that she was an adult of twenty-seven. But Nik had run so many rings round her that right now she might as well have been lurching one-legged through a swamp as she followed Damianos to the waiting limousine.

All of a sudden she saw herself as a fisherman, who had dangled a worm as bait and suffered the gut-wrenching shock of a man-eating shark rearing up out of the waves in front of her. And she couldn't believe, didn't believe, flatly refused to even *begin* to believe that Nik would carry through on such threats.

Olympia wakened with a heavy head the next morning.

When she had arrived home the night before, Irini Manoulis had already retired to bed. Olympia had lain awake far into the early hours, engaged in a frantic mental search for an escape. But there was only one possible escape route: she had to have the courage to call Nik's bluff. Why on earth hadn't she mentioned her mother's weak heart? However much he hated and despised Olympia, Nik would not threaten the health of a sick and fragile woman.

Olympia clawed up into a sitting position, using both hands to throw back the heavy mane of hair that rippled in tumbled mahogany waves almost to her waist. She grimaced. A grown woman of her age with hair still *that* long! She remembered her mother brushing it when she was a little girl, but most of all she remembered Nik skimming light fingertips through those glossy strands and saying, 'I love your hair...'

Ten years ago, ferocious bitterness and a mindless need to hit back at Nik Cozakis the only way she could had controlled her. That was why she hadn't defended herself when she'd been accused of betraying Nik with Lukas Theotokas. By then convinced that she had been used and abused by everyone who surrounded her, she had preferred the tag of being shameless to the reality of being exposed as she really was.

Number one wimp and patsy and fool! That was what she had been. She had only been a means to an end to her grandfather, human goods to be traded through marriage to the most prestigious bidder. Nik and his ambitious father had only seen the Manoulis empire, on offer for the price of a wedding ring. Hands had been shaken on the deal before she had even set foot on Greek soil.

And though she didn't want to relive the past, emotional

turmoil had released memories she usually kept buried, and her treacherous subconscious summoned up afresh her first sight of Nikos Cozakis at her grandfather's villa...

Nik by the pool, with a drink in his hand, sleek and designer casual in cream chinos and a black T-shirt. There had been at least ten other young people present that afternoon but Olympia, shy and self-conscious and nervous at being among so many strangers, had seen only Nik.

Nik, laughing at a friend's quip, jaguar eyes glittering in the sunshine. He had stared fixedly at her as she'd emerged from the villa. Deliberate slow cue to double take. Olympia reflected bitterly now on that moment. He had probably looked and thought, *She's even plainer than her photographs!* But back then Olympia had lacked all such perception, and she had been as transfixed by Nik as an eager new convert before a golden idol.

With a distinct lack of subtlety her grandfather had urged Nik over so that he could immediately introduce them. And Olympia had duly mumbled and stammered and blushed like an idiot, staring a hole in Nik's black T-shirt. Her mind had been a blank while she'd struggled without success to come up with something verbally witty and memorable to hold his attention. But she needn't have worried, Nik had done all the talking for her.

Pained by that memory of her own naivety, Olympia emerged from her reverie and made herself concentrate on the present. The even more hideous present. If she told her mother the *truth* of what had happened that summer, Irini Manoulis would be devastated. Her mother would believe her daughter's version of events, but the humiliation of what Olympia had endured would cause her deep distress. And her gentle parent would never, ever understand why Olympia had failed to hotly defend her own reputation.

But how *could* she have defended herself? Her supposed best friend, Katerina, had backed up Lukas's lying confession of having betrayed Nik with Olympia. Olympia had been sick to the heart, and so bitter after seeing Nik with that beautiful model that all she had cared about was hitting back. Revenge... Yes, Olympia understood both the concept and the craving. Her revenge, her punishment of Nik and her grandfather for misjudging her, had been allowing them to go on believing that she *was* the shameless little tramp they had already decided she was. Nik had been incandescent with stunned rage, his rampant ego severely dented by the shocking discovery that his plain and seemingly adoring fiancée could stray.

Only now did Olympia see how wrong she had been to try to punish them all with their own blind stupidity. Though she could not imagine even now how she could possibly have proved her innocence in the face of the lies that had been told, she knew that her frozen defiance that awful day must have contributed to that guilty verdict. And left Nik fired up with outrage and a desire for retribution that refused to dim even ten years on.

Well, he had given her a blasted good fright the previous evening, Olympia acknowledged. But in the light of day she was too practical, too down to earth to credit that he could have meant all that he had threatened. Giving him a son and heir, for goodness' sake! And what about that extraordinary kiss? The way he had just grabbed her? What point had he been trying to make? That he could kiss her and fantasise about some other infinitely more sexually appealing woman?

Bitterness black as bile consumed her. Of course Nik couldn't be serious...or could he be? He had taken her desperate offer and twisted it into something so threatening her brain had gone into freefall. Having a baby with Nik—worse, going to *bed* with Nik...sheer madness!

In the midst of her feverish thoughts, Olympia glanced at her alarm clock and gasped. Why hadn't her mother woken her up? It was ten to twelve in the morning! Scrambling off the bed, she hurried out of her bedroom and skidded into the lounge, hearing too late the deep burst of masculine laughter that might have forewarned her that her mother had a male visitor.

Lodged one step into the room, clad only in a short faded nightdress, Olympia felt her generous mouth fall open, sea-jade eyes huge at the sight that greeted her. The coffee pot and the best china were out on the dining table. Irini Manoulis was squeezing Nik Cozakis's hand and wiping tears from her eyes. Eyes that were not sad but sparkling, as if an inner light had been relit.

Supremely elegant in a charcoal-grey business suit cut to fit like the proverbial glove, Nik surveyed Olympia with the most supernatural calm she had ever seen. It was as if he was a regular visitor to her shabby home, a lifelong friend of the family, totally at ease with her mother, who was chattering away at speed in Greek, showing more animation than Olympia had witnessed in years.

His dark deepset eyes raked with total cool over Olympia's stricken face. 'Smile, *agape mou*. I'm afraid that when I discovered that you were still in bed I was too impatient to wait any longer to share our good news with your mother.'

'Good…news?' Olympia repeated, like a not very lifelike robot.

Belatedly aware of her daughter's presence, and raising her brows in dismay at the nightdress, Irini Manoulis urged, 'Olympia…go and get dressed! Nik is taking us out to lunch.'

Olympia fell back through her bedroom door like a drunk and dropped down on her bed before her wobbling legs collapsed beneath her. Evidently Nik had come here to tell her mother that they were getting married. Nik was a foe worthy of Machiavelli. And just then, Olympia was fully conscious that she was not Nik's equal in the manipulative stakes.

Barely a step in her wake, her mother entered her room. 'Nik's making the reservations on his portable phone…I need to get changed,' Irini Manoulis shared unsteadily, and then the older woman just flopped down beside her daughter and

shook her greying head in an apparent daze. 'Oh, Olympia,
I'm in shock...but in such *happy* shock I can't even reproach
you for keeping so much from me. What a wonderful young
man you are to have as a husband!'

And with that assurance Olympia received a heartfelt hug
from her mother, and she sat there like a stalactite in a cave,
frozen in time, registering that Nik had bricked up every potential escape route and trapped her with horrific speed and
dexterity.

'How long has Nik been here?' Olympia asked weakly.

'All morning...I would have woken you but we had so
much to discuss.' Too excited, it seemed, to notice that her
daughter appeared to be oddly silent, Irini drew back and
clasped Olympia's hands emotively between her own. 'He
invited me to live with you, but I said no... When I'm older,
who knows? But young couples deserve their privacy, and if
I ever return to Greece I would like my father to invite me.
For now, London is my home.'

'What...what did Nik tell you?' Olympia studied her
mother's workworn hands and gently patted them, struggling
to reason, finding it all but impossible.

Irini cleared her throat. 'Everything, Olympia. Indeed he
embarrassed me with his honesty, but I can truthfully say
now that I have no reservations about you marrying him.'

'Really?'

Her mother sighed. 'I know how terribly hurt you were
that night when you saw Nik with that other girl—'

Olympia's teeth ground together.

'You were both too young, Olympia. And the marriage
was not to take place until Nik had finished university,' the
older woman reminded her. 'A two-year engagement might
test even the most decent young man—'

'We'd only been engaged two months,' Olympia heard
herself interrupt.

An explosive surge of rage was rising inside her, threatening to choke her to death. How could Nik walk in cold

and introduce himself to her trusting mother and contrive to wash himself clean of his past sins? It wasn't fair. It was disgusting, calculating, *horrendous*…

'Yes, but there was alcohol involved. Sometimes when you're young, control is difficult to maintain,' her mother muttered uncomfortably. 'Who knows that better than I? Men have strong appetites…'

Olympia caught her tongue between her teeth before she could blow that dated sexist whopper out of the water.

'Nik had been strictly warned by your grandfather that prior to your marriage there were to be no intimacies between you,' Irini Manoulis pointed out, as if she was telling Olympia something she already knew. 'After what I had done, your grandfather wanted no risk of your marriage having to be brought forward because of a pregnancy.'

In an effort to contain herself, Olympia sucked in oxygen in a long, dragging gasp. The level of Nik's sheer inventiveness hit her like a punch in the stomach.

'It was right to protect you when you were so young.' Her mother sighed. 'But Nik was young too…'

And 'possessed of strong appetites', Olympia repeated, for her own benefit alone.

'Where's your ring?' her over-excited mother was already demanding.

Olympia got up and dug the diamond ring out of the drawer below the wardrobe.

'I told Nik that we had been burgled twice…he doesn't want us to spend one more night here.' Her mother's eyes shone with happy tears as she admired the beautiful diamond. 'It's just like a fairytale…you and Nik. Just like a fairytale, Olympia.'

Ten minutes later Olympia emerged from her bedroom, dressed in black trousers and a loose tunic top. Nik was in the lounge, still using his portable phone, talking in Greek. Olympia studied him, her temper running hot as lava. Just like a fairytale indeed! There would be no going back now.

It would break her poor mother's heart to have her hopes
raised so high and then dashed.

'I suppose you think you've been very, very clever,'
Olympia condemned as Nik switched off his phone.

He swung round, dark deepset eyes pinning to hers and
flaring to gold enquiry, his jawline hardening. Her tummy
muscles clenched, her heartbeat quickening. He let his keen
gaze roam down the taut length of her, lingering on the thrust
of her breasts that even her tunic top couldn't conceal, the
swell of her hips, the apex of her thighs, down and down,
and then slowly back up again. By that stage Olympia's face
was flaming and her teeth were practically chattering with
rage. He looked at her as if she was something he already
owned, a possession, something he had rights over when he
had no rights!

'Irini's happy,' Nik murmured flatly.

'What on earth have you told her about us?'

Nik loosed a soft, sardonic laugh. 'The cover story demanded a shrinking violet afraid to tell her mama that she
was again seeing a man whom she had once believed had
been less than faithful to her.'

'I will *not* give you a child—'

'You won't get a divorce until you do,' Nik countered,
smooth as silk. 'It's your choice.'

Olympia tore her attention from him and covered her furious face with unsteady hands. 'I really *hate* you—'

'Don't muddy the waters with emotions, Olympia. We
made a deal—'

'*You* made a deal.'

'To suit my needs...why not?' Nik fenced back with the
same unnerving cool. 'Now go back into your bedroom and
put on something more festive. This is your mother's day,
not yours. You can leave the talking to me, but you need to
work on smiling and pretending to be happy.'

'And what if I don't?'

Nik slung her an impatient look. 'You will. You'll pretend for her sake.'

We made a deal. What madness had taken her over that she had imagined they might somehow get married and never live together without anyone even commenting on the fact? What had she been thinking of that first day when she had left her grandfather and came up with that wild idea? What had she imagined she would tell her mother in such circumstances?

'I called Spyros last night,' Nik volunteered. 'He didn't ask a single question, but he said he was pleased and he thought that I would make you an excellent husband.'

'He probably hopes you're going to beat seven bells out of me every night!'

Nik dealt her a sardonically amused glance. 'When we have the mutual pleasure of announcing your first pregnancy, Spyros will appreciate that I was much more sensibly occupied.'

Olympia fled back to her bedroom before she lost her head and screamed at him. For her mother's benefit, she extracted a blue dress and light jacket from her restricted wardrobe and got changed.

Nik took them to the Savoy Hotel. They lunched in state. Just as he had promised, Nik did all the talking. They were to move into his London apartment as soon as possible. Irini would be able to decide where she wanted to live at her leisure. Their wedding was to be held in London in a fortnight. Unfortunately, Nik was far too busy to stay put in London until then, and was in fact flying back to Greece that very evening. Olympia studied her plate at the tone of regret he utilised to make that announcement. He was so clever, she grasped dully. He was ensuring that their supposed relationship was subjected to no closer scrutiny than it had already undergone.

Having escorted the two women back to their flat, Nik

watched his future mother-in-law excuse herself to go and lie down for a while.

'Get Irini to a specialist before the wedding,' Nik advised ruefully. 'I never thought I would say it, but your grandfather is stubborn to the point of cruelty. Surely he cannot be aware of how your mother has been living?'

'He wasn't interested in hearing how we were living…or anything else. Nik, please listen to me…' Olympia pressed her hands together, her sea-jade eyes open and unguarded. 'Feeling as we do about each other, how can we possibly live together?'

'Where did you get the outrageous idea that we were about to do that?' Nik demanded in a dark undertone, lean, strong face hardening. 'Do you honestly think I would want to *live* with a woman like you?'

Utter confusion claimed her. 'I don't understand…'

Nik vented a grim laugh. 'I have some pride. I'll share a bed with you, but I won't share anything else!'

Olympia gazed unseeingly into space. He believed a child could be conceived in mutual hatred? But what did it matter what Nik's plans were now? He might be able to railroad her into marriage on *his* terms but once that marriage existed he would find his mistake. She would not allow him to use her like that. She didn't owe him a child. She didn't owe him anything…

CHAPTER FOUR

ON THE morning of the day that Olympia's wedding was to take place, Spyros Manoulis arrived at Nik's apartment.

Not having heard his arrival, and simply wondering where her mother was, Olympia left the luxurious guest room she had been using swathed in a cotton wrap. She heard the low, tense exchange of Greek and, frowning, peered round the corner into the spacious hall. Her grandfather was standing, his white head bowed and what she could see of his face convulsed with strong emotion, as he gripped both her mother's hands. Instantly Olympia retreated back in the direction she had come.

She was pleased for her mother's sake that some sort of reconciliation was taking place, but Spyros had left it to the very last minute. Olympia was inclined to suspect that only the grotesque prospect of striving to ignore his estranged daughter at his granddaughter's wedding had finally broken down the older man's resistance. Indeed, though feeling intensely critical of *any* person capable of withholding forgiveness for twenty-eight years, Olympia was only humbled by the belated realisation that she had held spite against both her grandfather and Nik for *ten* years already. Her sense of superiority faded fast.

A week earlier she had visited the office of Nik's London lawyer and signed the pre-nuptial contract. She hadn't read it, nor had she sought independent legal advice. As long as her mother's future was secure, Olympia was indifferent to any financial arrangements made for herself. She had got all she wanted already, and she was eager to demonstrate to her bridegroom that she wasn't greedy.

Hopefully, when Nik was brought to appreciate that real-

54

ity, he would stop being greedy too, and he would see that the outrageous concept of conceiving a son and heir for his own convenience was quite unnecessary when he was still only twenty-nine years old. Having only spoken to Nik on the phone over the past two weeks, Olympia had been steadily recovering the calm and sensible outlook which came most naturally to her. Nik would see sense, of course he would...

'Darling, I'm so sorry...I lost all track of time!' Irini Manoulis entered her daughter's bedroom in a guilty rush and discovered that Olympia had got into her wedding gown all on her own.

Olympia smiled. 'I knew that my grandfather had arrived. I guessed that you would have a lot to talk about...'

In the space of a fortnight her mother had altered almost beyond recognition. She was eating better, sleeping better and, even more crucially, she had recovered her interest in life. True, she was still frail and easily tired, but an existence free of worry and stress was exactly what the heart specialist had advised and now it was hers.

'You look so lovely...no wonder Nik couldn't wait to marry you this time,' Irini sighed fondly.

All brides were lovely, most particularly in their own mother's eyes, Olympia conceded, unimpressed. And Nik was rushing her to the altar because he was eager for the fresh challenge of taking over her grandfather's companies. Hadn't he said so himself when she'd asked him why?

'Nik will restore your confidence in yourself,' Irini said with conviction.

Olympia almost forgot herself and snorted at that unlikelihood. Her wedding dress, purchased along with a modest new wardrobe on the credit cards Nik had had sent to her, *was* beautiful: slender and elegant in shape, with the most exquisite overlay of handmade lace. It was also dazzlingly white in colour, which would undoubtedly curl Nik's lip.

Indeed, Olympia had rejected other gowns purely on the grounds that they were not quite *white* enough.

It did not dawn on Olympia until the last possible moment that her grandfather was intending to accompany her to the church and walk her down the aisle. As she stepped into the limo while Spyros hovered uneasily on the pavement, the atmosphere between them dripped ice.

'I have been too hard on your mother,' the older man conceded curtly as the car drew away from the kerb. 'But I will make up for that now. If Irini wishes to do so, she can make her home with me again.'

'Good,' Olympia muttered grudgingly.

The silence hung.

'You are a very stubborn woman, Olympia. Very like my late and much loved wife—but in that way *alone*,' Spyros hastened to assure her, her supposed lack of morality clearly still so much on his mind he could think of little else even now.

'Thanks...I think.'

'I really do not want to know how you and Nik arrived at this astonishing *rapprochement*—'

'Good,' Olympia slotted in.

'But I feel it my duty to warn you that you may have troublesome in-laws.'

Olympia unfroze and turned. 'Sorry?'

Spyros grimaced. 'Nik's parents are not pleased, but no doubt in time they will come around. I feel sorry for him. They *were* a close family.'

Until he chose to marry the hussy, Olympia filled in, suddenly feeling hugely rejected and bitter. She had liked Nik's parents once, and his lively little brother, Peri, who had been a child of only ten back then.

'Yet they must feel a certain relief at the ending of the other connection...' her grandfather mused, half under his breath.'

'Other connection?'

Spyros frowned, as if she had been eavesdropping. 'I was talking out loud to myself.'

Nik had been having a wild affair with someone even more unsuitable than she was, she decided. Well, what was that to her? Why should she care? He was welcome to his women, who clung and begged. Her chin came up. Olympia could not imagine demeaning herself to that level with any man. But then Nik wasn't the celibate type, as she had discovered to her cost during their brief engagement. She was glad she would be living alone, sleeping alone.

The church was filled with flowers. The scent of them hung heavy on the air. Nik turned from the altar to watch her approach with grave dark eyes, so incredibly handsome he took her breath away. Tall, dark, beautifully built, his spectacular bone structure accentuated by the candlelight. Her heart turned over and skipped a beat. Hadn't she loved him once? Hadn't this once been her dream? How had it all gone so drastically wrong?

Disturbingly, just as they had discussed many years before, it was a traditional Greek wedding ceremony. Nik's godfather played a leading part in the rites, their wedding rings were blessed and then exchanged, and Nik held her hand throughout. Orange blossom crowns were placed solemnly on their heads. They drank from the same goblet of wine. Then they traversed the bible table three times in order to symbolise their promise to preserve their marriage for ever. By the end of it all Olympia was feeling like a real bride and very confused by the sensation.

Emerging from the church into the spring sunshine, and smiling widely for the waiting cameras, she said impulsively, 'I wasn't expecting anything like that...it was a beautiful ceremony.'

'Celebrating one's cultural heritage is fashionable these days,' Nik countered drily. 'Also a good way to personalise the corporate image.'

Olympia stiffened, no longer in any danger of forgetting

the fact that their marriage had more in common with a business merger than a personal event.

'But I believe I'll stop short of the flying of a flag on the roof tonight and having it lowered once I've enjoyed my bride,' Nik completed with dulcet cool.

Her cheeks burning, she turned outraged sea-jade eyes on him. 'You will *not* enjoy me!'

Joining her in the limousine, Nik dealt her a slumbrous look of amusement.

'I *mean* that,' Olympia warned him, staring rigidly out of the tinted windows as the car pulled out onto the road.

A lean hand closed over hers. She yanked her fingers free again. The next moment Nik closed his strong hands round her waist and simply lifted her across the back seat into his strong arms. 'You were saying, Olympia?'

'Let go of me!' she gasped in sincere shock, colliding with smouldering amber-gold eyes as he brought her down on his long hard thighs with shocking ease.

'When I'm ready.' Nik curved long fingers to her chin, bringing her so close she was gazing right into his stunning eyes. 'What beautiful skin you have...'

Her heart thudded against her ribs, her pulses leaping. 'Are we on the way to a reception?'

'Thank you for reminding me...' Dropping his hand to reach for the car phone, without releasing her from the hold of the powerful arm which still enclosed her waist, Nik stabbed a single button with his thumb and spoke with the chauffeur in Greek.

Then he turned his attention back to Olympia.

'Please let me sit on the seat,' she said, in an acidic tone which would have sent a weaker man into cringing retreat.

'You're going to have to work on that sour attitude, Olympia,' Nik censured in husky reproach. 'I don't like it.'

She breathed in very deep. 'Do you think I give a damn what you like?'

Engaged in pointedly surveying the provocative rise and

fall of her full breasts above the lace-edged bodice, Nik slowly lifted his spiky black lashes again, to rest his gaze on her flushed and furious face. 'I'll train you free of charge... after all, I expect to enjoy the results. Now, where were we?' he enquired lazily, his breath fanning her cheek, that dark deep drawl sending tiny little vibrations down her taut spine.

There was a soft snap as something whirred shut. 'What was that?' she muttered, already finding it difficult to concentrate. The atmosphere closed round her again, her throat catching, an extraordinary awareness of her own body taking hold of her.

'Just ensuring our privacy.' His tone was mesmeric as he framed her face with long fingers, letting a thumb intrude between her moistly parted lips. 'You have a very lush mouth, Olympia...'

Focusing helplessly on his golden eyes, a snaking little quiver assailed her. Heat curled low in the pit of her belly, making her push her thighs together to minimise the sudden ache. All her senses were centred on him with fierce intensity. As she recalled the taste and the feel of that wide, sensual mouth, she trembled, raised an involuntary hand and let her fingers slowly slide into his luxuriant black hair, drawing him closer, wanting, *needing*...

He let the tip of his tongue trace the tremulous fullness of her lower lip and she let her heavy head fall back, exposing her throat, jerking with a low gasp of tormented pleasure as he pressed his mouth hotly to the tiny pulse flickering wildly above her collarbone. The urgency inside her was building at an insane rate. She wanted his mouth so badly, and then he let his long fingers expertly explore the curve of her breast through the fitted bodice of her gown and trace the prominent bud of a straining nipple. She moaned out loud, pressing her hand to the back of his, struggling to get air back into her lungs, feeling as if she was on fire.

Nik withdrew his hand and leant back. 'Making love in

cars really does get you going fast...' he conceded lazily.
'Or maybe it's me you're hot for this time... What do you
think?'

As that insolent assessment penetrated, Olympia jerked her
head up so fast she wrenched her neck, her passion-glazed
eyes stricken. For a soundless beat of time Nik studied her
with measuring eyes of gold. 'Challenge me and I'm ruthless.'

Olympia dragged herself from him and over to the far corner of the seat, her abandoned body both throbbing and trembling. Perspiration beaded her short upper lip. She was devastated by the power he had over her, devastated by the
essential weakness which lay within her. Never one to deny
reality, she knew that the fact she had made no attempt to
stop him touching her had been as good as encouragement.
And that fact filled her with shame.

In the charged silence, Nik loosed a roughened laugh. 'A
demonstration that hurt me too, but I'm not planning to consummate our deal in the back seat of a limo.'

Sending the shutters that blanked out the glass division
between driver and passenger whirring back, Nik communi-
cated with the chauffeur again. He had toyed with the idea
of making love to her, Olympia realised in quivering shock.
'Our deal', not our marriage. *Not* making love either, she
adjusted sickly. Having sex would be a better description.
And how could she have responded to him as she had? That
insane craving for Nik Cozakis knew neither conscience nor
pride. It was an overwhelming hunger which had left her
pathetically weak in his eyes. And he had just dared to use
that weakness to demonstrate how empty her words of defiance could be.

When they arrived at the hotel where their reception was
to be held, Olympia was in line for further unpleasant surprises.

In a room set aside for the purpose, Spyros Manoulis
awaited their arrival in the company of two lawyers. The

dialogue was all in Greek. While Olympia looked on, feeling very uncomfortable, Nik and her grandfather put their signatures to several documents.

The older man took her aside before he left the room and murmured ruefully, 'I want you to know that this was not my choice, Olympia.'

A tide of colour burned her cheeks. She felt intensely humiliated. So even Spyros knew that his granddaughter was to be stripped of any possibility of being personally enriched by her marriage! Mortified by the older man's awareness of that revealing fact, she returned to the table and hurriedly scrawled her signature on the single sheet of paper set out for her. Having assumed that signing away her own rights of inheritance would be a complex matter when so large a business enterprise was involved, she was surprised but relieved that only one document appeared to be required.

But then what did any of it matter? It was foolish of her to be so sensitive, Olympia told herself irritably. She wanted nothing from her grandfather, nothing from Nik either. Nor did she plan to be her husband's beneficiary for one day longer than she could help. How long would it be before Nik tired of their pretence and agreed to a divorce? It wasn't that uncommon for marriages to break up in the very first year, she reasoned, eager to see a light at the end of what promised to be a long dark tunnel. After all, she hated Nik Cozakis, and even in the short term keeping up the charade of being his wife would be a considerable challenge.

Although her grandfather had forewarned her, when Olympia and Nik welcomed their guests she was embarrassed by the chilly reserve of Nik's patrician parents, Achilles and Alexandra Cozakis. They might have attended their son's wedding, but only, it seemed, in preference to publicising their disapproval by staying home.

At first glance she didn't recognise Nik's kid brother, Pericles. At twenty years of age, Peri Cozakis now towered over her. The younger man grinned, brown eyes sparkling with amusement, and only then did a sense of familiarity tug at her.

'Peri...?' she gasped.

'Catch you later...' he teased, well-satisfied by her double take and passing on.

'I wouldn't have known your brother,' she confided to Nik.

'Well, he doesn't *know* you either, except as the good-natured girl who let him slaughter her at basketball...so leave his illusions intact,' Nik responded very drily.

Olympia paled. Dear heaven, she thought in growing dismay and discomfiture, was what had supposedly happened in that wretched car park ten long years ago *never* out of Nik's thoughts for longer than ten seconds? They had been married for little more than an hour and already he had twice made references to that night.

Registering that Nick was speaking to another guest, she lifted her head again, only to freeze. Katerina Pallas stood before her, her hand already extended in greeting but her dark eyes carefully veiled. 'Olympia...'

As she surveyed her one-time best friend, Olympia's own hand simply dropped back to her side again without making contact. The memory of their broken friendship still pained her, and she had never had a friend that close again; betrayed so cruelly, and deeply hurt, she had lost faith in her own sex.

'Perhaps we could talk later...' Katerina suggested with an uncertain smile before she hurriedly moved on.

'How *dare* you?' Nik growled quietly, sending a wave of startled colour into Olympia's cheeks. 'How dare you insult a member of my family?'

Shaken out of her self-absorption by his reaction, Olympia frowned.

Nik dealt her a derisive look. 'I don't care how embarrassed you feel being faced with Katerina again, you will take care to greet her with the respect and civility she deserves!'

'No.'

'What do you mean...*no*?' Nik stared down at her in blunt disbelief.

'I'm not embarrassed and social niceties won't force me into insincerity for Katerina's benefit,' Olympia asserted tautly. 'So keep her away form me. She's just one big fake, and I wouldn't set out to be rude but I *do* have a temper!'

Taken aback by her defiance, Nik drew in a fractured breath, his hard bone structure rigid beneath his golden skin. Only the approach of Spyros Manoulis and the necessity of the bride and groom taking their seats at the top table forced Nik to let that assurance go unchallenged.

Olympia was surprised to register that she felt decidedly smug. Had Nik thought he had married a doormat he could wipe his feet on whenever he liked? Some things—well, plenty of things, Nik would discover he could *not* force. And he wouldn't like that. No, indeed, he wouldn't like that discovery at all. Even when Olympia had been head over heels in love with Nik Cozakis, she had recognised his innate conviction in his own essential male superiority. With blithe ease Nik had simply assumed that he could lay down the law and that she would naturally accept that he knew best in every way and in every situation.

'I really prefer you without make-up,' he had once told her. 'The natural look...'

She had got more subtle, but she had kept on wearing it.

'You're too young to go to clubs, under-age for alcohol as well,' he had reminded her, with an infuriating lack of sympathy. 'Your grandfather wouldn't approve, so you'll have to stay home.'

'I'll got out to a club with Katerina then.'

'You can forget that idea!' Nik had told her instantaneously.

And so they had had their one and only row, hours before the final break-up.

And then, encouraged by Katerina, Olympia had broken in on the boys' night out and what had she found? She tensed, bitter recollection nipping at her. She had found out exactly *why* her fiancé hadn't wanted her around, cramping his style…

After the long meal was over, Olympia was swept onto the floor by Nik to start off the dancing.

'I thought we'd be smashing plates by this stage…tradition and all that,' Olympia heard herself say snidely.

'One more crack of that nature…' His deep dark drawl sizzled above her head.

'And you'll *what*?' she breathed, not liking the sound of her own voice, but in the grip of an uncontrollable need to scratch and draw blood.

'You'll find out.'

'Promises…promises…such a shame you were never very good at *keeping* them!' It was as if Olympia's tongue had developed a life all of its own.

Long lean fingers curved to the nape of her neck, tipping her head back. Smouldering golden eyes blazed down into hers. And Nik caught her up into his arms and took her mouth with a dark, passionate force that went to her head like a drowning surge of alcohol. Taken by surprise, she had no time to put up the smallest defence and the world spun round her at dizzy speed.

The deep thrust of his tongue into her sensitive mouth imitated a far more basic possession. His erotic mastery took her by storm. Her heart-rate rocketed, her pulses leapt, and every inch of her quivering body was engulfed in fiery responsive heat. A need as relentless as it was cruel tore at her with shattering efficiency, leaving her weak and trembling, wholly at the mercy of the physical craving he had unleashed.

As the music came to an end Nik threw back his head and slowly peeled her hands from his shoulders. Brilliant dark eyes scanned her dazed face. 'I like it when you cling, Olympia.'

Gripped by a storm of sheer self-loathing, Olympia forgot that they had an audience and stalked away, only to find escape from the now crowded dance floor blocked by Nik's younger brother.

'It's time I got better acquainted with my new sister,' Peri told her as he folded her lightly into his arms.

'Peri, I...'

The young Greek gazed down at her with surprisingly serious eyes. 'I'm sorry my parents are spoiling your wedding day.'

Utterly taken aback, Olympia looked up at him in real discomfiture.

Peri shook his dark head. 'I can't get over the way they're behaving and I want you to know that I *don't* feel the same way.'

'Thank you,' Olympia muttered awkwardly.

'But I'd be grateful if you'd tell me what's going on...'

'Going on?'

'Come on, Olly,' Peri urged, employing the nickname he had tagged her with as a boy. 'I was a kid ten years ago but I'm not now. Why is my cousin Katerina sidling about looking shifty all of a sudden, and why all this crazy secrecy about what split you and Nik up back then?'

'Secrecy?' Olympia gulped, jolted by that faintly scornful reference to Katerina, not to mention the bald question which had followed. 'Looking shifty' was a remarkably good match of Olympia's opinion of Katerina. She had not enjoyed being forced to watch the other woman put on that convincing show of shy uncertainty in front of Nik.

'I'd also like to know why my parents are embarrassing the hell out of me today. But, more than anything else, I'd like to know *why* Nik is standing back and allowing them to treat you as they have.'

'Maybe your parents just don't approve of my background.' Olympia was desperate to head him off, and belatedly grateful that Nik had forewarned her. Naturally Peri was curious to learn what lay behind so much bad feeling in his own family circle, but she wished he hadn't chosen to open the subject with her.

'They're not out of the ark, Olly,' the younger man reproved. 'My mother wasn't choking back tears all the way through the ceremony just because you were born out of wedlock!'

Olympia compressed her lips, feeling she could have done without that news.

'And considering how she felt about Gisele Bonner being Nik's long-term squeeze, her attitude surprises me even more,' Peri confided, patently unaware that he might be referring to a relationship she had not known about.

Gisele Bonner. The name meant nothing to Olympia, but she somehow knew that she wouldn't forget it again in a hurry. Tilting back her head, she looked up at Peri and said with a cool she was far from feeling, 'You know, Peri…it's really not *that* unusual for parents to be disappointed with their new daughter-in-law.'

'You're stonewalling me,' Peri complained, unimpressed. 'But I warn you. I don't give up easily.'

'And I don't surrender my bride that easily, little brother,' Nik interposed, curving a long arm to Olympia's taut spine and detaching her from the younger man with ease.

Flushed and stiff, Olympia held herself back from Nik as he spun her away from Peri.

'Peri talks a mile a minute…and he's got no discretion,' Nik remarked curtly.

Olympia was aware of his tension but unable to understand its source. If it hadn't seemed such a ridiculous idea she might have wondered what Nik hadn't wanted her to hear. 'He wasn't indiscreet,' she said, and she meant it.

After all, poor Peri was even more out of touch with events than he realised. He didn't know his brother's marriage was a business deal, and a normal bride would have known of any lengthy relationship previously enjoyed by her new husband. Gisele Bonner, Olympia thought helplessly again, her soft, full mouth compressing as she grew rigid as a stick of rock in the circle of Nik's arms. Probably a blonde. Nik liked blondes. Long-legged beautiful blondes, with big blue eyes and not a lot of clothes coverage, she recalled, in her mind's eye recalling the Italian model she had seen him with so many years before.

'Excuse me…' Olympia said flatly, suddenly registering that she was still in desperate need of some breathing space.

Before Nik could guess her intention, she had slid out of his arms yet again and walked off the dance floor to head for the cloakroom. But she only actually got within ten feet of that potential sanctuary before yet another unwelcome event took place.

'Olympia?' Slender and petite in her stylish green suit, Katerina Pallas stepped right into her path.

Shaken, and angered by such a direct approach, Olympia murmured tautly, 'What do you want?'

'We used to be such close friends,' Katerina sighed in a plaintive little-girl voice, looking hurt.

'Save the act for someone who hasn't experienced your idea of friendship,' Olympia advised.

Katerina darted a careful glance around herself, anxious that their conversation should not be overheard. Only then did she risk giving Olympia a mocking smile. 'I almost died of fright when I was invited to your wedding. I thought it might be a trap, but when Nik greeted me just the same as ever I *knew* I was safe!'

'Safe?' Olympia queried.

Katerina tossed her head and laughed. 'It's so obvious that Nik *still* doesn't know what really went on ten years ago.'

'Is it really?' Although Olympia was struggling to look unconcerned, she was mortified by having that reality flung in her face.

But Katerina was too clever to be fooled. If Nik *had* been aware of the appalling lies his cousin had once told, he would naturally have confronted her.

'All hell would have broken loose if Nik had known that I fibbed about you and poor old Lukas!' Katerina gave a little mock shiver of apprehension, her dark eyes scornful as she sneered. 'So, if Nik's married you without knowing the truth, he can only have done it to get Manoulis Industries. You'd still take Nik at any price. Don't you have any pride?'

The knowledge that her lies still stood unchallenged had not only filled Katerina with triumph but had also given her a humiliating insight into the nature of Olympia's marriage. Olympia was cut to the bone.

'More pride than to stand here exchanging insults with you,' she answered tightly, starting to turn away.

But Katerina hadn't finished yet, and she giggled, 'What a come-down for Nik...I expect he'll have to close his eyes and try to pretend you're Gisele Bonner tonight!'

Olympia took refuge in the cloakroom. She felt sick. Her hands were trembling as she rinsed them in cooling water. Katerina hadn't changed one bit. Indeed, it was just a little scary to realise that the passage of ten years hadn't made *any* appreciable difference to the other woman. Katerina was sweet only when she had an audience she wanted to impress, and she still hated Olympia like poison.

However, Olympia did not want a rumour that her marriage was simply a business merger reaching her mother's tender ears. Which it might well do, if Irini Manoulis moved back into her father's home outside Athens. And judging by the way her grandfather was hovering round her mother today, his anxiety for her fragile health writ large in his every protective look and gesture, Olympia reckoned that her parent would not be living in London for much longer.

As she headed in the direction of the top table she saw Nik on the other side of the dance floor. He was scanning the crowds with a frown. Across that distance, brilliant dark eyes suddenly found and held hers. Her heart jumped and her mouth ran dry and she faltered to an unplanned halt. The innate power of that single look electrified her. Involuntarily, she relived the fierce hunger of his mouth on hers and felt the swift answering rise of heat surge at the centre of her trembling body. A wave of burning mortification sent hot colour flying into her cheeks.

No, she hadn't allowed herself to think about that kiss, until just looking at Nik forced her to remember what she would have much rather forgotten. That when Nik touched her, she couldn't yet control her own sexuality. That acknowledgement shamed and embarrassed her. At seventeen she had been able to control and stifle her physical reaction to Nik only because her ability to resist him had never been put to the test. But now the powerful responses she was experiencing frightened and confused Olympia. Nik made her feel like a wanton, and that terrified her. Only frozen indifference would hold Nik Cozakis at bay, and so far she was conscious that she wasn't doing very well in that department.

Nik crossed the floor to her side, black eyes grim. 'It's time for us to leave.'

Olympia tautened. 'But we've only been here a couple of hours—'

'Quite long enough,' Nik cut in with flat finality. 'You put on a lousy bridal act.'

'I don't know what you're talking about...' But even as she said it her memory was serving up taunting images: her silence throughout the meal, the way she had argued with him during that first dance and not once but twice broken free of him to walk away.

'Yes, you do.'

A sensation akin to panic surged up inside Olympia and she dropped her head to study the floor. 'I'm sorry...I'll make a bigger effort.'

'Why tax yourself?' Nik murmured silkily. 'You think I care what people think?'

'I just wasn't concentrating on how I should be behaving. Believe me, I *can* do better,' she asserted in haste, that panicky feeling increasing. All of a sudden the presence of a couple of hundred guests seemed like the best protection she had ever had, and she could not understand why she had been foolish enough to anger Nik by failing to behave like a normal bride.

'Too late. You had your chance and you blew it. Any notion I had of playing the proud bridegroom is long gone,' Nik spelt out very drily. 'So go and say goodbye to your mother.'

'I wanted to spend some time with her—'

'Tough.'

She began to turn away. 'I'll go and get changed first—'

'You'll stay as you are. Your luggage is already on board the helicopter.'

She frowned, taken aback. 'But I have a going-away outfit...I gave my cases to the driver before I left your apartment this morning and told him.'

'I countermanded your instructions,' Nik informed her with complete cool. 'I want to be the one to take you out of that wedding dress.'

Her head flew up, sea-jade eyes sparking. 'But I *told* you—'

'When are you going to learn to listen to what *I* tell *you*?' Eyes black as pitch raked over her and her tummy just flipped at the bleak coldness of that appraisal. 'And I'm not a happy camper right now.'

'H-happy camper?' Olympia stammered weakly.

'Just fifteen minutes ago I watched my cousin Katerina make a second, very generous attempt to reinstate a reasonably civil bond with you,' Nik related with a grim twist of his hard mouth, watching further colour fly into her startled face. 'I also watched her take off again in tears at your rebuff and then pretend that she wasn't feeling well so that she could leave our reception early without causing undue comment!'

Olympia was stunned by that revelation about Katerina. Katerina in tears at her rebuff and making an early departure

from their reception? It finally dawned on Olympia that
Katerina would still put her in the wrong whenever she got
the chance. She was shaken. 'Nik...that's not true. I said
nothing—'

'You behaved like a real bitch and I'm ashamed of you.
But don't worry about it. I won't be letting you loose socially
again,' Nik enunciated with icy clarity.

Olympia, who had never considered herself to be a fanciful
woman, felt the most chilling sense of foreboding spread
through her, but in angry discomfiture she tried to defend
herself. 'Nik, you're not being fair. *She*—'

'I have no interest in hearing your excuses. We're leaving
in ten minutes.'

'To go where?'

Belatedly, she recalled the helicopter he had mentioned.
'We're joining my yacht at Southampton. So I suggest you
spend those ten minutes with your mother,' Nik incised with
ruthless implacability.

Rigid-backed, Olympia approached her parent, who was
sitting with her grandfather. Her mother's eyes were troubled.
Spyros Manoulis stood up, his beetling brows set in a frown
of censure.

'Thankfully your behaviour is now your husband's responsibility, but allow me to tell you that no lady embarrasses
her husband in public.'

Olympia's teeth gritted behind her compressed lips. She
shot a pained look at her mother, who hurriedly scrambled
up to give her daughter a soothing hug. 'Don't let your pride
come between you and happiness,' she urged then, in an anxious whisper.

For a dismaying moment Olympia registered that she was
attracting censure from every conceivable source, and when
that censure also came from the mother she adored, it really
hurt. But an apologetic smile softened her mouth, for she was
genuinely sorry that anything she had done should have worried the older woman. 'When first we practise to deceive...'

she thought bitterly, for when honesty was forbidden, self-defence was impossible.

Indeed, more than anything else at that moment Olympia felt trapped. Her grandfather thought she was incredibly lucky to have got Nik to the altar, and he would always take Nik's side. Her mother was solely concerned with her daughter's happiness, but Olympia was in no doubt that she had just received a firm scold. Meanwhile, Nik was simmering like a volcano about what he saw as her ungenerous reaction to what he had assumed to be an olive branch from his cousin, Katerina. And, no matter what Olympia did or said, all of them would keep on seeing her as being the one in the wrong.

As Nik came to her side, depriving her of even the ten minutes he had promised, resentment currented through Olympia. Then a sharp and disturbing pang of fear assailed her as she appreciated that the very last thing she could face right now was being *alone* with her new husband.

And wasn't that ironic? she found herself thinking helplessly, as they took leave of all their guests. Ten years ago, the one thing she had most longed for was the chance to be alone with Nik, and the natural privacy offered to a newly married couple would have struck her as a heavenly blessing…

CHAPTER FIVE

At the age of seventeen Olympia had fallen for Nik Cozakis like a ton of bricks, and she had hardly believed her good luck at being accepted into the select group of his friends, for she had had nothing in common with them and she had been painfully shy.

Indeed, that summer in Greece she had entered a disturbingly different world. A world peopled with terrifyingly sophisticated teenagers with flash cars and designer wardrobes. And sometimes, looking on, listening to them agonise about their often incredibly superficial concerns, it had seemed to her that though cocooned by so much parental affluence and indulgence, none of them had the slightest idea about what real life was like. But Nik had been the exception. He hadn't *just* been gorgeous. His stunning dark good looks had been matched by an infinitely greater maturity and intelligence.

At the outset of their relationship it had not occurred to her that the regularity with which she'd ended up getting a lift in Nik's car meant anything more than kindness on his part. Then Katerina had told her that Spyros Manoulis had business connections with Nik's father and Olympia had cringed at the idea that her grandfather might have *asked* Nik to look after his English granddaughter.

'You know, I could've copped a lift in someone else's car this time,' she said, on one occasion.

'I don't want to be taking you so much out of your way,' she said on another, squirming with embarrassment when he stayed teetotal all evening at a party and then drove all the way across Athens to take her home. 'Couldn't I just jump on the bus?'

'Please don't feel you have to keep me company. I'm not

73

lonely. I'm quite happy watching everything that's going on,' she said with determination at a swimming party Lukas Theotokas staged at his home when his parents were abroad.

That night Nik flashed Olympia an incensed look and finally abandoned her to her own devices. Becoming tearful on the discovery that she was not at all happy watching Nik taking her advice and dancing with a very attractive girl, she fled indoors to find a quiet corner where she could break her jealous heart in private.

Lukas found her in the kitchen. 'I see Nik's got another fish to fry tonight,' he remarked, cruelly amused by her reddened eyes and pink nose. 'Someone should have warned you that he likes variety. But I've just had a really good idea…'

Olympia had never warmed to Lukas Theotokas, but she didn't understand why until it was too late; he was one of Nik's closest friends but he was jealous of him. Nik was richer, better-looking and more popular.

'A good idea?' she echoed.

'Why don't you and me have some fun?'

'What sort of fun?' she muttered, genuinely bewildered, for she was well aware that Lukas was crazy about Katerina, who flirted like mad with him but refused to go out with him.

'Yeah…I'd be interested in hearing the answer to that too,' Nik drawled from the doorway several feet away.

Stiffening in surprise, Lukas swung round. Nik said something guttural in Greek and his friend reddened and turned on his heel, leaving Nik and Olympia alone.

'What on earth did you say to him?' Olympia muttered uncomfortably.

'That I'd rip his head off if he said anything like that to you again.' Nik closed one hand over her tightly clenched fingers and drew her to him with cool, controlled determination. And then he kissed her. Lightly, gently and without the passion she had dimly imagined would figure in her very first kiss, but still her tender heart stopped dead for a split second before flying off into orbit.

'You're mine,' Nik sighed, in anything but a lover-like way. 'Don't you know that yet?'

'Yours?' she whispered shakily.

'My girlfriend,' he extended, looking exasperated by her need for that explanatory extension.

Struck dumb, she hovered, lips tingling, shyly studying their linked hands, still unable to meet his eyes. And then the joy hit her so hard she very nearly fell over with the force of it.

'Why do you think I've been running after you?' Nik demanded.

'I thought you were just being nice.'

Nik laughed outright. 'I always have a reason for being...*nice.*'

When she told her grandfather that she was dating Nik, Spyros Manoulis gave her a huge approving smile, and at the time she thought nothing of his lack of surprise. Nor did she smell a rat in the fact that her relationship with Nik stayed low-key and that they were only ever together in a group. On some abstract level she noted her friend Katerina's growing coolness, but she was too much in love and too wrapped up in Nik to pay proper heed.

Since they had only been dating six weeks, she was frankly stunned when Nik asked her to marry him. 'I really care about you...' he confided flatly, not exactly pushing the boat out in the New Age man emotional stakes, staring through the windscreen of his Ferrari as if his life depended on the view. 'I think when we're older we could be great together. You're a really caring person. You like kids and stuff.'

But then what choice had Nik had in that timing? By then she'd been within days of her scheduled return to London. He hadn't said that he loved her, but his marriage proposal had encouraged Olympia to take that belief for granted, and it had also freed her from all reserve. She'd been far too busy burbling about how passionately and devotedly she adored and loved him to notice his silence on that point.

Nik had liked that too. In fact, she could still recall him turning his bronzed classic profile towards her, a scorching smile slowly forming on his beautiful mouth, all his earlier tension put to flight. Nik had been relieved that he didn't have to be more verbal, demonstrative or persuasive. But Olympia had only been disconcerted when Nik had taken her home that evening and it had become obvious that Spyros had known Nik was planning to propose before *she* had.

'Of course I spoke to your grandfather first. He thought that perhaps you were too young, but I said we'd wait until I finished university before we got married,' Nik explained when she taxed him about that.

Indeed the serpent entered Olympia's private Eden only at the huge fancy party which Spyros Manoulis threw to announce his granddaughter's engagement.

'I'm just so relieved that Nik's parents like and accept me,' Olympia admitted to Katerina Pallas.

'And why wouldn't they?' Katerina vented a derisive laugh. 'I can't think of a single family in this room who would have said no to an alliance with the Manoulis heiress!'

'What do you mean?'

'Don't you ever get tired of acting like you're the poor little orphan girl without a blessing to your name? It's getting painful, Olympia,' Katerina said cuttingly. 'Everybody knows Spyros will be leaving his empire to you!'

The next morning Olympia uneasily broached the astonishing concept of her being an heiress with her grandfather.

'Yes, it's true. Who else do I have?' Spyros was amused by her unconcealed shock. 'You think I would let you join the Cozakis family with nothing but the clothes on your back? You think Nik's father would have been content to see his oldest son tie himself up *this* young without a little sweetener to the deal?'

'But...but—'

'I'm a self-made man, Olympia. I don't have any illustrious ancestors. The Cozakis family may be top-drawer high-society, but I can match them for every drachma and every tanker they've got!' her grandfather asserted with considerable satisfaction.

'I'm sure you can,' she muttered, thoroughly taken aback by what he was telling her. Suddenly her engagement was acquiring an extra dimension which she had never dreamt existed. A financial dimension...a *deal*?

'I'm proud that I can give you a dowry that puts you on their level. It's a good marriage for *both* families. I need someone to take over Manoulis Industries when I retire, and I can think of no young man who has already shown more promise than Nikos Cozakis. And now, instead of stealing profit from each other by staying in competition,' Spyros continued with positive triumph, 'Nik's father and I will work together.'

That same morning Katerina called in to apologise for her sharpness the night before. She found Olympia in a pensive, troubled mood.

'A dowry, for goodness' sake,' Olympia groaned. 'It's worse than the medieval barter system! Why did nobody mention it to me before now?'

'Women don't tend to get involved in that side of things. But money marries money in our world.' Katerina shrugged her own acceptance of that reality. 'Don't you appreciate how lucky you are? You're not exactly Helen of Troy, but you've still got Nik!'

But would she have got Nik if she had *not* been the Manoulis heiress? That fear powered Olympia's new insecurity. Her trusting assumption that Nik truly cared about her started seeming naive. She began looking to Nik for greater reassurance, but she did not open the subject of her massive dowry with him. She was afraid to confront the possibility of an awful truth. However, day by day that awful truth seeped in on her like a remorseless drowning tide...

Nik did not mention love. Nik did not seem to want to be on his own with her. When she said she'd like to go shopping, he just dumped her on his mother. When Spyros was away overnight on business she asked Nik over for dinner, but he took her out instead, totally ignoring the kind of invitation that most teenage boys could be depended on to take instant advantage of. She remembered all the teasing that had once gone on around Nik, all the earthy references to all the girls he'd supposedly slept with which had once embarrassed her. At one point, becoming desperate to justify his reluctance to so much as put a hand on her breast, she wondered if all that talk had just been fuelled by macho fantasy on his part for his friends' benefit, and if Nik was really still a virgin just like she was!

Indeed, so much did she like that explanation for his remarkable sexual restraint, she actually asked him if he *was* one evening.

'Don't be bloody stupid!' he launched at her in stunned outrage, springing out of his Ferrari as if she had grievously insulted his masculinity, striding up and down with fists clenched with fury before finally bending down to look back in at her with smouldering golden eyes full of sheer bewilderment. 'Where did you get a weird idea like that?'

Scarlet-faced, she mumbled in a mortified whisper, 'I just wondered...I mean, you don't...well, you know...with *me*...and I wondered why not—well...now that we're engaged.'

'We will wait until our wedding night because I respect you as my future wife,' Nik countered flatly. 'If you were Greek, I wouldn't have to tell you that.'

She didn't look at him. For the very first time Nik felt and sounded foreign to her, and he was making her feel like a brazen hussy even while her intelligence told her that she had had the right to ask that question.

'I'm starting to wonder what's going on here,' Nik

breathed harshly. 'Maybe I've been guilty of making false assumptions…are *you* a virgin, Olympia?'

'Yes,' she muttered, angry and confused and embarrassed.

Nik had literally held his breath until he got that confirming response, and she realised then for the very first time that her being a virgin was really, really important to him. And that bothered her. She was only seventeen, but just suppose she hadn't been a virgin? Just suppose she *had* experimented with sex at too young an age? Wouldn't Nik have been able to feel the same way about her? Would he still have asked her to marry him? Suddenly she didn't think so. And it was hard to believe that he could love her and feel like that…

'This is foolish…' Swinging back into the car, Nik reached for her tensely linked hands. 'Very foolish. But you're so shy I wasn't prepared for you to start talking like that, and for a crazy moment it made me suspicious. I just don't want anyone else *ever* to have touched you…'

And it was extraordinary how at that moment, even loving him as she did, and in the midst of struggling to understand his outlook, she felt the most powerful resentment stirring within her. What an idiot she had been to think for one moment that he too might be inexperienced! No, the pure and untouched aspect was to be hers alone! He was denying her what he himself had already enjoyed. He expected her to spend the next two years waiting for their wedding night.

'Suppose…suppose that we wait, and we get married and we find out we don't like each other *that* way?' she suddenly found herself demanding.

Nik withdrew his hand from hers with a jerk. He was disconcerted, not only by her return to the same subject but also by her attempt to argue her point when he had decided that the subject was closed. 'Don't be ridiculous!' he groaned, jaguar eyes golden and derisive. 'Christos…what's got into you today?'

And she might have let the matter drop sooner than risk an argument, but the first incendiary seeds of rebellion were springing up inside Olympia. Nik was defining her limits. She didn't like that. She didn't want to be treated like some untouchable vestal virgin kept in suspended animation until Nik finally told her that, yes, *now* she could have sexual feelings because they were married. He didn't own her. She might love him. But he didn't own her...

Olympia only emerged from her disturbing memories of the past when the helicopter in which she and Nik and Damianos had flown from London began to descend over the water at Southampton.

As the helicopter landed on the helipad on board Nik's yacht, Olympia was stunned by the sheer size of the ship. Indeed, the sleek, futuristic design of *Aurora* left her speechless. Nik had always been very fond of the sea. Yet ten years ago he had not shared that interest with her. In fact he had never once taken her sailing, she recalled wryly. It had been a surprising but telling oversight which Katerina Pallas had remarked on more than once.

About to clamber out of the helicopter, Olympia attempted to untangle her legs from the skirt of her wedding dress while reckoning that no woman had ever been forced to travel in less appropriate attire. Having already sprung out, Nik simply turned and scooped her up into his arms, ignoring her startled squawk to carry her across the deck.

An older man, clad in a smart uniform, greeted them with a wide smile. Quite unfazed, indeed his black eyes gleaming like a conqueror showing off his prize, Nik introduced Olympia to the Greek captain of his crew without putting her down and then strode on. Crossing an area furnished as the most opulent of sun decks, complete with richly upholstered seating and an overhead shading canopy, Nik entered a magnificent large room surrounded by windows on all sides. Olympia, who had naively expected to see little round portholes everywhere she looked, was quite transfixed by the floor-deep stretches of glass and the superb drapes.

'This is the main saloon,' Nik informed her as he lowered her down to stand on the soft deep carpet.

'It's just like a drawing room...' Olympia's annoyance with him was momentarily forgotten as she succumbed to a wide-eyed appraisal of the luxurious furniture, paintings and beautiful flower arrangements.

'*Aurora* was designed to offer all the comforts of home, so that I can work and live on board for long periods.'

Olympia walked over to a window. 'She's enormous... what length is she?'

'Three hundred and eighty-five feet. I'll be glad to give you the official inspection tour tomorrow,' Nik drawled lazily.

Tomorrow, Olympia reflected, her mouth running dry. His raincheck on the timing of any such tour had a significance she was in no hurry to examine. With reluctance, she turned back to face him, shoulders very straight, chin high.

Nik was looking at her. Lush ebony lashes semi-screened his gleaming dark gaze as he let it slowly, sensually roam over her steadily tautening figure. 'You make a beautiful bride, *yineka mou*—'

'Oh, please! Save it for the dummies who cling and beg!' Beneath that earthy all-male visual assessment, a surge of angry pink mantled Olympia's cheeks. She didn't like the way he looked at her; she didn't like it at all. It set every inch of her bristling and filled her with discomfiting heat. But even less did she appreciate the cruel mockery of such compliments. Maybe Nik thought he could *talk* her into bed to make his precious son and heir! No doubt he imagined she would be the same push-over she had been ten years back, still foolish enough to be taken in by his flattering pretence that he found her amazingly attractive!

'I beg your pardon?' Nik countered drily.

'You heard me.' Sea-jade eyes bright as jewels, Olympia stared back at him with a defiance born of growing desperation. Trying to sidestep the issue that this was their wedding night was foolish, she told herself urgently. Once again she needed to make her position clear. Nik was Greek, and bone-deep stubborn. She didn't want him turning up in her bedroom tonight with expectations. The further she allowed his mistaken assumption of supremacy to progress, the tougher it would be to disabuse him of that notion.

'Today you became my wife,' Nik breathed with dangerous softness.

Olympia clashed head-on with eyes that now smouldered like golden flames. She tried and failed to swallow. It was as if all the oxygen around her had been sucked up by the fire of his anger. She couldn't get air into her lungs. Her knees wobbled together and then locked. 'Yes, but there is no need for me to share a bed with you,' she extended in a breathless rush. 'No reasonable decent need, that is.'

'Very well,' Nik murmured without inflection, his lean, dark, handsome face taut with controlled power, and he turned on his heel to walk away from her.

Released from the terrifyingly intimidating hold of his charged gaze, Olympia slumped as if he had stolen the very backbone from her body. Her head whirled with the onslaught of sheer dizzy disbelief. *She had won!* For a split second she couldn't credit that reality, but then her common sense took charge to convince her of it. Naturally she had won. Nik was a civilised contemporary male. Sleeping with her and demanding that she give him a child would only have been a vengeful powerplay. All she had needed to do was stand fast and show him that she would not be bulldozed by his forceful personality into doing anything she did not choose to do.

'Are you coming?'

Intoxicated by the sense of triumph filling her, Olympia emerged from her thoughts to notice that Nik had paused to glance back at her in expectant enquiry.

'Oh...' So they were to go somewhere else now, she grasped. The farce of a honeymoon-style trip was no longer required from her. Nik would leave her in some discreet location and no doubt go off sailing instead with one of the clinging, begging little tarts he seemed to require to stoke his rapacious ego. He was going to let them lead the separate lives she had suggested from the outset. A strange hollowness formed inside Olympia at that prospect even as her steps quickened in his wake.

'You won't be able to change your mind again,' Nik delivered as she drew level with him. 'I hope you appreciate that.'

Mr Irresistible, Olympia christened him inwardly, while her face burned with the heat of her offended pride. Nothing like spelling out just how special he thought he was! Did he fondly imagine that she might have secretly craved an excuse to share his bed? Did he think she was one of those dithering women who said no and didn't really mean it? Well, she had got by for twenty-seven years without sex, and where *he* was concerned a hundred years would not be sufficient to change her view of him!

'I know exactly what I'm doing,' Olympia stated with ringing satisfaction.

Nik signalled to the trio of men working in and around the helicopter, where it sat parked about fifty feet away. They all stopped what they were doing. The one she recognised as the pilot approached, and Nik instructed him in Greek. Not quite quickly enough to conceal his surprise, the man dipped his head in agreement, and strode back to the helicopter to issue his own instructions.

'How brave you are...' Nik drawled, smooth as honey.

Inexplicably that tone shimmied down her stiff spine like the spectral hand of foreboding, but Olympia squashed the sensation and lifted her head high.

'You'll be a laughing stock,' Nik remarked with formidable cool.

Frowning in bewilderment, Olympia twisted her head back

round to look at him again. 'What are you talking about? A laughing stock?'

'If I fly you back to London and dump you back at your grandfather's feet, many of our wedding guests will be shocked, but an equal number will simply be amused.'

For an electrified instant Olympia just stared and stared up into those dark, deepset challenging eyes while her lips slowly parted company.

'Although I contrived to keep the media away from our wedding by various stratagems, such an unusual development will make headlines all round the world. Your mother and your grandfather will be aghast, but they will also appreciate that I am quite within my rights to return a bride who refuses to consummate our marriage.'

Olympia could not credit the evidence of her own ears. Her wide-eyed stare expanded to take in the hard, clean line of his sculpted mouth. He had not raised his voice and he revealed not one atom of anger. He simply spoke as a male describing an inevitable event.

'You c-can't be serious,' she stammered, in incredulous denial of the picture such a threat imposed on her. Their guests would still be partying late into the evening, and as host, Spyros would naturally remain to the end of the festivities.

'Why shouldn't I be?' Nik enquired with supreme calm. 'You're trying to take me for a fool within hours of our wedding. We made a deal and you're trying to back out on it. You picked the wrong guy.'

That assurance rang like a death knell over Olympia. Freedom yawned in the guise of the helicopter now being readied for take-off again. But freedom at *what* price?

'I wouldn't allow you to humiliate me like that,' she stated between clenched teeth of fury.

'I would carry you in kicking and screaming—'

'You're out of your mind...it would be medieval to stage

a scene like that in front of our guests!' Olympia countered in outraged condemnation. 'You wouldn't *dare!*'

'What would I have to lose? If you break the terms of our deal, all bets are off for me as well. I'm Greek. I'm better at winning than losing,' Nik shared gently.

A band of tension was tightening like a vice round Olympia's pounding temples. Her imagination, never so active until Nik had come back into her life again, was currently summoning up the barbaric image of Nik delivering her back to her family like a reject while a transfixed and titillated audience looked on. He wouldn't dare, she repeated inwardly, but, meeting the ruthless challenge of his hard dark eyes, she was no longer so sure.

'This is all crazy,' Olympia protested, abandoning fury in favour of a last-ditch appeal for rational, reasonable behaviour. 'So I stay on board this yacht and we pretend everything is normal in our marriage. Who is to know any different?'

'I don't have much time for cheats,' Nik murmured with measured derision.

Olympia paled. 'You're not being fair—'

'When did I say I'd play fair?'

'You *forced* me into agreeing to your terms for this marriage,' she reminded him tautly. 'You blackmailed me by threatening to tell my mother about—'

'I know...' His stunning eyes shimmered, giving him a coolly reflective aspect. 'But count your own sins first. You came to me and you begged me to marry you.'

'I didn't beg!'

'You begged,' Nik repeated drily.

An enormous tide of pain and frustration welled up inside Olympia. 'It doesn't *have* to be like this between us!'

'I like it this way,' Nik contradicted without hesitation, lean, hard-boned face set in implacable lines.

Olympia studied the helicopter, knowing it might as well be a thousand miles out of her reach. Slowly she turned away from that view and moved back into the main saloon. She parted her lips to speak again, and the words she had to say threatened to choke her. 'I'd like to see my room,' she framed woodenly.

Nik pressed a service button. A steward answered the call. Her thoughts in turmoil, Olympia followed in the steward's wake.

Her first impressions of the level of luxury on board *Aurora* were upgraded with every step she took. She saw a gymnasium and a library and a gleaming swimming pool. The state room she was shown into was exquisitely decorated. Two other doors connected with it. Dismissing the steward, she glanced at the gorgeous flower arrangement and the champagne bucket and grimaced.

She checked out the dressing room and was relieved to discover that only her own clothes hung in the wardrobes. At least Nik wasn't expecting to share the room with her! She walked through to the bathroom. Initially awed by the marble fittings, it took her a second or two to notice that there appeared to be something written on the mirror above the double vanity unit.

With a frown she drew closer.

'COMPETE IF YOU CAN!' was printed in crude letters across the highly polished reflective surface.

Compete with *what*? What on earth…?

Her bemused gaze fell on the glossy magazine spread open to one side. A full-page photograph of a gorgeous blonde in a provocative pose met her bemused eyes. 'Gisele Bonner' ran the scribe beneath. Olympia jerked in actual physical shock. Her brain gave her one brief message: wipe the mirror, put the magazine in the bin unread. She ignored the message.

Stomach flipping a sick somersault, Olympia focused on the picture. In a strappy, very short dress that barely covered her behind, never mind much else, Gisele's lithe, golden and perfect body showed to full advantage. She had incredibly long legs, huge baby-blue eyes set above exotically slanted cheekbones, and the sort of mouth cosmetic firms used to sell

very expensive lipstick. Her straight strawberry-blonde hair
fell like a sheet of polished silk to her elegant bony shoulders.

Olympia backed away from the magazine as if she had
been burnt. Don't look, don't read, screeched her brain, but
she couldn't control her overwhelming need to know what
was written on the opposite page. It was an article on Gisele
Bonner, famous catwalk model and long-term 'companion'
of Greek tycoon Nik Cozakis. She was thirty-two years old
and had sworn that she would never marry because she loved
her freedom and couldn't stand children. With a shaking
hand, Olympia reached out and turned the page. Faced with
a photo of Gisele curved round Nik like a boa constrictor at
the Cannes Film Festival, Olympia wished she hadn't bothered.

An audible gasp sounded behind her. Startled, she whirled
round. A youthful maid stood in the doorway, her attention
welded to what was written on the mirror, her hand flying
up to her mouth in apparent dismay. She started to speak in
a flood of anxious, apologetic Greek, afraid, it seemed, that
she was to receive the blame for that taunting message.
Hurrying forward, she swiped at the mirror with a towel,
smearing the printed words, rubbing fiercely to clear them
from view.

With a soothing but stilted phrase of very basic Greek,
Olympia retreated back into the state room. Why did she feel
so sick? She could not understand why she felt so sick, so
savaged! As the maid scurried out, clutching the magazine,
Olympia sighed. So Gisele had connections on board *Aurora*
Some member of the crew must have been bribed to plant
the magazine and the message. Olympia frowned then, as she
recalled Katerina's crack about Gisele earlier that day. Was
it possible that it could have been Katerina, rather than
Gisele, who had wanted to taunt Nik's bride on her wedding
night?

Compete if you can! Only what normal flesh and blood

woman would even *try* to compete with a female that gorgeous?

Thankfully, Olympia was not the competitive type. Her tremulous mouth compressed; Nik's former mistress was no business of hers. Refusing to waste any more time wondering who might have been responsible for that petty but nasty message, Olympia sat down jerkily in front of the dressing table. Her head ached from the weight of her hair. With impatient hands she began yanking out the pins which anchored the upswept style she had fixed it in earlier that day. Lifting a silver brush, she straightened out the tangles with a force that left her eyes watering.

Standing up, she reached her hands round her back to unzip her wedding dress.

Halfway out of the garment, she heard the door open. She spun round, words of angry rebuke on her lips at that unannounced entrance. As her gown slithered downward, she arrested its progress by spreading her fingers in a frantic movement. Without it she would have been bare to the waist, for the stiffly boned bodice had made the wearing of a bra superfluous.

Nik was lodged one step inside the door, which still stood ajar behind him.

Her mouth ran dry. Her mind went blank. She just gaped at him.

'I came to ask if you were planning to join me for dinner,' Nik drawled in a curiously hoarse undertone.

CHAPTER SIX

'*DINNER*?' Olympia queried shakily.

'In fifteen minutes...' Nik extended.

His attention was one hundred per cent welded to her. And, involuntarily, Olympia returned the compliment. Nik looked sensational, sleek and elegant as a jungle cat and intrinsically exotic. His black dinner jacket outlined his broad shoulders, well-cut trousers shaping his narrow hips and long powerful thighs with a smooth fidelity of fit that came only with the attention of a master tailor and the richest, smoothest cloth.

Exclusive, sexy, intensely male. She couldn't block him out any more. She couldn't drag her eyes from his lean, dark, devastating face. But then all women noticed Nik, turning their heads for a second lingering glance, often staring. His superb bone structure, level black brows and high cheekbones were matched to a narrow-bridged blade of a nose and a sculpted, sensual mouth that was pure temptation. But it was those molten gold eyes accentuated by the luxuriant fringe of spiky ebony lashes that stopped her heart dead in its tracks.

'Fifteen minutes...' Olympia repeated unevenly, fighting to concentrate as Nik stepped back and shouldered shut the door with a sharp, definitive snap.

A drumbeat of pulsing tension thundered in the atmosphere. As she collided with those burnished eyes, her every skin cell leapt. She could feel each breath quivering through her, the quickening crazy thump of her heart, the swelling mortifying ache of her breasts stirring below the stiff bodice. In desperation, she tore her gaze from his and lowered it.

'But right at this moment eating has to be the last thing on my mind...'

"Sorry?' she mumbled, knees trembling.

In the seething silence, Nik elbowed back his jacket, drawing her attention to a part of him she was not in the habit of studying, and to something that the fine tailoring of his trousers could not possibly conceal. The unmistakable thrust of overt male sexual arousal. And that recognition shocked Olympia rigid and sent a boiling blush rushing up her throat into her cheeks. She dredged her shaken scrutiny from him, expecting to feel disgusted, disconcerted even more when instead a sensation of hot liquid heat snaked up between her clenched thighs.

'*Theos*...you look like a pagan princess,' Nik asserted raggedly.

A pagan *what*? As she lifted her head, she caught a glimpse of herself in the dressing mirror. She stared at that unfamiliar reflection in astonishment. She had forgotten that her hair was loose. Her mahogany mane tumbled to her waist like a waving curtain, one pale naked shoulder displayed, the other concealed, the valley between her breasts accentuated by her folded arms.

'Look at me...' Nik urged thickly.

And she didn't intend to but somehow she did. The growling edge to his accented drawl sent a delicious little tremor running down her taut spine. She flung her head back and looked, encountering scorching golden eyes. She was stunned by the raw desire she saw there.

'Go...' she framed shakily.

'Do you honestly think that I'm about to sit down to dinner in *this* state?' Shifting his broad shoulders in a fluid movement, Nik peeled off his jacket and tossed it aside. Long brown fingers jerked loose the knot on his bow tie, unfastened the top button of his white silk shirt. 'Even you couldn't be that cruel—'

'Me...cruel?' Olympia interrupted in a bewildered daze. Although held by his smouldering gaze like a butterfly

pinned to a collector's board, she was hugely aware of the
tie dropping to the carpet, the shirt buttons being undone.

'Let the light of reality in here. Ten years back, while
you played Miss Prim and Proper Prude and brandished
your innocence at every opportunity, I was in absolute *agony*...in the grip of overpowering lust and unable to do
anything about it!' Nik's lean, powerful face hardened.
'Did that give you a kick, Olympia?'

'A...a kick?' Eyes huge pools of enquiry, she stared
back at him, struggling to absorb his assurance that he *had*
found her sexually attractive in those days. That claim ran
against everything she had ever believed, and she was paralysed by a sense of sheer disbelief.

'You kept me in a constant state of arousal. I never slept
after I was with you. My fantasies about what we were
going to do when we got married even embarrassed me!'
Nik admitted grimly. 'I wasn't used to going without
sex...it was torment; it was seriously painful.'

Olympia just gaped, bereft of all ability to conceal her
reactions. 'No...' she whispered in shaken denial. 'No, you
couldn't have felt like that—'

'And I don't intend to suffer that way *ever* again,' Nik
incised with husky vehemence as he crossed the room and
closed his arms round her from behind. 'Because you want
me too, *pethi mou.*'

'I don't!' she gasped strickenly.

Lowering his arrogant dark head, Nik pressed his sensual
mouth to one pale taut shoulder. A streaking dart of fiery
awareness flamed through her treacherous body. 'What's
the point of lying about the past now?' he murmured intently.

'I'm not lying!'

Nik progressed with wicked expertise from her taut
shoulderblade to a highly sensitive spot just below one
small ear. Her legs shook beneath her, her throat extending,
her head falling back against his chest.

'I need to hear you admit that you burned for me too,
that

only the fear that I wouldn't marry you or that you might lose your precious inheritance held you back,' Nik continued.

As he nipped at her tender flesh with his teeth Olympia shivered violently, and a muffled gasp broke from her parted lips. What he was doing to her put to flight all powers of reasoning. Her skin felt hot and stretched tight over her bones, and she was mesmerised by their reflection in the mirror. Nik with his proud, dark handsome head bent as she leant back against him for support. It was the stuff of a thousand of her secret teenage fantasies. She watched in trembling breathless excitement as he closed his hands to her crossed arms; his skin was so dark against her paler colouring.

'Olympia...' Nik gritted.

She squeezed her eyes tight shut in sudden shame, fighting for control and intelligence. But *still* the wave of unbearable heat and temptation beat at her. She was defenceless. For her, at that instant, there was nothing more important than the feel of Nik's lean, long-fingered hands on her, the hard, muscular strength of him, the sinful imagery flickering behind her eyelids.

'You've got it wrong,' she managed to frame jerkily.

'I've got nothing wrong. Ten years ago you played with me.'

There was no resistance in her as he eased her arms apart. Indeed she could hardly get air into her lungs. Her lashes lifted and she focused helplessly on the mirror again, watched her wedding gown dip to reveal her bare pouting breasts. Shame and excitement fought for precedence inside her. No man had ever seen her like that before, but then that was not a truth she had ever wanted to boast about.

'*Theos*...spectacular,' Nik rasped, with every evidence of sincerity.

Momentarily scientific interest overcame her burning self-consciousness. She watched Nik curve his hands to the full straining mounds which she had always despised. However, no such inhibition afflicted Nik. His frank appreciation of her lush curves was unconcealed. His thumbs rubbed in a skilled caress over her engorged pink nipples.

'Nik...' she whimpered between clenched teeth, the current of fiery response shooting to the very heart of her quivering body to leave her boneless and weak.

'Yes...*Nik*,' he spelt out with curious emphasis.

With a sure hand he eased her gown from her hips and let it shimmy down into a pool round her feet. Her skin warmed as she saw herself fully revealed in the pale silk stockings, blue garter and bikini briefs which her mother had presented her with. No longer could she watch like an onlooker.

'Definitely worth waiting a decade for, *yineka mou*,' Nik pronounced with roughened satisfaction. He lifted her up into his arms and tasted her soft mouth with slow erotic sensuality before he brought her down on the bed. 'Now tell me you don't want me.'

And she couldn't, not with her lips still swollen from his, not with her whole body thrumming as if it had a life of its own, craving more of what he had already given her. 'I can't...' she muttered, shattered by the raw power of what she was feeling in every fibre of her being.

Nik gave her a slashing smile that turned her heart over.

Nothing. She wanted nothing but Nik. In the back of her mind she knew it was a mistake, but that terrible hunger for him, fanned to a white-hot heat by his undeniable desire for her, was infinitely stronger. Nik cast off his shirt to reveal a magnificent hard muscular torso. His skin was the colour of living bronze. Black curls of hair hazed his pectoral muscles, petering down to a silken furrow over his hard, taut stomach. She ran out of breath as he unzipped his trousers. Unlike her, he had not an ounce of inhibition, and he moved with the lithe grace of a natural athlete. She liked watching him; she had always liked watching him. Little brown owl, she recalled painfully. But he was just *so* beautiful...

How could any other man have attracted her after Nik?

Nik had been the ultimate. But Nik had betrayed her, and would surely betray her again, yet still she watched and waited for him, feeling terrifying vulnerable.

'Why have you gone so quiet?' Nik murmured thickly, studying her with hot golden eyes.

Olympia emerged from her increasingly frantic thoughts and her sea-jade eyes widened as she focused on him. He was wearing not a stitch. And all that she had ever been curious about was now on view. She was stunned by the sheer size of him. Her face drenched with colour and she twisted her head away, but the image of him stayed with her, an image both threatening and exciting.

'I could be forgiven for thinking that you've never seen a guy stripped before!' Nik loosed a roughened laugh. 'Or did you find out a long time ago that some men turn on for that little hint of modesty and shyness?'

'That's not funny!' Olympia shot back at him, wounded by his derision and suddenly self-conscious, torn by conflicting needs.

Nik came down beside her and pulled her into his arms. 'I was out of line...but there's something going on here I don't understand. It's spooking me.'

She was more nervous than he had expected, she interpreted, but he wouldn't say that in case she read the comment as another attack. And tears stung her ears, because finally she was facing the fact that she wasn't in control any more. He threw himself back against the pillows, carrying her with him. She was engulfed in him, her breasts crushed by the hard wall of his chest, the hot, musky scent of his skin flaring her nostrils.

'I'm not a bastard in the bedroom,' Nik murmured rawly.

She shivered, the heat of his lean, powerful body percolating through her, the sharp ache of hunger intensifying.

'No?'

'No...so stop shivering,' Nik urged, knotting long fingers

nto her hair and tugging her lips hungrily up to the urgent demand of his.

And that kiss was pure naked seduction. He made love to her mouth, dipping his tongue between her readily parted lips to tantalise and torment. Her heart hammered, her tummy clenched and she twisted against him. He shifted in a fluid movement and lowered his dark head to find an achingly sensitive nipple. And she gasped, her back arching against that fierce tug of response she could not withstand.

'I want this to be good for you,' Nik intoned thickly. 'I want to be the best you've ever had.'

And even his dark rich drawl made her quiver. At mind-blowing speed Olympia found herself plunged into a world of sweet sensation, and all the time she was getting hotter and more restive. The feel of his hands on her tender breasts, the knowing expertise of his caressing mouth drove her wild. He traced her feminine mound beneath the thin silk panties and she almost passed out with excitement.

'Please…' she moaned.

Burnished golden eyes held hers then. He said something rough in Greek.

'Nik?' she muttered in a daze.

Lush lashes veiled his gaze. Stripping her of the last barrier between them, his fingers found the damp dark curls at the juncture of her thighs. She twisted and tossed beneath that intimate exploration. The fire inside her was voracious now. She was lost entirely in the hot, teasing torment of Nik's skilled foreplay. She couldn't breathe, couldn't speak, and her body spoke for her, her hips writhing. The need he had taught her to feel had become so powerful it hurt.

Like a lithe dark golden god, Nik came over her and slid between her parted thighs. 'You're so eager…so out of control. Now I finally know how easy it must have been for Lukas to take what should have been mine!'

His tone more than his words made her passion-glazed eyes widen. She gazed up into smouldering golden eyes. Lukas! The name jarred, but she hadn't caught enough of what Nik had said to understand. All that she grasped was that Nik was angry.

'What's wrong?' she gasped.

'Nothing...you're the perfect partner. Hot and willing.'

And, pushing his hands beneath her, he entered her then, in a powerful thrust, and she was so caught up in the newness of sensual invasion she couldn't concentrate. But a split second later she experienced a sharp, jagged pain, and she jerked in dismay under him, a startled cry escaping her.

Nik stilled, pushed himself up and swore in Greek. He studied her with fierce intensity. 'This *can't* be!'

Already the pain was ebbing, allowing her to unlock her tensed muscles.

'You can't be a virgin!' Nik gritted.

Olympia gulped. 'Nik, please...'

Clenching his teeth, Nik groaned with fracturing control, sinking deeper into her, forcing her tender flesh to yield more fully. And the sensation was so unbearably pleasurable that Olympia rose against him with a surprised cry of response. His hungry gaze blazed over her and suddenly he came back down to her again, to drive into her with long powerful strokes. The storm of desire was unleashed again as if it had never been interrupted.

And it was like nothing she had ever imagined. Caught up in the wild primitive rhythm he set, she was overwhelmed by intense excitement. Heart hammering, body burning with the onslaught of that fierce pleasure, she let him push her higher and higher towards the peak she craved with every sobbing gasp she uttered. And when she hit that ecstatic height, wave after wave of shuddering release engulfed her shaken body.

In the aftermath, she was simply stunned. She held Nik close, a crazy kind of joy already beginning to pierce the sense of peaceful satiation. She felt him brush a soft kiss across her brow like a caress. It felt so good to be in his arms, to share in the sort of intimacy she had never known before. Now, at the back of her mind, she was registering that Nik had actually recognised that he had been her first lover. Somehow, at her age, she hadn't expected there to still be any actual physical barrier. So she hadn't thought of that possibility or of what a difference it might make to their relationship. But now it occurred to her that Nik would surely have to accept that she had *not* betrayed him with Lukas ten years earlier.

In an abrupt movement that took her aback, Nik pulled away from her and sprang off the bed. With a frown, she flipped over. He yanked the bottle of champagne out of the ice-bucket and uncorked it, his lean, bronzed profile feverishly flushed and taut.

'Surprise…surprise. And of course you didn't warn me I would be the first. No doubt you imagine that being a virgin…technically speaking…wipes the slate clean!' Nik bit out in a charged undertone as he sent the champagne foaming down into a single goblet.

Noticing that his hand couldn't hold the goblet steady, Olympia sat up, clutching the sheet to her breasts, and simply stared, utterly disconcerted by this renewed attack.

Nik tossed back the champagne as if he was relieving a desperate thirst with water. He snapped the empty glass back on the table and finally looked at her, eyes as black and stormy as a wild wintry night. 'No wonder you were so quiet in bed. Did you think I'd be at your feet crawling and begging for forgiveness now?' he demanded rawly.

'I honestly don't know what you're talking about—'

'Like hell you don't!' Nik was ashen beneath his dark golden skin, his superb cheekbones rigid as he surveyed her. 'This changes nothing. Obviously Katerina interrupted you and Lukas before you could take full advantage of your sordid encounter. But it doesn't make you *innocent*. You still betrayed and dishonoured me…you still behaved like a shameless little whore without an ounce of remorse!'

Olympia was shaken by his reinterpretation of events, and for perhaps the very first time she registered a reality she had been reluctant to confront. 'You really do hate me...' she whispered in sick distress.

'After what you did to me, what did you expect?' As he hauled on his trousers, Nik loosed an unsteady laugh that sent a cold shiver down her spine. 'You covered us all with shame.'

Olympia was now pale as milk, but she still recalled that kiss he had brushed across her brow in the aftermath of their lovemaking, a salutation which to her had signified both tenderness and affection. 'But you...you just made love—'

'You think *that* was making love?' His expressive mouth curled with derision. 'I just consummated our deal, Olympia. You still excite me like mad, but what we shared is called sex. And, as I promised, we both enjoyed the experience, but don't start looking for anything more than that from me!'

Olympia sat there like a statue, not moving a muscle, knowing she couldn't afford to move in case she broke down. And if she broke down she might cry or scream or shout, and he would then know that he had *really* hurt her. Self-preservation kept her still, her face a very pale but smooth oval as she gazed back at him in frozen silence, unable to trust her voice enough to attempt speech.

Nik's penetrating dark scrutiny was one of ferocious intensity. She suspected that he was not getting the reaction he wanted from her and that gave her a bitter comfort. After all, she had sacrificed her pride only to be rewarded with a humiliation that smarted and stung even as her body ached from his intimate possession.

'You look just like you looked the morning after you were caught with Lukas. Cold as bloody charity,' Nik condemned with steadily fracturing cool, a flash of gold now illuminating his stunning eyes. 'You have no loyalty and even fewer principles...that lack in you turns me off most.'

It took every ounce of what little courage she had left but

Olympia lifted her chin and murmured glacially, 'I hope I conceive this month. I find this kind of scene a complete bore, but interesting for all that. Here you are, twenty-nine years old, and you're still stuck in the past which I left behind years ago, along with other childish things.'

A dark line of blood ran up over Nik's spectacular cheek-bones. He sent her a look of chilling dark fury and she jerked as if she had been struck. 'Be careful how you fight back, *pethi mou*. Too many people have already suffered at your hands. I don't intend to give you a second bite at the same cherry.'

He strode out. She leapt out of bed, raced about gathering up every item of clothing he had left behind and then, yanking open the door, she threw it all out in a heap in the corridor. Then she stood in the centre of the room, naked and shaking like a leaf. Pulling the sheet from the tumbled bed, she hauled it round herself. Next she poured herself a glass of champagne, hoping it would steady her ragged nerves.

But, try as she might, she could not prevent her memories from taking her back to the night which lay at the very heart of Nik's hatred for her. *Hatred.* She shivered and sank back on the bed to recall what had happened earlier that same day ten years earlier...

Katerina had asked Olympia to go shopping with her that morning.

'I just can't believe the way you let Nik boss you around,' Katerina had remarked over coffee in a café. 'Take his plans for his *own* entertainment tonight. If I was engaged to a guy as good-looking and volatile as Nik Cozakis, I wouldn't let him go out to a nightclub without me!'

'I don't want Nik to feel that being engaged means he has to take me everywhere with him—'

'Everywhere?' Katerina rolled her eyes in cynical disbelief. 'You already get left behind when he goes sailing. You also got left behind when he flew over to Paris to take care of some business for his father. Why don't we spring a   sur-

prise on the guys tonight? We could go to the same club
and see what they get up to without us.'

Olympia didn't fall for that idea at first. When Nik called
in that afternoon, she just asked him up front to let her
accompany him that evening. He told her no, she was too
young. So she threatened to go out clubbing with Katerina
instead.

'No way,' Nik countered. 'Her family wouldn't like it
either. We go out in a crowd to clubs. That way we all
look after each other.'

'But you've just said that I can't come with you tonight—'

'It's a boys' night…OK?'

And they argued and parted for the first time still angry
with each other. Olympia immediately phoned Katerina to
take her up on her suggestion that they gatecrash the evening. Katerina made it sound like a really fun thing to do,
but by the time the taxi dropped them off at the club
Olympia's strongest need was to smooth over the row she
had had with Nik.

They found Lukas sitting alone at a table with Nik's car
keys lying in front of him. When Olympia asked him in
surprise where the other boys were, he muttered something
about them having gone on to a party somewhere else.

Olympia had barely sat down when Katerina suddenly
gasped, 'Oh, no!'

Olympia looked in the same direction and saw Nik.
Lounging back against a pillar, her fiancé was in the act of
hauling a beautiful giggling blonde into his arms. Crushing
her to his lean, powerful frame, he then fell on her like a
sex-starved animal, demonstrating an enthusiasm which he
had never let loose in Olympia's radius. It was a process
which the luscious blonde openly revelled in.

'Who…wh-what?' Olympia stammered in sick disbelief.

'Ramona. She's an ex-girlfriend, an Italian model…let's
get out of here before they see us,' Katerina urged, snatching up Nik's car keys and thrusting them into Olympia's nerve-

less hands. 'We can talk outside about what to do. You *can't* make a scene in here!'

Hustled away at speed, Olympia was too distraught to protest. But a few feet from the exit Katerina stopped dead. 'Tell me, did you enjoy seeing Nik having a good time for a change?'

Olympia met her friend's glinting dark eyes and blinked, convinced she must have misheard her. 'Sorry?'

'Do you want to know what Nik *really* thinks of you?' Katerina enquired sweetly. 'I can tell you because he told me. He thinks you're fat and stupid and sexless, but worth your weight in gold!'

Olympia's stomach twisted. In deep shock, she stared back at the Greek girl.

'Your grandfather and Nik's father arranged your marriage before you even *arrived* in Athens. Everybody knows that.' Katerina gave her a contemptuous smile. 'Without your future inheritance you're nothing! If Nik needs to console himself with more attractive women, who can blame him?'

Stricken by such malice from the friend she trusted, Olympia whirled away and fled out to the car park. Taking refuge in Nik's Ferrari, as she had been primed to do, she burst into tears. Katerina's words stabbed her to the heart while her memory replayed the agonising image of Nik in an explicit clinch with a female ten times more beautiful than she herself could ever hope to be.

Katerina's spiteful assurances might have been discarded had they not fitted like a horrible blueprint to the flaws Olympia had been afraid to confront in her relationship with Nik. His seemingly instant attraction to her, the speed of their engagement, his sexual restraint which could easily be explained by her own lack of sex appeal. Nik had not only never loved her but had also discussed her and laughed about her with his cousin, Katerina. She felt as if she was dying inside herself, destroyed by her own blind, trusting stupidity.

She must have been sitting there a good twenty minutes

before the driver's door opened without warning. She froze, assuming it was Nik, but it was Lukas who climbed in beside her. 'Didn't want to do this, but here I am anyway,' he groaned, every word slurred by the amount of alcohol he had evidently consumed. 'You're standing on everybody's toes, Olympia. Why did you ever come to Greece?'

'Mind your own business—'

Lukas vented a humourless laugh. 'But it *is*...don't you see? My father says our company will be put *out* of business if your grandfather and Nik's father merge their empires. We won't be able to compete any more. Together, they'll be too powerful.'

'It's not likely to happen now,' Olympia whispered tremulously.

In silence, Lukas let his head loll back against the seat.

And then Katerina reappeared, and approached the car with a triumphant smile on her lips. 'All present and correct, I see. Guess what I plan to tell Nik now...'

'Go away...both of you!' Olympia urged brokenly.

'I'm not finished yet. But you and Nik *are*...I can promise you that. Just in case you were thinking of forgiving him for snogging the face off the blonde, I'm about to go back inside and tell him that I've just caught you and Lukas having a high old time of it here in his car!'

'Sorry,' Lukas framed thickly. 'Filthy set-up, but you didn't leave us much choice.'

'Why would you tell a mad story like that?' Olympia stared at the other girl in total disbelief and got out of the Ferrari to look her straight in the face.

'You're so dumb, Olympia.' Katerina dropped her voice to a level that Lukas could not hear. 'Nik and I were getting really close until you muscled in and pushed me out. Who do you think he'll turn to when you're gone?'

It was the last straw for Olympia. No longer in the mood to confront Nik, feeling as gutted as she did, she was desperate just to get away from *all* of them—Nik and Lukas and

Katerina—each of whom had betrayed her. Leaving Katerina and Lukas in possession of Nik's Ferrari, she took off across the car park. Unable to face returning to her grandfather's villa, she ended up walking into a park and spending what remained of the night on a bench.

And when she finally arrived home, at seven the next morning, Nik and her grandfather were waiting for her together. All emotion drained from her by then, she clung to the defensive shell supplied by her battered pride and her seething bitterness. Indeed, that day she genuinely didn't care about Katerina's lies or what she herself stood condemned for doing with Lukas if it enraged Nik and outraged Spyros and got her back home to her mother and London more quickly.

Olympia emerged from her recollection of that ghastly evening of revelation to find that she had had two glasses of champagne and that all of a sudden she wasn't feeling very well. Idiot to drink on an empty stomach! she castigated herself. Why was it that when Nik came into her life she went haywire and made a total hash of everything?

Normally she was quiet, sensible and reasonably mature. She didn't fight with people. She didn't make waves. In the grip of emotional turmoil, Olympia's mind flailed about in a half a dozen different directions. Things from the past didn't fit together as neatly any more, she acknowledged, while wondering why the bed appeared to be lurching beneath her. Was it the effect of the champagne? Standing up, she watched the carpet ripple with incredulous eyes and plotted a swerving path into the marble bathroom.

As she ran a bath for herself and got in, she struggled to concentrate on the shattering confession which Nik had made. His staggering claim that she, the plain Jane that she was, had given him sleepless nights of sexual frustration ten years back. That did *not* make sense—not when she looked back on their excruciatingly proper engagement, during which Nik had behaved as if she'd had a repelling force field surrounding her.

Indeed, she might well have called him a liar this evening had Nik not been demonstrating a most impressive amount of *current* desire for her! Was that why she had lost control and ended up in bed with him? Learning that she could actually *be* attractive to Nik had demolished her defences. Somewhere inside her still lurked the hurt and humiliated teenager who had been forced to see herself as fat and sexless.

Only now, when sanity returned in the aftermath, did she despise herself for surrendering to her own most basic urges, not to mention his. At what price too? 'Consummating their deal'? She shuddered, mortified, tears welling up and running down her cheeks.

Why didn't she *know* more about men? She had spent ten years sitting home with her mother, ten years distrusting the motives of every man who asked her out, and oh, yes, even with her restricted social outlets there *had* been invitations. She had succumbed to a handful of first dates but had invariably seen so many faults in the man she'd then said no to a second date. Yet now she had the horrible suspicion that the only flaw one or two of the nicer men had suffered from had been an inability to be Nik Cozakis! And if that was true, that meant she was a bigger fool than even *he* thought she was!

As she clambered out of the bath a wave of dizziness engulfed Olympia. In the act of wrapping herself in a fleecy towel, she overbalanced and fell. A cry of fright broke from her lips as she hit the floor. She was winded and she was hurt. She lay there sobbing with pain and self-loathing.

'*Theos mou!*' The first she knew of Nik's arrival was the outburst of Greek, swiftly followed by the domineering command to lie still while a pair of infuriatingly invasive hands roamed over her legs and her arms.

'Haven't you had enough of that yet?' Olympia muttered,

reddened eyes squeezed tight shut while she lay there like
a corpse.

'You might have broken something...I heard you
scream!'

'Go away!'

'I'm going to make you comfortable here on the floor
and have a doctor flown in,' Nik announced, sounding
strangely breathless.

'That would be stupid.' Olympia planted both hands on
the floor and slowly raised herself. She felt bruised and
battered but knew she had done no lasting damage.

Her head was still swimming. She opened her eyes to
get her bearings and registered that the bathroom walls
were heaving around her. That optical illusion made her
feel horribly nauseous.

'Oh...' Nik sighed, suddenly recognising what was really wrong and propelling her in the right direction so that
he could offer support while she was ingloriously ill.

He was a true prince when she would have given anything for a male who was squeamish and had simply cut
and run to leave her to it. He mopped her brow with a cool
cloth, murmured what sounded like concerned things in
Greek, and stood by while she freshened up again.

'I'm drunk,' Olympia breathed, rebelling against a sympathy which stung her pride. Glancing up, she collided with
liquid dark golden eyes framed by the most astonishingly
long dark lashes, and even in the weakened state she was
in her heart skipped a beat.

'No, you're seasick,' Nik contradicted without hesitation.
'I should have thought of this, and I'm about to hit the first-
aid supplies and make you feel much better.'

He carried her back to the bed, rolled her out of the towel
and flipped the duvet over her. The entire manoeuvre was
carried out with such dexterity that it was done before she
knew what he was about.

'If I had ever got to take you sailing I'd have been better
prepared for this,' Nik commented with wry amusement.

'Who stopped you?' she muttered, tongue-in-cheek.

'Spyros,' Nik responded, startling her with that answer 'Your grandmother *and* your uncle drowned in the sea Your grandfather didn't trust a teenager to look after you on the water, and with losses like that in the family how could I argue with him?'

As Nik left the state room, Olympia stared into space with shaken eyes. Such a simple explanation for his failure to take her sailing all those years ago, and yet it had never once occurred to her.

Five minutes later Nik reappeared with a glass of water and a tablet. She took them and lay back against the pillows.

Sheathed in tight black jeans and a beige T-shirt, Nik looked younger, more approachable, even more gorgeous than he usually looked. She turned her head away, her pinched profile taut, knowing that she had to look her plainest at that moment.

'I'll be fine now. You can leave me.'

'No. I'll stay until you go to sleep.'

Her lip curled. Nik had been brought up to have wonderful manners. Confronted with apparent female fragility he went into automatic protective male mode. It meant nothing. It meant no more than the consummation of their marriage *deal*, she conceded grimly. So Nik enjoyed sex So Nik wanted a son and heir. All she had really learnt wa that she didn't need to be beautiful, like his ex-mistress Gisele Bonner, to get Nik in the mood, but since men had the reputation of being less choosy than women were about their sexual partners she was in no danger of seeing herself as irresistible.

'If you wanted me so much ten years ago, why did you never do anything about it?' she whispered suddenly, since he seemed to be in a more approachable mood.

'Get real, Olympia,' Nik urged lazily. 'If your grandfather had found out that we were sleeping together, he'd have sent you home in disgrace. I didn't want to be responsible fo causing another family rift, nor did I want you thousands of miles away in London.'

'Yes,' she acknowledged, shutting her eyes.

'Do you want any more good reasons? Like the fact that a pregnancy would have been a disaster for both of us at that age? Or the simple truth that I honestly did want to *try* to wait until we were married?'

Olympia was so disconcerted by the ease with which he offered those explanations that she said nothing. On yet another count Katerina had lied. Nik had never found her unattractive. Indeed, Nik had merely been a remarkably sensible teenager.

She drifted off to sleep without being aware of it and awakened in the early hours to the dim glow of a lamp somewhere close by. When she opened her eyes, she tensed in dismay to find Nik barely a foot away. Still clothed, he was lying on top of the duvet in an indolent sprawl, hooded dark eyes coolly intent on her face.

'What are you thinking about?' she heard herself whisper.

His beautiful mouth twisted. 'Lukas…'

'Magic!' Olympia snapped, and flipped over to present him with a defensively turned back.

'We grew up together. He was a clown but I was fond of him,' Nik breathed in a driven undertone. 'When he died, I felt like I'd let him down.'

'Died?' Olympia flipped back over to focus on him with shocked eyes. 'When did he die?'

'In a drunken car smash a few weeks after you left Greece.' Nik grimaced as he sat up. 'Apparently he was rarely seen sober after that night. I don't think he could cope with what he had done.'

Her face drained of all colour. 'So you're blaming me for that as well.'

'No, I'm not.'

But she didn't believe him. She felt hollow inside. Lukas Theotokas had been Katerina's dupe. Had Lukas even appre-

ciated what he was getting involved in that night ten years
ago? He had had to get very drunk to play his part in the
brunette's plans. It was sad, terribly sad. And if she told
Nik now that his one-time friend had deliberately set out
to break them up by the nastiest means available, Nik
would no doubt go through the roof. She sensed that Nik
now saw Lukas as more sinned against than sinning.

'So much grief followed from that night,' Nik stated
curtly. 'Katerina failed her exams, and for a while her fam
ily were very concerned about her. She was upset about
Lukas—'

'I bet she was.'

Nik dealt her a chilling appraisal. 'You think that
Katerina should have lied to protect you because you were
friends, but for a Greek family loyalty always takes prec
edence.'

Olympia's face shuttered, bitterness choking her. No
longer did she regret her own failure to defend herself
against Katerina's lies. What hope would she have had of
being believed with a blood relative lying in the role of a
witness?

'Katerina lied, and so did Lukas. They both had their
reasons, reasons you don't seem to want to find or exam
ine!'

Untouched by that accusation, Nik regarded her with re
flective cool. 'There's only one thing which doesn't add up
for me—'

'And what's that?'

'No Greek woman would have failed to defend her own
reputation. Why didn't you proclaim the fact that you were
still a virgin when I confronted you the next day?'

Olympia studied him with incredulous eyes. 'You're kid
ding me...do you really think I still cared enough about
you to demean myself to that level?'

'So you *did* see me in the club with that blonde.'

Twin spots of red mantled her cheekbones as she belat
edly realised how much she had revealed with that outburst.

'And you *were* out for revenge when you went with Lu
kas.'

Infuriated, Olympia began to turn away again, but Nik

forestalled her by closing a strong hand over her forearm.
'So I wanted to satisfy my curiosity. Why not? I have very
little memory of that night.'

'I beg your pardon?'

'Someone spiked my drink. If you saw me with Ramona,
it must have been shortly before I passed out.'

Olympia nodded slowly. 'Mr Innocent…Mr Clean. You
know, my mother may have fallen for that storybook explanation, but I'm a lot less easy to impress!'

Nik's level dark brows drew together in a frown, a disconcerted light in his brilliant dark eyes. 'Are you saying
you don't believe me?'

'Got it in one. Not a nice feeling, is it?' Taking advantage of his loosened grip, Olympia rolled over and stuffed
her face in the pillow.

He swore in guttural Greek.

'Oh, you're so sensitive…' Olympia raised her head to
comment, tongue-in-cheek.

Hard dark eyes struck hers in a raw collision. 'You are
one calculating little witch—'

'There's the door…use it,' Olympia suggested, her furious eyes glittering like jewels.

Instead, Nik knotted his long brown fingers into the
glossy mahogany strands of hair tumbling down onto the
pillow beside him, effectively imprisoning her.

'Nik…wh-what?' she stammered, taken aback.

'Nik, yes—but say it in Greek. _Né_,' he intoned, smouldering dark golden eyes gazing down into hers. He found
her still reddened lips with his mouth and tasted her with
hungry, driving intensity. On a scale of one to ten it was
an eleven-plus kiss. Her head spun; she could think of no
pressing reason why she should breathe if it meant sepa-
rating from Nik for a single second. Her heart hammering,
her pulses racing, she was simply overwhelmed by the explosive excitement channelling through her.

'We don't talk about the past from now on,' Nik instructed

thickly as he ripped off his T-shirt and snaked up his lean hips to unzip his jeans beneath her bemused gaze.

Olympia was utterly disconcerted by a danger she had not foreseen. 'No…we shouldn't…we *can't*,' she stressed, pushing out that more forceful negative, one hand palm down, fingers splayed on the warm, hard muscular wall of his chest. She could feel the steady thump of his heart. Without any prompting from her brain, her fingertips were already flirting with the curling black springy hair hazing his bronzed chest.

'No problem…' Nik murmured silkily, reclining back against the pillows all lithe and dark and dangerous.

She made the mistake of meeting his eyes: a jaguar-gold challenge. Her breath feathered in her dry throat and her breasts tingled, their sensitive peaks pinching into taut little buds. She was shaken to realise that the sort of hunger she had only ever experienced when Nik was actually touching her could now surge through her in a mortifying instantaneous tide even when he *wasn't*.

Like a sleek jungle predator biding his time while an unwary prey circled round him, Nik began to smile. It was the smile of the male who knew exactly what effect he could have on her sex. It was unashamedly primal. Her mind recoiled and urged her to slap him hard, but it was an incredibly sexy smile which made her agonisingly aware of her own femininity.

'I think…' Olympia began tremulously. 'I think…'

'Yes, what do you think, *yineka mou*?' Nik lazily coiled one fine strand of her hair round an indolent forefinger, regarding her with glinting dark eyes semi-screened by spiky black lashes.

Dear heaven, she *wanted* him. The answers came in a flood inside her own head! She wanted to rip his jeans off, she wanted him everywhere at once, she wanted to relive every glorious, greedy minute of the ecstasy he had given her the night before.

'I'm not thinking…I'm not thinking anything right now,' Olympia swore in feverish haste, her cheeks burning.

'I *am*…' Pillowing his tousled dark head back on one elbow with a relaxation that shrieked in comparison with her own frantic tension, Nik watched her steadily with a world of intimate knowledge in his slumbrous gaze. 'Why fight what you're feeling?'

'Is this like your…er…standard seduction routine?' Olympia enquired, struggling to get her mind and her body back under safe lock and key again, failing miserably in an atmosphere so alive with sexual awareness she was trembling.

'At the risk of sounding like a jerk, I've never needed a routine.'

The awful thing was that she believed him, which in turn drew her attention to all the reasons *why* Nik had never needed to go to that much effort. Those stunning dark good looks, that high-voltage sexual aura, the charismatic personality which had been noticeably absent with her in recent times but which she recalled from the past with a deep hurting ache of loss. The teasing, the warmth, the easy smiles…

And suddenly out of that memory came an absolutely unbearable longing to be in Nik's arms again, the kind of sharp, desperate craving which she had no hope of resisting that close to him. She lifted her hand almost clumsily and pushed her fingers slowly, almost fearfully, into his luxuriant black hair, leaning over him awkwardly, her heart banging against her ribs as if she was about to plunge off a cliff.

Nik was gracious. He didn't laugh. He didn't speak. He reached up and drew her down to him and let the tip of his tongue dart and flicker between her parted lips in an erotic invitation that turned her bones to water and made her shiver as if she was in a force ten gale. He set her back from him then, and peeled off his jeans with the sort of loaded, unhurried cool that somehow excited her even more. He kicked back the duvet she was still sheltering beneath and came down beside her with fluid predatory grace.

'I might have asked what you like...' Nik husked in his accented drawl, burnished eyes blazingly intent on her as he spread her out beneath him with a care that sent tormented little ripples of anticipation down her taut spine. 'But you don't know what you like yet, which means we have *so* much to discover together, *yineka mou.*'

Olympia was already boneless, but she was halfway to mindless as well by the time he finished speaking. Breathing took major concentration. Nik teased the corner of her mouth with his own. Unable to bear that teasing, she twisted her eagerly parted lips under his and kissed him with all the untutored eagerness that was flaming through her like an attack force. Fantasy was running riot in her brain. She imagined flattening him to the bed, forcing him to do exactly what she wanted him to do.

'On the other hand, we could race for the finishing line...just this once,' Nik qualified raggedly.

'Please...' was all she said.

CHAPTER SEVEN

WHEN stray sounds penetrated Olympia's slumber, she would have ignored them but for the extra-sensory mental jab that urged her to take heed.

She was so exhausted it took huge will-power just to lift her eyelashes. The curtains were wide, sunlight spilling in. She was tense until she found and focused on Nik. Happiness bubbled up inside her with the force of an unrestrained oil gusher. It didn't strike her as odd that she should be happy. Every time she had stirred in Nik's arms during the night she had experienced that feeling and she had become accustomed to it before she had had the chance or the need to question the sensation.

A stray shard of sunlight gleamed over blue-black hair still wet from the shower, curved like a caress over a powerful shoulder and darted down over the long sweep of Nik's back, gilding his bronzed skin to pure gold. His classic profile was hard, very masculine, until that playful sunshine accentuated black lashes as long and lush as silk fans. And she smiled then, a sleepy, secretive smile, while she watched him haul on his jeans. She just adored those lashes; she always had.

She rolled over to the side of the bed closest to him, lying on her tummy, sleepy face propped on one hand, sea-jade eyes open and unguarded. 'Nik...what time is it?'

'Afternoon. Two o'clock. We haven't eaten since we came on board, nor have we emerged from this state room. I imagine my crew are well satisfied with my virility.'

Olympia didn't really think that dry comment through, merely interrupting on impulse to say shyly, '*I* certainly am!'

Nik stilled. She dropped her eyes, reddened fiercely. Odd how daylight could banish all sense of intimacy, she recog-

nised too late. She was annoyed that she had made a com
ment that would make her mother faint dead away in ladylike
disbelief. She had sounded so gauche as well. That final
awareness plunged her into an agony of embarrassment.

'It was good,' Nik conceded, without any expression at all.

Good? she almost shrieked back at him in shock. Good?
Like a meal, a nice day out, a satisfactory piece of work?
Suddenly she was marvelling at the happy contentment she
had woken up with only minutes earlier. Had her brain and
her memory gone on holiday while she slept?

'But then why shouldn't it have been?' Nik remarked with
a slight dismissive shrug. 'I knew we would be sexually com
patible.'

Her swollen mouth trembled. She compressed her lips
hard. A hollow and sick sense of rejection was swallowing
her up like a big black hole. The chill in the air raised goose
flesh on her exposed arms. She had to force herself to look
directly at Nik again. She discovered that she needed armour
cladding to protect herself from the cool distance in those
black eyes, and unfortunately she only had flesh.

Pale and taut now, she muttered, 'I thought we understood
each other better now.'

Hadn't there been a closeness which might not have been
spelt out in actual words but which had surely been shared
not just in the breathtaking intensity of their lovemaking but
in the aftermath too, when he had continued to hold her in
his arms?

'Only when we're in the same bed,' Nik delineated with
precision.

Olympia felt as if he had slid a knife beneath her ribs and
she was fighting not to bleed in front of him. 'I get the mes
sage,' she said tightly.

'I'm leaving for a few days,' Nik divulged smoothly, lean
strong features cool as glass. 'Don't ask me when I'll be
back. I don't know.'

'I do hope it won't be any time soon,' Olympia told him

sincerely, temper beginning to mount in response to the treatment she was receiving.

Nik froze in his path to the door.

'I'll call you if I'm pregnant. With a little bit of luck you won't have to come back at all!' Olympia added for good measure.

In one accelerated movement Nik swung back. Outraged black eyes lanced into her flushed and furious face.

'However, I should warn you that all that flattering effort you expended on me during the early hours may well prove to have been unsuccessful as it's not really the most promising time of the month for me,' Olympia shared in a tone of bitter satisfaction.

'*Christos*...how can you be so crude?' Nik launched with a flash of white gritted teeth. 'You will not refer to the conception of our child in such offensive terms!'

'Silly me...' Olympia barely recognised herself in the provocative persona which had sprung up inside her own skin. 'I forgot what a feeling and sensitive guy you were. I'm so sorry.'

Nik's big hands coiled into fists. Olympia surveyed that evidence of vulnerability and her heart truly sang a triumphant chorus.

'You are my wife,' Nik growled, not quite levelly.

'No...no...no, I'm not. I'm your partner in this deal, the *sleeping* partner,' Olympia reminded him gently, but her own rage was as fierce as his own. Fury poured through her like petrol ready to ignite, blaze and burn him up, for he had hurt her, he had humiliated her, and he wasn't allowed to do that. No. Not this time. Not ever again.

Nik studied her with smouldering penetration, jaguar-gold eyes rising to the challenge. 'No doubt you would like me to lose control and turn violent. Then you could divorce me and take off to freedom with millions of banknotes...is that what you think?'

Olympia frowned, giving the suggestion serious thought.

Strange how the prospect of freedom, even accompanied by millions of banknotes, failed to tempt her, she conceded worriedly.

'Get down and dirty with good legal counsel,' Nik advised in abrasive continuance. 'As you should have done *before* you signed our marriage contract.'

Completely in the dark as to his meaning, Olympia muttered, 'Sorry?'

'I can be the biggest bastard on the surface of this earth, but if you choose to walk out you leave our children behind and you leave the marriage as poor as you entered it,' Nik informed her with grim satisfaction. 'My lawyers said you'd never sign so punitive a contract. They said you'd throw hysterics when you read the first clause and that by the time you read the final one you'd be in need of resuscitation. But then, they don't know you the way *I* know you.'

Olympia was now hanging on his every word. 'Don't they?'

'All you were thinking about was the money,' Nik completed with derision.

'No...not that,' she muttered.

Nik reached the door.

Her blood ran cold as she recognised the amount of control Nik wanted over her; he was even willing to use any children they might have as a weapon against her. He might be fond of calling their marriage a deal, but it was not a term she should take literally. Nik had no plans to treat her as a partner, even of the junior variety. Nik was more into ownership than partnership.

In genuine shock at that realisation, Olympia whispered shakily, 'How can you still hate me this much?'

Teach me, she was thinking crazily, teach me how to hate as hard and for as long as you have hated. It was a lesson she seemed in dire need of learning.

Nik turned back his arrogant dark head. Black eyes without a single softening shade of liquid gold met hers with a coldness that frightened the life out of her. 'I really loved you once. Or is that too deep and sensitive a connection for you to understand?'

Three days later, Olympia congratulated herself: she wasn't crying any more.

I really loved you once. An admission made with the darkest, deepest and most bitter sincerity. A statement she could not dismiss, protest or doubt. And, not to put too fine a point on it, that confession had slaughtered Olympia where she sat. It had ruined her appetite and destroyed her ability to sleep. It had ripped apart the entire fabric of her view of the past and in so doing had sunk her into deep emotional turmoil.

She slid from the extreme of wanting to kill Nik for telling her ten years too late to the extreme of wanting to kill Nik for telling her and then taking off in his wretched helicopter, leaving neither forwarding address nor phone number. Why had he left her? Where had he gone?

Meanwhile *Aurora* kept on sailing, without ever putting into port. Olympia became acquainted with the gym, the sauna, the swimming pool, the library, the fantastic meals and the level of luxury and personal care now available to her at any hour of the day and night. If she wanted her hair done her maid was a hairdresser, with two dozen styles at her fingertips. If she wanted to listen to music the yacht had two bars, a dance floor and a state-of-the-art sound system. And if she wanted to phone her mother the satellite communications systems could handle anything.

Unfortunately talking to Irini Manoulis entailed skilled diplomacy as Olympia bent over backwards not to actually tell a lie. Yes, she was having a wonderful, stupendous time on her honeymoon. Just one problem—and that she did not choose to share with her mother. She was enjoying it solo.

So Nik had *loved* her. Never mentioned it though, never brought himself to the dangerous brink of saying the words

which might have kept them together and encouraged her to
fight Katerina's lies. The fiancé who had never held hands
with her, who had backed off fast when she threatened to get
slushy, who had never given her flowers, cute gifts, cards,
anything that might have spoke for him! Nik had been such
a cool guy at nineteen. *Except* when he'd proposed...

And she put her head down and wept again, because at
twenty-seven, armed with the knowledge of the love she had
doubted at seventeen, she found that clumsy, unromantic
marriage proposal of Nik's back then especially poignant,
especially painful. She remembered his intense relief when
she'd just said yes and then proceeded to do all his talking
for him.

And now, in the present, she agonised over *why* Nik had
left her alone on *Aurora*. After the night they had shared, she
hadn't expected that. Maybe getting her to bed had just been
a challenge for Nik. Or maybe he had simply got bored with
her, bored with the whole set-up. She hadn't been much of
a challenge. Nor could she had been an exciting partner for
so experienced a lover. What had been so special for her had
not necessarily been remotely special for Nik, and she was
ashamed of her own naivety. She had been so happy when
she'd wakened, but Nik had been stone-cold and remote.

Out of bed, he truly did hate her. Why? Once he had loved
her and she had *hurt* him. Forgiving and forgetting wasn't
on his agenda. Nik was ready to fight to the last ditch to hang
on to his bitter desire for revenge. She had compromised his
sense of honour, shamed him in front of others. Too late did
she recognise the intensity with which her Greek husband
still felt those wounds on his masculinity. What a number
Katerina and Lukas had worked on them both that night!
Only now did Olympia find that she *could* accept Nik's side
of the story. Lukas must have spiked Nik's drink and invited
Nik's ex-girlfriend to join them at that club. It was all so far
in the past, yet that night was still poisoning the present and
causing her unimaginable pain.

Why so much pain? And why was she missing Nik so dreadfully? She ought to have been glad to see him go, grateful that he stayed away. But she wasn't. She was hurting too, shaken that Nik was as bitter if not more bitter than she had been. Her own emotions were all over the place. Either she had never got over Nik or she was falling for him again. And that suspicion made her very angry with herself. Nik had married her to gain the Manoulis empire and Nik would divorce her as soon as she gave him a son and heir. It was a straight business deal that had no room for emotion.

When Nik had been gone for five days, Olympia decided it was time to abandon ship. Given the opportunity to travel, she ought to be taking full advantage of it, not sitting around on board *Aurora* with nothing to do but sunbathe and think about a husband who had dumped her for more exciting things within a day of their wedding.

Nik's captain spoke excellent English, and when Olympia told him that she would like to visit the port of Malaga on the Spanish coast he was happy to be furnished with a destination and even mentioned the necessity of taking on fresh supplies. Evidently Nik had not been in touch since his departure, a state of affairs which was the perfect vehicle for her own intentions.

When the yacht docked at Malaga, as an act of exorcism and a statement of her new independence, Olympia asked her maid to cut twelve inches off her hair; she liked the results. However, the Captain looked dismayed when Olympia appeared, to disembark with a travelling bag in her hand. She told him that she would return in exactly a week and then she hastened towards the gangway like an escaping prisoner. It rather spoiled the moment when the older man intercepted her to point out that there were certain formalities to be observed before she set foot in a country of which she was not a resident.

However, within half an hour Olympia had satisfied those requirements and she was on her way. Having read Washington Irving's *Tales of the Alhambra* the previous year, and renewed her acquaintance with the book during Nik's absence, Olympia had her itinerary all worked out. She was heading for Granada, to see the wonderful gardens and the palace-fortress of the legendary Moorish sultans. She caught the train from Malaga, but when she arrived it was late afternoon. Wanting more than a couple of hours to explore the Alhambra complex, she found a small city *pensione* in which to spend the night.

The next morning, coolly clad in a lilac dress in a light floaty fabric, she was walking past the car parks at the entrance to the historic site when a long silver limousine pulled up beside her. His broad face expressionless, Damianos climbed out and flipped open the rear passenger door for her. 'Kyria Cozakis…'

Having stilled in astonishment at first glimpse of Nik's bodyguard, Olympia was frozen to the pavement. How on earth had she been found at such speed?

'Olympia…' A dark, deep familiar drawl murmured from the interior. 'I'll give you a count of five to join me inside the limo *without* argument.'

A furious flush lit Olympia's cheeks. Outraged at being addressed as if she were a spoilt child likely to throw a tantrum, she took a hasty couple of steps closer. 'Someone followed me off the yacht…right?'

'One,' Nik sounded, infuriating her even more.

'Someone's been spying on me. Well, I think that was really low and contemptible—'

'Two.'

Out of the corner of her eye, she noticed Damianos retreat back round the limo and fold into the front seat. 'Furthermore, I have plans of my own—'

'Three.'

'I just want to see the Alhambra…OK?'

'Four.'

'There's no way you are going to tell me to get in that car

when I don't want to, Nik Cozakis!' Olympia slung fierily, with her hands planted on her hips.

'Five...'

Snatching in a ragged breath, Olympia crossed her arms and thrust up her chin. Nik emerged in one fluid but forceful movement. Sheathed in a tailored suit the colour of pale honey, he looked spectacular, and, even mad as she was with him, her heartbeat quickened and her mouth ran dry. Taking note of the curious tourists nearby, Nik assumed a studious air of solicitude.

Lifting her into his arms with exaggerated care, he drawled with fake anxiety, 'You never could take the heat, darling...you need to lie down for a while. Preferably *under* me,' he completed for her ears alone.

Stowed inside the limo because she honestly didn't have the nerve to fight him in a public place, but incensed at the growling arrogance of that conclusion, Olympia gasped, 'I'm getting straight back out again—'

Slamming the door, Nik swung back to her, brilliant eyes hard and angry. 'You took your life in your hands when you left the security of the yacht yesterday!'

Olympia bridled. 'What on earth are you talking about?'

His lean, strong face set in grim lines, Nik continued to study her with unconcealed censure. 'Whether you like it or not, you are the wife of a very rich man and the granddaughter of another, and that makes you an extremely vulnerable target.'

'For what?'

'For kidnappers, thieves and aggressive paparazzi!' Nik spelt out with wrathful bite. 'The instant I learnt you had left *Aurora* alone, I was seriously worried about your personal safety! The crew member who followed you for your own protection was unable to report your whereabouts until late last night.'

Involuntarily, Olympia had paled. 'No thief would find anything worth stealing on me.'

'And how would you like to find yourself at the mercy of a gang of thieves who couldn't even get a Rolex watch for their trouble?' Nik demanded rawly.

Olympia's tummy curdled and she dropped her head. His genuine concern made her feel ashamed, for if she was truthful her primary objective in getting off the yacht had been to infuriate Nik with a taste of the same treatment he had given her. 'I wouldn't...I'm sorry, I honestly didn't think.'

Nik expelled a slow, fracturing hiss. 'At least you are all right...apart from your hair.'

'My hair?' The sudden change of subject disconcerted her.

Nik skimmed lean brown fingers down the foreshortened length of the glossy mahogany strands now hanging just below her shoulderblades. 'You butchered your beautiful hair. How could you *do* that?'

Hot pink flooded Olympia's cheeks. She hadn't been prepared for Nik to be that blunt, nor for the strength of his unconcealed regret.

'You knew how much I loved your hair.' Nik withdrew his hand with a heavy sigh. 'I suppose I'm lucky I didn't hold your throat in the same regard. No doubt you would have cut it and bled to death.'

It was ridiculous, but, feeling like a woman who had sacrificed her sole attraction, she found her eyes smarting with tears. 'It'll grow...' she heard herself say in a wobbly voice, even though she preferred her hair shorter and found it far easier to handle.

'So now we go and see the Alhambra,' Nik murmured flatly.

'No, never mind...you're not even dressed for—'

'I insist, *pethi mou*. Today we take up where we left off a week ago and start learning to be married.'

Olympia flicked a startled glance at him.

Dark, deepset eyes met hers levelly. 'I had some stuff to work out but I should not have stayed away for so long.'

With Damianos and another bodyguard trailing them at a

discreet distance, Nik and Olympia went off to explore the Alhambra. It was a gorgeous day. The sun shone down on wooded walks with the green freshness of spring. Olympia was enchanted by all that she saw: the haunting inner courts with their tranquil fountains and the sand-coloured towers mirrored on the surface of still, silent pools.

They wandered through the lush gardens of the Generalife. In a cool rose-shaded arbour, sunlight sparkling through the drops of a water spout, Olympia glanced up and found Nik's intent gaze welded to her.

'What?' she muttered self-consciously.

'You are quite unaware of your own power,' Nik asserted with an amused shake of his dark head. 'In many ways, still so innocent. That day in my office I would have recognised that if I hadn't been so angry with you.'

Olympia tautened. She recognised the change in his outlook with slow, wondering relief. In his time away from her, Nik seemed to have shaken free of his anger and his bitterness and his desire to wound. 'I did *try* to tell you that nothing happp—'

'No...' Nik pressed a cool forefinger against her eagerly parted lips. 'Leave it all in the past, where it belongs.'

Her eyes shadowed. 'But—'

'No more bad memories.' Brushing back the smooth hair falling across her cheekbone as she frowned, he murmured grimly, 'We were just kids, and kids do stupid things when they get in too deep too young.'

For a split second she wanted to protest that she hadn't done anything stupid, had indeed done nothing to deserve the condemnation she had suffered, but she sensed that it was neither the time nor the place to press that argument again. Nik had moved on, and in the short term so must she, unless she was prepared to risk the promise of a new and better understanding. As she lifted her head again, she collided with smouldering dark golden eyes.

Instantly she was divorced from everything but her intense

awareness of him. His lean, lithe powerful physique, the proud tilt of his well-groomed dark head, the strong cheekbones which stamped his bronzed features with such strength and character and the wicked sensuality of his beautiful mouth.

'I want you, *yineka mou*,' Nik admitted with a boldness that shook her, his brilliant gaze roaming over her shapely figure with explicit hunger.

Just as suddenly, the atmosphere crackled with electric energy.

Olympia felt her face burn and her skin dampen. All sound around them was distanced, just as if the world had stopped. No longer did she hear the soft rush of playing water, the distant hum of voices in the hot still air. Her heartbeat thudded as she snatched in a stark breath. Embarrassment seized her as she became conscious of the heaviness of her breasts and the tormenting throb of her swollen nipples.

His hands on her tense shoulders, Nik drew her closer, a world of intimate knowledge in his stunning eyes. She trembled, the power of every sense heightened, an almost choking excitement currenting through her. But she found it unbearable to be held and not touched.

'It may hurt to wait, but anticipation makes the pleasure all the keener,' Nik muttered thickly, linking his fingers tautly to hers and urging her back into the sunlight.

Later she didn't recall that walk back to the limo, only that it left her with legs that felt as weak as cottonwool. Damianos mentioned something about lunch and Nik vented a ragged laugh. She looked at her watch, but she couldn't interest herself enough to focus and think. Nothing mattered but the burn of Nik's jaguar eyes on her, the possessive hold of his hand, a proximity which was as much a torture to her as a necessity.

She leant towards him in the back of the limo. His fabulous bone structure taut below his golden skin, he held her back. 'Not enough time,' he spelt out with roughened urgency. 'I don't want to be interrupted.'

Olympia snatched in a wavering breath as the limousine sped away. The silence sizzled. She was trembling. She skimmed a fascinated glance down at their still linked hands and felt as if her heart was expanding inside her constricted chest. A wealth of emotion was welling up within her. Fierce longing mingled with even fiercer hope.

For the first time in a month she truly understood herself. She didn't question from where her feelings had come, or even how, she simply accepted the reality of their existence. She *loved* Nik Cozakis. Not with the uncritical adulation of her youth but with the deep desperation of a woman, who knew the pitfalls and the probable hurt that lay ahead. Love wasn't on the agenda in their marriage deal.

The limousine pulled up in front of a palatial building built of ancient weathered stone. Nik tugged her out into the sunlight. With an inclination of his imperious dark head he acknowledged the respectful greeting of an older man standing on the steps and swept her straight through the imposing entrance into a dim interior. On his impatient passage to the stairs she glimpsed ornate dark antique furniture and a vast Persian rug lying on worn flagstones. From the stairs, she saw upturned curious faces studying them across the vast reception hall, and finally realised that they were in a very grand and no doubt very exclusive hotel.

She coloured. 'People are staring at us—'

The shift of one broad shoulder signifying his supreme uninterest in the curiosity of strangers, Nik strode across the magnificent landing. A maid waiting there bobbed the equivalent of a curtsy and hastened to throw wide the double doors of a beautifully furnished reception room.

'This is really lovely—' Olympia began, just a tiny bit taken aback by the indecent speed with which they had arrived within reach of a bedroom and striving to play it cool.

But Nik swung her back to him, cupped her cheekbones with hard, impatient hands and drove his lips down on hers with an explosive hunger that blew her away. She clung to his suit jacket to stay upright, whimpering low in her throat in startled response as his tongue stabbed sensually deep into the tender interior of her mouth.

'*Theos mou…I need to be inside you,*' Nik groaned in frustration as she lay against him, struggling to get air back into her lungs, her whole body weak with aftershocks and the kind of anticipation that reduced all self-discipline to rubble.

He gathered her up into his arms and strode with purpose into the bedroom. Lowering her back on to her feet, he pulled down the zip on her dress and brushed it from her shoulders so that it slid into a heap round her ankles. He scanned her scantily clad figure with heavily lidded golden eyes that made her entire skin surface burn and tingle and slowly settled her back on to the foot of the big bed.

Struggling to concentrate, Olympia muttered anxiously, 'Shouldn't we have checked in at Reception?'

Nik frowned. 'Why?'

'Because that's what people usually do…*isn't it*?'

''Not when they own the hotel.'

'Oh…' Olympia watched him discard his superb tailored suit with the same sort of pent-up excitement she might have felt at the highest point of a rollercoaster ride. Her heart was hammering so hard it was literally a challenge to breathe. Her tongue couldn't form words. Her body trembled, awake and eager and utterly outside her control.

Across the room, she encountered dark golden eyes that made her head spin. She was weak with a wanting so powerful it hurt, but still she attempted to be sensible. 'We…we should talk first,' she whispered unevenly.

'At this particular moment?' Nik demanded in frank disbelief. 'No chance!'

Hot-faced, she surveyed him, her heartbeat pounding at an insane rate in her own eardrums, her swollen lips parted, her mouth dry as a bone.

'This past week has felt like six months,' Nik imparted,

his Greek accent thick as molasses as he stripped off his boxer shorts and strode back to her, naked and glorious.

'I feel like I'm going to die of excitement,' Olympia mumbled in honest shame, shattered by the strength of the craving he could rouse in her. With his eyes, with his words, with the hard, sleek urgent masculinity of his magnificent physique. He was pure, packaged sexual enticement at that moment, and she was enthralled.

As he came down to her, Nik treated her to a primal smile of promise. 'Not yet, *pethi mou*...but soon.'

Already she ached for him, feverishly aware of the hot pulse between her thighs. She held herself very still as he skimmed the straps of her bra out of his path and eased away the embroidered cups to expose her full breasts and their prominent pink peaks.

Venting a groan of satisfaction, Nik captured a sensitive bud between his lips and laved it with the tip of his tongue. With a gasp of reaction, she arched her hips off the bed. Raising his head, Nik pushed his hands beneath her hips and removed her briefs. He let his tongue delve into the sucked-in hollow of her navel while his skilled fingers went on to explore the straining length of one taut thigh. She jerked, almost out of her mind with excitement. Then without warning found herself wondering if it was always like this for him with a woman, indeed, if he was the same with other women, and she tensed, coldness touching the fire burning through her.

She looked up at him, lifted an unsteady hand to stroke her fingers through the black hair she had already tousled and let her fingertips trail back down over one high, proud cheekbone to the firm curve of his chiselled mouth.

For a split second, eyes as dark as jet assailed hers. Nik ravished her mouth with his again. It drove her mind blank, shut out everything but the all-consuming power of sensation and her own needy response. Casting aside her bra, he directed his attention back to the tender flesh he had already sensitised. She squirmed and gasped out loud, the heat building in the pit of her stomach sending a message of fire to the very heart of her.

'*Theos*...if I had touched you in the car, I would have had you,' Nik swore with a ragged laugh. 'Sometimes you turn me on so fast and hard, I feel like an animal.'

'I want you too...' she confided unsteadily, desperate need digging talon claws of impatience into her.

He touched her then, where she so needed to be touched. He discovered the swollen damp welcome that already awaited him and with a hungry growl he shifted and pushed her thighs back with determined hands.

She saw the wildness in him as he came down over her. It was a savage hunger for possession that melted her skin to her bones. His cheekbones were taut and flushed, his brilliant eyes blazing. She lay there pliant and exposed, exulting in his forceful maleness with every fibre of her being.

'I am burning for this,' Nik intoned quietly, with feeling fervour.

He entered her with a single driving thrust that wrenched a keening moan of shaken response from her. Buried deep inside her, he gazed down at her with burning satisfaction and rasped, 'You feel like hot silk. *This*...being with you again...is all I've thought about since I left you.'

She couldn't speak. The intimacy of his bold possession brought a wave of delight that was blindingly intense. Every inch of her quivering body was leaping with crazy excitement, and with his every virile stroke the level of her craving for him increased. Heart banging, pulses pounding, she clung to him. Wild sensation overwhelmed her with hot, drowning pleasure. Then a shooting starburst of explosive heat consumed the last of her awareness and left her freefalling from mindless ecstasy back to the real world again.

Hauling back the covers on the bed in the aftermath, Nik swept her up and laid her down on an exquisitely cool sheet. As he urged her back into his arms, Nik vented a husky laugh. 'It was worth thinking about all week as well, *yineka mou*,' he confided, with very male appreciation.

Olympia's heartbeat was only slowly subsiding to a less maddened pace. She discovered that once more she could think. Her joy at being with Nik again spilt over into momentary sadness, for, looking back ten years, she realised that she now saw a different picture. At seventeen, her ultimate dream guy had asked her out and put an engagement ring on her finger. Nik had genuinely been attracted to her, Nik had genuinely loved her, but she hadn't been equal to the starring role in what had felt too much like a fairy story. So, aided and abetted by her grandfather and Katerina, she had questioned the dream, doubted the dream, and ended up losing the dream through her own sense of unworthiness.

Nik shifted with sinuous sensuality against her. The faraway look of regret in Olympia's eyes was replaced by one of shaken sexual awareness. In the wake of that acknowledgement of loss, she was gripped by a fierce desire to make the most of every moment and live it to the full. 'I loved you so much—'

'Did you?' His lush lashes dipped, screening his spectacular eyes to the merest glimmer of reflective light.

She sensed Nik's withdrawal and knew that once again she had got too close to the fire. She wanted to offer him feverish confirmation and tell him that she loved him still, but fear and pride held her back from that brink. Unable to voice what was on her mind, she took refuge in touching him instead. She wrapped her arms round him in an almost clumsy gesture of affection.

'You're driving me insane with all this intense rave-from-the-grave stuff...it's like the clock stopped ticking for you when you were seventeen,' Nik framed with blunt censure, sliding over on to his back and carrying her with him, rearranging her with confident hands to his own satisfaction.

Olympia was desperately hurt by an accusation that was, she registered belatedly, all too accurate. Yet on their wedding night *she* had been the one to accuse Nik of being obsessed with the past. Now their roles had been reversed. But, perhaps mercifully, her weak body was already reacting with brazen hussy efficiency to the urgent arousal of his. A wave of responsive heat gripped her, blurring all thought. Her breasts were crushed into his chest, her tender nipples tingling at that sensation. She was so close to him, but not anything like close enough.

Nik surveyed her with deceptively indolent sexuality and teasing expectation. 'Now I would like to demonstrate all the many wonderful ways I can give you incredible pleasure, Kyria Cozakis.'

His supreme confidence blazed over her like a scorching golden aura, and she could not hold back the tender smile curving her mouth.

CHAPTER EIGHT

FOUR weeks later, Olympia sat up, sipping the iced water she had poured from the flask by the bed.

They had arrived at Nik's magnificent villa on the island of Kritos late the night before. Olympia had slept well, but now she felt slightly dizzy and nauseous. And she knew *why*, didn't she? Frowning at that acknowledgement, Olympia tugged on a light robe and slid back the doors that gave access to the superb balcony beyond the bedroom. A sea breeze wafted in, the cooling air bliss on her clammy skin. As the voile drapes she had brushed back fluttered, she stilled them with a careful hand and glanced back at the bed.

Nik was still asleep in an indolent sprawl of long, lithe bronzed limbs, the pale linen sheet tangled round his lean hips. A dreamy smile curved her mouth. After an entire month spend cruising the Mediterranean, she was happier than she had ever dreamt of being again. Yet if that was true, why was she holding back on telling Nik that she was pregnant?

It was only eight, but Olympia was too restive to return to bed and went for a bath. Lying back in the scented water, she recalled the terms of their marriage deal and sighed heavily. Nik had been breaking those same rules for the past month. He was *living* with her! Although he had flown in several staff, and begun making use of his office on board *Aurora*, he still spent an enormous amount of time with her. Now that they were back on dry land again, she saw no reason why that shouldn't continue.

Towelling herself dry, she acknowledged that recently Nik had indulged her every wish to the hilt. Such freedom of choice had rather gone to her head, for all her life she had

131

longed to travel and see the sights she had only read about. Over the past weeks the yacht had docked at Majorca, Corsica, Sardinia and finally Sicily. In retrospect, a bewildering jumble of memories engulfed Olympia. Sunlit beaches, shimmering seas, twisting roads and extravagant and beautiful scenery.

Certain memories stood out in sharp definition. Nik linking his hand with hers as they walked through the exclusive resort of Porto Cervo in Sardinia a week ago…his fury at the sudden appearance of paparazzi with flashing cameras and the protective way he had screened her from that unpleasant invasion. Nik laughing, teasing, caring and attentive in all sorts of little ways. Nik telling her off for not wearing a higher factor suncream when she got burned, his concern palpable. And, oh, at least a hundred memories of his lovemaking. Occasionally gentle, sometimes wild, but always passionate.

He loved her body. She accepted that now. At every opportunity he made her feel sexually irresistible. There had been days when her plans to explore new places hadn't even got off the ground, days when Nik had taken one incredulous glance at the itinerary she had mapped out and rebelled, taking her back to bed instead. Nights when they'd never made the dinner table and had eaten in the early hours.

Yet still she was in no hurry to share the news that she had conceived their first child. It was forty-eight hours since Nik had insisted that a doctor examine her sunburned shoulders. Conscious that she hadn't had a period since before their wedding, Olympia had made full use of that consultation. A brief examination and one little test had followed, and then the confirmation had been given: she was going to have a baby. She was both thrilled and terrified. Before their marriage Nik had made her getting pregnant sound like a likely halfway post to divorce.

And what if they didn't really *have* a new understanding? How could she tell for sure? Nik never mentioned the future.

Nik never mentioned the deal he had forced upon her. They could well have been living in a time capsule, where only the immediate present existed. And for now he was charming, the ultimate in entertaining company. But then why shouldn't he be? she thought with a sinking heart. He had already got her pregnant in record time.

'I've got a complaint to make. Where *were* you when I woke up?'

Olympia jumped halfway out of her skin and spun round from the mirror. Nik was poised in the doorway, black hair wildly tousled, strong jawline dark with stubble, slumbrous dark golden eyes gleaming, a wolfish grin of amusement curving his mouth. He looked heartbreakingly gorgeous.

'Nik—'

'I've ordered breakfast…for later.' Strolling across the spectacular mosaic-tiled bathroom, Nik closed his hands over hers and urged her into his arms. 'Join me in the shower and tell me who you were daydreaming about…it had better have been me, *pethi mou.*'

Delicate colour burnished her cheeks. She buried her face in his shoulder, loving the hot, musky evocative scent of his brown skin. 'Who else?'

Disposing of her robe, he swept her under the shower with him. 'I have so much work to catch up on,' he muttered raggedly between hard, drugging kisses that left her taut and trembling, caught up and inflamed by his hungry urgency. 'We have guests coming too. *Theos mou*…to hell with all that!'

A long while later, they breakfasted out on the beautiful stone terrace, shaded by tulip trees and a lush, colourful tangle of bougainvillea. The day was glorious, hot and still, the very light golden. In every direction the views were breathtaking. Set high on a mountainside studded with cypress groves, which stretched down to the blue green waters of the Aegean, the villa was surrounded by lush natural gardens which blended into the landscape.

In the distance she could see the harbour, adorned by a picturesque collection of houses, and the most lovely little church with a domed campanile. In the deep natural bay *Aurora* towered like a giant ocean-going liner in a sea of brightly coloured fishing boats. From her first glimpse of Kritos by moonlight the night before, Olympia had been utterly enchanted.

Only then recalling Nik's reference to guests, Olympia frowned in sudden mingled dismay and amusement at her own inability to concentrate earlier. 'You mentioned guests... who's coming and when?'

'Markos Stapoulos and his wife, Samantha. She's British. I think you'll like her,' Nik drawled levelly. 'They couldn't make our wedding because Markos's father was ill, but they're flying in to lunch with us. They should be here in about half an hour.'

Olympia had already stiffened. Ten years back, Markos Stapoulos had been Nik's best friend. Filled with strong discomfiture at the prospect of meeting him again, she said sharply, 'I suppose Markos knows all about that pathetic car park story as well!'

If ever a silence could have been said to sizzle like the string leading to a stick of dynamite, the endless yawning silence which followed that exclamation sizzled.

Studying her with stunned and disconcerted eyes, Nik rammed his hands down on the surface of the table and leapt up to his full intimidating height. '*Christos!* Do you think I dined out on that particular story?' he grated, with an explosive fury that shook her. 'Apart from your grandfather, only my parents and Katerina know about that night!'

As Olympia watched, pale but unbowed, Nik strode out from beneath the shade of the tulip trees and into full sunlight. He swung back to face her, his bone structure rigid beneath his bronzed skin, brilliant dark eyes hard with condemnation as he spread his arms in a striking show of raw incomprehension. 'Why are you dragging all this up again?'

'Because you still won't either listen to or believe in my version,' Olympia whispered ruefully. 'And I resent that.'

A dark line of colour scored Nik's hard cheekbones. '*Theos mou*...you have no right to resent anything! You're damn lucky I decided to put that tawdry episode behind us and appreciate you for the woman you are today!'

'If you put it behind you, why are you still shouting at me?'

'I...am...not...shouting,' Nik asserted, with such thickened and challenged self-restraint behind that assurance that she could barely distinguish his words.

'Good, because I was never with Lukas and I'm going to keep on telling you that until you listen!'

'But I'll *never* believe you.' His black eyes glittered like banked twin fires over her, his derision unconcealed. 'I remember the way you looked at me the morning after. You were guilty and proud of it!'

And Olympia remembered her bitter, silent defiance and recognised that Nik's bone-deep conviction that she was now lying stemmed as much from what he had seen in her as from the nonsense he had been told. A great weariness enfolded her then.

'Yet looking back, knowing what I know now...it was nothing!' Nik shrugged with expressive dismissal. 'I should have said it before now, but naturally being your first lover made up—'

'It made up for so much you vanished for a whole week!' Olympia slotted in. *You have no right to resent anything.*

She shivered, trembling fingers curling round her glass of fresh orange juice. Nice to finally find out what lay behind the smooth and charming façade. A stubborn Greek male as unforgiving as a rock that stood through the centuries, weathered but immovable. She was so furious with him she had to weld her back to the seat to stop herself from flying upright and screaming back at him.

'Why don't you just tell me exactly what you *did* do with Lukas?' Nik demanded with sudden splintering force.

In total shock at that blunt invitation, Olympia's eyes opened very wide.

In response, Nik jerked both his hands up in the air in a speaking gesture of savage frustration. 'It's *your* fault I'm thinking like this again!' he condemned with raw violence. 'Why the hell couldn't you just leave it alone?'

He strode past the table and then stilled, wide shoulders rigid beneath the fine, expensive cloth of his well-cut jacket. He swung back, dug something from his pocket. He tossed a leather jeweller's box down on the table in front of her. It was a careless, understated move that nonetheless contrived to shout censure, reproach and arrogant male superiority. 'I was planning to give you that after breakfast.'

Olympia had never liked one-upmanship. 'What's in the box...a *truth* drug?'

Nik swore long and low in guttural Greek and strode back into the villa.

Olympia flipped open the box and found herself looking at an exquisite diamond-studded locket. She lifted it out, more or less to occupy her shaking hands, and flipped it open. Inside were two tiny photos of her mother and her grandfather. She was incredibly touched by that thoughtful and personalised extra. Had she overreacted or had he? Who was more guilty? The tears overflowed.

Resolving to pull herself together, Olympia went back indoors. Passing through the superb galleried hall, she went upstairs to their bedroom. What did Nik feel for her? Did he feel *anything* of any importance? Or was she just another bed partner for a highly-sexed male? Was the dark side of Nik's volatile temperament getting a kick out of the fact that she couldn't resist him? For, if he cared at all, how could he still distrust her to such an extent? That hurt her very much. It also seemed to make a complete charade of the wonderful weeks they had spent together.

In search of her make-up, Olympia reached for the handbag she had used the night before. It was a capacious holdall, and with a moan of impatience she tipped out the entire contents on to the bed. In the act of reaching for her cosmetics purse, she stilled in surprise to study the medium-sized brown envelope which had also fallen out of her bag. The envelope was sealed and she had never seen it before.

With a frown, she tore it open. A newspaper cutting and a pair of glossy colour snaps tumbled out on to the smooth silk bedspread. Olympia stared fixedly at the topmost photo, its rather fuzzy quality suggesting the use of a long-range camera. It was Gisele Bonner, lying topless on a sun lounger in the arms of a male who looked remarkably like Nik. Remarkably. She peered at that male image with straining eyes and then bent to examine the other photograph. Another shot of a bare bosom she would sooner not have seen, she conceded, with what felt like a hysterical laugh building like a giant bubble in her tight throat. But in the foreground of that second photo, now standing full face to that clever, intrusive camera lens, she saw Nik. Not a male who bore a remarkable resemblance to Nik but a male who was without a single shadow of doubt Nik Cozakis!

Her heart sounded a dulled, thunderous thud. Without warning, the door at the other side of the room opened. 'Olympia...?' It was Nik's rich dark drawl.

Without the slightest thought or hesitation, Olympia flung herself face down on the bed across the photos, the newspaper cutting, her handbag and its jumbled contents.

Nik drew to a halt and regarded her prone position with a slight frown. 'Are you feeling OK?'

'Fine...'

When she made no move to get up, Nik hunkered down by the side of the bed, his stunning dark eyes level. 'You've been crying—'

'No, I haven't been.'

'Liar,' he groaned, one forefinger gently tracing a silvered tear-track marking her cheek. 'I'm sorry I lost my head. I just can't think straight when you mention…' His lean strong face shadowed and darkened, his tension returning. 'I know it's not reasonable, but just please don't mention it again. It makes me…unreasonable,' he selected, after a long hesitation and perceptible difficulty in coming up with an alternative word.

'Yes…' She wasn't really listening; the facts of that stupid business with Lukas ten years back now seemed unimportant. She was staring deep into Nik's gorgeous dark golden eyes and praying, praying that the photos she was concealing from him were *old* photos, sent by his vindictive ex-mistress merely to taunt and distress his new wife.

'Are you sure you're OK?'

Olympia's fingernails curled into the bedspread. 'Just give me five minutes to fix my face—'

'Did you like the locket? Damianos said lockets went out with parasols and fans, but I thought it was *you*…'

'It's me,' she confirmed tightly.

His brows pleating, Nik vaulted slowly back upright.

As soon as he had gone, Olympia rose into a crouch to snatch at the crumpled newspaper cutting lying beneath her. Sinking back on to her knees, she spread it, surprised to see that there were two photos set side by side in the cutting. One the pool scene featuring Nik and Gisele in a clinch and the other of Nik and Olympia emerging from the church after their wedding.

As Olympia registered the proof that the picture of Nik about to snog Gisele must have been taken after she herself had married him, she sucked in oxygen in a great gulp, perspiration dampening her brow. Her stomach curdled. Sick, deep shock engulfed her. Beneath the pool photo, in confirmation of her worst suspicions, ran the immortal words; *'Nik Cozakis breaks his honeymoon in the Med to comfort his mistress.'*

That first week they had been married, the week when he

had left her alone on the yacht. When else? Nik had been with his mistress, Gisele Bonner. A mistress not former but *current*. Getting up from the bed, Olympia thrust the photos and the cutting back into her handbag. Then she hovered like a sleepwalker. She went into the bathroom to freshen up. But when she got there she discovered she hadn't brought her cosmetics purse with her and she had to walk back to the bed to fetch it. Then she found that her hands were shaking so badly she was powdering her eyes instead of her shiny nose.

Who had planted that envelope in her bag? Her maid? Five weeks earlier, greeted on the yacht on her wedding day with that 'Compete if you can!' message and the magazine article on Gisele, Olympia had believed the young Greek woman was innocent of any involvement. Now she was less naive. Only her maid had enjoyed such free access to her state room. Only her maid could have easily put anything inside her handbag. But right then the identity of Gisele's helpmate seemed relatively unimportant. It *had* to be Gisele who was doing this to her, didn't it? Surely Katerina could not be responsible for these photos as well?

Olympia was so shattered she could barely think straight. I'm pregnant. I'm pregnant by him now, she kept on thinking dizzily, panic threatening. When she heard the whirring, clacking beat of a helicopter getting louder overhead, she had to force herself to leave the bedroom; their guests were arriving. As she went downstairs, she pressed a tremulous hand to her pounding brow. She breathed in very slowly and deeply. She had to get a hold of herself fast, because there was no way, absolutely no way, that she could confront Nik with other people around.

Elegant in her peacock-blue shift dress, Olympia stared across the stone terrace at Nik as he approached the helipad to welcome the arrivals. In a lightweight suit the colour of honey, superbly tailored to outline his broad shoulders and long, long legs, Nik looked sensational. Her heart lurched. A male possessed of devastating attraction who might well have no more sensibility than an animal in the mating season when it came to satisfying his own sexual inclinations. Undersexed he wasn't. She knew that for herself. Her husband, her lover. Time she came back to the real world again, she decided numbly...

Nik Cozakis was a Greek tycoon. One of a rarefied breed of very rich and powerful men, little given to the virtues of self-denial and fidelity. On the very day Nik had blackmailed her into agreeing to *his* marital terms he had said with cool satisfaction, 'I also get a wife who really knows how to behave herself, a wife who never, ever questions where I go or what I do because we have a business deal, *not* a marriage.' Just when had she chosen to forget those horribly revealing words of warning? At what point had she chosen to ditch all memory of that ruthless blackmail and those threats?

Her tummy tied itself into knots and her fingers closed in tightly on themselves. Only as Markos Stapoulos and his wife emerged from their helicopter did Olympia move forward to stand by Nik's side. Markos was a short, thickset cheerful bear of a man, already going grey, Samantha an effervescent Scottish redhead.

Olympia was grateful for the other couple's enlivening presence. She needed time, time in which to get a grip on her flailing emotions. On several occasions she became conscious of Nik's dark, questioning gaze on her and she cursed his perceptive powers. She couldn't bring herself to look at him, and no doubt he had noticed the brittle quality she could hear in her own voice as she endeavoured to respond appropriately to Samantha's friendly chatter.

After lunch, the two men vanished into Nik's office.

'Business, everything is always *business* with Greek men!' Samantha shook her head in rueful acceptance.

'How did you meet Markos?' Olympia asked, just a little of her highwire tension evaporating with Nik's removal from the scene.

'I was a nurse in the London clinic where he had his appendix out. Between you and me and the gatepost, he was terrified! That was three years ago.' Smiling, Samantha relaxed back into her well-upholstered seat. 'You have no idea how much more comfortable I feel here now that Nik has a wife too.'

'You must've met Gisele Bonner,' Olympia heard herself say, and it was as much of a shock to her to hear that comment escape as it was to her companion, who stilled in surprise. 'Please…just forget I said that. I really wasn't fishing!' Olympia hastened to assert.

'No, you can say anything to me. I *do* understand how you must feel.' With an air of ready sympathy which increased Olympia's embarrassment, Samantha leant forward and began to talk in a confidential manner. 'Ex-girlfriends who look as stunning as Gisele and who continue to hog the headlines long after their sell-by date are hard to swallow. Of course you don't like that. The first time we met Gisele, Markos was *mesmerised*…I could have strangled him! I didn't speak to him for a week!'

Olympia felt torn into two, both wanting and not wanting to hear more.

'Gisele's clever, and very ambitious. She got her claws into Nik and hung on in there even when his attention strayed!' her companion divulged.

Olympia nodded, wondering in dulled horror whether she was supposed to be cheered by the news that Nik hadn't been faithful to his mistress either.

'Gisele knows how to please a man. That was the secret of her staying power.' Samantha pulled a face. 'Have you ever met a Greek male who *didn't* love having his ego stroked by a woman who hangs on his every word and treats him like a god?'

Olympia shook her head and closely studied her tightly linked hands.

'You really shouldn't be worrying about her, Olympia.'

'I'm not.' Olympia was beyond worrying. Having learnt the secret of Gisele's success, she knew her marriage was over. The chances of her treating Nik like a god in the near future were slim to none.

'Nik lives very much in the limelight and Gisele adores sharing it with him. It did a lot for her career. I bet she was behind that ridiculous story printed in that downmarket tabloid last month,' the other woman continued with visible distaste. 'But who on earth would believe that Nik was with *her* when you and Nik had only just gone off on your honeymoon?'

'Who?' Olympia echoed with a sickly smile. Yet that was exactly what Nik had done. After one night, he had abandoned his bride in favour of his mistress. A tiny tremor ran through her tense frame.

'That kind of horrible lie appearing in newsprint makes me grateful that Markos and I aren't glitzy enough to be a target for the paparazzi.' Samantha sighed.

At that point Nik strode in through the doors standing wide on the stone terrace. Olympia jerked in dismay and liquid spilled from the glass in her hand, staining her dress. 'Oh heck…' she mumbled, rising hurriedly from her seat with averted eyes. 'Excuse me, I'll have to change.'

'We've all been invited to join a wedding party in the village,' Nik imparted.

'I'd love that,' Samantha responded warmly. 'But did Markos mention that we have to leave by seven?'

Slipping quietly from the room, Olympia breathed in deep. A *wedding*? For a dangerous split-second, the crushing pressure of the emotional turmoil she was struggling to contain threatened to break its boundaries. Like a living nightmare she saw warning flashes of what might happen if she lost control. She would shout, she would scream, she would break things. In response to the rising level of her distress, she felt violent. Angry, bitter, outraged. Why couldn't he love her? Why couldn't he love her the way she loved him? Would this day, this enforced pretence of harmony for the benefit of their guests *never* end? she wondered wretchedly.

Upstairs, she wrenched an elaborate backless black cocktail dress with a bolero jacket from a hanger, knowing that she would be expected to dress up for such an occasion. Having been welcomed ashore by a party of villagers when they arrived the night before, Olympia was under no illusions as to Nik's status on the island of Kritos. If Gisele treated Nik Cozakis like a god, the islanders treated him like their king!

He had made island life viable for another generation. He had rebuilt the school, brought in an extra teacher, dredged the silted-up harbour and persuaded a doctor to take up residence in the state-of-the-art surgery he had supplied as a lure. He had also allowed the development of a small exclusive resort on the other side of the island, which was providing employment for many of the younger people. He had done more for Kritos in five years than his father had done in his entire lifetime. And, in true heroic tradition, Olympia thought bitterly, Nik had personally told her none of those things. Markos Stapoulos had let those facts drop over lunch. But then Markos had always *hugely* admired Nik.

'Olympia…'

Olympia froze and slowly turned. Nik leant back against the bedroom door to close it. His lean, strong face taut, black eyes chillingly intent, he surveyed her. 'What the hell is the matter with you?'

'I beg your pardon?'

'Don't be facetious!' Nik countered with biting derision. 'You can't treat me like the invisible man without making our guests uncomfortable. Hospitality is a serious matter to all Greeks, a service we undertake with pride and pleasure. I can only be ashamed of a wife behaving like a sulky little brat!'

Olympia shivered and clenched her teeth together.

'And don't you *dare* give me that little fishwife look!' Nik growled, incensed.

Burning colour mantling her cheeks, her hands coiled into tight, hurting fists, Olympia murmured thickly, 'Maybe you should have asked Gisele Bonner to be your hostess instead.'

'You have a point. Gisele never let me down in front of my friends,' Nik responded, without a second of hesitation.

'That was really low, Nik...' Olympia whispered unsteadily, shaken even in the mood she was in by that smooth retaliation.

His stubborn jawline hardened. 'No woman treats me as you have today. We had a stupid argument and I apologised sincerely for my part in it. I have no time and even less patience for the way you're behaving now!'

Stiff-backed, Olympia spun away to lift the bolero lying on the bed. 'Go to hell...' she said succinctly.

A hand like an iron vice closed over her taut shoulder and turned her back. Nik gazed down at her with eyes as hot as golden flames. '*Christos*...do you have a death wish?' he grated incredulously. 'Or is it just that you don't like your own sex? Am I getting the big freeze because Samantha was bantering with me over lunch?'

Olympia was trembling. Nik was emanating rage in sizzling waves. 'I don't know what you're talking about—'

'You couldn't make even a polite pretence of forgiving Katerina either! Was that because she once had a crush on me?' Nik demanded. 'I want to know what the problem is. Is it jealousy that makes you act like this?'

Olympia dredged her eyes from his and focused on his caramel silk tie. 'You'd better go downstairs and join our guests again—'

'Markos knows I'm mad with you. *Theos mou*...I will go nowhere until you tell me what is the matter with you!' Nik swore in a savage undertone, sliding long fingers into the glossy fall of her hair and tipping up her face to his when she would have looked away. 'This morning you were smiling, laughing...*happy*!'

The tension in the atmosphere pulsed like a ticking time bomb. Against her will, she met scorching dark golden eyes and her heartbeat accelerated, her breathing quickening. She read the blunt masculine bewilderment in his angry gaze and something twisted inside her, filling her with wild despair and pain. 'Let...go...of...me,' she framed jerkily.

'I don't think so, *yineka mou*,' Nik breathed, lowering his arrogant dark head and prying her lips apart with the driving force of his mouth.

It was the very last thing Olympia had expected. She wasn't prepared. She had no time to muster her defences. The fierce turmoil inside her ignited as if he had thrown a match into a bale of hay. Shock flashed through her, and then suddenly she found that her hands were biting into his shoulders and she was kissing him back in a devastating melding of fury and hatred and hunger.

Tipping her back on to the bed, Nik pinned her arms to the mattress and plundered the tender interior of her mouth with an erotic urgency that drove her halfway out of her mind. She couldn't think. Her pent-up feelings were finding vent in a primal passion that smashed all boundaries, leaving her at the mercy of what felt like an uncontrollable need.

'You are mine...' Nik rasped, jack-knifing back from her to thrust up the skirt of her dress and hook his fingers to the waistband of her panties. He wrenched her out of them with unashamed impatience.

And she lay there quivering, every nerve-ending crying out for the satisfaction only he could give. Nothing else mattered, nothing but the desperate craving which had tightened her nipples to distended points and set up an agonising throbbing ache between her thighs.

'You understand this OK...' Nik gritted, running his burning, intent gaze over her, his scorching hunger hot as fire licking at her super-sensitive skin.

He came back to her with a driving kiss that consumed her. He was rough, and she had never known him rough before, and he excited her beyond belief. She was out of control, but so was he and she loved that. It answered the wildness leaping through her. He was hard and hot and full and he sank into her tender welcoming flesh with a forceful maleness that made her sob out his name in ecstasy. Her back arched as the blinding excitement peaked on a shivering storming tide of mindless pleasure.

In the aftermath, she opened her eyes and blinked.

For a split-second, as Nik stared down at her, she saw a shell-shocked look in his stunning dark deepset eyes that could only have mirrored her own. Rolling off her without a word, he headed for the bathroom. She lay there immobile struggling to breathe again, feeling ravished, feeling the sweet, heavy satiation of her own body with shattered recognition. She tottered upright and smoothed down her dress with unsteady hands.

Tossing the towel he had dried his face with on the floor, Nik studied her from the bathroom doorway. 'Come here...' he urged raggedly, opening his arms with pure Greek expansiveness.

'You don't need to say sorry...I liked it,' Olympia admitted, half under her breath, her voice wobbling.

He crossed the room, curved an arm round her and bent his dark head to brush his mouth sensually across one feverishly flushed cheekbone. 'Sometimes you make me so angry I could self-destruct. I can handle that...but I can't handle what I don't understand,' he murmured in a raw-edged undertone, his accent very thick.

'It's OK...' And she meant it, but not in the way she knew he would read it. She loved him more than she had ever loved anything or anybody. But she also knew at that moment that she would never live with him again, never let him touch her again, that there had never been any big decision to make. Only her own weak and fearful reluctance to confront reality

ad allowed her to spend a few hours in a turmoil of inde-
cision.

'It's not like I...like I don't care about you,' Nik said
gruffly, after a long silence which had screeched with his
tension, his struggle to find something he could bear to say.
'You're my wife.'

He hovered for a moment, as if he hoped that statement
would dredge some response from her. When it didn't, he
left the room.

Olympia studied her panties where they lay on the carpet.
She wasn't shocked by that wild bout of sex they had just
shared. She had wanted him, needed him, and had briefly
found an outlet for an agony beyond what she could bear.

And Nik? Nik was terrific at handing out orders and reading the riot act, marvellous at sticking to the light and charming in conversation, but when serious communication beckoned Nik Cozakis was almost as inarticulate as a toddler. So
grabbing her and kissing her like Neanderthal man and venting his emotions in a purely physical way had provided a
necessary escape route. Odd, she reflected, that he should be
so attuned to her that he had seen right through her efforts
to behave normally. By rights, Nik should have been easily
taken in.

But he didn't *hate* her anymore. A shaken laugh escaped
Olympia as she restored her appearance to one of respecta-
bility. She thought of her baby, the baby that Nik had ensured
she conceived. She pressed her hand protectively against her
stomach. No wonder Nik had spent four whole weeks *living*
with her! Had he marooned her in separate accommodation
and only made flying visits to her bed, getting her pregnant
might well have taken months. But all that was over now.
The deed was done. She would love her baby, she would
look after her baby, but she would not give house-room to a
husband who had slept with another woman.

Before she went downstairs, she marvelled at the strange
tranquillity of acceptance which now enfolded her. She found

the housekeeper in the kitchen and gave her clear and concise
instructions; Nik would hate her again by the end of the evening.

They drove down to the village taverna, where the wedding festivities were in full swing, in a Toyota Landcruiser
with Nik at the wheel. Settled at a large table in the seat of
honour, Nik found his attention much in demand, and Markos
swiftly became involved too, in what was an overwhelmingly
male-dominated dialogue.

Beside Olympia, Samantha released a little gurgle of
laughter.

Olympia glanced at her.

Samantha's eyes danced with amusement. 'Do you know
what I was just thinking? What an awful shame it is that
Gisele can't see how Nik acts around you! But then I doubt
if she's ever heard your story—'

'My story?' Olympia repeated.

'Yours and Nik's. What you were like together as teenagers. Markos told me Nik was like...totally overboard in
the way he went for you...and I just couldn't *imagine* Nik
like that with a woman. Since I've known him he's always
been very cool and casual in the emotion department,' the
redhead confessed, shaking her head in apparent wonderment. 'But around you he's a different guy...he's really intense, locked on to your every move.'

Olympia forced a smile. 'Really, Samantha...'

'No, I'm loving seeing him like this,' Samantha asserted
with an only slightly guilty grin. 'Your Nik's broken plenty
of hearts in his time. I'm quite transfixed, watching him surge
forward to open car doors and pull out chairs for you, and
you just take it *all* as your due.'

Olympia nodded without comprehension or indeed much
interest. She liked Samantha, wished she had met her under
other circumstances, but reckoned she would never meet her
again. The day had been one of interminable strain and she
could not wait for its end. Furthermore, Nik had always

opened car doors and pulled out chairs for her, and she could not see anything worthy of comment in the fact. 'He has very good manners.'

Samantha sighed. 'Oh, why don't you put him out of his misery and make up with him, Olympia? I've never seen Nik as on edge as he is today.'

Olympia flushed with discomfiture. 'So it was obvious we'd had a row—'

'Oh, it wasn't you who gave it away, it was *him*.' Samantha patted Olympia's hand soothingly. 'Don't worry about it. Markos and I had several major blow-ups the first few months we were married. Getting used to living together takes time. Greek men can be incredibly bossy.'

Hands were clapping in time to the music. Olympia glanced up just as Nik was urged from his seat by their host. He shrugged out of his jacket, discarded his tie and loosened his collar before striding across the floor to join the other men.

Olympia watched the men begin to dance, the music initially sombre, the tempo slow. Nik knew every step, every turn. He was as at home dancing shoulder to shoulder with fishermen in a taverna as he was talking business on board his fabulous yacht. A rare quality which inspired respect, but she was equally conscious of the appreciative female eyes fixed to him. Nik, with his vibrant dark looks and magnetism, the potent and inescapable sexuality of that lean, muscular body accentuated by the lithe, rhythmic grace with which he moved. And it was at that point, just as the music began almost imperceptibly to quicken, that the pain inside Olympia began to break through to the surface.

She did not believe that Nik loved Gisele Bonner. She did not even believe that Nik *needed* Gisele Bonner. But Nik had betrayed her all the same. Nik did not respect either his wife or his marriage. *You have no right to resent anything.* No, no respect there. What a fool she had been to think otherwise! She could have wept at her own eagerness to believe that something true and real might be made of a marriage which had only ever been a business deal! Nik had the Manoulis empire. Nik had a wife he believed he could treat like the dirt beneath his feet when it suited him.

He hadn't even thought to warn her about that tabloid newspaper article which Samantha had referred to with such naive dismissal. How could she love someone who treated her as if she was *nothing*? How, knowing what he had done, could she have lain under him sobbing with pleasure? Her temples pounded as the music speeded up.

It was as if an explosion was taking place inside her. Suddenly she was being bombarded by all the images that she had shut out in self-protection. Nik pawing that skinny blonde tart in some South of France love-nest. That skinny blonde tart pawing Nik with the sort of expertise he was used to and which his wife didn't have. She felt sick to the stomach, wrenched by such violent bitter jealousy she shuddered.

The music reached a soaring crescendo and came to a sudden halt. In the outbreak of vociferous applause Olympia stood up and turned away from the table.

'Kyria Cozakis?' It was Damianos, clutching a mobile phone in one hand, who intercepted her on her passage to the cloakroom. 'Nik's luggage to go out to *Aurora*?' he queried uncertainly. 'The villa staff to go off duty in the middle of the evening? Have I got this right or has there been a mistake?'

All colour receded from Olympia's face. 'You've got it right.'

'But Nik has no plans—'

'I have other plans, Damianos.'

The older man gazed down at her, thunderstruck by the only possible construction he could put on that assurance.

'I suppose you're going to go and warn him now.'

'Not in a public place, *kyria*. Forgive me...' Damianos gathered steam, his appraisal of her set features betraying

honest if incredulous concern. 'But can you have thought of
what you are doing?'

Olympia nodded jerkily.

'He will go mad...'

Olympia breathed in deep and nodded. Out of the corner
of her eye, she watched Damianos walk away, shoulders and
back still rigid with incredulity. He had been looking after
Nik for twenty years and there was a strong paternal streak
in the older man's make-up, but it had been foolish of her to
worry that Damianos would interfere. He would play dumb
sooner than add insult to mortal injury by revealing prior
knowledge of Olympia's plans.

Markos and Samantha had already risen from the table.
Working his way through the crowd, a rueful smile curving
his lips, Nik reached for Olympia with a confident arm and
pulled her close. 'I've been neglecting you,' he said with
perfect truth, dropping a careless kiss down on the crown of
her head.

A salutation of approval, she recognised with a squirming
sensation that took her aback. She had not committed the
heresy of trying to break in on the male bonding session. She
hadn't pouted and sighed like Samantha had either. Nik was
relieved and pleased. Nik, she registered as she climbed into
the back of the Landcruiser with Samantha, had not a *clue*
of what was coming his way.

Twenty minutes later, their guests seen off on their flight
home, Olympia walked hurriedly back into the villa, her hand
already digging into her handbag for the photos and the
newspaper cutting. Nik was only a step in her wake...

CHAPTER NINE

AFTER an instant of hesitation, Nik slung his jacket on a chair in the hall, ebony brows rising at the absence of the usual phalanx of servants who greeted his every arrival and departure. 'Where is everybody? This place feels like the *Marie Celeste*.'

Olympia snatched in a deep breath. 'I gave the staff the rest of the night off.'

Nik frowned. 'I hope you can cook…I'm hungry.'

Olympia's grip on the photos was threatening to crumple them. 'Nik—'

'Why don't you rustle up something in the food department?' Nik qualified with a shift of a vague but expectant hand. ''I could do with a shower.'

Olympia absorbed that expressive gesture. He had the body language of a male who had never needed to enter a kitchen in his entire life and who had not the slightest conception as to what went on there. Why that should strike her as endearingly naive rather than fantastically spoilt escaped her. Why, indeed, it should make her eyes sting with tears was even more of a challenge to work out. Unless it was his descent to the prosaic when she herself was wired to the skies with an impending sense of doom and drama.

One lean hand already resting on the balustrade of the staircase, Nik glanced back at Olympia, where she stood still and graven as a status. 'Olympia?'

'There's no point in you going upstairs!' Olympia exclaimed abruptly. 'I've had all your clothes packed up and sent out to *Aurora*!'

'Have you gone crazy?' Nik enquired slowly, his bemusement patent.

'No, I haven't gone crazy,' Olympia said tautly. 'I got these this morning…'

Nik studied her outstretched hand with puzzled brows.

'And if you still think that my reserved manner was sufficient to embarrass you in front of your friends, you should be feeling like a very lucky guy right now,' Olympia informed him tremulously.

Nik gave her a withering look and still made no attempt to move forward and investigate what she was holding in her hand. In fact he was making a decided point of not even looking in that direction. 'But I sense I'm *not* going to be a lucky guy as we speak,' he derided with lashings of cutting cool. 'I also see that you were being less than honest earlier when you refused to admit that there was something wrong. But I still intend to have a shower, Olympia.'

'A *shower*?' Olympia echoed in a strangled undertone.

'And that gives you fifteen minutes max to get my clothes back off *Aurora*, because I want to change,' Nik extended gently. 'Or there's going to be a hell of a row.'

In sheer disbelief, Olympia watched Nik mount the stairs. Then frustration galvanised her frozen muscles into action and she sped upstairs as well, hurrying past him to reach the landing first.

'I am sure there's a very good reason why you're acting like a child desperate to throw a tantrum in my face—'

'Don't you send me up!' Olympia seethed as rage came to her rescue. She slung the crumpled photos and the newspaper cutting at his feet. '*There!* You and your bunny-boiler! Now do you get the picture?'

'Bunny-boiler?' Nik repeated, deigning to glance down in the direction of the photos, only one of which had landed the right way up on the carpet, but not deigning to stoop to pick them up. 'What are you talking about?'

And Olympia hit him. She didn't plan to; she didn't think about it. Consumed by a head-spinning surge of rage, she clenched her fists and struck out wildly at him, connecting with his shoulder and his chest. So unprepared was Nik for that sudden attack that he almost over-balanced, and had to make a frantic grab for the banister to steady himself. Then he strode up on to the landing, snapped strong hands over her wrists and held her back from him, outrage blazing in his eyes.

'*Christos!* Are you out of your mind?' he launched at her rawly. 'What does who I slept with before our marriage have to do with you?'

Shaking like a leaf in that firm hold, Olympia gritted her teeth, shocked at herself, shocked at the fact that she wasn't getting the reaction she had expected to get. He was acting as if she was nuts and he was innocent. 'You were with her the week after our wedding!'

Without making any response, Nik released her and crouched down to gather up the photos and the cutting, treating only the second photo, which had not appeared in print, to a proper appraisal. He sprang back up again. 'Where the hell did you get these photos from?'

'The bunny-boiler.'

'The only female acting like a bunny-boiler is you,' Nik delineated with chilling cool. 'Now, take a big, deep calming breath and tell me how you got hold of these photos.'

'You're not going to talk your way out of this, Nik,' Olympia swore with quivering vehemence, and she went on to describe the message on the mirror and the magazine article which had been awaiting her in her state room on *Aurora* on their wedding day.

'And the photos?' Nik prompted, steady as a rock, but the line of his well-shaped mouth was forbidding and hard, his strong bone structure fiercely delineated beneath his bronzed skin, his increasing anger tangible.

'Planted in my handbag.'

Nik crunched the photos in a gesture of pure contemptuous dismissal and let them fall to the carpet again. Swinging on his heel, he strode downstairs with the speed and determination of a man who now had a purpose.

Both white-knuckled hands grasping the landing banister, Olympia watched him snatch his mobile phone from the pocket of his jacket, stab out a number and then start talking in Greek.

'*What* were you doing on the phone?' she demanded, when he finally slung the mobile aside again.

'Damianos will deal with this sleazy invasion of our privacy and identify the culprit,' Nik imparted with whip-like clarity, staring up at her with a thunderous frown. 'You should have told me about this immediately! That *any* employee of mine should have the insolence to play a part in such disgusting behaviour outrages me! I am not surprised that you are out of your head with…distress.'

'I'm not distressed, Nik…I'm so angry—'

'You can't punch straight…I got the message. You're very Greek when you're angry, Olympia.' Breathing in deep on that sentiment, Nik sent her a gleaming look of grim amusement. 'And as I can understand that this unpleasant campaign has been working on your mind, I can excuse your loss of control, and indeed marvel at your ability to remain even *polite* in my radius today.'

'Do you think talking all round the real issue here is going to deflect me?' Olympia demanded, her wrath and confusion only rising to ever more dangerous heights at the lowering suspicion that she was being patronised. 'Do you think I'm stupid or something?'

'These photos were taken well over a year ago,' Nik murmured very drily. 'Unfortunately the first I knew of their existence was when that tabloid chose to publish one of them. I was *not* with another woman that week. And, with regard to that offensive newspaper story, a retraction and a humble apology has since appeared in print. If I chose to discuss the matter with my lawyers rather than with you, put it down to my consideration for your feelings.'

'My feelings?' Olympia squeezed out shakily.

'I didn't want you to feel that you had been humiliated by a sleazy rag that calls itself a newspaper! I will tell you something else too,' Nik continued with a preoccupied frown. 'I can't see Gisele as the instigator of all this.'

Olympia looked unsurprised by his defence of the other woman. 'Naturally not.'

'I tell you…she's not the type. Gisele is not spiteful and we parted on good terms. Yet who *else* would have reason to target you like this?' Nik questioned for himself, mollifying Olympia slightly with that concession.

'Katerina…' Olympia suggested, unable to withhold the suggestion.

Nik's mouth compressed. 'Don't be ridiculous!'

Silence fell. Having now explained himself to his own satisfaction, Nik dealt Olympia an expectant appraisal.

A laugh with a ragged edge was torn from Olympia. 'Yes, you do think I'm stupid, don't you?'

Nik frowned. 'I've just about had enough of this, Olympia. Naturally I can produce the retraction and apology which were printed. I was *not* with Gisele the week after our wedding!'

Olympia was unimpressed. 'So you say. But you could've bribed the photographer to say he'd lied about *where* he took that photograph. You could have intimidated the newspaper editor with the threat of a big costly court case. Maybe that one photo they printed was the *only* proof they had and, let's face it, photos don't carry dates! Without further supporting evidence that you had been with Gisele, what could the newspaper do but cave in to your threats?'

'You're accusing me of lying…'

The way Nik stared at her, he couldn't seem to credit that she could dare.

'You warned me that you would do whatever you liked when you married me,' Olympia reminded him flatly.

'If I was doing what I liked right now you would be down

at my feet begging me for forgiveness!' Nik exploded with an abruptness that shook her. 'How *dare* you doubt my word?'

'Being caught out once is careless...being caught out twice is one hundred per cent proof that you're a womaniser as far as I'm concerned,' Olympia informed him fiercely. 'And I have no intention of living with a womaniser!'

Nik strode back towards the stairs. '*Twice?* Where the hell does that come from?'

'I was foolish enough to swallow your story about someone having spiked your drink ten years ago in that nightclub...but don't ask me to swallow another dose of the same nonsense where that flat-chested bunny-boiler is concerned!' Olympia spelt out bitterly.

'You are linking this peculiar business with Gisele back to—?'

'Why so incredulous, Nik? You couldn't even believe me once...you took everybody's word over mine about Lukas,' she reminded him in a voice that trembled with the force of her resentment and pain. 'If I was accused of the *same* thing again you would slaughter me where I stood and you wouldn't listen to any explanation I tried to give!'

'So we're back to squabbling over what did or did not happen in that bloody car park...I don't believe this!' Nik thrust long fingers through his luxuriant black hair, smouldering eyes fixed to her in dark, disbelieving fury.

'I don't trust you because you don't trust me. I don't trust you because we don't have a marriage; we have a business deal—'

'You shut up and you listen to me...' Nik broke in with barely leashed savagery.

Olympia shook her dark head. 'I've fulfilled my part of the deal.'

Nik threw both his arms wide apart in dark fury. 'If you use that word "deal" just *one* more time—'

'I'm pregnant, and now I want you to get out of this house and leave me alone.'

Nik froze, his stunning dark-as-night eyes flying to her pale frozen face and staying there for long, timeless moments. 'You're pregnant?' he echoed in open disconcertion and doubt. *'Already?'*

'Well, you put in a lot of overtime on the project, didn't you?' Olympia shivered with loathing and hurt, chilled to the bone.

Nik was appraising her with eyes that had turned dark liquid gold. 'You're so strung up you barely know what you're saying. *Theos mou*...you're pregnant,' he said again, still in shock from that revelation but beginning to show a growing sense of male satisfaction. 'You crazy, foolish woman, you could have hurt yourself hitting me!'

Olympia blinked in disconcertion.

Nik bent and lifted her off her feet with strong and very careful hands. 'You shouldn't be throwing scenes like this either. You need to lie down and stay calm...think of the baby,' he urged, taking advantage of her complete bewilderment at this sudden change in tack to stride down the corridor towards their bedroom.

'Nik...I just asked you to leave this house *and* me.'

'You don't mean it.'

'I do mean it!'

With a heavy sigh, Nik settled her down on the bed. 'You're hysterical.'

Olympia thrust her hands beneath her and reared up off the pillows. 'I am not hysterical!' she shrieked at him full blast.

'I'm not going to argue with you about this. Naturally you're upset. You're feeling suspicious and with good reason. You're right. Gisele was obviously a secret bunny-boiler who fooled me,' Nik conceded, spreading soothing hands, his calm, his control, his lack of anger now hitting her with striking effect.

'You think you've got me where you want me because I'm pregnant!' Olympia launched at him. 'Well, you haven't! My grandfather will look after my mother, so you can't get me on that, and if you don't get out of this house I'm going to take off in your yacht!'

'The crew are on leave…it would be difficult for anybody to take off anywhere in *Aurora* right now. Only the helicopter is available.'

Olympia trembled. 'You've got no right to do anything more to me than you have already done—'

'I hate to descend to this level…but if you feel like that, why did you let me make love to you this afternoon?' Nik angled a cool, enquiring scrutiny at her.

Her face burned as red as fire. 'That was sex. I *used* you because I felt like it!'

His ridiculously long black lashes lowered. He averted his head, stiffened his shoulders.

'You think that's funny, don't you? I bet you think I'm crazy about you and that this is just a lot of empty shouting and threatening…but it's not. Do you really imagine that I could be foolish enough to *care* in any way for a guy who married me just so that he get hold of my grandfather's money?'

Nik's proud head came up fast. If he had been trying to stifle amusement, he wasn't now.

'You're a laugh…you're a real laugh,' Olympia condemned with ferocious bitterness. 'So superior in every way, and yet you were willing to marry a woman you think of as a *tramp* to gain Manoulis Industries!'

Momentarily, Nik was immobile. Pallor was spreading round his rigid mouth. His eyes glittered like ice, his distaste palpable. The temperature had dropped to freezing point. Without another word, he swung on his heel and strode out of the room.

'And don't come back!' Olympia shouted after him, her voice breaking.

She sat there hunched on the bed, listening to the silence. Her eyes shimmered with tears and the blankness of shock, her emotional turmoil getting worse rather than abating. Just suppose he was telling the truth about Gisele? She crushed out that traitorous voice and hugged herself. If Nik wouldn't trust her, how could she trust him? Why, though, had he no longer been content to hear their marriage termed a 'deal'?

He had had four weeks to tell her that he wanted something more. He *hadn't*. Not a single word in that line had escaped him. She had her pride to think about. Her nose tickled, her throat closing over with tears. Pride was all she had left now that she was carrying Nik's baby. He had hurt her very badly ten years ago. She wasn't going to be hurt like that again. So she was hurting now, but by breakfast time tomorrow, after she had had a good long sleep, she would be feeling much better.

Nik's kid brother, Peri, flew in five days later.

'Hi, Peri...' Olympia said with a wobbly smile as she showed him into the impressive lounge with its spectacular vaulted ceiling.

Peri studied her shadowed, swollen eyes and her red-tipped nose. His level brown gaze was rueful. 'You're not looking good, Olly. You'd know I was lying if I said otherwise.'

To her horror, the tickly sensation of threatening tears made itself felt. She swallowed and gulped.

'Nik's not crying...but his temper's on a hair trigger and everybody with freedom of choice is staying well out of his way.'

'Where is he?'

'Athens—working, using his own apartment. My mother implied that your marriage had been a mistake,' Peri volunteered wryly. 'Nik shouted at her for the first time in his life. Then my father tried to defend my mother and I swear that Nik came within inches of hitting him. So if you're not happy, Olly...do try to remember that you're not the only member of this family suffering. We don't usually have punch-ups at the dinner table!'

'It's not my fault that it didn't work out,' Olympia muttered, very much on the defensive.

'May I sit down, or do I belong to the enemy camp now?'

Olympia flushed and remembered her manners. 'Of course you can sit down. Would you like something to drink?'

'No, thanks. Just give me five minutes of your time,' Peri urged. 'Nik doesn't know I'm here, and if he did know, he'd rip my head off!'

'I can't discuss Nik with you. It wouldn't feel right.'

'But you can listen, can't you? Did that filthy blurb in the papers the week after your wedding cause all this trouble between you and my brother? You nod or you shake your head, Olly,' Peri told her. 'That is *not* discussing Nik.'

Olympia stiffened, and then both nodded and shook her head.

'How am I supposed to read that?' Peri groaned.

Olympia shrugged, determined not to be drawn. She was desperate to confide in somebody, but it wouldn't be fair to use Peri. Her sense of fairness prevented her from telling tales of Nik to his kid brother.

'OK...Nik spent the first five days he was away from you getting drunk as a skunk in a rented chalet in Switzerland.' As Olympia's sea-jade eyes opened very wide, Peri added, 'I discovered he'd taken time out from your honeymoon quite accidentally. The minute that tabloid story broke I tried to contact Nik to warn him, and then found out that I couldn't get hold of him. Being the really nosy guy I am, I didn't let up until I tracked him down. He wasn't very happy to be found.'

'I expect not drunk...*alone*?'

'Oh, no, Nik never gets to be alone, not with Damianos around. And Damianos very much disapproves of alcohol, so as you can imagine the atmosphere in Switzerland was not one of companionable insobriety. Nik was getting drunk and

Damianos was pouring black coffee down him with punitive regularity.'

'Why was he getting drunk?' Olympia prompted shakily.

'He had some "stuff to work out"…that's a direct quote from Nik.'

'I got the same.' Her shoulders slumped. 'Why Switzerland?'

'Not many places you can hole up when you're supposed to be on your honeymoon and are very newsworthy. I don't think Nik saw the alpine pastures except through an alcoholic haze.'

Silence stretched. Peri looked at Olympia. Olympia looked hopefully at Peri.

'He sobered up into a rage when I told him about that gutter press article. He spent the last day sorting that out with his lawyers. At no stage was he in a position to enjoy a lusty poolside clinch with Gisele…' Peri's mouth quirked. 'In fact I doubt he'll enjoy a lusty clinch outdoors ever again now that that photo's come back to haunt him. It would make *me* think twice, I can tell you!'

Olympia reddened. 'You'd lie for Nik—'

'If he had been with Gisele, I'd take the view that it was none of my business and you were better off out of it.'

Olympia chewed at her lower lip. 'Nik's a womaniser.'

'Well, before you came along ten years ago, *yes*…after you broke up, *yes*…but never when you were around. Not at present either!' Peri hastened to assure her.

The tears welled up and rolled down her cheeks. 'It's not that I don't appreciate what you're trying to do, Peri,' Olympia admitted chokily. 'I do, but it's too late for Nik and me. Something rotten happened a long time ago and it's always going to be there between us and it can't be fixed. I *made* Nik go…I practically threw him out and I deliberately said what I knew would drive him away.'

Emanating intense curiosity, Peri studied her with anticipation.

'I'm not saying any more. I've said too much already. Will you stay for dinner?' she asked hopefully, because she was so lonely.

'Sorry. If I don't want Nik to ask where I've been, I need to get back.' Peri rose upright.

Olympia stretched up and kissed his cheek, loving him for trying to help. 'You're so different from Nik.'

'I was the unexpected baby when my parents had given up all hope of the patter of tiny feet sounding again. I was *ruined*!' Peri emphasised.

'Wasn't Nik?'

'No. Nik was told to act like a *man* when he was scared of the dark as a kid. I got an open door, a night light, and my father held my hand and told me an extra story,' Peri reeled off with a comical grimace. 'Nik got sent to a military academy where a rigorous macho regime of cold showers and assault courses was aimed at honing his competitive instincts to a killing edge! I doubt if he got much encouragement to share his deepest feelings there.'

'Where did you go to school?' Olympia was fascinated.

'A mile from home and I never boarded. I burst into tears when they mentioned the academy and it was never mentioned again.'

Peri left Olympia with a lot to consider. Even the most suspicious wife would have been challenged to continue believing that Nik had been unfaithful. Olympia had been challenged to believe that even *before* Peri arrived.

Nik had not shown a hint of guilt or discomfiture when she'd accused him of being with Gisele. Nik had just been furious. All he had cared about was finding out how she had got hold of those wretched photos and ensuring that the culprit who had aided his former mistress in her campaign was identified. And the oddest thing was that Olympia was no longer even sure that she had *ever* really believed at heart that Nik had been unfaithful.

It was as though her mounting resentment at Nik's refusal

to listen to her explanation about Katerina and Lukas had destroyed her usual common sense. She had also been feeling increasingly insecure. Yes, she had been very, very happy with Nik during their weeks on *Aurora*, but underneath there had always been the sinking awareness that Nik had not actually *said* anything to reassure her that he had overcome his medieval desire to avenge his honour.

And somehow…in retrospect, she didn't really know *how*…her emotions had just taken over and everything had mushroomed out of all proportion. So she had got rid of him. And the minute Nik had gone out of the door, loweringly, she had wanted him back, but had been too stubborn and proud to admit it. She had spent the night telling herself that she had done the right thing and the early hours worrying that she had been too hasty in throwing him out. She had spent breakfast weeping like a wimp over the acknowledgement that Nik had positively glowed like a proud father-to-be once he had realised that she was pregnant.

But, ironically, Olympia was most upset by something which Peri had dropped quite casually: if Alexandra Cozakis had commented that their marriage had been a mistake, Nik had evidently informed his parents that their marriage was in trouble. Announcing that to the wider family circle seemed so final, so horribly, immovably final. Was Nik thinking about a divorce now?

Olympia was still keeping in touch with her own mother on an almost daily basis, and going to enormous lengths not to lie but not to tell the whole truth either! Irini Manoulis was currently living outside Athens with Olympia's grandfather, and naturally awaiting some kind of invitation from her newly married daughter. Olympia had been reduced to saying that Nik was away on business and that she was incredibly busy…

The phone was brought to her at two that afternoon. Expecting the caller to be her mother, Olympia answered in a bright upbeat tone. 'Mum?'

'It's Nik.'

He didn't sound like himself. He sounded flat, taut, expressionless.

'Are you all right?' she pressed instantly.

Silence sizzled on the line.

Olympia was holding the phone so tight she was hurting her fingers. She had just heard his voice and all pride and self-discipline had vanished. She was thinking of crawling, and hating herself for it. 'Maybe you think that in the light of what I said and did that is a funny thing for me to ask,' she began, hoping to draw out the dialogue as long as possible—which meant she had to do all the talking because it didn't sound as if *he* was going to be much help in that field.

'I'm *not* all right,' Nik informed her. 'Look, the helicopter will bring you to Athens for eight. I'll see you then.'

'Nik?'

'What?'

She breathed in jaggedly, eyes ready to overflow again. 'I'm just so miserable!'

'You got what you wanted. You got my favourite house. You got my baby. You haven't got me,' Nik enumerated curtly.

'But I *want* you!' Olympia sobbed, before she could swallow that despairing cry back again.

The silence stretched and stretched like a giant elastic band attached to her sensitive nerve-endings. At any moment she expected it to snap and rip her down the middle.

She heard Nik clear his throat, but he still said nothing.

'I just don't know what to say,' he finally advanced gruffly when she had practically given up all hope of a response.

'Fine…don't worry about it…I know I shan't!' In a flood of tears, she stuffed the phone under two cushions, listening to it ring and ring and ignoring it. The roof had fallen in on her just as Nik had always forecast. Reckless to the point of self-destruction. He'd been right. She had trashed the relationship they had built up. If there had ever been any hope of them staying together she had destroyed that hope all on her own. And it was going to be precious little comfort to her in the future that she had held on to her principles. Already loving Nik, needing Nik, was starting to feel like a life sentence of craving what she couldn't have.

The housekeeper entered the lounge with a gentle knock on the door and another phone. Olympia accepted it with writhing reluctance.

'Olympia?' Nik grated rawly.

'I'll see you at eight. I only said I wanted you because of the baby!' Olympia lied, and after a couple of seconds the phone went dead.

So they would discuss their divorce, or their separation. No, the lawyers would see to the technicalities. Why had she lied like that about the baby? Nik hadn't deserved to be insulted again just so that she could save face.

Olympia dressed in unrelieved black to fly to Athens. A stretch limo ferried her through the busy streets at a snail's pace. There was plenty of time for her to ponder her mistakes and her misery and she didn't bother looking out of the window. So when the limo finally drew to a halt, and she climbed out to gaze up at the huge stone mansion in front of her, it was a horrible shock to realise that she had been brought to the Cozakis *family* home, rather than Nik's apartment or even his office.

A very correct manservant ushered her into the classical hall with its chilly but impressive decor and sculptured heads set on plinths. Olympia could feel herself dwindling in stature right back down into the nervous and intimidated teenager whom Nik had brought home to meet his parents. She had tried to edge back out through the door again, muttering that maybe it was a bit too soon for such a meeting, and Nik had yanked her back.

Momentarily, her eyes shimmered with tears over the memory. For a crazy instant she wanted to be transported back into her seventeen-year-old self, strengthened with all the knowledge she had acquired since their marriage. Most of all, she wanted to experience just once what she had been far too insecure to recognise then...that Nik had truly *loved* her.

'Olympia...'

She jerked round. Nik was in a doorway staring at her. She stopped breathing. Her heart just jumped and raced. She connected with his spectacular gaze, those jaguar-gold eyes surrounded by inky black lashes. She went weak at the knees. Her attention expanded to rove all over him. The bold, dark features, the intrinsic aura of intense maleness which made breathing such a challenge, the palest grey suit exquisitely tailored to his magnificent athletic physique.

'All four limbs still present and correct, head better screwed on...' Nik muttered tautly.

She didn't know what he was talking about. She didn't *care*. She just walked across the hall as if he had yanked on a string.

'There's only a few things I need to say to you...'

She froze, stricken eyes veiling. 'Better keep the limo waiting, then.'

How had she missed out on noticing straight off how much strain Nik was betraying? It was etched in the clean, tight lines of his bone structure and the set of his mouth. He had lost weight since she had last seen him and he was pale.

He showed her into a book-lined room. 'Firstly, I've torn up all the copies of that offensive pre-marital contract I made you sign.'

Olympia was not noticeably cheered by that announcement. He was feeling guilty, she thought. He was now willing to offer generous financial compensation in place of himself. She was obviously going to be a *rich* ex-wife.

Nik reached for her hand. 'You accused me of marrying you for what I would gain. I asked for that by not telling you the truth about the deal I made with Spyros. I may *control* your grandfather's business empire but he still *owns* it and can still dispose of it as he wishes.'

Olympia was astonished by that admission. 'But—'

'Spyros didn't want it that way but I insisted. At the time, I assumed that our marriage would end in divorce,' Nik completed heavily.

That made a great deal of sense to Olympia. Nik had wanted revenge more than he'd wanted profit. It had also suited him to let her believe that she was wholly dependent on him for security. Furthermore, when their marriage broke up, her grandfather could not feel cheated for he would have lost nothing by such an agreement.

Olympia was now paper-pale. Nik was dealing with all the remaining sources of resentment and misunderstanding that still lay between them.

'One last point...without doubt the most important point...' Nik hesitated.

The baby. Access arrangements? The necessity of maintaining a civil relationship in spite of their no longer living together? Her throat convulsed.

'It took me a long time to learn what should have been a very simple lesson,' Nik confided with driven urgency. 'Lukas? That was nothing—indeed, when set against more important matters, a complete triviality.'

'A c-complete triviality?' Olympia stammered with sheer incredulity.

'You saw me in the arms of an ex-girlfriend...*you hit back*. At least that's how I saw it then, and it made complete sense at the time to me,' Nik spelt out in a charged, almost bitter undertone. 'I had you on this pure, perfect pedestal, and when you seemed to jump off it I was gutted. I carried that feeling for ten years, nourished it, hated you beyond all reason—'

'I understand,' she broke in, lowering her head wearily even as something in his wording nagged at the back of her mind. 'I felt the same way about you.'

'And when it came to Lukas and you,' Nik continued tautly. 'When it came to trying to deal with that here, in the present, I was still frozen in time at the age of nineteen. So I reacted like a boy, *not* like a man. I need you to understand that.'

Olympia's head was spinning. Nik was being so open, so honest. He seemed to be trying to prove that he had finally forgiven her for what she hadn't actually done. He was even attempting to foist some of the blame for the episode on himself. He was offering an unconditional acceptance of both her and the past which she had never expected to receive. And then what had nagged at her in Nik's wording a minute earlier was clarified. 'You *seemed* to jump off…it made complete sense *at the time…*' Nik was talking as though he now doubted her guilt.

'You said you wanted me…' Nik breathed roughly, throwing her thoughts into confusion again. *'Back?'*

Olympia's sea-jade eyes connected with dark golden eyes. His tension was strong as her own. 'Back,' she confirmed instantaneously.

Nik released his breath audibly and closed both arms tightly round her. She could feel his heart going thump-thump-thump against her as if he had just run a marathon. Slowly he lifted his proud dark head. The look of intense strain was back in his taut gaze. He lifted his hands to her face, curving his fingers round her cheekbones.

'Katerina is here,' he told her then, startling her.

'Katerina?'

'Spyros is here as well.'

'My grandfather?' Olympia was in shock at those twin announcements.

'With the obvious exception of Lukas, I have assembled everybody who was originally involved in our broken engagement ten years ago,' Nik advanced as he walked her back into the hall and towards the drawing room. 'They have

all simply had dinner together and your arrival will be unexpected. That is how I planned it.'

'Planned it?' she questioned, but Nik was already opening
the door and standing back for her entrance.

CHAPTER TEN

FIVE heads turned towards the door, and with only two exceptions all faces betrayed discomfiture of varying degrees when Olympia appeared.

Spyros Manoulis looked the least surprised and the most pleased. Nik's brother, Peri, greeted her with a wide grin of approval. Achilles, Nik's father, who always looked forbidding, merely stiffened. Nik's mother, Alexandra, cosily seated beside Katerina, froze with unease. And Katerina? Katerina stared, and then pinned a bright smile to her lips.

The other woman had no fear, either of Olympia or of her lies being exposed, Olympia recognised bitterly. In pleased receipt of a warm hug from her grandfather, and a cooler acknowledgement of her arrival from the other parties present, she took a seat. How was she supposed to confront Katerina without any proof that she had lied? Why should Nik's cousin confess anything when she had so much to lose? While Olympia was frantically wondering what she could say that might provoke the brunette into showing her true colours, Nik started talking.

'I have a story to tell you all,' Nik drawled lazily from his stance by the marble fireplace.

Curiosity awakened, everybody sat up a little straighter to listen. But when Olympia realised what story it was that Nik intended to tell she was disconcerted and embarrassed. She decided that the minute she got him out of the room she would kill him! It was purgatory to be forced to sit there while Nik told the tale of the message on the mirror on their wedding night, and then went on to mention the newspaper article which he had tried to protect Olympia from. By the

171

time he got round to the photos which she had found hidden in her handbag Olympia was squirming.

Achilles Cozakis breathed with distaste. 'A most unpleasant business.'

Alexandra Cozakis, who had turned to ice at the mere mention of her eldest son featuring in an intimate photograph with Gisele Bonner, said without hesitation, 'That was the behaviour of a very malicious woman.'

'Disgraceful!' Spyros Manoulis pronounced, with sincere annoyance on his granddaughter's behalf.

'Now I know why I never really took to Gisele,' Peri mused with a grimace.

'How *awful* for you!' Katerina gasped in turn, giving Olympia a look of caring commiseration.

Katerina's exclamation seemed to draw everybody's attention to the fact that neither of Nik's parents had offered their daughter-in-law sympathy for what she had suffered.

'Who do you think was behind that campaign against my wife?' Nik enquired softly.

Everybody frowned while they tried to work out why he was asking what appeared to be a stupid question.

'It *wasn't* Gisele,' Nik emphasised, and he drew a folded document from the inside pocket of his jacket. 'It was a member of this family. Someone who has run tame in this house since I was a child. Someone we trust, someone we care about.'

Comprehension hit Olympia as she looked across the room and recognised that Katerina had turned as white as milk. The brunette was sitting forward on her seat, her tension palpable. Dear heaven, Olympia realised then. It hadn't been Gisele behind that campaign; it had been Katerina!

'You shouldn't have been so careless, Katerina. Damianos is a very thorough investigator,' Nik delivered.

The whole room seemed to erupt then. Nik's parents spoke up in furious Greek, most probably defending Katerina, who had burst into instant floods of tears.

'Use English,' Nik cut in with quiet authority. 'Olympia's Greek is much improved, but you are speaking too quickly and nobody has a greater right to understand all that is said here. And before anybody gets carried away with the need to comfort my cousin, let me tell you how she contrived to wage such a campaign.'

Katerina had been on board *Aurora* with Achilles and Alexandra Cozakis the week before the wedding. She had bribed Olympia's maid into carrying out her instructions. Nik handed the document in his hand to his father. 'The maid was in regular contact with Katerina during our honeymoon. Katerina flew to Spain to meet up with the maid and pass over the photos. That meeting was witnessed by another crew member. The photographer who sold the photos to Katerina was willing to identify her. The evidence against my cousin is incontrovertible.'

'How could you imagine that I would do such dreadful things?' Katerina wept brokenly.

'Because it wasn't the first time, was it?' Olympia heard herself answer, and slowly she rose to her feet.

'What's that supposed to mean?' the brunette demanded, her voice stronger the instant she saw Olympia in front of her, her hostility unconcealed.

'When Nik and I got engaged ten years ago, you decided to break us up.'

'I have no idea what you're talking about,' Katerina said woodenly.

'Like hell you haven't!' Nik launched without warning at his cousin. 'Ten years ago you *swore* in front of witnesses that you caught Lukas and Olympia having sex in my car!'

Such plain speaking provoked a moan of reproof from Nik's already shaken mother.

'I'm sorry.' Olympia was sympathetic towards the older woman's embarrassment. 'Of course you don't want to be forced to listen to anything more unpleasant, but this does have to be cleared up. I was unjustly accused and I do want the truth to be known and accepted.'

'Katerina!' Nik thundered impatiently.

'All right!' Katerina said flatly. 'For what its worth, I got together with Lukas and we set you both up. Nothing happened between Lukas and Olympia...I just made the whole story up! Are you satisfied now?'

An unearthly silence fell at that unemotional rendering of such offensive facts.

'*Why?* Nik demanded with sudden rawness. 'Why would you make such filthy allegations about my fiancé? You're my cousin. Lukas was my friend.'

Katerina turned her head away in mute refusal to respond. In silence, Spyros Manoulis ushered Olympia back into her seat and remained beside her.

'She was in love with you, Nik,' Olympia sighed ruefully. 'I'm afraid it was a little more than just a crush. I moved in on what she saw as her territory and she's hated me for that ever since.'

'I am appalled by this,' Achilles Cozakis admitted to Olympia, making no attempt to conceal his horrified embarrassment at the lies which the brunette had told. 'We accepted everything Katerina said without question.'

'I too am filled with disgust, Katerina,' Alexandra Cozakis stated with tear-filled eyes but a cold, steady voice. 'You hurt and distressed my son and destroyed Olympia's good reputation. Yet I remember how warmly Olympia received your offer of friendship. She did you no harm and neither did Nik. Your lack of shame even now shocks me most.'

Beneath that onslaught of censure, Katerina's face hardened.

'What was Lukas's part in all this?' Nik breathed with a roughened edge to his dark drawl, ashen pale now beneath his bronzed skin.

'Lukas had to get very drunk to do what he did that night, Nik,' Olympia answered in gentle consolation. 'He was very unhappy about it, but he seemed to believe that if the Cozakis and Manoulis families got together in business, his family's company would be unable to compete.'

Nik awarded Olympia a stunned look of comprehension. 'Yes, when I think of it, that *would* have been a possibility, but it did not occur to any of us at the time. *Christos*...where were my wits?'

'We can be grateful that at least Lukas's parents don't have to live with the knowledge of their dead son's part in this sordid affair,' Achilles Cozakis stepped in to say, his tone one of finality before he turned to address Katerina. 'I have called a car for you. You will not be welcome in this house again!'

'You were *still* telling lies about Olympia on our wedding day!' Nik suddenly erupted in an outraged roar, taking everybody by surprise.

Katerina jumped up, her face twisting with sudden fury and violent resentment as she stalked to the door. 'You could have had me as a wife but you picked a nothing, a bastard from a backstreet in London, and you got what you deserved!'

Nik's parents reared back in almost comical horror from Katerina's rage and abuse. It was clear that neither had ever seen that side of the younger woman.

'No, Olympia got what I deserved,' Nik muttered with sick distaste, and turned away as the door slammed on his cousin's exit.

'What a *lively* family you have, Achilles!' Spyros Manoulis said to Nik's father in apparent wonderment. 'But that one who has just gone out is a snake. I would not like to think that Katerina would again be in a position where she might harm Olympia.'

'She leapt up like a madwoman!' Alexandra Cozakis gasped with a stricken sob. 'Who would ever have thought that Katerina could be like that?'

'Be assured that that young woman will cause no further

trouble,' Achilles Cozakis asserted in considerable mortification, patting his distraught wife's shoulder. 'But I think we
have all had enough of her for one evening.'

Nik was by the window, silent, still, and not looking in
anybody's direction.

'Yes, indeed.' Spyros extended a hand down to Olympia,
who clasped it and stood up. 'By the way, I'm taking my
granddaughter home with me.'

'Home with you...' Olympia echoed, thunderstruck by that
casual announcement.

Nik seemed to emerge from his abstraction. Swinging
round, he took an almost clumsy step forward, as totally
taken aback by that development as everybody else. 'What
are you saying, Spyros?'

'I'm taking her back. You don't deserve her. In my home
she will be properly valued and protected.'

'Spyros...Nik is in shock, as we all are,' Achilles Cozakis
intervened in dismay. 'We are *all* very much aware that
amends must be made to Olympia for her treatment, not only
in the past but in the present. We are painfully conscious of
our mistakes and prejudices.'

'Come on, Olympia...' Olympia found herself being hustled towards the door at speed by her determined grandfather,
who paused in the doorway only to say in conclusion, 'You
have lost yourself a fine woman, Nik Cozakis!'

'That'll give my son-in-law something more sensible to
worry about!' Spyros chuckled as he swept them both out of
the Cozakis mansion. 'Did you see their faces? All that weeping and wailing! We Manoulises are people of action.'

'But I don't want to leave Nik,' Olympia protested shakily,
the evening's events beginning to catch up with her as well,
leaving her feeling momentarily weak and weepy and out of
touch with what was happening around her.

'I know what I'm doing.' Her grandfather urged her with
gentle hands into the limo waiting outside. 'I'm stealing you

back for an hour. Now that you're married, Nik's welcome
to spend the night in my home.'

'How can he spend the night when he's not with us?'

'Olympia...tonight Nik was so weighed down with his
guilt and his bitterness he was in a stupor, and I felt sorry
for him. When he saw his wife being trailed away, he went
from the stupor into panic...much more healthy!' Spyros asserted, patting her tightly linked hands in a comforting gesture. 'I have no doubt that Nik will be pounding my front
door long before midnight! However, I also cruelly misjudged you, and we *also* have fences to mend.'

And Olympia and her grandfather did mend those fences,
quite happily, and, being both of a blunt disposition, they did
the mending within a very few words. Had Olympia had Nik
by her side she would have felt happier; she did not have her
grandfather's faith in the belief that Nik would immediately
chase after her.

Arriving at Spyros's villa, she was engulfed in a rapturous
welcome by her mother, who was looking terrific.

'Doesn't she look well?' Spyros said proudly of his daughter, Irini. 'Good Greek air performed the miracle.'

Neither Olympia nor her grandfather saw any point in distressing Irini Manoulis with the evening's events. Olympia
chose to share the news of her pregnancy instead. Spyros
was ecstatic, and broke out a bottle of champagne. Her
mother glowed with excitement and briefly wondered where
Nik was.

'You'll see Nik over the breakfast table,' Spyros promised,
ignoring Olympia's strained look.

Her mother showed her into a spacious guest room and sat
down on the edge of the divan to chat to her daughter at
length about babies. She began to yawn a little then, and
Olympia persuaded her to go to bed. Soon after that, a loud
knock sounded on the door and her grandfather appeared
looking very smug. He said nothing, though. He just stepped
back, and only then did Nik move into view.

His tie was missing, his black hair ruffled, half his shirt undone, a definable dark shadow now roughening his strong jawline. He was far from immaculate but, being Nik, he still contrived to look absolutely gorgeous. Her heart started beating so fast she felt as if she couldn't breathe.

The silence was too much for Spyros. He slapped Nik on the back. 'Even I didn't expect a grandchild on the way this soon!' he admitted, before mercifully closing the door to leave them alone.

Olympia was cringing with mortification.

Nik had frozen in receipt of that congratulatory slap. Haunted night-dark eyes rested on Olympia. 'I didn't give you much choice, did I?'

'I'm really pleased about the baby...' Olympia told him.

'You have to be, don't you?' Nik sighed.

'I am really happy about our baby,' Olympia repeated doggedly, recognising the strain etched in his vibrant dark features. 'Why did it take you so long to get over here?'

'The limo broke down. I had to get a cab, and then it got stuck in a traffic jam, and I ended up walking the rest of the way with Damianos grousing in my wake.'

Olympia had to gulp back a nervous laugh.

Nik swallowed. One of his hands moved in an awkward gesture and then stilled again. He watched her with intense and beautiful dark eyes and then he breathed in very deep. 'You know I love you so much it hurts...' he said with ragged sincerity.

She flew off the edge of the bed and flung herself at him.

Nik caught her into his arms and held her so close she almost couldn't breathe. 'I was planning to say a lot of other things, but when it comes down to it loving you is about the only thing I've got to offer in my favour.'

'Rubbish,' Olympia scolded chokily.

'I thought I knew so much ten years ago and I didn't know anything. I should have *known* they were lying!' Nik groaned into her hair. 'I can't forgive myself for being that stupid. How can you? I wrecked everything for us—'

'We were so young, and we were both so desperate to save face we couldn't be honest with each other.' She smoothed possessive fingers through his black hair, allowing happiness to channel through her in an exhilarating wave. 'I don't want to look back any more, Nik. You can't look out for the Katerinas of this world. She was very clever and very convincing. I really trusted her as a friend and I was shattered at the way she just turned on me that night.'

'When Damianos found the photo trail led back to her I was devastated, and I knew instantly that everything you had ever tried to tell me about her had to be true,' Nik confided tautly.

'When did you find out?'

'Late last night. My first urge was to fly straight out to Kritos, but I decided it would be better to confront Katerina and that you had the right to be there too.' His beautiful mouth tightened. 'I didn't want to tell you in advance in case in some way you alerted her and put her on her guard. I knew we didn't have a shred of proof about what she did ten years ago, but I was determined to get the truth out of her for your sake.'

'I'm so grateful you had the evidence that it was her behind those photos.'

Nik looked down at her with immense regret. 'She caused us so much misery. But there's never been anybody but you in my heart...nobody else even came close.'

Olympia hugged him tight, his gruff honesty bringing tears to her eyes.

'I really had already overcome my...my—'

'Unreasonable feelings about what you thought I had done with Lukas?' Olympia put in helpfully. 'I *know* you had. You made that quite clear—'

'The day you threw me out of the house.'

'I know.' Olympia sighed lovingly. 'You got no credit at

all. The fact sort of got lost in what I was feeling about those photos.'

'Katerina again,' Nik ground out.

Olympia snuggled past his jacket into his shirtfront, drinking in the achingly familiar scent of him, wonderfully aware of the tall, hard, lean length of him. 'Do you know she actually told me that our marriage was arranged before you even met me?'

'What nonsense is that?' Nik held her back from him.

'I know,' Olympia sighed shame-facedly. 'How could I have believed something so far-fetched?'

'There was no arranged marriage.' Nik cupped her cheekbones. His gorgeous dark eyes sought hers with glimmering amusement. 'But I did see a photo of you in Spyros's office the year before we met,' he confided. 'You were sitting with a white cat on your knee. You had such a glorious smile that I had to ask your grandfather who you were.'

Olympia stared up at him in surprise, for she recalled that photo.

'Your grandfather knew I was impressed, and that may be why he invited me over to meet you as soon as you arrived in Greece...I wouldn't put it past him.'

'Neither would I...' But Olympia smiled, tickled pink by the idea of Nik having admired her that much even before he met her. 'Were your parents feeling better by the time you left?'

'They're very upset about the way they've treated you, and concerned that they may inadvertently have encouraged Katerina. Possibly there was a time when my mother thought she wouldn't mind if I married her,' Nik acknowledged grimly. 'However, I never had the slightest interest in her in that way.'

'But she doesn't ever seem to have faced that, which is very strange.' Olympia frowned, feeling sorry for the other woman as she recognised how irrational Katerina's behaviour had been.

'Because she's obsessed. My father will talk to her family and suggest that she has professional help. It's not a problem that can be ignored. I suspect that guilt over Lukas's death may have hit Katerina harder than any of us could have appreciated,' Nik conceded ruefully. 'He was infatuated with her. How must she have felt when he crashed that car?'

Olympia shivered, and decided a change of subject was overdue. 'Tell me, would you *really* have dumped me back at my family's feet in front of our wedding guests?'

A dark flush scored Nik's fabulous cheekbones. 'I wanted you to think I would. *Christos*...the minute you forced your way into my office it all started up again for me. But it had to be on my terms this time, so that I felt I was in control. Then the minute we made love, on our wedding night, everything just went haywire for me...'

'How?'

'You were seasick and all I wanted to do was look after you.' Nik groaned. 'And then we lay talking on the bed and it felt completely right, not strange at all. It actually felt as if we'd never been apart.'

'Really?' Olympia was delighted by that admission.

'All of a sudden I couldn't kid myself that I was still in control. That's why I took off the next day.' Nik grimaced. 'I didn't like what I was feeling.'

'What were you feeling?'

Nik released a self-mocking laugh. 'If I'd known I wouldn't have had to go away. I went to Switzerland and I was absolutely bloody miserable, sitting drowning my sorrows.'

'I'm glad you were miserable because I was too. What conclusions did you come to?'

'That I was in trouble, *agape mou*. That I wanted to be with you rather than in Switzerland. That I still had feelings I didn't want to examine too closely,' Nik admitted with a rueful twist of his sensual mouth. 'And then we got together again in Spain and I didn't bother beating myself up any more about what I might or might not have been feeling.'

Olympia looked up at him in reluctant fascination and reproach.

Nik said defensively, 'I was really happy, but I know I should have mentioned that that outrageous marriage deal idea was history as far as I was concerned. But then I didn't know how you felt...'

'And no way were *you* going to say anything before *I* did...' Olympia recognised, giving him a teasing look of comprehension.

'You *still* haven't said anything,' Nik reminded her, studying her with brilliant dark eyes.

Olympia's eyes danced. 'It was your turn this time...I did all the talking ten years ago!' She stretched up on her tiptoes and linked her arms round his neck. 'I love you, Nik Cozakis...'

Liquid dark golden eyes gazed down into her. 'Madly, totally and for ever?'

'What a memory you've got!' Olympia was thrilled he could recall her saying those words to him ten years earlier. He must have treasured them to remember them so well, and that really touched her.

'That's how much I love you,' Nik confessed, bending his dark head to taste her mouth with aching slowness. Her heart sang and her knees trembled, and suddenly she was moving backwards, well aware that there was a bed behind her.

Nik came down beside her with a wolfish grin. 'We've still got talking to do...'

Olympia flicked a button loose on his shirt. 'I'm listening.'

He grasped her hand, eyes suddenly level and serious again. 'These last few days away from you were hell. I was really scared I'd lost you. When you said you wanted me back, on the phone, I felt so sick with relief I couldn't think of a thing to say.'

'Sometimes actions speak louder.' Olympia lay back

against the pillows with the faint air of a woman arranging herself to her best advantage. 'You're not great on the phone, but you have your talents in other places.'

'Picking bunny-boilers?' Nik asked with glinting eyes, shrugging out of his jacket with fluid sexy ease.

'Are you ever going to let me forget that scene I made?' She groaned, her face burning. 'I never said sorry for hitting you either.'

'And I never said sorry for going on like a jerk about the way you were acting that day. It's just I didn't know what was wrong and I was panicking.' Nik sighed and kissed her with slow, sensual intensity.

'I saw that,' she whispered tenderly.

'You won't get the chance to accuse me of straying again. I don't like being away from you. I'll cut down on travel so that we can base ourselves on the island,' Nik shared huskily, resting the palm of his hand on her still flat stomach and smiling at her with unconcealed contentment at that prospect. 'You and me and the baby together.'

It sounded like paradise to Olympia. They exchanged another kiss. It went on a little longer than the previous one. They shifted closer and closer. Nik admitted he felt very strange, getting put into a bedroom with her in her grandfather's home, and they both started laughing. And when the laughing stopped they lost themselves in each other, the experience all the more intense and all the sweeter for the love they now openly shared.

Olympia settled their infant daughter into her cradle. Alyssa had loads of dark curly hair and eyes the colour of sea jade. And from the hour of her birth she had drawn both Nik and Olympia's families closer together.

Spyros Manoulis was a regular visitor. Spyros, who had had little to do with his own children because he had been too busy building his empire while they were growing up, had succumbed to a fever of adoration for his great-granddaughter, whose every tiny move he applauded. Olympia's mother, Irini, whose health had improved in step with her increasing sense of wellbeing, was an equally keen grandmother, but currently had another interest in her life as well.

Olympia smiled at the memory of her grandfather's shock the previous winter, when his middle-aged daughter had gone out to dinner with a retired widower she had met through friends. Irini was getting married to Sotiris in a few weeks' time and Olympia was looking forward to the wedding.

Achilles and Alexandra Cozakis could not have done more than they had done over the past year to establish a close and loving relationship with their daughter-in-law. Peri's irreverent sense of humour had done much to lessen the strain which Katerina had left in her wake. And Alyssa, adored by all, had been a wonderful blessing.

About six months after that night when Katerina's lies had been exposed, Katerina had written to Nik and Olympia offering them her assurance that never again would she seek to interfere in their lives and saying that she now deeply regretted all the trouble she had caused. Since then Katerina had moved to London, to live with her elder sister and her family, and was apparently embarking on a new life.

There was not a single cloud in Olympia's world. Exactly a year ago she had married Nik, expecting nothing but hurt and pain to result, and since then she had gained the loving support of two families, a gorgeous baby daughter and a husband she loved more with every passing day. This was their wedding anniversary, but they were staying home on Kritos because with the number of social invitations they received staying home alone was more of a treat than going out.

Olympia fingered the diamond necklace round her throat and looked in the mirror with a secretive smile. Once she wouldn't have thought she suited diamonds. Then she had begun seeing herself through Nik's eyes, and finally through her own, and her old lack of confidence was long gone. Her reflection showed a woman with very long dark hair—Nik's pleas had prevailed—wearing a beautiful designer gown that made the most of her lush breasts and hips.

'Sensational...' Nik purred from the doorway.

Olympia gave a sensuous little wriggle of appreciation as he kissed one smooth bare shoulder.

Nik gazed down at their baby daughter with softened eyes. 'She's tremendous. Do you know what my first thought was when you threw me out of the house nearly a year ago?'

'I didn't know Olympia had the guts?' Olympia teased, turning round to study him, her attention roaming over his vibrant good looks with possessive appreciation and, even now, a heart which developed a distinctly rapid beat at his proximity.

'No. What if she has a boy and says, Right, that's it. You've got your son and heir, where's my divorce?' Nik confessed with a rueful groan of remembrance. 'I started praying for a whole succession of girls the same moment!'

Olympia was entranced by that admission. She liked him to know that he had almost shot himself in the foot with that marriage deal he had proposed. But as a bridge to a shared future which he couldn't have brought himself to reach for otherwise the marriage deal had worked just great, in her opinion. They had enjoyed such a blissfully happy first year together, and she had been fortunate enough to have an easy pregnancy and delivery.

Nik laced his fingers with hers and kissed her with all the considerable skill in his repertoire. 'I love you, *agape mou.*'

'Madly, totally and for ever,' she confided, quivering a little with a heat that was all too familiar and pulling herself back from him by exerting every means of self-control she knew. 'Dinner,' she reminded him, colouring.

'It was just one kiss,' Nik pointed out.

It rarely stopped at one kiss, though.

They strolled out to the stone terrace and took their seats at the beautifully set table awaiting them. In the drowsing heat of early evening, Olympia took in the magnificent views which had so enchanted her on her first morning on the island. And then she gazed at Nik, more enchanted than ever.

He was the love of her life, and on that thought she began to eat the exquisitely cooked meal which was being served to them. Their eyes met, jaguar-gold into green, with increasing frequency. And if they ate a little more quickly than was expected, and got a bit impatient between courses, and vanished altogether before the coffee arrived, the staff weren't surprised. They had seen it all so many times before.